The DRAGON Society

Tor Books by Lawrence Watt-Evans

Dragon Weather
The Dragon Society
Touched by the Gods
Night of Madness

Split Heirs (with Esther M. Friesner)

The DRAGON Society

LAWRENCE WATT-EVANS

A Tom Doherty Associates Book
New York

THE DRAGON SOCIETY

Copyright © 2001 by Lawrence Watt-Evans

This book is printed on acid-free paper.

Edited by Jenna A. Felice.

A Tor Book
Published by Tom Doherty Associates, LLC
175 Fifth Avenue
New York, NY 10010

www.tor.com

Tor® is a registered trademark of Tom Doherty Associates, LLC.

Library of Congress Cataloging-in-Publication Data

Watt-Evans, Lawrence.
        The Dragon Society / Lawrence Watt-Evans.—1st ed.
            p. cm.
        "A Tom Doherty Associates book."
        ISBN 0-765-30007-9
        1. Dragons—Fiction.   I. Title.

        PS3573.A859 D68 2001
        813'.54—dc21   2001041536

First Edition: December 2001

Printed in the United States of America

0   9   8   7   6   5   4   3   2   1

Dedicated to my son,
Julian Samuel Goodwin Evans,
who has been very patient with me

The
DRAGON
Society

Secrets

Strangers at the Gate

Late one winter night, at an hour when all sensible folk were long abed, a man stood yawning atop the city wall beside the gates of Manfort, leaning against the gate tower and peering every so often into the darkness outside the city. He was wrapped in a thick coat and wore a broad-brimmed black felt hat, but still shivered with the cold, occasionally stamping his feet on the stone battlement.

Then a dull, distant creaking drew his attention. The streets inside the gates and the paved square outside were dark, cold, and empty, but somewhere to the south, far down one of the roads leading out of the plaza, he could see a dim flicker of light. Suddenly alert, he stared at it, shuttering his lantern so that his eyes could adjust more completely to the darkness—and so he would not be seen so easily.

The light drew nearer, and the creaking grew louder, until at last the man on the wall could make out a wagon trundling up the road toward the city. The wagon was large and boxy, drawn by oxen—the sort of wagon used by the caravans that brought goods from all over the Lands of Man. A single lantern dangled from a long iron hook above the driver's seat, providing just enough light to let the tired oxen see where to set their feet.

Caravans did not travel by night, of course—but the man on the wall was not waiting for a caravan. He unslung the bow on his back and strung it without ever taking his eyes off the approaching vehicle.

The wagon drew steadily nearer, the oxen trudging stolidly up the street toward the plaza, through occasional patches of half-melted slush that had fallen from the roofs on either side; the wheels slipped sideways on the wet cobblestones now and then, but the wagon moved steadily forward.

The two men on the driver's bench sat side by side, huddled against the cold. One, the driver, was a stocky, crop-haired man of indeterminate age clad entirely in black leather; he stared into the darkness ahead, as calm and stolid as the oxen pulling the vehicle. Beside him, alternately drowsing and starting into intense alertness, slumped a tall young man wrapped in a black woolen cloak piped with white; a scar marred this man's right cheek. He came alert as the wagon neared the gates and scanned the towers carefully.

The man on the wall beside the tower ducked behind the parapet, out of sight, and drew an arrow from the quiver on his back.

"We should have stopped at an inn," the driver said as the wagon bumped into the plaza. "Dawn can't be more than two hours away. You're exhausted, the oxen are exhausted, I'm tired myself, and we still have to get to the Upper City and get everyone inside."

The young man shook his head sharply. "No," he replied. "I might still have enemies here. If we had arrived by daylight the news of our return would be everywhere in minutes, and they could have had assassins in the crowds on the street before we could get inside the gates, let alone reach the Old Palace."

"They could have assassins on the wall or the rooftops right now, Ari, and we'd never know it in the dark."

"Only if they knew we were coming," the other said, but he threw a quick glance at the stone parapet, which was little more than a black shape against the starry night sky.

"Lord Toribor is a sorcerer, isn't he?"

The young man snorted. "Lord Belly? Not much of one. He left the sorcery to Enziet and Drisheen."

"You swore to kill Lord Nail, as well as Belly, and surely he knows some sorcery."

"True. I suppose he might know enough to know we were coming."

"Then why don't you think Lord Nail might have archers on the rooftops, waiting for us?"

The younger man sighed. "He might. But he's still sworn not to kill me in Manfort itself, and I think he'll probably keep that oath."

"What about the others, then? Do you think any of them might decide to avenge Enziet or Drisheen?"

"I don't know. I don't know what the rest of the Dragon Society knows, or what they would think of any of it . . ."

He was interrupted by the slap of a bowstring. The young man was too tired to recognize the sound immediately, but his leather-clad companion reacted instantly, shoving Arlian to one side while he dove to the other. Arlian's hat fell to the pavement.

An arrow whirred between them and embedded itself with a thump in the back of the driver's bench.

"Damn!" Arlian said, fumbling at his belt as if expecting to find a sword there. "Black, where did it come from?"

"There," Black said, pointing at the archer on the wall—who had risen from concealment with another arrow nocked. Arlian tumbled completely out of the wagon, and the arrow smacked into the seat where he had been a moment before.

"If he's smart, he'll shoot the oxen," Black hissed, as he crouched half on and half off the driver's bench. "Let's hope he's a fool. We can dodge better than they can."

Arlian had gotten to his feet and stepped back beside the still-moving wagon, out of the light. "Thirif! Shibiel!" he called quietly as he walked alongside.

No one responded.

"Don't wake them," Black said. "They'll stick their heads out, half-asleep, to see what's happening. You could get them killed."

"*We* could get killed! They might have some magic that would help—maybe an illusion of some sort, like the one they used at the inn in Cork Tree."

"I think we can handle one bowman without magicians, Ari."

"I don't have a sword, Black—it broke back there in the cave, remember? And how do you know there's only one?"

Black didn't reply at first, and Arlian called, "Black?"

"Hush," Black said. "Listen!"

Arlian listened, and heard creaking wheels, ox hooves slapping on wet pavement . . .

And something else, farther away. Footsteps. Running footsteps at street level.

"It isn't just one," Black said.

"I sincerely regret being right about that," Arlian said. "Black, I'm completely unarmed."

Another arrow whirred past Arlian's ear, uncomfortably close; apparently he wasn't as well hidden by the wagon as he had hoped.

"Can you use a whip?" Black called.

"To drive oxen, yes; to fight, no."

"I'll keep it, then."

A fourth arrow chipped a splinter from the wagon inches from Arlian's nose.

"I notice he's only shooting at *me*," Arlian said.

"Yes, I know," Black said. "You're the one someone set assassins on."

Arlian noticed that Black's voice seemed to be receding. He risked poking his head forward and looking around.

Black was no longer on the driver's bench. His black leather clothing, black hair, and black beard blended into the darkness, and Arlian could not spot him for several seconds, but finally he made out a low shape moving rapidly forward, bent over and moving with amazing stealth, his drover's whip clutched in one hand. Arlian watched him run a zigzag path across the plaza toward the gates.

He could no longer hear any footsteps; he peered into the darkness, trying to guess where the assassins were. He heard the snap of a bowstring, but did not hear or see the arrow's flight, and the click of a steel point striking stone seemed distant—was this some other bowman at work? The first archer was presumably still on the wall, but those other footsteps had not been . . .

Someone shouted, and he thought he heard a scuffle; he looked for Black, but could not locate him in the darkness.

Then an unfamiliar voice called from some distance, "Lord Obsidian!"

Puzzled, Arlian hesitated, then shouted back, "Who calls?"

"I'm called Horn," came the reply. "I work for Lord Wither."

"Lord *Wither* sent assassins?" Arlian was startled; while he and Wither had had their disagreements, he had not thought the old man wished him any serious harm.

"No, my lord—we have captured the assassin. I have my knife at his throat. What would you have me do with him?"

This was all far too confusing in Arlian's exhausted condition. "Black?" he called.

There was no reply for a moment; then he heard voices muttering in the distance, too low for him to make out any words. Then Black's voice called, "Wait there, Ari."

Arlian waited, baffled. He glanced up at the battlements just as a light flared, and saw several men, one of them with his hands raised while the others surrounded him. The light came from a lantern in one man's raised hand.

Then the light vanished behind the gate tower, to reappear moments later at the tower's base, where Arlian could see that it was now Black who held the lantern. There were two others with him, both strangers—but one of them did, as he had said, hold a knife at the other's throat.

Arlian had thought there were more people than that in the lantern's glow atop the wall, but there were only the three approaching now. Arlian stood and waited for them.

"Lord Obsidian," the man with the knife said as they drew near the wagon. "This is the assassin."

"And you are Horn?" Arlian asked.

"Yes."

"Would you mind telling me why you are out here in the middle of the night, saving me from assassins? How did you know who I was?"

"Sorcery, my lord," Horn replied. "Lord Wither grew impatient for your return, and used sorcery to determine when you would arrive—and in so doing, he learned of this ambush, and sent me to ensure your safe arrival."

"That was kind of him," Arlian said. "And is Lord Wither here?"

"No, my lord. He is safely home in bed. He trusted me and my men to deal with matters here."

"Your men?"

"I have others with me. They have remained on the battlements, in case other dangers still lurk."

Arlian nodded. Then he turned his attention to the other stranger, the man with the knife at his throat.

"You meant to kill me?" he asked.

"Yes, my lord." The man's eyes were downcast, staring at the paving stones.

"Why?"

"I was hired to do so, my lord."

"By whom?"

The assassin looked up and met Arlian's gaze.

"My lord, you understand that revealing that would ordinarily put my friends and family at risk, and since you are surely going to kill me in any case . . ."

"No, I am not," Arlian interrupted.

That seemed to disconcert the assassin; he stammered, then said, "I cannot . . . I . . . This is a special circumstance, my lord."

"In what way?"

"The man who hired me is dead, my lord. You killed him."

Arlian blinked wearily at him. "Did I? Who was he?"

"Lord Drisheen, my lord."

Arlian nodded. "So I did."

"If he were still alive I would not betray him, but he is dead, and left no family . . ."

Arlian snorted at the very idea of Lord Drisheen having a family.

"He paid us half before he left," the assassin continued. "The other half was put in trust, to be delivered when your death was confirmed—if you came back to Manfort; if you died elsewhere, we would not be involved. But we were to kill you outside the gate—he insisted upon that—so my brother and I have been taking turns freezing up on that wall for months. If we had been able to strike in your home . . ."

"I'm sure you'd have done better," Arlian said. He noticed that this fellow seemed to have no compunctions about betraying his brother's role in the scheme. "I don't suppose Drisheen told you *why* I was to be killed?"

The assassin's surprise was plain even by lantern-light. "Revenge, of course. He knew you meant to kill him."

"Of course." Arlian sighed. He looked at the waiting wagon—the oxen had stopped when Black made his dash across the plaza—and at the arrow embedded in the back of the driver's bench.

"Shall I kill him now?" Horn asked.

"No," Arlian said. "Let him go."

"My lord?" Horn said, startled.

"Release him. He's unarmed, of course?"

"Of course," Horn said. "Well, at least we took his sword and knife and bow—he might have other weapons hidden. But surely, my lord, you cannot mean to let him go free?"

"I can and I do. You heard me say I did not mean to kill him, and I don't. Let him go."

Horn hesitated, then lowered the knife and released his hold on the assassin's arm.

"One thing," Arlian said, as the man stood staring stupidly at him. "You are no longer an assassin. If you ever attempt another murder, I will hunt you down and kill you. You heard how Lord Wither's sorcery warned him of your intent—well, I have two Aritheian magicians in this wagon whose magic makes Lord Wither's mightiest sorcery look like a child's game. I have had my fill of vengeance for the nonce, but I am being merciful, not stupid. Do not test me on this; my mercy is limited. Do you understand me?"

"Yes, my lord." The assassin bowed deeply.

"You got half your money; enjoy that, and make no further attempt at the rest."

"Yes, my lord."

"Now, go away."

The assassin hesitated, then turned and ran for the gate.

Arlian, Black, and Horn watched him go.

"I had heard, my lord, that you were *obsessed* with revenge," Horn said. "It would appear I was misinformed."

"You were not misinformed," Arlian said. "My obsession has become more specific than that. I am obsessed with revenge upon the dragons, not upon men."

"In other words, he's mad," Black said cheerfully. "But he pays well."

Horn grimaced. Arlian studied him.

"So I am under Lord Wither's protection?"

"For the moment, yes," Horn said.

"Why?"

"He says you have something he wants, my lord."

"And has he asked you to collect it for him, or to bring me to him, so that I can pay him for saving my life?"

"I am not at all sure we did save your life, my lord—your man here seemed well on his way to settling the matter, had we not done so first. At any rate, we are not to trouble you. Lord Wither will wait upon you in his own good time, when you have had a chance to recover from your journey."

"Will he, indeed?" Arlian had a fairly strong suspicion that Lord Wither's courtesy and consideration was not entirely unselfish. The old man probably thought that a polite approach was more likely to be effective in cozening Arlian. Arlian also had a fairly strong suspicion that he knew what Lord Wither wanted, and that he was not going to get it.

"Thank you for your help, Horn," Arlian said, "and my thanks to Lord Wither for his intervention. Tell him I will be happy to see him in a few days."

Horn bowed.

"Can we go now?" Black asked, gesturing at the wagon.

Horn stepped aside. Arlian retrieved his fallen hat, then hurried to the driver's bench. A moment later he and Black were back in their seats, the arrow embedded in the back of the bench between them had been pulled free and tossed aside, and the oxen were trudging onward as if nothing had happened.

2

Homecoming

The wagon rolled slowly up the streets of Manfort, toward Arlian's home in the Upper City. "I told you we should have stayed at an inn tonight," Black said. "I don't think he would have attacked us if we had arrived by daylight, with people everywhere."

"Oh, I think he would," Arlian said. "He could have lost himself in the crowds and escaped."

Black clearly didn't believe this, but did not actually say so. Arlian glanced at him, then said, "We had to come through the gate sometime, and I thought our chances were better late at night. I may have erred."

"I think you just didn't want to wait any longer than necessary to get home," Black replied. "Not even a few hours."

"That's part of it," Arlian admitted. "After all, Hasty's child is due at any time, if it hasn't come already. But also, I have a reputation to keep up as Lord Obsidian." He caught himself on the edge of the seat as the wagon bumped over a loose paving stone. "Which do *you* think is a better entrance—riding in openly at midday, dirty and tired, in a cheap old trader's wagon, or simply reappearing without warning, back in place at the Old Palace?"

"Why do you still care what anyone thinks?" Black demanded, throwing his companion an angry glance. "Enziet and Drisheen and the others are dead, and Nail and Belly know you for who you are. Who are you trying to impress?"

"Everyone I can. If I intend to hunt down and kill the dragons that destroyed my village, I'm going to need help. I can't do it alone."

Black glanced at him, and saw that his companion's expression was intent, although he was staring into empty darkness. Clearly, Arlian was seeing something other than the street ahead of them, and Black suspected it had something to do with dragons. "You probably can't do it at *all*, Ari," he said gently.

"I have to try."

Black's manner turned harsher. "And just who do you think could possibly help? Lord Wither? He seems to be eager enough to help you as it is, at least against Drisheen's assassins, but what could he do against a dragon? Who *are* you trying to impress?"

"The Duke of Manfort, for one," Arlian replied. "His ancestors led humanity in the wars against the dragons, seven hundred years ago. He might welcome a chance to continue the job."

Black grimaced. "He's more likely to hang you. After all, you hunted down and killed his chief adviser. If he's sufficiently annoyed about that I don't think it will matter whether he finds you in your palace or in the gutter. It's lucky for you that he probably doesn't have the wits to find anything but wine, food, and women without an adviser telling him where to look—and unlucky for your plans that I don't think he has the nerve to do anything about the dragons."

Arlian shrugged. "If his advisers urge him on, who knows what he might do?"

"Arlian, why would his advisers urge him to do anything as insane as hunting dragons? The only one mad enough to even consider it is sitting beside me on this wagon."

Arlian did not argue with that; instead he asked, "Who *are* the Duke's advisers now? The names I knew were Lord Enziet, Lord Drisheen, Lord Hardior, and Lady Rime."

"Well, you've just named the four best known."

Arlian smiled wryly. "And it would seem I've killed two of them."

"So you did," Black acknowledged. "And I believe Lord Hardior fell out of favor last year. That leaves Lady Rime."

"Who sleeps behind us," Arlian said. He glanced over his shoulder at the interior of the wagon. "I'm amazed she didn't wake during our little encounter at the gate."

"She might well have awakened and had the sense to stay quiet."

"So she might," Arlian agreed. He glanced back into the wagon again, but could not make out any of the passengers—the lantern was positioned so that its light did not penetrate far into the interior.

"At any rate, Lady Rime was not here to maintain her position or claim Enziet's," Black said, "and somehow I doubt that void went unfilled. There is undoubtedly some sweet-tongued scoundrel who has wormed his way into the Duke's favor in our absence—Lord Hardior, reclaiming his position, or perhaps some other courtier."

"And we don't know who that might be, nor whether he's kindly disposed toward us, so wouldn't you say it would be best to impress him?"

"Oh, I suppose so," Black muttered.

"One might expect that whoever it is would be grateful to us for removing Enziet and Drisheen and creating an opportunity for advancement in the Duke's favor," Arlian suggested hopefully.

"Gratitude is a virtue that is expected more than practiced," Black remarked dryly.

"I've noticed that," Arlian admitted. He looked around at the deserted streets.

Here and there a torch or lantern cast an orange glow across the gray stone walls and stone-paved streets of Manfort, or the mounds of dirty, melting snow, but for the most part the city was dark. There was no sign of any further ambush, nor any sign of Horn or Lord Wither's other men—but then, why should there be? Drisheen had left the city hurriedly, and had little time to prepare; furthermore, like all members of the Dragon Society, he had been sworn not to seriously harm another member within the city walls. He had probably only had time to commission the one pair of assassins, and would not have arranged an attack to take place within the city—he had surely expected to return, and to take up his place once more in the Society, so he would not have broken his oath so openly.

And Lord Wither would know that.

Arlian, Wither, Drisheen, Enziet—they were all members of the Dragon Society, all dragonhearts. Each of them had survived an encounter with a dragon. Each had at some point swallowed a mixture of human blood and dragon venom, and had been transformed thereby. Long ago a few dragonhearts—Enziet, Wither, and the long-dead Rehirian—had founded the Society with the stated purpose of opposing the dragons however they might, of avenging the attacks they had survived, the attacks that had slain their friends and families. For centuries, every known dragonheart in the Lands of Man had eventually joined the Society.

And those dragonhearts were no longer entirely human.

Dragonhearts did not age. They were immune to poisons and disease. They all had, to varying degrees, a supernatural vigor—dragonhearts were a shade stronger and faster than ordinary men, and did not tire as easily. They possessed an unnatural charisma, so that all of them, over the centuries of life the elixir granted them, were able to become wealthy and powerful. Every member of the Society, no matter how lowly born, was now a lord or lady, as the terms were used in the Lands of Man—owners of profitable businesses, with multiple employees they did not oversee directly.

Those were the positive effects of the heart of the dragon. The less pleasant consequences included sterility, toxic blood—and other things, secrets that most of them did not yet know. Further, dragonhearts tended to grow cold and detached from normal society over the years, and had therefore banded together in their own secret society—though even there, their relationships were often less than cordial.

Arlian, for example, had vowed to kill five of his fellow members, as well as various other people, in vengeance for certain crimes. He had dealt with three of those five—Horim, Drisheen, and Enziet.

Drisheen, it seemed, had attempted to return the favor.

That left Lord Stiam, known as Nail, and Lord Toribor, also called Belly, at least nominally Arlian's sworn foes—but he was certain that neither of them would try to kill him inside the walls, either directly or through hirelings. They took their oaths seriously.

So he was safe, for the moment, and had only to get home to the Old Palace. He peered around in the darkness, trying to recognize where he was. After an absence of more than four months Arlian was not entirely certain he could have found his own way to his estate by night; he had lived in Manfort only briefly.

Black, though, seemed to know every twist and turn of the route. He guided the oxen unhesitatingly up the slope toward the Upper City. It occurred to Arlian that he didn't know whether Black was a native of Manfort, or whether he had come from somewhere else originally. Black was not particularly prone to talk about his own past, beyond a few amusing anecdotes he would sometimes retail when drunk.

Arlian respected that. After all, his own history was not something he wanted widely known. He had told Black and Rime and a few others the entire story, and much of it had been revealed during his initiation into the Dragon Society, but to most of the population of Manfort Lord Obsidian was a figure of mystery, his background unknown.

And since he was an escaped slave, that was a very good thing. Arlian doubted that a runaway mine slave who had stolen and adventured his way into a fortune would get the same respect as someone whose background was entirely unknown.

He had not been born a slave; he had been born Arlian of the Smoking Mountain, a free citizen in the mining village known to outsiders as Obsidian. The natives had never bothered with a name among themselves, since there was only the one village on the Smoking Mountain; Arlian had not known that anyone called it Obsidian until long after the place was destroyed.

He had been a boy of eleven when three dragons swooped down from the overcast sky of a sweltering summer day and burned the village to the ground. He had survived in his family's cellar, where he had been trapped beneath his grandfather's corpse—and where he had swallowed a mixture of his grandfather's blood and a dragon's venom.

It was in the aftermath of that destruction that Arlian had been captured by looters and sold into slavery. He had spent seven years in the mines of Deep Delving before an overseer, grateful that Arlian had saved his life, had helped the young man escape.

Arlian had not dared to use his real name for a time after his escape, and had gone through several other names before finally arriving in Manfort, wealthy from adventures in Westguard and the magic-haunted south, and adopting the identity of Lord Obsidian.

As a boy he had sworn to avenge his home's destruction, and his own enslavement. He had later also sworn to avenge the murder of friends in Westguard, and the abuses suffered by the slaves kept in the brothel there known as the House of Carnal Society and the House of the Six Lords.

A sadistic overseer from the mines in Deep Delving, a young man known as Lampspiller, was also on Arlian's list of people who deserved punishment for their crimes, but he was only a minor concern.

Arlian had made a good start on fulfilling those oaths of vengeance. Most of the looters were dead; the last two, Dagger and Tooth, had long since vanished from Manfort and were perhaps dead as well.

Of the six lords who had been behind the atrocities in Westguard, Arlian had rid the world of four—three dragonhearts, and Lord Kuruvan.

The other two were the least of the lot—Nail had gone so far as to apologize for his actions and turn over the two women he had still held as household slaves, and Arlian had fought and wounded Toribor once already, almost three months ago, in a nighttime duel in the streets of a town called Cork Tree. Toribor's pair of maimed slaves, Cricket and Brook, were now safely in the back of Arlian's wagon, with Lady Rime and two Aritheian magicians, and pursuing their former master did not seem especially urgent. As he had told the assassin, Arlian had had his fill of vengeance, at least for now, and at least against men and women.

But then there were the dragons—not merely the three who had burned Obsidian and slaughtered Arlian's family, but all the dragons that still lived deep beneath the earth, and ventured forth to kill and burn when the whim struck them. Arlian wanted them all dead.

No man, it was said, had ever slain a dragon, in all of human history—not in the old days when the dragons ruled the world, nor in modern times when the dragons had retired to their caverns and left humanity to mind its own affairs.

So it was said—but it wasn't true.

Arlian had killed a dragon.

Admittedly it had been only a newborn dragon, a mere infant, and even so he had almost died fighting it, but he had killed a dragon.

Save for the venom scar on his face, his injuries from that battle were healed now—or at least, the injuries to his flesh; he was not sure just how much damage had been done to his spirit. He had learned things in that conflict that troubled him deeply.

He had also learned secrets that he thought might enable him to someday slay the dragons that had destroyed his home and family, as he had slain the infant—secrets that might eventually allow the complete extermination of dragons—but there were complications, very severe complications.

Arlian wanted to think everything out very carefully before continuing his quest for vengeance—and he definitely intended to continue.

He could do that thinking anywhere, but he preferred to do it in Manfort, heart of the Lands of Man, in his home the Old Palace, a rambling monstrosity that the current Duke of Manfort's grandfather had abandoned as too expensive to maintain, but which Lord Obsidian had bought and restored.

It was in Manfort that Lord Toribor and Lord Nail lived. It was in Manfort that Lord Enziet had served as chief adviser to the

Duke. It was in Manfort that the Dragon Society, the sorcerous secret masters of the Lands of Man, met—and it was inside Manfort's walls that the members were sworn not to kill one another. If Arlian stayed elsewhere, his enemies in the Society could send assassins after him, but here, they could not.

It was in Manfort that his potential allies dwelt, as well. If he hoped to wipe out the dragons, he would almost certainly need a great deal of assistance, and the Dragon Society—at least, those members, like Lord Wither or Lady Rime, who had no reason to hate or fear him—seemed a likely source for that aid.

Though there were complications.

And it was in Manfort that he had a household awaiting him—his hired servants, and four of the women he had saved from the House of the Six Lords.

He held no slaves, of course; after his years in the mines Arlian could hardly allow slavery in his own home. His four guests had been brothel slaves for years, their feet amputated to prevent any attempt at flight, but he had freed them.

He had freed those four—but it should have been more. Arlian's gut knotted at the memory of poor Sweet, who had died in his arms; of Sweet's friend Dove, whose bones still lay in Lord Enziet's house; and of Sparkle and Ferret, whom Lord Drisheen had hanged out of spite rather than permit Arlian to rescue them.

There were the two in the wagon, Cricket and Brook, which made six in all, but still, the House of the Six Lords had had sixteen unwilling occupants. Arlian had been unable to save ten of them.

He sat, silently remembering, as the wagon moved slowly up the street, and then dozed briefly and unhappily, the faces of dead women drifting through fragmented dreams.

He jerked awake again as the wagon bumped across a gutter as it crossed an intersection. He glimpsed the familiar outline of the Old Palace ahead, a black shape barely distinguishable from the black night sky behind it. The windows were dark, and no lantern hung at the gate or in the forecourt.

"We're almost there," he remarked.

"Almost," Black agreed.

"I hope someone's awake to admit us."

"I have the keys," Black said.

Arlian nodded. He should have expected as much, he told himself; Black was always prepared. A man of great foresight; Arlian knew he had been very lucky to stumble into such a companion, and even luckier that Black had stayed with him for so long.

Oh, he paid Black a generous salary, and Black was moderately susceptible to the superhuman charisma of anyone possessing the heart of the dragon, but there was no question that Black had the willpower and common sense to leave if he chose.

That he did not so choose flattered Arlian immensely. He wondered sometimes whether he deserved such an honor.

"I think the postern would be appropriate," Black suggested, breaking into Arlian's thoughts. "Given the hour."

"Of course," Arlian agreed—though if he had been driving in his current weary state he would have taken the wagon directly to the front gate without thinking about it.

Black clucked and pulled at the reins, and the oxen turned in to the alley, bound for the kitchen entrance.

A moment later the wagon creaked to a stop, and Black leapt to the ground. "You wake the others," he said. "I'll unlock the doors and see if there's a fire."

Arlian, who had been poised to jump down after his steward, caught himself. "Of course," he said. He turned and ducked down into the body of the wagon, dodging the arrow that still stood in the floorboards.

The Arithean magicians were curled up on one side, Lady Rime on the other; at the back, sleeping on cushions atop the luggage, were Cricket and Brook.

There was no sense in waking the younger women until someone was available to carry them; Arlian turned to the magicians, Thirif and Shibiel, first. He shook Thirif's shoulder gently. The Aritheian stirred and sat up, then awakened his companion while Arlian turned his attention to Lady Rime. Rime came awake instantly and stared up at him.

"We're at the Old Palace," he told her. "You're welcome to stay as long as you like, or we can take you to your own home once we have the others safely inside."

Rime shot a glance at the sleeping women, and another at the magicians. "I'll stay here tonight," she said.

"It's almost dawn," Arlian said.

"Then I'll stay the morning," Rime replied. She twisted around, pulled her wooden leg from the corner where she had secured it, and set about strapping it onto the stump of her left leg.

"Good," Arlian said. He turned toward the others, and found Cricket already stirring, her sleep disturbed by their voices.

A moment later Black returned to announce that the postern was open, the kitchen fire burning, and the staff alerted. "Will you want breakfast, my lord?" he asked.

Arlian blinked at him.

"I want sleep," he said. "Have my bed readied, and places found for all of us. Anything else can wait."

"As you will, my lord," Black said.

Arlian stared at him for a moment. Black had slipped easily back into his formal role as steward after months of casual equality on the road; Arlian, in his exhausted condition, could not make the adjustment so readily. "Let us fetch the women," he said, gesturing toward Cricket and Brook.

Black nodded.

Everyone was awake now, and the Aritheans lent a hand in getting Brook and Cricket down from their perch and out of the wagon.

Brook stared at the arrow, but said nothing. The others seemed not to notice it. Arlian suspected that Rime had been awake for at least a portion of their encounter with Drisheen's assassin, and had already seen it.

"We're really here?" Cricket asked sleepily, as Black lifted her and started for the postern. "I'll really see Lily and Kitten and Hasty and Musk?"

"You really will," Black assured her.

She smiled happily. "That's wonderful! What else could I ask for?"

"Feet," Brook said grumpily as Arlian hoisted her in his arms, the stumps of her ankles waving in the air.

And on that note, Lord Obsidian re-entered his home.

3

An Unexpected Legacy

Arlian came awake with the odd impression that he had coughed. His throat felt entirely fine, however. He blinked up at the plaster nymphs on the dimly lit ceiling.

"Ahem."

That explained it, he realized. *He* hadn't coughed; someone else had, to awaken him. He lifted his head.

He saw at once that the light in his chamber was only dim because the curtains were drawn. The narrow gap where one pair failed to close completely allowed a beam of sunlight, like a bright golden screen, to cut across the far end of the room at a steep angle.

From that, Arlian judged it to be roughly midday.

It was good to be home, he thought, where he could sleep away the morning in a real bed, untroubled by innkeepers or the exigencies of travel. He stretched beneath the covers, enjoying the feel and smell of the fine linen sheets, then looked around for the source of the cough.

Old Venlin, Arlian's chief footman, was standing at his bedside, carefully not looking at his lord and master.

"Good morning, Venlin," Arlian said. "Assuming, of course, that it *is* still morning."

"It is, my lord," Venlin said, "though in another hour or so the sun will indeed be past its zenith."

"Then it's time I was up and about my business, wouldn't you say?"

"It's not my place to instruct you, my lord," Venlin said.

"Of course," Arlian said, flinging aside the sheet and counterpane and swinging his bare feet over the side of the bed. "Still, I won't fault you for offering your opinion when asked. And right now, I wouldn't fault you for fetching my robe."

"As you wish, my lord," Venlin said, stepping to the wardrobe. "Might I suggest, if you do indeed welcome my opinion, that you might wish to dress immediately? You have a visitor waiting."

"Ah!" Arlian smiled as he stood, clad only in his shirt. "That's why you're here at my bedside, then. I thought perhaps the kitchen staff had simply become impatient about keeping my breakfast warm. Who is it, then? Lord Wither?" Horn had said Wither would wait until Arlian had had time to recover from his journey, which should have meant at least a day or two, but Arlian supposed Wither might have yielded to impatience.

"No, my lord."

"Oh? Then one of our unfortunate female guests, perhaps?"

"No, my lord—your steward has explained to them that you need to rest after your journey, and they are accordingly restraining their eagerness to see you. Your visitor is a gentleman who says he represents Lord Enziet."

Arlian's smile and good mood vanished; for one nightmarish instant he thought he had dreamed his long pursuit of his enemies southward along the caravan road, had imagined that horrific final battle with Lord Enziet, most appropriately also known as Lord Dragon . . .

But he could feel the scar on his cheek, could remember it all far more clearly than any dream, and he knew Enziet was in fact dead.

But the people of Manfort, and of Enziet's household and estates, might not know it yet. And even if they did, they might well still have posthumous missions, as Drisheen's hired assassin had.

He did not think Enziet had hired assassins—he would have left that to Drisheen. Presumably this visitor was some servant of Enziet's, here on some long-delayed business—or to demand any news Arlian might have of Enziet's whereabouts. Whatever he wanted, Arlian could not see how it could be good.

The news of Arlian's return must have spread quickly, even more quickly than he had expected, if someone from Enziet's household had already heard of it and come to call. Perhaps Drisheen's assassin—Arlian wished he had thought to get the archer's name—had carried the word.

"I'll meet him in the small salon in ten minutes," Arlian said, heading for his wardrobe. "Never mind the robe; I'll dress myself."

Venlin bowed, and departed.

This meeting with the dead man's representative seemed to demand a certain degree of formality, so it was actually closer to twenty minutes before Arlian strode into the small salon, washed and brushed, resplendent in his best black velvets, his vest and jacket trimmed with white lace and worn over a white silk blouse.

Just outside the door of the salon he had passed a pair of his servants, a woman called Stammer and a youth named Wolt, obviously planning to eavesdrop; he pretended not to be aware of their presence. He doubted anything would be said that he didn't want them to hear, and he could always chase them away later if it became necessary.

In the salon he found two men waiting for him. One was Black, of course, in the white-piped black livery of the household. The other was a thin, gray-haired man Arlian had seen before, also dressed in black. His coat was trimmed with gold, however, rather than with white.

Arlian knew those colors, and after a second he recognized the face, as well—this was Enziet's own steward. He had been expecting a mere messenger, not the head of Enziet's staff.

Arlian stopped dead.

Enziet's steward bowed, and said, "My lord Obsidian."

"Good day, sir," Arlian said. "I understand you wish to speak to me." He kept his tone formal, but not openly hostile; after all, this man was a mere hireling.

"Indeed, my lord. I am here at the direction of Lord Enziet—who, I am told, is dead." He glanced at Black.

"He is," Arlian said. "I saw him plunge his swordbreaker into his chest and tear out his own heart, in service of dark sorcery."

The steward swallowed. "Ah," he said.

"Did you think I had killed him, then?" Arlian asked mildly. "We fought, yes, but in the end it was his own blade that slew him." This was technically true, but highly misleading; Arlian had no intention of explaining the actual circumstances of Enziet's demise. He did not want to encourage any sort of retribution.

He wished he could have denied killing Lord Drisheen, as well, but alas, there had been several witnesses to that. And of course, Lord Drisheen had arranged his own attempt at retribution.

"I am not unduly concerned with the manner of his death, my lord," Enziet's steward replied. "Merely the certainty that it occurred."

"It did," Arlian said. "In a cave beneath the Desolation. I witnessed it, as I have said, and my man Black saw the body as well, and can attest that the heart had been ripped out and that Lord Enziet is no more."

The steward nodded. "We had reason to believe that my lord Enziet was dead some time ago," he said. "Through sorcerous means."

"That does not surprise me," Arlian said. "Lord Enziet was a sorcerer of renown."

"Yes." The steward's reply was a flat acceptance of Arlian's statement, with nothing of surprise or flattery or displeasure in it.

"And why does this bring you here?" Arlian asked. "Did your master leave a message for me, to be delivered upon my return? A threat, perhaps, or a curse?"

It occurred to him that there had been time for a message to be delivered before he left Manfort in pursuit of Lord Enziet; he had not rushed out on the other man's heels, but days later. Whatever brought this man here was something intended to follow Enziet's death.

"A curse? On the contrary," the steward said. "As Lord Enziet was preparing to depart, I asked him when we should expect his return, and he said he did not know, and explained the sorcery that would allow us to determine that he yet lived. I asked what we should do if he never returned, and he said these words: 'If I die and Obsidian lives, then let it be *his* problem.'"

Arlian frowned, but before he could speak the steward continued, "I asked him to explain that further, and he did. My lord Obsidian, Lord Enziet has named you his sole heir in all things."

"He . . ." Arlian stopped after that single word, and his mouth snapped shut. He stared at the steward.

As he stared, though, he was thinking about what the man had said and realizing that it was very much the sort of thing Enziet might have done. Arlian had been his bitterest foe, certainly—at least, his bitterest human foe—but Enziet had not been inclined to anger or hatred. His passions were colder than that, cold and cunning as a dragon, any human warmth he might once have had long since dead.

Enziet could have had no natural heir, after all. His blood and heart tainted by the venom of a dragon, he had lived for nearly a thousand years; any family he might once have had was long dead. And while the venom bestowed long life and immunity to poison and disease, another effect was sterility—for the past several centuries Enziet had been unable to sire children.

Nor had he had any friends or colleagues he would have trusted to succeed him. The few comrades he viewed as anything near his equals had all been ancient dragonhearts like himself, cold and treacherous—his closest companion, Lord Drisheen, had accompanied him on his final journey, and had died on Arlian's blade at an inn in Cork Tree.

Arlian had slain Lord Horim, whom Enziet had used as his proxy in duels, in a duel outside Manfort's gates. Later he had severely wounded Lord Toribor, another of Enziet's sometime companions. Enziet could not have relied upon any of his friends surviving Arlian's thirst for revenge, save perhaps the Duke of Manfort, and Enziet was hardly foolish enough to rely on the Duke for anything at all.

And Arlian could easily imagine that Enziet would consider his killer his only equal. It was very much his way of thinking. Nor would Enziet have thought he was doing anyone any great favor by naming him his heir. He knew Arlian had all the wealth he wanted.

The real question here was just what else Enziet's legacy might contain, besides mere riches. Drisheen's legacy had been an assassin of limited competence; Enziet's, while seemingly far more benevolent, might well prove more troublesome.

"His heir in all things, you say," Arlian said.

"Indeed, my lord," the steward said with a bow.

"Do you know what he meant by that?"

The steward hesitated, then said, "I assumed that he meant precisely what he said, my lord—that you are now the master of all his enterprises, of whatever sort, and that his estates and all their contents are now yours, to do with as you please. It is with that understanding that I place myself at your service, my lord."

"I already have a steward," Arlian said, with a wave at Black. "Tell me, though—do you think Lord Enziet meant me to assume his obligations, as well?"

The steward, discomfited, glanced at Black before replying, "I am not aware that my former master had any significant obligations, my lord."

Arlian's mouth twisted wryly. "Oh, he had obligations, indeed. And vows, and secrets. And I'm not at all sure I know enough of those secrets to keep up with the obligations."

"I don't understand, my lord."

"Of course you don't," Arlian said. "I'm not sure *I* do." He gestured at the chairs. "Do sit down," he said. "I need to think, and there's no need for us all to tire our feet while I do it."

Enziet's steward—Arlian realized he had no idea of the man's name—bowed, then obeyed, sinking into a chair of gilded oak and dark leather. Arlian took a seat on one of the blue silk couches for himself, and Black settled on the other.

Black cleared his throat, and Arlian glanced at him.

"My lord," he said, "do you intend to claim this legacy?"

"Of course," Arlian said, leaning back in his chair.

"Has it occurred to you that Lord Enziet might have prepared some elaborate vengeance? A deadfall tripped by entering his private chambers, perhaps, or some subtle poison on his personal papers?"

"An interesting suggestion," Arlian said, glancing at Enziet's steward, "especially in view of certain events last night."

"I can assure you, my lord, that . . ."

Arlian held up a hand to silence him.

"I am quite sure that you are not aware of any such traps," Arlian said. "Furthermore, I think it very unlikely that any exist. Lord Enziet intended to dispose of me far more directly, and was far too pragmatic to concern himself with any elaborate revenge—at least, any revenge so lacking in subtlety as killing me outright; he was not as simple as Lord Drisheen. I think Enziet might well have taken some aesthetic pleasure in leaving me heir to his own problems, though."

"Ari . . ." Black began, but Arlian cut him off.

"There may be traps. There may even be assassins. We will check for them carefully. However, I think them unlikely. Enziet expected me to die, and himself to live, and disarming such traps or paying off hired killers upon his return would be a nuisance I'm sure he would have preferred to avoid. Furthermore, dear Black, if you'll recall, Lord Enziet left quite hastily; I don't think he would have taken the time to devise and implement such a thing."

"He was in quite a hurry," Enziet's steward confirmed.

Arlian nodded, and for a moment the three men were silent as they contemplated the situation. Then Arlian said, "Tell me, does Lord Enziet's legacy include slaves?"

"Of course," the steward said. "I believe there are eight here in the city, and hundreds on his country estates."

"They're all to be freed immediately."

The steward's mouth opened, then snapped shut. "As you say," he said.

"Are you one of them?" Black asked.

The steward hesitated, then said, "Lord Enziet gave me my freedom some time ago."

"Ah. You *were* a slave once," Black said.

"Then perhaps you understand my distaste for that institution," Arlian said.

The steward replied with an ambiguous gesture, not quite a nod, not quite a shrug.

"Whether you understand or not, as Enziet's heir, I am now your employer, am I not?"

"If you'll have me, my lord."

"You wish to remain? You understand that I have a steward in whom I am well pleased, and that you will serve merely as chamberlain of certain properties."

"I do, my lord."

"Then do as I say. Every slave is to be freed *immediately*. Furthermore, they are to be offered employment as free men and women, but are by no means to be coerced in their decision to accept or reject that employment. I cannot emphasize this strongly enough."

"As you say, my lord," the steward said, bowing his head.

Arlian did not think the man looked entirely convinced that the order was a good idea, but at least he seemed to accept that Arlian was serious.

"What's your name?" Arlian asked.

"Ferrezin, my lord."

"Good. Once the slaves have been dealt with, I will need an inventory of my legacy."

"I will see to it."

A thought struck Arlian. "When time permits, I wish to know who is heir to Lord Drisheen, as well."

Ferrezin looked up. "Then Lord Drisheen . . ."

"... is dead, as well," Arlian concluded. "I slew him myself." There was no point in trying to conceal the fact, since there had been several witnesses. "He did not see me as kindly as your late master; we have already met and disposed of an assassin he had hired before his departure."

Ferrezin nodded. "I had heard rumors. I will inquire as to his heirs, my lord."

"Excellent. Is there anything more you wish to tell me, then?"

Ferrezin thought for a moment. "I have no further instructions," he said. "I would ask, though, when we might expect Lord Obsidian to visit his new holdings, in Manfort and elsewhere."

"I will come by Lord Enziet's manor tomorrow afternoon, I believe, by which time I trust a preliminary outline of that inventory will be ready."

"Very good, my lord." Ferrezin rose and bowed.

"Black will see you to the door," Arlian said, rising as well. That would give the two men a chance to exchange any steward-to-steward remarks that were inappropriate for the master's ear—and it would give him time to think.

Ferrezin bowed again, then snapped upright and wheeled on one heel. He and Black left the salon, and Arlian stood, looking after them.

So he was Lord Enziet's heir—and in more ways than Ferrezin could possibly know.

In that cave beneath the Desolation, far south of the walls of Manfort, he had learned a secret that Enziet had guarded for centuries—and other secrets, as well. That first great secret was a burden and a power, and on the long journey north, as his wounds had healed and he and his companions had made their slow way back to Manfort, he had thought about it often. Now, though, the news that he had become heir to Enziet's goods as well as his knowledge seemed to bring a new clarity.

The secret was simple enough—the method by which the dragons, once rulers of much of the world but now sleeping in their caverns beneath the earth, reproduced themselves.

Enziet had known that secret, and with it he had, centuries ago, compelled the dragons to leave the Lands of Man. He had put an end to the Man-Dragon Wars by exchanging oaths with the dragons—if they departed from the Lands of Man and allowed him to live, then he would permit them to live and breed, and would keep their secret safe.

Enziet had kept his end of the bargain up to the very instant of his death, when all had become clear to Arlian.

Dragons reproduced by contaminating humans with their venom, mixed with human blood. The elixir that bestowed the "heart of the dragon" upon any ordinary mortal who drank it—as Arlian had, when he lay trapped beneath his grandfather's bleeding, venom-drenched corpse—did more than anyone else had known.

Every member of the Dragon Society knew that a dragonheart was immune to disease and lived for centuries—and during that extended lifespan a dragonheart became ever more detached from humanity, ever more like a dragon. A dragonheart's blood was inhuman, toxic to normal humans, and became more so over time. They knew that, too.

What they did not know was that at the end of a thousand years, more or less, that poisoned blood became a dragon, and burst forth from its human shell.

Arlian had seen the dragon that sprang from Enziet's heart, had seen Enziet's mind behind its eyes—and had slain it, there in the caves beneath the Desolation.

That was the second great secret, the one Enziet had guessed at but never known for certain. All his life Arlian had heard that no man had ever slain a dragon; he did not know whether it had been true before Enziet's death, but it was true no longer. He had done what even Enziet had never managed.

Dragons were an incarnation of fire and darkness, immune to all weapons of wood or steel—but obsidian, the volcanic glass for which Arlian's home had been named, was fire and darkness made stone, and could cut a dragon's flesh. Enziet had made an obsidian dagger, and Arlian had found it and with it killed the dragon Enziet had become.

These were the two great secrets Arlian knew about the dragons—how they were born, and how they could die. These were Enziet's true legacy, far more precious than his house or lands.

When the dragons destroyed the village of Obsidian and slaughtered Arlian's family, he had sworn to destroy the dragons or die in the attempt. For years, everyone who learned of this oath told him he was mad.

Arlian thought it was entirely possible that he *was* mad—there could be no question that he had lived through experiences that could drive a man mad—but he also saw that thanks to Enziet, he did indeed have a chance to destroy the dragons, once and for all. In theory, he could hunt them down in their caverns, deep beneath the earth, and kill them while they slept—obsidian weapons should, he hoped, be sufficient.

He could not be *certain* of that until he tried it, but an obsidian blade thrust into its heart had been enough to kill a newborn dragon, and he could only hope that this vulnerability was not something dragons outgrew.

Finding their underground lairs would be a challenge, but he thought it could be done—by following rumors, by using sorcery, *somehow* he was sure he could find the dragons.

Furthermore, once he found and slew the existing dragons, he could end the entire race of dragons forever, free humanity of any threat of their resurgence, by destroying all the dragonhearts in the Lands of Man.

Of course, *he* was one of those dragonhearts, as was his friend Rime, as were all the other members of the Dragon Society.

There might be some way to cure them of the draconic taint, by sorcery or other means, to turn them back to mere mortal men and women again so that they would not undergo the hideous transformation Enziet had—but there might not be any such possibility, and if Arlian could not find a cure he would have to kill them all, and then end his campaign by destroying himself, as well.

Slaughtering the entire Society would take careful planning, and probably some treachery, since he was sworn not to kill any of the Society's members inside the walls of Manfort. He would there-fore leave that until later; he would start by hunting down the drag-ons. That would be a daunting challenge in itself, certainly.

If he survived it and completed the hunt, only then, when the dragons were gone, would he turn his attention to the Society. And only when he was certain that he had exterminated all the others would he take his own life.

This would take a very long time, but after all, there was no hurry. He had a thousand years or so.

Household Accounts

When Ferrezin had departed, Arlian began the business of restoring the Old Palace to its proper operation. He waited until Black had seen Ferrezin out, then inquired as to the condition of the staff. As steward, Black was responsible for overseeing the household, and even though Black had, like himself, only just returned from an absence of months, Arlian was certain that he would have arisen earlier and already seen to his business.

Arlian was correct in that assumption.

"I haven't spoken to everyone," he said, "but Stammer assures me the pantries and larders are well stocked and the ovens and cookware all in good condition."

Stammer was a young widow Arlian had hired after her husband's death of a fever; the deceased, Cover, had been one of the looters Lord Enziet had brought to the ruins of Arlian's village, but Arlian did not blame Stammer for her spouse's crimes. She had proven loyal and competent, and now ran the kitchens.

"Venlin reports the formal coach is in good repair and the horses all healthy," Black continued. "The footmen are all well and at their posts."

Arlian nodded.

"Hasty appears to have taken charge of the housemaids. The house appears clean, but beyond that I can't say."

That was no surprise; Hasty was not the sort to give succinct summaries of anything. She was not a servant, but a guest—one of the former inmates of the House of Carnal Society, her feet amputated to prevent any possibility of escape. When the House was burned Hasty and another woman, Kitten, were taken by Lord Kuruvan, the only ordinary mortal among the six proprietors.

Arlian had dueled Lord Kuruvan and won, freeing the two women. Hasty, however, carried the late Lord Kuruvan's unborn child—who surely could not remain unborn much longer. Arlian felt considerable responsibility for the coming child, since he had killed its father.

"Hasty—has her child been born?" Arlian asked.

"Not yet."

"I should visit her."

"Yes, you should," Black agreed. "You should also talk to Qulu and Isein at the first opportunity."

Qulu and Isein were two of the three Aritheian magicians in Arlian's direct employ; the third, Shibiel, had accompanied Arlian into the Desolation, and would have nothing to report.

Qulu and Isein, though, had had charge of the trade in magical devices that was the basis for much of Lord Obsidian's immense fortune. Arlian had been the first person in decades to make the perilous journey across the Dreaming Mountains to Arithei, reopening the trade route between that mysterious realm where wild magic was everywhere, and the Lands of Man, where magic was scarce and expensive. He had brought back three wagonloads of magical devices, but was no magician himself, and had hired Qulu, Isein, and Shibiel to use and sell those devices.

"Of course. Have you seen them?"

"My responsibilities are the household and your person, Ari; your business enterprises are none of my concern."

"Now, does that mean that they wouldn't talk to you, or that you haven't yet found the time to track them down?"

"It means I delegated that to Thirif and Shibiel, whom I saw at breakfast, and Thirif later told me that Qulu and Isein are glad you have returned, and want to discuss matters with you."

"Very good." Arlian smiled. Thirif was not actually in Arlian's employ, but he had nonetheless joined the pursuit of Lord Enziet, and had provided invaluable assistance. "Is Rime still here?"

"Lady Rime left about an hour ago, to attend to her own estates. She said to tell you that she expects to be quite busy for some time, catching up on matters neglected during her absence."

That was no great surprise, although Arlian would have liked a chance to say a farewell and thank Rime for her assistance on the road—and to ask whether she had, in fact, been awake during the events on the plaza outside the gate.

Perhaps, after months spent in close quarters, she had wanted to waste no time in putting a little space between Arlian and herself. If so, he could scarcely blame her. The wagon had been quite crowded.

"And what else?"

The two of them ran quickly through other household matters—not all of which Black had yet investigated. That done, Arlian hesitated. He wanted to see the guests he had left behind—Hasty, Kitten, Lily, and Musk. He also wanted to make sure Cricket and Brook were settling in comfortably.

But business, in the form of Isein and Qulu, beckoned. He left Black to attend to other matters while he turned his own steps toward what had once been the ducal treasury and accounting offices, back when the Old Palace had been the seat of government for the city of Manfort. Arlian had established his own businesses in that wing.

He found Isein and Shibiel talking quietly in their native language in the old tax assessor's hearing chamber; they looked up when he entered, but neither woman spoke immediately—probably because, Arlian thought, neither of them was entirely comfortable speaking Man's Tongue as yet.

Arlian stepped into the room, then bowed.

"My best to you both," he said. "Isein, it is a pleasure to see you again after so long an absence!"

"Welcome home, my lord," Isein said, and Arlian noticed her resisting the temptation to stare at the venom scar on his cheek. "It is good to see you."

"I understand you and Qulu wished to speak to me?"

"Yes." Isein glanced at Shibiel, then faced Arlian once again. "We must return to Arithei," she said.

Arlian frowned, slightly startled. "You wish to leave my employ?"

"No, no." Isein waved a hand in the air helplessly. "We need to go and come back."

Puzzled, Arlian asked, "Why?"

"Because we have sold it all!" Isein said. "We must get more magic."

Comprehension dawned on Arlian's face.

Encouraged, Isein said, "Two, maybe three months ago, we ran low. All the best magic was gone then. Now the rest is gone. Nothing is left. Qulu and I tried to make more, but the . . . the air here has so little magic we could do nothing."

"Of course," Arlian said. "So you wish to return to Arithei, and bring back more magic. Excellent. We will assemble a caravan at once."

"Good, good," Isein said. "But Arithei is beyond the mountains."

"A very long way," Arlian agreed. "You should start immediately."

"Yes, but . . ." Isein looked at Shibiel.

"Amethysts," Shibiel said. "To cross the Dreaming Mountains."

"And silver," Isein added.

"You have your pendants . . ." Arlian began. He stopped when he saw Isein and Shibiel exchanging glances.

"*Caravan*," Isein said. "Not just four of us. Four is not enough to be safe. When we came north we were twelve, and had swords and silver and amethysts. Now we are four, with silver and amethysts, but we have no swords now, and two of us . . ." She gestured at herself and Shibiel. "Two of us are women, not warriors."

Arlian stroked his beard, thereby reminding himself that it needed trimming. Isein had a point—of the dozen Aritheians Arlian had led north, half had scattered across the Borderlands on business of their own. Hlur and her husband had come all the way to Manfort, but Hlur had taken up her post as the Aritheian ambassador here, and would not want to join a trade caravan. That left only the four in the Old Palace—Qulu, Isein, Shibiel, and Thirif. Each of them had a silver necklace with an amethyst pendant—silver kept away some varieties of night-creature that roamed beyond the border, while amethyst, and nothing else, protected the bearer from the mind-destroying nightmares and dream-things that gave the Dreaming Mountains their name.

The Aritheians kept the knowledge of the power of amethysts a secret, so that the Dreaming Mountains would protect them from any outsiders who might seek to exploit or conquer them; no one in the Lands of Man knew, save Arlian and his companions.

Unfortunately, there were no longer any amethysts to be found in Arithei. It was a lack of amethysts that had closed the trade routes, and Arlian's bag of stones, inherited from a dead Aritheian named Hathet, that had reopened them.

And in addition to amethyst and silver, cold steel blades would be needed to handle some of the other monsters along the way—not to mention the bandits who lurked along the southern edge of the Desolation.

Four magicians who had used up their magic would not be much of a caravan, as Isein said, and anyone else who accompanied them would need to carry silver and amethyst to cross the mountains. The silver was no great problem, but amethysts? In the Lands of Man amethysts were considered just pretty rocks, not even fit for cheap jewelry. The Aritheians' secrecy had worked against them in that regard.

"Also," Isein said, "how do we pay for new magic?"

"Silver," Arlian said. That, at least, was simple.

"Your money is all in gold. In Arithei silver is worth more."

"Changing it is no problem. But amethysts . . ." Arlian tried to recall whether he had ever seen amethysts in the possession of any-one in the Lands of Man other than himself or the Aritheians.

He didn't remember any.

Arlian had gone to Arithei with one hundred and sixty-eight amethysts; he had returned home with two he had kept for himself, and each of the Aritheians had had one. Now he needed to replace some of the ones he had sold.

Well, he knew where those one hundred and sixty-eight had come from—the mines in Deep Delving, where he and Hathet had been enslaved. He could presumably commission the miners to find him more.

He could inquire of the jewelers in Manfort, as well, but he had little hope of finding much that way.

Returning to the mines . . . perhaps it was time he did that. There were old debts to be settled there. There was an overseer called Lampspiller who was on Arlian's list of cruel and abusive people who deserved to be punished, and the old man who had bought Arlian and put him to work in the mines had been a candidate for the list, as well.

Until now Arlian had focused his attention on the people who looted his ruined village, and the six lords who had owned the brothel in Westguard, and of course the dragons, but Lampspiller and the old man might be due for a visit.

Two of the looters had vanished, and the rest were dead. Two of the six lords still lived, here in Manfort, and four were dead. Progress had been made on both those fronts—but the mine was untouched.

And there were two people there, the brothers who had helped him escape, to whom Arlian owed a debt. He had saved Bloody Hand's life, but Bloody Hand had given him his freedom, which was even more precious. Perhaps it was time to see whether Lord Obsidian could do anything for Enir, called Bloody Hand, and his brother, Linnas.

As for the miners themselves—Arlian frowned. He didn't approve of slavery. He hated the idea that there were still people living out their lives down there in the dark, sleeping in the tunnels, spending their waking hours chiseling lead and silver ore out of the rock. On the other hand, the only slave who might still be alive there who had been anything close to a friend to him was Wark, and Arlian needed someone down there to find the amethysts for him.

Perhaps he could make some arrangement to have the slaves freed after they had provided enough amethysts—but to do that, he would need to control the mine . . .

Arlian wondered how much money he actually had. He had tried, ever since he had first arrived in Manfort as Lord Obsidian, to give the impression that his wealth was infinite, so that he could buy his way into the attention of the six lords he had sworn to find and kill; in fact, his journey to Arithei had made him very, very rich, but he had spent freely, and his magic business had now dried up for lack of goods to sell.

But on the other hand, he had just inherited Lord Enziet's estates. Presumably he was now as rich as ever.

Maybe he could *buy* the entire mine. He would need to find out who owned it.

It was possible that as Lord Enziet's heir, he *already* owned it. After all, why had Enziet chosen that particular place to sell a young slave?

But if Enziet had owned it, he wouldn't have needed to *sell* Arlian at all; he could simply have put him to work.

It would definitely call for further investigation.

"We will get more amethysts," he said. "But it may take some time. I'll need to make arrangements, perhaps travel to Deep Delving. For now, you and Qulu should make whatever preparations you can for a caravan to Arithei to buy more magic—buy silver and wagons and so on, but nothing perishable, and don't hire any guards or drivers yet."

"Yes, my lord," Isein said, with a slight bow.

A thought struck Arlian. "Thirif may still have a few items he took with him to the Desolation. And . . . Shibiel? Do you have anything left?"

"A few things," Shibiel admitted. "Not many. Not easy things to sell."

"Then perhaps we should just keep those for an emergency," Arlian said. "Thank you both for bringing this to my attention. And since you cannot devote your full attention to selling magic we no longer have, I hope to see more of the three of you!"

With that, he took his leave, and made his way to the south wing of the palace to see that Cricket and Brook were comfortable.

5

Petty Concerns

Arlian found Cricket and Brook, his new guests, in a sitting room with Lily, Musk, Kitten, and Hasty. He had come to see whether they were comfortable, but it was instantly apparent that Hasty was *not* comfortable. There was little Arlian could do about that—the discomforts of late pregnancy were not something that could be remedied by rearranging furniture.

The six women were talking rapidly when he arrived, their conversation punctuated by frequent laughter, as they brought each other up to date on all that had befallen them since they were carried out of the House of Carnal Society almost three years ago.

Arlian stood unnoticed for a moment in the sitting room doorway, listening to their happy voices and enjoying the scent of their hair and clothing and powders, and decided he did not want to interrupt this cheerful reunion. He was about to turn away when Hasty, shifting in her chair as she tried to find a more comfortable position, noticed him and called, "Triv! It's Triv!"

All six women turned to look, and all six voices were raised in greetings and invitations. Arlian could hardly refuse, and stepped into the room, where he found himself the target of a barrage of questions and exclamations.

The four who had stayed at the Old Palace during his absence all remarked on the new scar on his cheek; Musk and Kitten gave cries of sympathy, while Lily wanted to know how it happened, and Hasty said, "I think it's very dashing!"

He smiled, but did not explain how he had acquired it, and they were happy to drop the subject and barrage him with other questions, comments, and news.

He tried to leave after a few moments' chatter, pleading the need to attend to household business, but Hasty forestalled that by pointing out that he ought to eat a proper luncheon, and he could do that as well in the sitting room as anywhere. She beckoned to a footman standing quietly to one side, and Arlian found himself compelled to stay and eat with the six women.

This was no great hardship; in truth, he found their company delightful.

The meal was brought, eaten, and cleared away while Arlian was subjected to detailed accounts of all he had missed while traveling, including the progress of Hasty's pregnancy, the romantic misadventures of various servants, the city's gossip about the Duke and his court, various preposterous rumors about Lord Enziet, Lord Drisheen, Lord Hardior, Lady Rime, Lord Belly, and Arlian himself, and a great deal of other trivia. He did not manage to leave the room until late in the afternoon.

He wondered how four women who could not walk, and who presumably never left the palace, had gathered so much news, but did not ask them directly.

Cricket and Brook seemed to be quite happy with their new surroundings, he thought, and happy to be reunited with the other women. Arlian was glad he had been able to give them this; he wished he were able to make others happy more often.

He could not waste any time on happiness for himself, of course, until the dragons were all dead—and then he would die, so that the dragon within him would perish. His life, his strength, and his wealth were committed to that goal. The simple joys of life, of friends and family, were not for him, he knew that, but he took pleasure in seeing others experience them, and tearing himself away required an effort.

The remainder of the day was devoted to reestablishing his own routine, and making sure his servants understood what was expected of them in regard to his wardrobe, his meals, his privacy, and so on.

It was astonishing how many small matters needing his attention had accumulated in his absence—questions about replacing broken crockery, about what to plant in the gardens now that spring was almost upon them, about what to tell tradesmen and messengers regarding his return. He had scarcely begun on these when he found himself yawning uncontrollably and resolved to go to bed.

He told himself that he would get everything in shape the next day, and then begin planning his attacks on the dragons, recruiting other dragonhearts to help him, gathering information . . .

The following morning Arlian went over the household accounts, which appeared to be in order. By the time he was able to tear himself away from that it was well past noon, and time to live up to his announced intentions and inspect his unexpected inheritance. He left instructions for what to do if Lord Wither or his representative came by during his absence, then wrapped his cloak around him and walked alone down the familiar streets of damp stone to Enziet's estate.

His arrival was unlike any previous visit. Once he had broken in to this forbidding gray stone house, climbing up to the roof and lowering himself to a balcony overlooking the central courtyard; once he had come to the front door with a knife at the gate-guard's throat. He had never before been made welcome.

This time he was greeted with deference, with bows and courtesies, which he acknowledged politely as he was shown inside. He was not certain, though, that even now he was actually welcome—the servants' faces were carefully blank as they answered his questions.

The estate, he learned, was called the Grey House—a name that was apt, if unimaginative.

This visit, his first as the owner, was brief. He spoke to a few members of the staff to be sure that Ferrezin had obeyed his order to free the slaves, and then spoke to Ferrezin himself to be sure that the promised inventory of Enziet's holdings had been begun.

Guided by a footman, he found Ferrezin in the counting room behind the kitchens, in a state approaching panic because in fact the inventory, though started, was nowhere near complete. Rather than try to go over this meager beginning, Arlian decided it best to give the man more time to prepare. After all, given his own experiences in trying to manage the Old Palace, he well understood how little things could eat away at one's time.

He did, however, ask Ferrezin about mine holdings in Deep Delving.

Ferrezin frowned. "Lord Enziet did not own any mines there out-right," he said, "but he did have a share in several mining operations."

"Look into that first, then," Arlian said. "I want to know what I own there." He pulled a silver pendant from his pocket, and held it out so that the former steward could see the amethyst set into it. "In particular, I want more of these purple stones. This one came from a lead mine in Deep Delving—they sometimes occur in the galena, in the ore that yields lead and silver. I want you to send anyone who is not needed here out and around the city, to see whether any similar stones can be had from any of the jewelers in Manfort—or for that matter, in any of the surrounding towns, though I wouldn't bother with anything much farther than Westguard. And I want to know whether any of the miners in Deep Delving have bothered to collect these stones. I know they're considered worthless, but I have reasons for wanting them."

Ferrezin blinked at the pendant, then looked up at his new master's face.

"Of course," he said. "Ah . . . will any purple crystals serve?"

"I need this particular variety," Arlian said. "I will leave you the pendant, for comparison." He tossed the necklace to Ferrezin, who almost dropped it, snagging the chain at the last possible instant.

"I will begin the search as soon as the inventory . . ." Ferrezin began.

"No," Arlian interrupted. "The stones are of the utmost urgency. I want you to send someone intelligent and trustworthy to Deep Delving at once—go yourself, if you cannot think of anyone else suitable. I want a search of the jewelers begun at once. The inventory is *second* in importance; the purple stones are first. If you need another sample, I may be able to provide one."

Ferrezin nodded. "I see," he said.

"I'll leave you to begin, then," Arlian said.

Ferrezin watched him go, then looked down at the pendant and shook his head. It appeared his new employer was going to be at least as demanding and eccentric as the old.

6

Lord Wither

Three days after his return Arlian had not found time to return to the Grey House a second time, nor had he found an opportunity to visit the hall of the Dragon Society at all, to see for himself what the current situation was among his fellow dragonhearts and what reports of the events in the south had made their way into those chambers. He had not yet called upon Lord Wither, to thank him for Horn's assistance; nor had he had any further contact with Lady Rime, to inquire after her well-being.

He saw no need for haste in these matters. He had attended to the most urgent concerns in his own home and business and in Enziet's, and felt it entirely sensible to take a few days to rest and recover from his journey before launching upon any major new activities. Horn had said Lord Wither would call upon him, rather than expecting a visit at his own estate or a meeting in the Dragon Society's hall on the Street of the Black Spire, so he was under no obligation to speak with his benefactor.

When he had everything back to normal, though, he promised himself that he would call on Wither and Rime, and visit the Society's hall, and go over his inheritance.

And when that was done he would begin preparations to kill the dragons—to hunt them down in their lairs and see whether obsidian really would kill them.

Of course, he would need to find more obsidian and shape it into weapons, and even then he couldn't really be sure it would kill full-grown dragons as it had a newborn—he could only *hope* that it would.

And he would need to find the dragons. He knew where one lair was, beneath the Desolation, and he could try his luck there. If he found them asleep, and killed them, and survived the experience—and managing all three of these did not seem very likely—then he could worry about finding the others.

For that, he would need help, he was sure—he would want to question the other members of the Dragon Society, and go through their archives, for information that might be useful in locating the other caverns.

And that led, obviously, to the rather vexed question of just what he intended to do about the Dragon Society in the long run, and just how much he would want to tell them about his plans. He could not allow any of them to transform into dragons, but he had no desire to harm any of them any sooner than necessary.

And of course, he now had his two great secrets about the dragons, and as a member of the Society he was obligated to share anything he knew of the great beasts—but how could he tell them that they were all doomed?

He was still thinking about this, rather than actually doing anything about it, when Venlin informed him that he had another visitor.

"Lord Wither, my lord," Venlin said.

Arlian, sprawled comfortably on a silk-upholstered couch in the small salon, looked up at the old man, then glanced at the others in the room. Cricket was perched on the oak and leather chair by the hearth, and Lily curled up on the other couch; they had been discussing plans for the women's future when Venlin entered and announced this arrival.

It was not unexpected, of course, and Arlian suspected that he knew what Wither wanted, why the old man had sent Horn to Arlian's aid, and why he had been using his sorcery to track Arlian.

Arlian sighed, and gathered himself up.

"I will speak with him in my study," he said. While he usually preferred to speak with guests in the small salon and keep his study more private, thanks to the late Lord Drisheen's clever idea of amputating feet to keep the brothel slaves from attempting to escape it was far easier for Arlian to move himself and Lord Wither than the two women.

The study seemed somehow appropriate, in any case; that was where he had first met Lord Wither, shortly after Lord Obsidian had first arrived in Manfort.

It was odd to remember that meeting, Arlian thought as he ambled down the passage to the study. He had been so young then, and so naïve—yet how long ago had it really been? Just a few months, not even a year.

He had not yet fought a duel when he first met with Lord Wither. He had not yet joined the Dragon Society—it had been Lord Wither who first told him how to find the secretive organization.

Oh, he had not been a total innocent—he had already spent years working in the mines and months hidden in a brothel, had already stolen Lord Kuruvan's gold and journeyed across the Desolation to the magic-haunted Borderlands, and beyond the Dreaming Mountains to Arithei. He had survived dragons and slavery and made himself wealthy, and he had burned for revenge against those who had wronged him. He had killed a man in battle.

But he had not been weighed down with secrets. He had not had half a dozen mutilated women dependent upon him, and had not had another die in his arms. He had not seen so much death and horror.

Venlin had gone to fetch Lord Wither, and for a moment Arlian was alone. He stood in the entrance to the study, looking about.

The desk and the cabinets and the bookshelves were all clean and tidy, the varnished wood gleaming in the midday sun that thrust in through the two tall windows. Arlian crossed the room and pulled the draperies across the panes; somehow he didn't think Lord Wither was fond of daylight.

As he did, though, he paused, hands still clutching the maroon velvet, to consider that thought. Why was he so certain that Lord Wither would not care for the sun?

When he realized what his unconscious logic had been his jaw tightened, his teeth pressed hard shut.

Lord Wither had lived for centuries with the heart of the dragon—how many centuries Arlian was not entirely certain, but at least eight hundred years had passed since Lord Wither reached manhood. The venom had festered and grown within him, and now, while his shape was as human as ever, Arlian knew that the toxic ichor of a dragon flowed in his veins where human blood had once been. By now Wither was surely as much dragon as human in many ways—and dragons did not abide direct sunlight; they dwelt in caverns and emerged only when the skies were darkened with clouds. He still stood, hands on the drapes, when Venlin announced, "Lord Wither."

Arlian's hands dropped, and he turned to face his guest.

Lord Wither was a stooped old man; never tall to begin with, he was shrunk and bent with age, fitting the name he had borne for centuries. The name had originally been applied to him not only because of the ravages of time, but because his right arm was shriveled and almost lifeless, ruined in the draconic encounter that had given him his extended lifespan.

Still, despite his stature and condition, Lord Wither was not a man to be trifled with. Beneath his thick mass of gray hair blazed a pair of fierce, deep-set green eyes, intimidating in their intensity; the heart of the dragon was strong in him.

He was master of more ordinary power as well—political connections, and immense wealth that was reflected in his attire. He wore his hair pulled back in a simple ponytail nothing like the current fashionable styles, but his clothing was in the latest mode, and extravagantly well made. His coat was green velvet trimmed with gold, with long white lace cuffs and a collar faced with white silk;

the sleeves and cuffs were skillfully tailored to obscure his deformity. The shirt beneath was white as snow, elaborately ruffled, and his breeches were fine black wool.

Over his coat he wore a black leather sword belt set with emeralds, and the left-handed sword hilt protruding from the beaded scabbard was inlaid with silver, pearl, and diamond. Wearing a sword into another lord's home would ordinarily have been a grave breach of etiquette, but an exception was invariably made for Lord Wither; the customary excuse was that it would be unkind to ask a person with but one useful hand to unbuckle and buckle a belt, but Arlian was fairly sure that it was really because no one dared argue with such a man. Those eyes were enough to deter anyone.

Lord Wither stepped into the room, and Venlin quietly closed the door from without, leaving the two lords alone in the study, standing a few feet apart, gazing intently at one another.

"Lord Wither," Arlian said, taking a step away from the window. "How good to see you!" He did not extend a hand; Wither, with his crippled arm, never shook hands.

"Let us dispense with the usual polite lies," Wither replied, looking up at Arlian's face, and more specifically at the scar on Arlian's cheek. Wither's voice was deeper and richer than one would expect from so small a man. "You are not pleased to see me at all, and we both know it."

"You misjudge, my lord," Arlian said. "I will not pretend to take any great pleasure in your company for its own sake, but I am nonetheless glad to see you. I am grateful for your assistance upon my arrival at the city gate; I acknowledge myself in your debt, and I prefer to pay my debts promptly. Further, I am hopeful that we may be able to exchange information or other intangibles to our mutual benefit."

"I'm not here for intangibles," Wither snapped. "What I want from you is quite real and substantial."

"Indeed," Arlian replied. "And what would that be?"

"Dragon venom," Wither said. "Lord Enziet promised to fetch me venom, and *you*, I am informed, are Enziet's heir and successor.

You pursued him into the Desolation, and saw where he died. You are a dealer in magic, you've made your fortune at it, and you are a dragonheart obsessed with gaining vengeance upon the dragons—you would surely not have passed up a chance to learn more of their secrets. Furthermore, I can see with my own eyes that you have encountered a dragon's venom since last we met, for nothing else could have scarred a dragonheart's face that way. If anyone can provide the venom Enziet promised me, you are that man. If you have it, name your price! You say you are in my debt—well, this is how you can repay me."

"Ah," Arlian said. He leaned back against his desk. "I feared as much. And this is why you sent your man Horn to protect me?"

"Of course. If Drisheen's hireling had slain you, who knows what would have become of any venom you carried? If you have none in your possession, what would become of the knowledge of its whereabouts? I saw you safely into the city so that we could have this conversation, and you could repay me with venom. If you do not think your life alone to be worth it, I will pay you anything in my power. I *must* have it!"

Arlian sighed. "I would offer you a seat, my lord, but I suspect this conversation will be brief. It seems to neatly parallel our first, some months ago. Once again, you seek this dragon venom to extend the life of your mistress, yes? And once again, I must confess that I have no venom to sell you."

"You killed Enziet before he could get it? Then what marked your cheek?"

"I have not said that I killed Enziet. He thrust the blade into his own chest, my lord—and yes, he did so before entering the cavern where the dragons slept. If he had any of the venom in his possession, I am unaware of it."

"But you saw him die. You know where he was going."

"I saw him die," Arlian admitted warily.

"And that scar . . ."

". . . is none of your concern. I must insist on that." Arlian had already refused to explain the mark several times, to various people;

it had, in fact, been left by the venom of the dragon Enziet had become, and Arlian was not yet ready to reveal that to anyone—certainly not to Lord Wither.

Wither hesitated, then reluctantly accepted that and continued, "But you saw Enziet die, and you knew where he was going. Then do you know where he intended to find the venom he promised me? Can *you* obtain it, now that I have reminded you that I am determined to have it, and you acknowledge yourself in my debt?"

Arlian paused for a moment before replying.

In fact, while he knew none of their other lairs, he did know the location of that one cavern beneath the Desolation where dragons slept; Lord Enziet had led him to the entrance, and it was there that the two men had fought their final duel. With a little sorcerous aid and the cool air of winter to keep the great beasts asleep, it should be possible to slip in, collect a few drams of venom, and escape safely—but Arlian had no intention of doing so.

He would not do so because drinking the mixture of venom and blood, the elixir that Wither sought, would transform Lady Opal into a dragonheart, which would mean that in a thousand years or so, if she were not slain, her blood would give birth to a dragon. Arlian would not willingly help in the creation of another dragon, even at a distance of a thousand years. This was one magic he had no intention of restocking.

His brief hesitation was not due to any uncertainty about whether or not he would sell Lord Wither the venom; it was instead because he was unsure how much of the truth to tell the old man.

Lord Wither was impulsive, despite his age, and selfish and stubborn, like virtually all those who had tasted a dragon's venom and lived. Indebted or not, Arlian did not feel he could trust him.

"I am sorry, my lord," Arlian said. "I have no venom to sell you, nor will I fetch any. Lady Opal must live out her natural span without any draconic assistance."

The thought struck him as he spoke that perhaps that brief mortal lifetime might yet be enough to outlive Lord Wither. For the most part the dragonhearts thought themselves effectively immortal, since they did not visibly age; Wither probably thought he had another eight or nine centuries of life stretching before him, perhaps even more.

Arlian knew that to be false. He knew, from Lord Enziet, that it took a millennium or so for dragon venom to transform a man's blood into a dragon, and that that marked the span of years Lord Wither could expect to live—but *Lord Wither* did not know it; it was all part of the complex of secrets that Enziet had hidden from the Society, and that only Arlian now knew.

Wither had lived at least eight hundred years, perhaps more, already. If Lady Opal were to be contaminated, as Wither proposed, she would outlive him by centuries. If Arlian's estimate of Wither's age was low, or if the dragon within him developed somewhat faster than Enziet's had, then Wither might not see out another fifty years. In that case, Opal might survive him even without any unnatural meddling.

Arlian was not about to say as much, though. These were hardly appropriate circumstances to reveal such things. Instead he finished his refusal and explained no further. He stood against his desk and watched a red flush of anger suffuse Wither's features.

"May the dead gods curse you, Obsidian!" Wither shouted, raising his left hand to shake a finger in Arlian's face. "Why do you refuse me this? You say you are in my debt, yet you refuse me the one thing I ask. I know you, know the way you twist your words— you say you *will* not, not you *can* not. You know more than you say. Am I to watch another woman grow old and die because you have some secret you wish to keep? Is that it? Or would aiding me somehow interfere in that ridiculous vengeance you still pursue?"

Arlian wished now he had lied outright, instead of trying to remain in the vicinity of the truth. He raised both his own hands, palms out. "Calm yourself, my lord," he said. "I am not withholding anything for the sake of vengeance, nor is it merely to conceal a secret that I refuse you. I have my reasons for declining to bring you venom, and I think them good—as did Enziet before me, I am sure, for remember, he knew for centuries where venom could be obtained, and knew for years that you sought it, yet he did not offer to fetch it until circumstances drove him to it. I believe I know his reasons, and that they were the same as my own. The risks involved in such a venture, for myself and Lady Opal both, are so great that I do not care to attempt the feat. I *am* in your debt, and will gladly perform some other service, or grant you what I may grant—but I cannot give you the venom you seek."

"And is there *no* way I can convince you otherwise?" Wither demanded. "No price that would be sufficient? Ungrateful wretch! If you fear the dragons, you need not go yourself; merely guide a servant to the proper location, and I will pay you handsomely. Horn would be glad to accompany you and go where you direct him."

Arlian shook his head. "I will not do it, my lord. Perhaps some-day, when your temper has cooled, I will explain my reasons, but for now you must simply accept my decision."

Wither lowered his hand and his gaze met Arlian's. "Indeed I must," he said, his tone bitter, "for I have sworn not to harm you within Manfort's walls, and I have no way to compel you. But I am patient, my lord Obsidian, and Opal is still young, scarcely thirty. We will wait. We will wait for you to come to your senses, and we will pursue every other avenue open to us, and we *will* have our way!"

With that, he turned on his heel, snatched open the door, and marched out of the room, brushing past the waiting Venlin in the passage beyond. Venlin, startled, hurried down the corridor after the departing guest.

Arlian watched them go, and frowned.

Wither was a resourceful man. He might well find a way to obtain venom for Lady Opal—which would add her name to the long list of those Arlian might someday need to kill. Whether Opal herself would, given the option, choose a natural life or an extended one marked with the dragon taint and ending in violent death, Arlian could not guess—he had never met the woman.

He doubted, though, that she would defy Lord Wither's obvi-ous wishes. Wither had the unnatural charm and intensity of the heart of the dragon; ordinary mortals would be hard put to refuse him anything he wanted.

Arlian did not want to kill anyone, really—at least, no one human. Even the deaths of the handful of people he had sworn vengeance upon and had not yet slain, should they come about, would not be something he enjoyed. Lord Enziet's death had been necessary, and satisfying in its way, but it had sated his bloodlust. Any further killing would be an unpleasant duty, required by the need to force justice upon an unjust world, and to keep humanity free from any threat from the dragons.

Unless he could find some miraculous cure for the venom's effects, he would have to kill Wither in time. He would have to kill Rime and Nail and Toribor and all the rest of the Dragon Society before they could undergo the bloody transformation from human host to newborn dragon. He would have to kill *himself* before he became sufficiently draconic to lose sight of the necessity.

He shuddered, then swallowed—not at the prospect of his own death, a prospect he had lived intimately with since he was a boy of eleven, but at the thought that he might misjudge, and allow himself to complete his own eventual transformation.

He would need to kill all the dragonhearts before that change could occur—and he would have to find and kill the dragons themselves, as well.

It was a daunting task, to say the least.

He had perhaps as much as a thousand years or so before he became a dragon, but when would his nature have altered enough to vitiate the drive for vengeance and put an end to the project? That might happen far sooner.

He had been thinking that he was in no hurry, but perhaps there were reasons not to dawdle. The palace was largely restored to its proper order, and the servants could handle any remaining details; it was time to attend to all the other matters that delayed his assault on the dragons. It was time to investigate Enziet's legacy further, and to see what could be done about obtaining amethysts from the

mines of Deep Delving and perhaps meting out some overdue justice there. It was time to send a caravan guarded by silver and
amethyst to Arithei, so that his fortune could be enlarged and his
magical arsenal restocked—he might need both money and magic
to carry out an attack on the dragons.

And then, when all that was done, it would be time to begin the
extermination of his draconic foes—or to die trying.

7

Taking Up Arms

Arlian wondered, as he turned the dusty pages of yet another encrypted notebook, whether Enziet had accumulated secrets deliberately, as another man might collect gems or concubines, or whether it was simply a natural consequence of living for so very long.

Ferrezin had completed a rough inventory of Enziet's major holdings, and the list was impressive, but for the most part Arlian had only scanned it briefly. He was not interested in farms or taverns, or mines in the western mountains. Mines in Deep Delving, especially one particular mine, were another matter, but he could not tell from the list whether Enziet had had any financial interest in the Old Man's mine there. There were properties in Deep Delving, some of them clearly related to mining, but their exact nature was not stated.

Ferrezin had assured him that two trusted men were already on their way to inquire further.

An inn in Westguard was also of some interest, since Arlian knew that it had been built from the burned-out ruins of the House of Carnal Society. It was odd to think that he now owned Enziet's share of the building where he had spent months hidden in the attic.

And Enziet, using the Duke's ancient right to bestow abandoned property upon his retainers, had laid claim to the ruins of the village of Obsidian, on the Smoking Mountain, and to the obsidian workings there. No one had contested the claim, so that Arlian now owned what remained of his own childhood home, as well.

In a way it was almost comforting to know that Enziet had at least taken the trouble to keep what he had stolen, rather than casting it aside after looting it. And it was oddly satisfying to know that it had now returned to the village's only survivor and rightful heir.

Those emotional interests aside, Arlian thought that owning the ruined village might be useful, since sooner or later he would need obsidian.

Those properties were all of interest, in their way, and stood out on the long list of holdings, but for the moment Arlian was more concerned with the contents of the Grey House itself—Enziet's walled estate here in Manfort, the ancient fortified home where Arlian now sat at one of Enziet's desks, looking through his dead foe's notebooks, hoping to find further information about just what Enziet's arrangements with the dragons had been.

There were innumerable books, and several sealed chests—Ferrezin had worked with sorcery enough to know better than to open any—and an amazing collection of miscellany. Poor Dove's bones were still in a box on the third floor, and Arlian intended to give those a proper burial eventually.

For now, though, he was going through Enziet's journals and accounts, trying to puzzle out the dead man's systems.

Enziet had had an annoying habit of using ciphers and codes and other tricks, and of course no one had the keys to any of them, but Arlian was able to puzzle out some things, and there were often hastily written entries in plain Man's Tongue scattered among the indecipherable material.

While most of the writing in the notebooks might not be readily understandable, it was quite clear to Arlian that Enziet had gathered a great many secrets, only a few of which had anything to do with dragons. Many of them appeared to be related to blackmail or scandal of one sort or another—but then, Enziet had been active in politics, so that was hardly surprising. Several notebooks appeared to describe the misdeeds of various long-dead courtiers, and Arlian wondered why Enziet had bothered to preserve them.

Enziet had also been a sorcerer, and there were notes on many of his experiments. While Arlian's own knowledge of magic was severely limited, and mostly concerned the wild southern magic rather than the subtle sorcery of the Lands of Man, he was fairly certain that some of the things Enziet's notes described went beyond what the other sorcerers of Manfort knew to be possible.

It had already become clear to Arlian that if he wanted to recapture Enziet's knowledge of the dragons, he would need to study sorcery. And he *did* want to recapture that knowledge, so that he could use it in exterminating the monsters and eliminating their threat forever. He knew how to destroy their offspring by killing the human hosts, and he knew that weapons of obsidian could pierce the hides of young dragons, but he did not know how to find all the deep caverns where the dragons slept. He did not know just how effective obsidian blades would be against full-grown dragons. An obsidian dagger had slain the beast that emerged from Lord Enziet's corrupt heart, but that dragon had been a mere hatchling, not very much larger than a man, its hide still soft and red, while the three that had destroyed Arlian's birthplace had measured at least fifty feet, and perhaps as much as a hundred, from snout to tail, and had been black and hard and ancient. Arlian did not think a mere dagger, no matter what its substance, could kill such a creature. A spear might, if thrust directly into the heart . . .

He reached the last page of the notebook and slapped it shut, stirring a flurry of dust. He sneezed, and wiped his nose with a lace-trimmed handkerchief.

He had had enough of poring over these frustrating tomes, at least for the moment, he decided as he slid the notebook back into its place on the shelf. The secrets he needed might be right here in front of him, lost amid the hundreds for which he had no use, hidden by Enziet's codes and ciphers—or they might be somewhere else entirely, or perhaps Enziet had only carried them in his head.

He rose from his seat, brushed dust from his linen blouse, and turned his attention to the row of three trunks that stood against the wainscotting to the left of Enziet's desk. According to the inventory, these chests contained sorcerous apparatus—Ferrezin had not been any more specific than that.

Ferrezin had not dared to open them.

Sorcery did not generally require much in the way of apparatus. Sorcery was subtle. The Lands of Man, all the lands that had been taken from the dragons centuries ago, were poor in magic, and required that subtlety. In the lands beyond the borders, places like Arithei and Tirikindaro and Pon Ashti, magic ran wild, raging across the sky and flowing through the earth, and all the power a mage could want was there for the taking; in fact, Aritheian magicians Arlian had spoken with had explained to him that the hardest part of wielding magic in their homeland was restraining the sheer raw energy that would, if given any leeway, destroy or transform the magician and everything else in the area. Roads and cities in Arithei had to be protected by elaborate networks of wards and cold iron to keep wild magic in check. Silver and iron and certain stones, not just amethysts but a variety of gemstones, were used to contain the wild magic, and spells involved the use of a wide variety of symbols and talismans to bind the mystic energies.

In Manfort, though, and throughout most of the Lands of Man, there was so little magic that most people could not sense or use it at all, and the delicate art of sorcery had developed to exploit the tiny trace that remained. Anything that would restrict the flow of magic would be useless in sorcery, and anything that might confine it would be impossible to use with any frequency. Most sorcery relied on the sorcerer's own skill, and a few common objects.

It took a normal man's lifetime to learn to coax any significant effects from so limited a resource—but because dragonhearts lived many times longer than normal men, many of them were adept in the sorcerous arts.

Enziet had been very adept indeed. He had used sorcery in this very house to communicate with the dragons in their caverns—but the only visible tool he had used for that, according to the only witness Arlian had heard describe the feat, was a bowl of water. He had maintained spells of warning and protection, but those had required nothing but words, gestures, and the stones of the house and wall to anchor them.

What, then, was in the chests?

Arlian took from his belt the ring of keys that Ferrezin had provided, and knelt before the first chest, eyeing the lock. He lifted an oil lamp down from the desk and turned up the flame to provide more light.

The lock appeared ordinary enough, but sorcery was usually invisible. Arlian debated sending for Thirif or Shibiel or Isein, or perhaps inviting a local sorcerer to take a look at it, to see whether there might be some sort of sorcerous trap—but that would take too long. Pawing through dozens of incomprehensible notebooks had left him impatient, and after all, he did have the key, and Enziet was dead. Sorcery was delicate work, so delicate that much of Enziet's lesser magic might well have died with him, and Arlian certainly could not sense anything magical about the lock.

Besides, he simply did not think Enziet would have bothered with traps. It did not seem his style.

Arlian judged the size and shape of the keyhole, then looked at the three dozen keys to find one that would fit.

There were several that looked possible, but Arlian chose one immediately, for a very simple reason—it was black iron banded with silver, where the others were brass or steel. Iron and silver were protections against magic.

Sure enough, the key slid easily into the lock and snugged tightly against the wards; when Arlian turned it he heard a satisfying series of clicks, and the hasp sprang free.

No magic manifested itself; whatever protective sorcery the trunk might have had placed upon it either was gone or had yielded before the key. Smiling, Arlian lifted the lid unhindered, and peered into the chest, holding the lamp high.

For a moment he didn't recognize what he saw; the gleaming

black shapes refused to resolve into intelligible forms. He shifted the lamp, and saw its light glitter on sharp, curved edges.

At last, though, he realized what he was seeing.

The chest was full of obsidian.

This was what Lord Dragon had looted from the Smoking Mountain all those years ago. This was what he had been seeking when he found young Arlian, trapped in the cellars of his ruined home—and sold the boy into slavery.

For an instant that long-ago scene came back to Arlian in all its terrifying detail. He remembered the sight of the dragon's face as one of the three monsters looked directly at him. He remembered the horrible warm weight of his grandfather's corpse, and the pressure of the hot stone floor beneath him, as he lay pinned at the foot of the fallen ladder. He remembered the unspeakably hideous taste of blood and venom dripping into his open mouth, and his stomach wrenched at the memory.

And he remembered being pulled from the cellar to see his home in flaming ruins, the entire village destroyed, while Lord Dragon, with his fine clothes and scarred face and cold voice, directed half a dozen looters in stripping away what few valuables remained. He remembered Enziet demanding to know where the workshops were, where the obsidian was.

And he, Arlian, had shown him, to escape a beating, so as not to risk being crippled—because a cripple would never be able to avenge the wrongs done that day.

He stared at the black glass shards in that trunk in Manfort and felt all the cold hatred he had nursed for years rise up afresh in his bosom, all the thirst for justice, all the lust for bloody vengeance.

He had slain Enziet, or at least the dragon Enziet had become. He had let Cover die of a fever, had let Hide be murdered. He had killed Shamble and Stonehand.

Dagger and Tooth might still live; Arlian had been unable to locate them. Dagger had fled from Manfort years ago, and Tooth simply vanished. Tracking them down would probably require sorcery, if it could be done at all, and if they still lived—which Arlian thought unlikely.

The looters, then, had been dealt with; all were dead or gone.

But the dragons still lived.

And here, in this chest, was the material Arlian needed to make weapons that could kill them.

This was a part of what Enziet had left him, part of the legacy—surely a part that Enziet had intended to be used when he named Arlian as his heir. Despite his dealings with them, despite his betrayal of the old Order of the Dragon that had fought them, Arlian knew that Enziet had hated the dragons even as he was becoming one. For centuries, he had sought a way to destroy them.

He had found one—but had never had a chance to use it. Clearly, he had hoped Arlian would do it in his stead.

Arlian grimaced. Lord Obsidian, he called himself. This volcanic glass was his namesake—and his destiny.

He reached down and picked up a piece, and realized that it had already been shaped into a fine long spearhead. Beside it lay a black stone dagger, and a broken shard that appeared to have been intended as a sword-blade—but obsidian did not have the strength to make a sword.

Knives and spears. That would be enough. A good sword was a nobleman's weapon, meant for honest combat—and Arlian did not want to *fight* dragons. He wanted to *slaughter* them, as they had slaughtered his family and townsfolk.

He had been thinking that killing Enziet had been enough to satisfy his lust for revenge, and that he would continue his campaign against the dragons simply for the greater good of humanity, but now he realized that it had merely been enough *human* blood. He still wanted to see the dragons die for what they had done.

And with obsidian weapons and a thousand years, he might achieve that goal.

He was holding the obsidian spearhead and gazing contemplatively at the chest when a knock sounded on the door. He glanced up.

"Yes?" he asked.

The door opened, and a servant peered in nervously. Arlian did not know the man's name; he had not yet learned who everyone in Enziet's household was.

"Your pardon, my lord," the servant said, "but your steward wishes to speak with you."

"Ferrezin, you mean? He's not . . ."

"Your *steward*, my lord, not the chamberlain." The reproach in his tone was subtle, but definite.

"Black? Here?"

"Yes, my lord."

"What does he want?"

"He did not say, my lord."

Arlian frowned, puzzled. This did not bode well. "I will be down presently," he said.

"Very good, my lord." The door closed again.

Arlian put the spearhead back in the trunk, looked at the two chests that were still unopened, then at the shelf of notebooks and ledgers.

There would be plenty of time for all that later. He straightened his cuffs and reached for the door. He did not bother locking the chest; who would want to steal obsidian blades?

And who would *dare*, even now, to steal anything from Lord Enziet's house?

A few moments later he arrived in the gray stone foyer and found Black waiting for him.

"My apologies for any inconvenience, Lord Ari," Black said. "I had thought I could come in and wait until you wandered downstairs on your own, but I'm afraid that the staff here does not tolerate such informality."

Arlian waved away Black's apology, and directed him toward the inner door. "I'll tell them that you are to have the freedom of the house," he said, as he led the way to a small parlor, "but what is it that brings you here? Is there a problem at the Old Palace?"

"Well, I don't believe he's there anymore," Black said, "but he might well have slipped back."

"A problem you call 'he'? Of whom do we speak?"

"Your dear friend, Lord Wither."

Arlian turned his head to peer sideways at his friend. "Wither? He came to the palace again?"

"Indeed he did."

"Did you direct him here, then?"

"He wasn't looking for *you*, Ari," Black said, smiling crookedly. "He came to speak to *me*."

"Indeed?" Arlian settled into an age-blackened oak chair, and gestured for Black to take a seat as well. "And what did Lord Wither want with you?"

"He made me a business proposition. He believes I have a piece of information for which he offered to pay very generously indeed."

"And what information would this be?" Arlian asked, though he thought he knew.

"The exact location where Lord Enziet died. He wanted me to lead him there."

Arlian nodded. "I suspected as much. Did he say why?"

"He did not." Black eyed his employer. "I take it there is something he believes Lord Enziet had with him when he died, and which Lord Wither wants very much. When he spoke to you the day before yesterday, I suppose he thought you had whatever this mysterious thing might be? I suppose this is why he sent Horn to protect us?"

"He *hoped* I had it. I didn't. And for that matter, Lord Enziet didn't have it yet when he died, either—he was on his way to fetch it, and fell short of his goal."

"Ah." Black sat back in his chair. "I had wondered why Enziet sought out that particular cave in the Desolation. Should I ask what this precious thing was?"

"I think you would be better off if you did not. And when Lord Wither made his offer, what did you tell him?"

"Why, that I would consider it, of course! Am I so foolish that I would casually discard an offer of great wealth?"

Arlian smiled crookedly. "Indeed, Black, you are no fool at all, and well do I know it—though your willingness to remain in my service does perhaps cast some doubt upon the matter. Am I to bid for your services in this, then, to see whether I will match Lord Wither's offer?" His tone and smile were openly sardonic, to avoid any possible misunderstanding of his attitude.

"Of course not, Ari! You already *know* where Enziet died!" Black replied, mirroring that smile. Then his expression turned grave.

"Seriously, Ari," he said, "I really wasn't sure what to make of this. I know something of your history, and I've aided you in your pursuit of vengeance, but you have always kept secrets from me, and more than ever since Enziet's death. There are clearly issues here of which I know nothing; plainly, as plain as that scar on your cheek, events occurred in that cave I do not understand, and it seems reasonable to assume that Lord Wither's ferocious interest in the place, and in you, is somehow connected. When I travel through unfamiliar land I prefer to have a guide, and you would seem to be the only person I know to be familiar with these paths. Would it harm you if I led Wither to the cave, or would it aid you in your schemes? Would it harm *me*? Would it harm Wither? I can't serve your interests effectively when I don't know what they are."

Arlian contemplated his steward for a long moment, then sighed.

"I do wonder sometimes why you put up with me," he said.

"You pay well," Black responded immediately, before Arlian could continue.

Arlian smiled wryly. "Not *that* well—and as you say, I do keep some secrets from you, a great many of them, while burdening you with others. And I'm afraid I intend to continue doing so for some time yet. This one is one I think I can reveal, however, and one that should not prove burdensome. That cave was just an antechamber; what Lord Wither seeks lies below."

"A deeper cavern?"

Arlian nodded.

"One where dragons sleep? Was Enziet trying to wake them?"

"I'm not certain just what Enziet intended," Arlian admitted. "Waking the dragons is one possibility. What he had told Wither, however, was that he merely intended to fetch back a dragon's venom."

"And that's what Wither wants? Dragon venom?"

"Exactly."

"But why? He *already* has the heart of a dragon, and all the money he needs. Does the magic eventually need renewal, then?"

Arlian shook his head. "He also has a mistress," he said.

"Lady Marasa, called Opal."

"Exactly."

Black did not reply, and Arlian felt the need to add, "Wither has seen several women grow old and die, and has developed a distaste for the process."

"Understandably," Black said. "Shall I tell him, then, where to find the cave?"

Arlian frowned. "No. The world needs no more dragonhearts."

Black gazed thoughtfully at his employer for a long moment.

"It occurs to me to wonder, Ari, why you would object to bestowing long life and exceptional health and impressive strength of character upon anyone. It occurs to me to wonder why I, for example, should not seek out this venom for my own use."

Arlian had feared this might be coming. It would be simpler if he just told Black the truth, but although Arlian trusted Black more than he had trusted any other man he had met since escaping the mines of Deep Delving, he was not yet ready to share these particular secrets. Enziet had kept the knowledge of draconic reproduction hidden for centuries, and Arlian was not so hasty as to casually throw that secrecy away.

At least, not yet.

He met his steward's eye. "I have my reasons, my dear Black, and I think them good. I ask you to trust me in this, for now. Perhaps in time I shall bring myself to explain it all to you, and you can decide for yourself. If there comes a time when you can no longer rely on my unsupported word and I still will not explain, I won't stop you—but if the results of your experiment are what I fear, I may well do my best to slay you upon your return. I would really very much prefer not to do that."

Black made a wordless noise.

"And do remember, please, that what you propose is to slip into a cavern where several dragons are sleeping—a cavern with no natural light whatsoever. Do you plan to bumble about in the dark, perhaps stumbling over an outstretched talon while groping for the venom-dripping fangs, or do you intend to bring a light? I have no idea how soundly dragons sleep, nor how sensitive they might be to torchlight . . ."

Black grimaced. "You have a point," he said. "So I am not to seek out the caverns for either myself or Lord Wither and his woman. Shall I lead him hither and yon across the Desolation, then, pretending I've lost my way? It might discourage him."

"No," Arlian said. "I suspect that would merely make him more determined, and we owe him better than such a deception—he did send Horn and his men to our aid, and has not pressed that claim on my service. No, simply refuse his request. Let him find some other way to damn Lady Marasa; we will have no part in it."

He did not mention that he doubted even a man as reliable as Black could resist Wither's superhuman charisma indefinitely. The possibility that the heart of the dragon would be enough to sway Black to Wither's will if the two were to travel together in the Desolation for any length of time was not one Arlian cared to risk. Black might not appreciate hearing this stated aloud, though.

Arlian was so focused on the question of Black's susceptibility to Wither's authority that he did not think anything of his own words until Black replied, "*Damn* her?" Black's eyes widened. "What an interesting turn of phrase. Are *you* damned, then?"

Arlian's face grew still as he remembered all he had been through in the past ten years—fire, death, and horror; his family, his friends in the mines, the woman he had loved, all dead. He saw his own life, empty of almost everything but an obsessive need for revenge; he saw that he could not trust even his best and most loyal friend, but instead withheld secrets from him and calmly considered the possibility that Black would betray him to Lord Wither—and the possibility that he might someday kill Black.

Arlian looked Black in the eye. "Do you really need to ask?" he said.

Black's gaze fell, and the dialogue was at an end.

The Last of Lord Drisheen

For the next several days Lord Wither did not intrude on Arlian's attention—nor did anyone else outside his own households. Instead Arlian concerned himself with his preparations for his eventual war against dragonkind, and seeing to the needs of his guests and staff. Freeing Enziet's slaves had left that house shorthanded, but he hesitated to hire new servants.

He supposed that in time he would dispose of one house or the other, but he had not yet decided which. The Old Palace was much more comfortable, but far larger than he needed, and far more difficult to maintain. It had stood empty for years before he acquired it, because it was simply too big for any ordinary lord.

If he could not obtain more Aritheian magic to sell, and if Enziet's holdings did not yield sufficient income, he might not be able to *afford* to keep the Old Palace; and the Grey House, while lacking in charm, was large enough for himself and the six women.

If money was no object he would prefer to keep the Old Palace and sell the Grey House, but he certainly wasn't going to dispose of anything until he was sure he had dealt appropriately with its contents.

A box of bones and other remains in an upstairs prison chamber of Enziet's house were, Arlian knew, all that was left of a woman named Dove; on his third visit he retrieved that receptacle and began arrangements for a private burial in a garden behind the Old Palace, beside Sweet's grave, where Cricket, Brook, Hasty, Lily, Kitten, and Musk could attend without attracting unwanted attention to their maimed condition—or to Hasty's extremely pregnant condition. The funeral took place without incident on a raw, blustery day.

The evening after the burial Hasty went into labor, and Arlian sent for the midwife. Little Vanniari was safely delivered the following morning, and served to usurp much of everyone's attention for some time thereafter.

Arlian did find time to purchase a new sword and swordbreaker to replace the set he had lost in the cave beneath the Desolation, and to make a few experimental obsidian weapons from the supplies Enziet had left.

He received preliminary word from Deep Delving—Lord Enziet's holdings included a one-fifth share in the Old Man's mine, and the other owners would be willing to sell if the price was right.

The mine's manager, whom Arlian and the other miners had known only as the Old Man but whose real name proved to be Lithuil, had agreed to collect amethysts for Lord Obsidian, the exact price to be negotiated later. It was clear that Arlian would eventually want to make a trip to Deep Delving in person to deal with this—but it could wait. He did, however, send word that he would be interested in acquiring the other four shares, and that he wanted silver stockpiled for his use.

He did not visit the Dragon Society's hall on the Street of the Black Spire. He knew that he should, to assess his own reputation there and to inquire as to whether the locations of the dragons' lairs were known, but he could not bring himself to face the other dragonhearts yet. After all, he was seriously considering trying to kill them all eventually. A cure for the dragon's taint would be better, but he could not imagine how one might be found—in all its seven hundred years, the Dragon Society had not found one.

Of course, most of them probably hadn't tried, since it was the

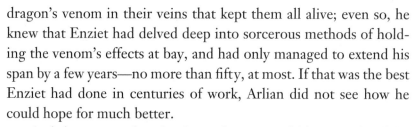

dragon's venom in their veins that kept them all alive; even so, he knew that Enziet had delved deep into sorcerous methods of holding the venom's effects at bay, and had only managed to extend his span by a few years—no more than fifty, at most. If that was the best Enziet had done in centuries of work, Arlian did not see how he could hope for much better.

And that meant that the dragonhearts would have to die if the dragons were to be exterminated.

Which also meant that he, Arlian of the Smoking Mountain, would have to kill them all.

Furthermore, as a member of the Society Arlian was sworn to share any information he might acquire about the dragons, and he was not yet ready to reveal the great secrets he had learned from Enziet, any more than Enziet had. Enziet had found it expedient to ignore that part of his own member's oath; Arlian did not like to think himself similar to his late foe, but he could certainly understand why Enziet had held his peace. In time Arlian thought he would find it necessary to reveal the truth, but he hoped it would not be soon; he needed time to think, to plan, to prepare himself and anticipate the actions of the others. Fortunately, the oath did not say that he must reveal what he learned *immediately*. He would tell them all eventually, if only to explain why he was killing them.

To walk into their hall now and pretend that all was as before, to face their questions about how Enziet had died, to look at them and talk to them in full knowledge that someday he would kill them . . . Arlian was not ready for that.

He did not go to the Society's hall, nor did he invite any of the Society's members to his home—not even Rime—nor did he call on any. Had anyone come to call at the Old Palace he would have admitted his visitor and been as polite as he could contrive, but he could not bring himself to seek out the company of men and women he meant to kill.

He did wonder what was being said among them, whether Nail

and Belly were concerned about their fates—they *knew* he meant to kill them someday, where the others did not. He did not seek them out, but he did listen when his guests or his servants gossiped, and he asked a few questions intended to elicit the latest news about them.

Since the members of the Society were all among the city's wealthy and powerful, gossip did circulate—Cricket and Stammer seemed to be the best sources, though Arlian could not imagine how Cricket, newly arrived and confined to the palace by her inability to walk, heard as much as she did.

Arlian was interested to learn that Lord Drisheen had named no heir. This was hardly surprising in a man with no family who had intended to live forever, but it was interesting, nonetheless.

Thus neglected, under ancient custom Lord Drisheen's estates had therefore fallen to the Duke of Manfort, and once a decent period was allowed for notice to be circulated, and for the Duke's representatives to sort through and remove anything that they thought the Duke would prefer to keep for himself, the residue was to be auctioned off at the Duke's convenience.

That convenience happened to occur some nineteen days after Arlian's return to Manfort, when the novelty of Vanniari's presence was beginning to wear thin, but before Arlian was ready to return to the tedium of sorting through the remainder of Lord Enziet's belongings, or to venture out of the city to visit Deep Delving.

While Drisheen's lack of an heir did not startle Arlian, this date struck him as a pleasant surprise; he had assumed, until learning otherwise, that Drisheen's estates had long since been dealt with, since Lord Toribor and the others had brought word of the man's death back to Manfort long ago. Drisheen's hired assassin had certainly known his employer was dead, so the news was hardly secret.

Arlian supposed he had underestimated the time needed to prepare for the auction, but whatever the reason for the delay, it suited him. The discovery that matters were not settled meant he would have a chance to see whether Drisheen, who had been one of

Enziet's closest companions, had left anything relevant to Arlian's own inheritance—perhaps Enziet had used one of his ciphers to send messages to Drisheen, and Drisheen had kept a key; or perhaps Drisheen had a diary recording observations about dragons, or about Enziet. Enziet had known where at least one nest of dragons lurked; perhaps Drisheen had known others. And Arlian admitted to a certain curiosity regarding any record Drisheen might have left of hiring an assassin.

Accordingly, on the appropriate morning Arlian made his way through the cold gray streets to Drisheen's mansion to attend the first session of the auction; the quantity of goods involved meant that several days would be needed to dispose of everything, with each day's proceedings including a mix of personal effects, furnishings, and business property, and continuing until the auctioneer judged the buyers to be losing interest.

Arlian went alone; Black was busy with the household and took no interest in what he called ghoulish proceedings, and Arlian had had no one else suitable to accompany him on such an errand. He had had no contact with Lady Rime since returning to Manfort, and his female houseguests could hardly manage an event where people were expected to stand while bidding, and to walk from room to room. Arlian realized he had no other friends in Manfort—a rather depressing discovery—so he walked down the hill to Drisheen's estate alone, his cloak wrapped about him.

The gate and door stood open when he arrived, attended only by one harried footman. Arlian handed this fellow his cloak, and did not wait to be shown to the auction; he found it easily enough by following the sound of the auctioneer's chant. He made his way through the foyer, down a passage walled in white stone, into a good-sized but overcrowded parlor, where at least a dozen potential buyers clustered around the auctioneer.

Other buyers were wandering through the various rooms, Arlian saw, and as he had no interest in parlor furniture he strolled on into a mirror-lined gallery where assorted lords and ladies were scattered, looking over the furnishings. No one acknowledged his presence, and he did not intrude, but studied the attendees.

Most were unfamiliar. He knew all the members of the Dragon Society, and had met a good many of Manfort's wealthiest and most powerful residents at the ball he had held in the Old Palace, but the people here to bid were mostly a little lower on the social scale, looking to acquire cheaply things they could not properly afford.

He moved through the gallery to the door of a salon, and stopped without entering.

The Duke of Manfort was in the salon, chatting with a portion of his court. Arlian thought better of intruding, and turned away.

It made sense that the Duke himself would be here, since the auction was for his benefit; presumably he had come to oversee the sales and ensure that adequate prices were paid. It made sense, but Arlian had not really thought about it. He cursed himself for this oversight—this might have been a chance to sound out the Duke's attitude about aiding Arlian's planned war against the dragons. Simply walking in unprepared might well end in disaster if he said the wrong thing . . .

But he would have time to consider, while the auction continued. Perhaps he could work out a sound approach.

For now, he decided to join the main body of bidders. He returned to the parlor, only to find that they were moving on to the drawing room beyond.

Arlian followed, joining the crowd for the next hour, but for the most part he made only a few desultory bids, and those only on books and certain personal effects, in hopes of acquiring information about Drisheen's sorcerous pursuits. He had no use for second-hand furnishings, and nothing with any discernable connection to Enziet was offered.

He purchased nothing in the drawing room but a bundle of papers that, upon investigation, proved to be household accounts, all utterly useless.

From there the auctioneer moved on into Lord Drisheen's

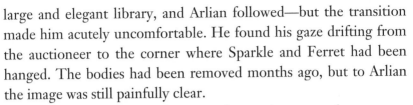

large and elegant library, and Arlian followed—but the transition made him acutely uncomfortable. He found his gaze drifting from the auctioneer to the corner where Sparkle and Ferret had been hanged. The bodies had been removed months ago, but to Arlian the image was still painfully clear.

He forced himself to focus on the auctioneer, and a moment later on the Duke's own little party. The Duke and his half dozen courtiers had climbed up a concealed stair to the balcony behind the auctioneer and now stood there, looking out at the crowd, the better to observe the bidding.

That brought the memory of the hanged women back even more forcefully. A lordling in pale green satin, the farthest of the party from the Duke, stood with his elbow not six inches from where the noose that killed Ferret had been looped across the balcony rail. Arlian tried not to think about that as he looked over the Duke's party.

About half of the Duke's companions were dragonhearts, Arlian saw. The crowd of potential buyers on the floor below included a handful more of these. The Dragon Society controlled most of the wealth and power in Manfort, after all; Arlian had suspected at least a few of them would attend.

As in the gallery, none of them acknowledged his presence, even though the dragonhearts, unlike those others, unquestionably knew who he was. He was unsure whether they were caught up in the bidding and had honestly not noticed him, or whether they were deliberately ignoring him. Snubbing the man who had killed four prominent lords, three of them dragonhearts, was not unreasonable, Arlian supposed—but it might be that his presence had truly been unobserved, as he was not making himself obvious and had come without retinue.

In any case, Arlian found himself with an opportunity to observe the dynamics of the city's elite, the Duke's entourage and the Dragon Society, that was probably more use than any chance to buy anything. What he immediately saw was that Lord Hardior, who had been out of favor not long before, had obviously taken up the role of chief adviser now that both Enziet and Drisheen were gone.

Lady Rime, once also a senior adviser, was not present, and the other courtiers in attendance were clearly not significant. Hardior alone stood at the Duke's side, rather than a respectful step back.

Arlian had first met Lord Hardior at the elaborate ball held to introduce Lord Obsidian to Manfort's rulers, but had not dealt with him much after that. Lord Hardior was a member of the Dragon Society, of course—the Society, working behind the scenes, held almost all real power in Manfort—but had not been present for Arlian's initiation, and had therefore not participated in the ritual questioning there. Arlian thought he might have exchanged a few polite words with Hardior on various other occasions, though.

He remembered that Lord Hardior had reportedly been cast out of the Duke's inner circle a year or two back, and that Lord Enziet had been rumored to be responsible. Now, though, Enziet was dead, and here was Lord Hardior, impeccably dressed in white lace and brown velvet, pressed close up beside the Duke, whispering jokes into the Duke's ear, unobtrusively pointing out the prettiest women in the crowd, while the other advisers maintained a respectful distance and the Duke smiled and chuckled in response; clearly, Lord Hardior had seized on the opportunity presented by Enziet's absence.

At that moment, as the auctioneer droned on about a tedious volume of genealogy, Hardior happened to glance out at the crowd and notice Arlian looking up at him.

Their eyes met, and Hardior smiled.

Arlian wondered what that smile meant; it seemed friendly enough, but he knew better than to trust any dragonheart to be what he appeared. This was not the cold smile of an enemy sighting his prey, or the ironic disdain Arlian had often seen Enziet display; it seemed a sincere display of warmth.

That warmth could be false, of course, intended to deceive

Arlian into thinking he had an ally until the jaws of a trap closed around him. It might well be that Hardior was preparing to arrest Arlian for the murder of Lord Drisheen, and found it ironically satisfying to see Arlian here in Drisheen's home.

If he were to be charged with any crime it would probably be Drisheen's death, since Arlian's other significant killings had all been in fair and honorable combat. He had slain Drisheen in cold blood, Drisheen's sword undrawn, before witnesses; if Hardior wanted to destroy Arlian, that would be the best accusation to bring to bear.

On the other hand, it could be that Lord Hardior did indeed feel some appreciation for Arlian's actions in removing Enziet and Drisheen permanently, and taking Rime out of the city for several months, leaving the Duke virtually unattended by those he trusted.

That could be useful. A political ally might be very helpful indeed in making preparations to destroy the dragons and the Dragon Society. Arlian cocked his head and smiled back.

For a moment the two men stood smiling at one another; then Hardior leaned over and whispered in the Duke's ear. He pointed at Arlian.

The Duke's gaze followed Hardior's finger until it found Arlian, whereupon the Duke smiled and waved.

Arlian made a small bow in response. A few heads turned his direction at this, but no one commented. He thought he saw a few surprised faces among the dragonhearts, but any such expression was quickly suppressed.

Then all of them returned their attention to the auction as the genealogy sold for a mere seven ducats, and a volume of Lady Arinia's infamous erotic tales, the cause of much scandal three centuries before, was put up for bid.

The Duke had seemed favorably disposed toward him, and Arlian wondered whether there was any way to take advantage of this—but he was down here, pretending to bid, and the Duke was up on the balcony, watching, and he could not see any way to get close enough to speak without violating the etiquette of the occasion.

Besides, there was no chance of speaking with the Duke here

without Lord Hardior being a party to the conversation, and Arlian did not know enough of Hardior's intentions and attitudes to risk that.

He frowned, and tried to politely ignore the men on the balcony—and the unwanted image of Ferret, dangling there . . .

A Conversation with Lord Hardior

Not long after that Arlian grew bored, and turned to leave. Nothing of interest was for sale, so far as he could determine, and he had seen what he came to see in other matters—the elite of Manfort seemed to have accepted the loss of Lord Enziet and Lord Drisheen without any great disruption, and it was plain that the Duke of Manfort remained an easily guided fool securely in the grip of the Dragon Society.

And no one had been openly hostile toward him; in fact, Hardior and the Duke had seemed quite friendly. If anyone intended to avenge the men Arlian had slain, they were not being obvious about it. That would make his life easier; there would be no distractions as he prepared his campaign against the dragons. He had half expected to find that Lord Toribor, perhaps with the aid of Lord Nail, had stirred up the Society against him, making him an outcast—but there was no sign of any such thing.

Neither Toribor nor Nail had been present at the auction, however, nor had most of the other dragonhearts. Arlian reminded himself that he could not allow himself to be *too* confident of his own safety. They might well still have plans to deal with the man who had sworn to slay them. Wither wanted him alive, but no one else had sent anyone to stop Drisheen's assassin.

He paused in the doorway to pull his cloak about him; the sky outside was leaden gray, as gray as the stone streets beyond the gate, and the air was chill, as the dying winter managed one last gasp. He was about to step out and let the footman close the door when he heard a footstep and a polite cough behind him.

He turned to find Lord Hardior standing at the far side of the little foyer, one arm draped gracefully against the doorframe.

"My lord Hardior," Arlian said. "A pleasure to see you!"

"Lord Obsidian," Hardior said, stepping forward, out of the doorway. "I had hoped to catch you."

Arlian glanced at the waiting footman, and said, "I was just leaving; shall I stay, then?"

"Oh, pray don't let me keep you—but might I walk with you as far as the gate, perhaps? A few words make any journey more pleasant, no matter how brief, don't you think?"

"Indeed," Arlian said. "I would be glad of your company." He bowed slightly, then turned and stepped outside. He took two paces down the path toward the gate, then paused until Lord Hardior appeared at his side.

"Is your coach waiting?" Hardior asked.

"I walked," Arlian said. "And yourself?"

"I rode with His Grace," Hardior replied. "Since I have forgone the pleasure of his company for the remainder of the afternoon, I, too, am on foot."

"Then if you like, our stroll need not end at the gate. I take it that if you abandoned His Grace in my favor, there was some fairly urgent matter you wished to speak of with me?" Arlian set out down the path at a leisurely pace as he spoke, and Hardior accompanied him.

This was a perfect opportunity to sound out Lord Hardior, to learn a little of how he was viewed in the Duke's court and in the Dragon Society. Arlian tried not to grin, limiting himself instead to a polite little smile.

Hardior smiled as well. "Perhaps not urgent, my lord, but of some importance, yes."

"Then tell me of it, I pray."

"It's simple enough. I wish to know your intentions."

Arlian glanced sideways at him. This was a more direct approach than he had expected. "My intentions?"

"Indeed. You have deprived His Grace of two trusted advisers, and while he does not doubt your honor or question your justification, he is concerned lest you remove more. He wonders whether perhaps it is your intent to gain power in Manfort by thus removing rivals."

The two had reached the gate, where a gatekeeper stood by watching silently as they passed. He had not been there when Arlian arrived, and Arlian would have preferred it had he not been there now.

Arlian said, "My dear Hardior, I am not interested in gaining power at all, by any means. I know you were not present at my . . . arrival on the Street of the Black Spire, but surely you heard some of what was said there?" He did not think it wise to mention the Dragon Society by name while the gatekeeper was still within earshot, but he was sure Hardior would recognize the reference.

"One hears so many tales, Obsidian, that one scarcely knows what to believe. I would prefer you tell me directly why you came to Manfort, and what you hope to accomplish."

"I came in pursuit of vengeance, my lord," Arlian said. He could see no reason to evade the question; his purposes were hardly secret within the Society, and they were now too far down the street for the gatekeeper to overhear. The street was not utterly deserted, but the other citizens abroad on this gloomy day were few, and all seemed more concerned with getting home out of the damp chill than with listening to the conversation of the two lords. "As a child I was wrongly sold into slavery in the mines of Deep Delving, and I swore to find and slay the seven people who participated in that shameful act. Later I befriended women who were maimed and then murdered at the whim of six lords, and further swore to avenge those poor dead souls, as well as my own enslavement."

"Thirteen men, then," Hardior said.

Arlian shook his head. "No," he said. "Ten men, and two women, for one of the six lords was Lord Enziet, who was also the man who sold me into slavery."

"And have you disposed of them all, then?"

"I have found all the ten men," Arlian said, "and eight of them are dead. Two of the lords, Nail and Belly, still live, and I have been unable to locate the two women—one is thought to have died years ago, and the other fled Manfort and has never returned."

He belatedly remembered Lampspiller—his envoys to Deep Delving had not been instructed to inquire after the overseer, so he had no idea whether Lampspiller still lived.

If he did . . . well, it was a minor matter compared to the dragons, and he was unsure whether he would pursue it or not. He decided not to mention it.

"And where does this leave you, then?" Hardior asked. "As a member of the Dragon Society you are sworn not to kill Nail and Belly within the city walls; do you propose to hunt down these two women?"

"I have had enough of vengeance against men and women, my lord. It may well happen someday that I will kill Nail and Belly— Nail has agreed to meet me outside the wall when I have dealt with Belly, and I may take him up on that, or I may not. Belly and I have fought before, and I think we have each other's measure; at this point I think it might be possible to let the matter end there, but it may be that we will fight again at some point." The memory of that duel in the night-dark streets of Cork Tree, which had ended with Toribor lying bleeding in the dirt, rushed back, and Arlian found himself thinking that he should pay Lord Toribor a visit, and discuss matters left unresolved between them. He should have done so sooner, in fact, but since his return to Manfort he had been distracted—by Enziet's legacy, by Isein's news about the dearth of magic, by Wither's visit, by Vanniari's birth.

He did not particularly want to kill Lord Toribor anymore, but he had said, there in the streets of Cork Tree, that their dispute was

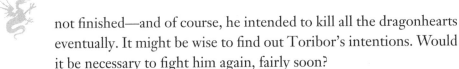

not finished—and of course, he intended to kill all the dragonhearts eventually. It might be wise to find out Toribor's intentions. Would it be necessary to fight him again, fairly soon?

He remembered that he had made a promise to Toribor, there in Cork Tree—that he would hear Enziet out before killing him. Toribor had believed that Enziet's death would unleash all the dragons upon the Lands of Man, and end the peace between humanity and the dragons that had lasted seven centuries now.

That had actually been a fairly reasonable belief—it had been Enziet's bargain that had ended the old Man-Dragon Wars. Enziet had been dead for months, though, and Arlian had heard no reports that the dragons had emerged from their caves. It would seem that the predicted catastrophe had not come. Arlian wondered what Toribor thought of that.

These were definitely matters to be discussed.

None of them were anything he wished to discuss with Hardior, though. His concerns with Toribor were his own affair, and none of Hardior's business.

"Those two women, if they live, I no longer think worth the trouble of pursuit," he added as an afterthought. "Though if I happen across them, I will deal with them as seems appropriate at that time." Dagger and Tooth had merely been tools of Enziet, of Lord Dragon; with their master gone they were no more than two scoundrels in a world awash with their like.

"Then when you have met and slain Belly and Nail, assuming you do contrive to accomplish this and survive, what will you do?" Hardior asked. "Have you plans beyond this vengeance you've pursued so diligently?"

Arlian smiled crookedly. "Indeed I do, my lord, for I have not yet mentioned the greater revenge I seek. The men are my lesser foes. My family was slain by three dragons when I was a boy, and I have sworn to find and destroy those dragons, or die in the attempt." He did not mention that he intended to kill *all* the dragons; that would sound far too grandiose.

"Ah!" Hardior spread his hands. "I had heard this, my lord, but I could scarcely credit that the man who slew Lord Enziet could be so mad."

So much for restraint in declaring his intentions. Arlian threw Hardior a quick, wary glance. "Lord Enziet cut out his own heart," he said. "I have not said I killed him, merely that he is dead."

"I am not seeking to trick a confession from you, Obsidian. There are obviously mysteries here I do not understand—that fact is written on your cheek, for no blade made that mark. I do not ask you to explain. I may never truly know what happened to Lord Enziet, and this does not greatly trouble me. From my own point of view it is enough that he is gone, and that you do not seek to take his place."

"I have no interest in replacing him in the Duke's court," Arlian said. "He did, however, name me heir to his possessions and estates, and I have accepted that role."

"And you are welcome to it. Better to have them in your hands than disputed, or auctioned to fill the Duke's overflowing coffers as Drisheen's are."

Arlian stopped walking and turned to face Hardior.

"My lord," he said, "let us speak plainly. You said you wished to speak to me of a matter of some importance, yet you ask only about my own intentions. While plainly these are of importance to *me*, I fail to see their significance to *you*. Were I truly hoping to usurp your position at court, or subvert your influence in some other way, surely I would not *tell* you? You would not trouble yourself solely to hear my protestations of innocence—what *else* could I say? Why, then, are we having this conversation?"

Hardior grinned at him.

"As blunt as Enziet, aren't you?" he said. "Very well, then. Yes, I expected you to deny any aspirations to power here in Manfort, but I thought myself capable of judging your sincerity. Furthermore, since you do indeed appear to be mad, I thought you might voluntarily provide me with a list of whom you still intend to murder, so that I might plan accordingly. You appear to have done so.

You have named Nail and Belly and said there are no others, and I believe you. Nail is of no political consequence whatsoever, having withdrawn from court before the present Duke was even born; Belly is committed to no faction since Enziet's death, and indeed appears to be almost a broken man, one who can be easily dealt with, spending his time practicing swordplay rather than politics. I have hopes, my lord, that you, as Enziet's heir and a very wealthy man in your own right, can be convinced to openly support my position at court—it would strengthen my standing, and in exchange I would ensure that there will be no investigation into Lord Drisheen's death in a Cork Tree tavern."

"Indeed," Arlian said. He had to admit to himself that such a bargain would have its advantages, freeing him of any worries about the Duke's interference in his affairs, but he could not resist adding sarcastically, "And how do the dragons figure into your calculations?"

"As yet they do not," Hardior said. "While it's true that Belly has babbled about secrets and bargains that Lord Enziet had made, I expect that matters will go on much as they have for centuries— the dragons will stay in their caverns much of the time, emerging once in a while when the weather is right to destroy some unfortunate hamlet, and we will ignore them and go about our business. If you seriously do attempt to destroy them you will, of course, die in the attempt, which will be unfortunate, but the rest of us will continue without you—I only hope that you do not thereby stir them sufficiently to provoke the destruction of a village or two. If, as I rather expect, you find it expedient to spend a good many years in planning and preparation, then we will have the pleasure of your company that much longer."

Arlian stared at him silently for a moment, and Hardior's smile slipped under that gaze.

"There are secrets here you do not know, my lord," Arlian said at last. "What Enziet told Belly was, if not lies, at best only part of the truth, but Enziet did spend almost a thousand years researching the nature of dragons, and he named me heir to what he learned. I may be mad, my lord, but I believe I do in fact know a means of killing dragons. If it proves that I am *not* mad, and I do indeed slay one or more of the monsters, what then?"

Hardior's smile vanished.

"Are you asking what I would do if you killed a dragon?"

"Yes. And let me also ask what you would do if I slew *all* the dragons."

Hardior hesitated, his expression unreadable, before replying, "Why, you would be the greatest hero in Manfort's history, of course! Anything you asked would be yours."

"Anything? Even the deaths of certain people?"

"Nail and Belly?"

"Perhaps. And perhaps others."

Hardior swallowed, then shook his head. "This is absurd. Your madness is catching, my lord. Let us leave such matters until such time as they move out of the realm of sheerest fantasy."

"As you please, my lord." Arlian turned and began walking.

Hardior hesitated, then turned the other way.

"Good day to you, my lord," he called.

Arlian waved a silent response, and marched on.

That suggestion that he might spend years in planning his assault on the dragons—the implication that he would never, in fact, attempt it—aggravated him.

He would take his time in preparing, since rushing in unprepared would almost certainly get him killed, but he would not put it off indefinitely. The temptation to do so was real, certainly, but it was not a temptation he would yield to. He would demonstrate to Hardior, and to everyone else in Manfort, that he might be mad, but he was neither a fool nor a coward. He *would* go hunting dragons, and he would do it soon.

Perhaps he and the Aritheians would go to Deep Delving together, settle matters at the mines there, equip a caravan with silver and amethysts for the journey to Arithei, and then head south.

And once in the Desolation the Aritheians would continue on to the Borderlands, while he would turn east, to the cave where Enziet had died, and the dragons' lair beneath it.

Within a year, he promised himself. He would head south within a year.

In the Hall of the Dragon Society

Vanniari was a happy baby, plump and healthy, feeding well at her mother's breast. Hasty doted upon her, but was limited in how well she could care for the child by her own maimed condition; Lord Obsidian's other crippled guests, Cricket and Brook and Musk and Lily and Kitten, were of little assistance, and instead the palace servants were called upon to handle the fetching and carrying involved. Stammer took charge of the situation, ensuring that Hasty's daughter had a steady supply of clean clothing and was properly provided with bedding.

Arlian made a point of visiting Hasty and Vanniari at least once a day, but he devoted most of his attention to other matters.

One of the first things he did after returning home from his conversation with Lord Hardior was to begin composing a message to Lord Toribor, a message that asked for a meeting.

This composition was difficult; the usual forms, with their expressions of friendship, were clearly impossible when the last contact between the two men had been a duel that had ended with Arlian declaring their dispute unresolved. Furthermore, it would not do to put down in writing exactly what Arlian wanted to discuss, as servants might well read the note. Even reassuring Toribor that his life was still protected by the Dragon Society's oath was diffi-

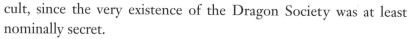

cult, since the very existence of the Dragon Society was at least nominally secret.

At last, though, after a full day's effort, Arlian felt he had achieved a satisfactory phrasing, and dispatched the message in Black's care.

Two hours later, as Arlian was conferring with the kitchen staff regarding when and where dinner would be served, Black returned with Toribor's reply. He handed it to Arlian without comment.

Arlian opened the note and read, "I had wondered when I would hear from you. For reasons I trust are clear, I will not set foot in the Old Palace, nor in the house that once belonged to Lord Enziet, nor will I allow you in my own home; but I will, if you choose, meet with you tomorrow at an address we both know on the Street of the Black Spire."

Arlian considered this briefly, then handed it to Black. "Fair enough," he said. "Tell him I will see him tomorrow afternoon." He glanced at the preparations going on a few feet away, and added, "Don't go now, though. After supper will be soon enough."

The following day was bright and warm, a perfect day in early spring, and between the weather and the impending meeting with Lord Belly, Arlian could not concentrate on his schemes of vengeance against the dragons; instead he visited the graves in the garden where Sweet and Dove were interred, and marveled at the green shoots poking up in the flower beds, and the buds on the trees, and the rich smell of the moist earth.

He had not often had the opportunities and time to look at such things. A year ago when the first spring greenery appeared he had been returning to Manfort a wealthy man, and had been too concerned with establishing his household in the Old Palace, establishing his business connections for his dealing in Aritheian magic, and establishing his reputation as one of Manfort's wealthy eccentrics, to pay attention to nature's changes.

The year before that he had been fleeing the House of the Six Lords, and finding refuge with Black in a rented room in the stony streets of Manfort, as the world outside the city turned green.

And for the seven springs before that he had been deep beneath the ground, in the bare rock tunnels of the mines at Deep Delving, where the seasons meant nothing.

Now he stood in the garden, staring at the tiny green points pushing up through the dead leaves on either side of Sweet's grave, unable to decide just what he was feeling. Sweet's death still left a raw wound in his heart, a ragged hole in his soul—but she was at peace, free forever of Lord Enziet, free of her pain and fear and horrific memories, and around her the world was renewing itself, going on without her.

He, too, had to go on without her. He had avenged her, had killed the man who had tormented her for so long, and who had fatally poisoned her. He had as well killed three of the others who had held her in bondage, crippled her, and abused her—only Nail and Belly remained alive. He had done everything he could to repay her for her kindness and love.

It didn't bring her back. It didn't give her the happy life she had deserved. Nothing could; she was dead and gone.

Arlian was not. He still lived. He had a home, and wealth, and friends, and he was a dragonheart, immune to poison and disease. The world was a wonderful place that was renewing itself, turning green and lush. There was a new baby upstairs with her mother, just starting out on life.

His life should be long and happy. He was free to do anything he chose.

And he intended to commit dozens of murders, culminating in his own suicide. That assumed, of course, that he didn't die in his attacks on the dragons.

Over the past ten years any number of people had told him he was mad, and as he looked at Sweet's grave he suspected they were right. He had done as much as anyone could reasonably ask of him; he had destroyed Enziet and Drisheen, and rescued six women from slavery. He had freed all Enziet's slaves, as well.

But it wasn't enough to satisfy him; obviously, he wasn't anyone reasonable.

He was still awash in confusion and uncertainty of the wisdom of his cause when he marched down the Street of the Black Spire to the black iron door with the red bar that guarded the hall of the Dragon Society.

He knew it might not be wise, that it could only end badly, but he never seriously contemplated abandoning his vengeance against the dragons. He merely debated whether or not he was insane to pursue it.

He was thus distracted when he was admitted to the Society's great chamber, and the sudden hush that fell over the room startled him out of his thoughts. He paused, standing just inside the inner door, and looked over the room, where a dozen faces stared silently back at him.

None of the spring sunlight penetrated here; instead the windowless room was lit by a hundred or so assorted candles, their light sparkling dully from the gilding on the coffered ceiling and from the polished wood of the walls and cabinetry, bright on hundreds of carvings and curios. The air was still and heavy with the scent of dust and hot candle wax. The room's occupants were scattered among the dozens of heavy tables and chairs, their footsteps silent on the thick carpets.

But all of them were staring at him.

Arlian, concerned with his own thoughts and his upcoming meeting with Toribor, had not stopped to consider what the effect of his appearance here might be. Now he realized he should have.

He was the man who had denounced Lord Enziet, the Society's most senior member and one of its founders, as a traitor. He was the man who had pursued Enziet into the Desolation, and presumably driven him to his death. He was the man who had slain Lord Drisheen, another senior member, in a tavern in Cork Tree, and who had survived the assassin Drisheen had loosed upon him. He was the man who had slain the notorious Lord Horim in a duel outside the gates, and who had sworn to kill Lords Stiam and Toribor as well.

And he had not set foot in this room since he set out after Enziet.

Furthermore, he was a dragonheart who reportedly had a *new* scar on his face, and it was the Society's long-held belief that only a dragon could scar a dragonheart. Naturally, the others wanted to look at him, to see what he would do, and whether the scar was really there.

He looked slowly around the room, at the faces amid the statuary and bric-a-brac, and in a far corner he saw the big square face with the eyepatch, the face he was seeking. Wordlessly, he made his way across the room, winding between the tables until he reached Lord Toribor, who sat behind one of the several tables.

A dozen pairs of eyes followed his movements closely.

"May I join you?" Arlian asked, gesturing at a chair at Toribor's table.

"Sit down," Toribor said. "Let's get on with it."

Arlian took a seat, and for a moment the two men simply looked at one another.

"I take it you're not interested in polite pleasantries," Arlian said at last, speaking quietly.

"You stabbed me in the leg last time we met," Toribor said, a good deal more loudly, "and you've promised to kill me. I find that sufficiently unpleasant to make any sort of social niceties very difficult."

"Of course." Arlian nodded. "Nonetheless, I think there are matters we should discuss. I think you'll recall that when last we spoke, as you lay bleeding profusely, you made me swear an oath—that I would not kill Lord Enziet without hearing him out." His voice remained low.

"I remember it," Toribor said, matching his tones to Arlian's own.

"I listened to what he had to say."

"And . . ."

Before Toribor could say any more, the two were interrupted by another, a man of medium height, his black hair going grey, who had marched up to the side of the table. Arlian recognized the features, but could not immediately recall the man's name.

"Is Obsidian threatening you?" the new arrival demanded.

Toribor looked up at him. "No," he said.

"We all know he intends to kill you . . ."

"And he's sworn not to attempt it inside the city walls. Thank you for your concern, Lord Zaner, but I can handle this young pup."

Zaner looked from one man to the other, then spread his hands. "I'm trying to help, but if you don't want it . . ."

"I don't," Toribor said, glaring at Arlian. "The offer is appreciated, but we have private business."

"If you change your mind, just let me know."

"I will, my lord."

Zaner hesitated, then turned away, saying, "I just want to help. There's no need for any trouble here."

Toribor and Arlian watched Zaner retreat; when he was out of earshot, Toribor leaned across the table and said, his voice low but intense, "What did Enziet tell you?"

"A great deal, actually." He remembered that conversation in the utter blackness of an unlit cave, how Enziet had laughed at him, and told him that the dragons had been driven from the Lands of Man all those centuries ago not because the first Duke of Manfort and his warriors had fought them so bravely, but because Enziet had blackmailed them, had threatened to destroy their young.

He had no intention of telling Toribor all that, nor of describing how Enziet had died releasing a dragon from his own heart's blood.

"The point I wanted to mention to you," he said, "is that Enziet lied to you. He said that if he died, the dragons would return. Well, look around you—he's been dead for months, and has there been a single report of a dragon awake? He told me, there in the Desolation, that he *didn't know* what the dragons would do when he died. Yes, he had made a pact with them, and it ended with his death, so the dragons are no longer bound by its terms—but they're old and tired, and they still sleep."

Toribor stared at him for a moment, then said, "Why should I believe you?"

Arlian blinked in surprise.

"Because I have no reason to lie," he said. "I will swear, if you like, by the dead gods or whatever you choose, that Enziet admitted to me that he did not know what the dragons would do when he was dead."

"And why are you telling me this?"

That was a harder question, and Arlian struggled for a moment to compose a response.

"Because this was unresolved between us," he said at last. "When last we spoke, in the streets of Cork Tree, I made you a promise. I wanted you to know that, however it might appear, I kept that promise, and your concern, the concern that seemed more important to you than your life at the time, was baseless."

"You don't know that," Toribor said flatly.

Arlian stared blankly at him. "The dragons have not returned," he said at last.

Toribor snorted. "Of course not," he said. "Look outside, my lord—winter is just now passing away! You should know, as well as any of us, that this is not dragon weather, that it has been too cold for them since well before you caught up with Enziet."

Arlian stared anew—not at Toribor, not at anything, but blindly, as he realized his own foolishness.

He had not thought of that, obvious as it was. When Black had first assisted him from the cave he had been too concerned with simply staying alive to worry about the possibility that the dragons might emerge from their own deeper caves to reassert their rule over the Lands of Man, and by the time he had recovered sufficiently to worry about other things the everyday business of traveling in an overcrowded ox-drawn wagon had distracted him. When at last he had begun to think of larger matters, enough time had passed that he had simply assumed the dragons were not coming. He had thought they might not yet know of Enziet's death, or might be planning to negotiate a bargain with Arlian in Enziet's stead. He had considered it most likely, however, that they were simply too old and weary to be bothered with the outside world, despite Enziet's death.

After all, no dragon had been seen in the ten years since three of the creatures had destroyed the village of Obsidian, on the Smoking Mountain. According to everything he had heard, all the dragons that yet survived were the black of ancients; none were still the green of a dragon's vigorous prime. The youngest were at least seven hundred years old. Surely, even dragons did not live forever, and even dragons must grow tired and feeble with age. He had hoped to find and kill them while they still slept.

But he had not considered what was obvious to Toribor—that dragons were creatures of heat, and for centuries had only emerged in high summer, when the air was hot and thick and the sky dark with clouds.

Which meant that when summer came, the dragons might well come with it.

Suddenly, his plans to make obsidian weapons and find the dragons' lairs seemed far more urgent. He had assumed that, as Hardior had said, he could take his time in preparation, years or even decades if necessary—though he had never intended to wait that long. But now he had to consider the possibility that he had only two or three months, that when the cool green of spring gave way to summer's heat the dragons would emerge.

He knew how they reproduced, and could surely, with the help of the rest of the city's population once they were alerted, destroy all their potential offspring by slaughtering the Dragon Society— but that would still leave the dragons themselves unchecked, and while he thought he might be able to drive an obsidian-tipped spear into the heart of a *sleeping* dragon, killing a dragon when it was awake would be far more difficult.

And it also assumed that anyone *believed* him when he explained draconic reproduction—it occurred to him that they might not. If he tried to stir up a crusade against the Dragon Society it would probably only serve to confirm the widespread belief that he was insane.

Killing dragons might be far more urgent than he had thought.

"Listen, Belly," he said, leaning forward, his eyes focusing again, "you may be right. I hadn't thought of that, and I feel like a fool that I didn't. And that makes it all the more important that we make common cause now. Yes, I have still sworn to avenge the wrongs you did to the women in the House of Carnal Society, but for now I would put that aside. I defeated you once, and took your two women and a horse, but I let you live; now I would let you live again, for a time, so that we can work together, so that all the Dragon Society can work together if the dragons *do* come back."

"And what can we do, then?" Toribor demanded angrily. "We are not the warriors our ancestors were; we don't even know how they fought the dragons, or how they drove the dragons away. No man has ever killed a dragon; how can we even begin to fight them? If they return, we will all be enslaved, as the ancients were . . ."

"No," Arlian interrupted, "we will not. I told you Enziet told me many things. He had been researching for centuries, and had learned that obsidian blades can pierce a dragon's hide."

It was Toribor's turn to stare, though his expression showed more doubt than surprise.

"Obsidian can cut a dragon?" he said. "As Lord Obsidian slew Lord Dragon?"

"Indeed," Arlian said, a trifle uncomfortable at the comparison. He contemplated denying, once again, that he had killed Enziet, but decided there was no point in distracting the conversation with anything so irrelevant to the matter at hand.

"And you propose to arm us all with obsidian blades, then?"

"As many as possible, yes."

"And the possibility that these black weapons might be ensorcelled, that this might be some scheme of your own, is not supposed to occur to me?"

Arlian sighed.

"I am no sorcerer," he said. "You know that. I'm scarcely into my third decade, and it takes centuries to master sorcery."

"You have magicians in your household," Toribor pointed out. "Aritheian mages. Who knows what they might do with obsidian?"

"Not I," Arlian said. "All *I* know is that it should be able to kill dragons. I would like to arm the Dragon Society with obsidian."

"I think not," Toribor said. "We have all known since you first joined that you're mad, Lord Obsidian; I, for one, do not care to join you in that madness." He pushed his chair back and rose to his feet. "I do not think we have anything more to say to one another. I believe you when you say that Enziet did not know what would happen after he died, but beyond that I have no idea what is truth and what a madman's ravings. If the dragons do return, I will face them as best I can. If obsidian will indeed cut them, then I will accept a black blade and do what I can. Until then, my lord, I want nothing to do with you. We did not speak all winter; let us see whether we can better that record."

With that, he turned and marched away.

Arlian watched him go, dismayed and confused.

Ensorcelled weapons? The idea had never occurred to him, yet it had seemed obvious to Toribor. *Could* the Aritheians enchant weapons? Might that help against the dragons?

Could their magic help in any other way? He had not really considered the possibility. There were no dragons in Arithei, so the magicians could have no practical experience with them; he had not thought about whether they might know something of *why* the dragons did not travel beyond the Borderlands. Sorcery was useless against the dragons, so far as anyone knew, but southern magic was far more powerful than sorcery.

It was an interesting possibility—but not what he had come for. He had hoped to convince Toribor that they were all, as human beings, on the same side, but Toribor was clearly not ready to hear that.

He looked around at the other dragonhearts. Several of them were staring openly at him, and none of those stares were friendly.

Arlian sighed. He had done what he came to do; though the attempt had been an utter failure, it had given him a great deal to think about, and had added considerable urgency to his preparations. There was no point in sitting here, a target for hostile stares; he rose and headed for the door.

11

Preparations and Alarms

After his meeting with Toribor, Arlian put aside most of his other concerns and threw both his households into the business of making obsidian weapons, while he devoted much of his own attention to searching Lord Enziet's books and papers for any sort of map or guidance to the whereabouts of any sleeping dragons other than that one cave.

The possibility of going to the one cave he *did* know about was obvious, but he put it off—at this point he could not get there much before midsummer and, for all he knew, by the time he reached it the dragons might be out marauding while he searched their empty lair.

He had intended to travel to Deep Delving to buy amethysts and attend to other matters; his agents had acquired three more shares in the Old Man's mine, so he would be able to do as he pleased with it. He had also thought he might perhaps go on from there, but if Manfort was to be attacked that summer he did not feel he could spare the time. A caravan to Arithei could leave later in the year, cross the Desolation in the fall, winter in the warm southern lands, and return in the spring. If the summer had passed safely, he could accompany such a caravan into the Desolation, and divert himself from it in the cool of autumn.

But if the dragons were coming to besiege Manfort this summer, he wanted to be here to face them. For now, obsidian seemed more important than amethyst.

He did not explain to his staff *why* he wanted obsidian weapons. The very mention of dragons was enough to frighten or upset some people, and the idea of making weapons intended specifically for fighting dragons would probably have thrown a few of the more impressionable servants into fits. Fortunately, his reputation for eccentricity was well established, and allowed him to make this seemingly pointless demand without provoking undue comment.

Except, that is, from Black.

"I don't need to know all your secrets," Black said, in a private meeting in Arlian's study at the Old Palace, "but this one I really do think calls for an explanation. I know where this stone came from, but I still don't know why Enziet wanted it in the first place, or why *you* want it made into weapons. It smacks of sorcery, and that worries me—*you* aren't a sorcerer, but Enziet and Drisheen were both formidable in the art. For all I know, their spells might have survived them, and if so I don't like it."

"There's no sorcery," Arlian said. "At least, not the sort you mean. It's a discovery Enziet made—obsidian is the one thing that can pierce a dragon's hide."

Black considered that, and looked down at the obsidian dagger he had brought to the discussion. Then he looked back at Arlian. "Have you tested this, or are you taking Enziet's word?"

"I've tested it," Arlian said.

"This is connected with that scar on your cheek, and what happened in the cave, isn't it?"

"It is."

"And you aren't going to tell me the details, are you?"

"Not yet."

"So these weapons are for use against dragons."

"Yes."

"You really do intend to hunt down and kill the dragons who destroyed your home."

"Yes."

Black nodded thoughtfully. "But you don't need dozens of spears to do that. You're just one man; you can't carry all the weapons you're having made."

"I'm aware of that."

Black tapped the black glass dagger against the nails of his left hand as he silently studied Arlian's face.

"Just how bad is it?" he asked at last.

"I don't know," Arlian admitted. "It may be nothing. But I want to have the weapons ready if the worst comes to pass."

"And what about the men to wield the weapons?"

Arlian sighed. "I can't raise and train a private army," he said. "I am viewed with quite enough suspicion as it is. If the weapons are needed, there will be men who want them—and probably women, too, for that matter."

"*That* bad?"

"I hope not."

"Do you have enough obsidian?"

"I think so."

"I could inquire after more."

"That might be wise."

"Lord Wither's man Horn has been talking to the staff, you know, hoping someone will tell him where to find the dragons. I believe some of them have been invited to meet Wither himself and discuss the matter."

"I know where the entrance to one cavern is, holding no more than half a dozen of the great beasts; if Lord Wither locates any others, I would be pleased to hear of it."

"I doubt he has any way of finding others, but what if he learns where that one is?"

"Then presumably he'll attempt to fetch some venom, either in person or by hiring others to make the journey on his behalf. But who on the staff could direct him? You and I were the only ones to set foot in the cave there. I doubt Rime or Shibiel or Thirif could give useful directions; I'm not entirely sure *I* can find it again without a great deal of effort."

"Cricket and Brook were with us."

"And, being amputees, they cannot walk and therefore never left the wagon; what could *they* tell him?"

"You may misjudge Brook's abilities."

That struck Arlian as curious, that Black would single out Brook. Arlian remembered Brook as a clever and usually cheerful woman who liked to hum quietly or talk to herself when focused on some task; he remembered that she had been quick to help him out in Cork Tree, when he had rescued her from Toribor's party. On the long ride back from the Desolation to Manfort, Brook had helped tend Arlian's wounds and had been good company for them all.

But Arlian did not remember any indication that she would be any better at navigating the Desolation than anyone else, and how would Black know her any better than he did? Perhaps, since arriving at the Old Palace, the two had spoken when Arlian wasn't present.

Perhaps, it suddenly occurred to Arlian, they had done more than merely speak.

"And if I do misjudge, if Brook could somehow lead Wither to that cave, why would she?"

"For gold, Arlian."

"I give her whatever she needs here."

"But she might prefer to be entirely in command of her own destiny, and not dependent on you. You freed her from slavery, but she may want more freedom than you can give her."

"She may, at that," Arlian acknowledged. "And she has every right to earn her own way however she can. If you would be so kind as to inform her that I would prefer she not sell that particular bit of information, I would appreciate it—but on the other hand, I will not stop her. If Lord Wither does find that cavern, he does so at his own risk. It's a two-month journey, more or less, and by then the weather will be much warmer, especially in the south; *I* would not care to venture into a dragon's cave in warm weather. It's not entirely coincidental that Enziet led us there in winter. You might mention that to Lord Wither."

"Indeed I might," Black agreed. "He's a patient man, and he may well decide to wait until autumn."

"By which time the matter may be moot."

Black hesitated, then asked, "And suppose, Ari, that Lord Wither does seek out a dragon's cave, either the one you know or another, and finds what he's after. What will you do?"

"That depends what use he chooses to make of it," Arlian said.

"And would you provide him with some of the weapons you have Ferrezin and the others preparing?"

Arlian leaned back against the desk.

"Now, *that* is an interesting question," he said. "I think that if asked, I would sell him a few, yes. I have no great dislike for Lord Wither, even though I would prefer he not obtain what he seeks."

"You prefer him to the dragons, at any rate."

"Yes."

"And you're making obsidian weapons because you expect a need for them?"

"Rather, I think a need may arise; to say I *expect* it is to overstate the case. And I would prefer it if you did not mention any of this to others."

Black snorted. "They would probably think me as mad as you."

And with that, the conversation was at an end.

Days passed, each a little longer and a trifle warmer than the one before, and Arlian accumulated a sizeable arsenal of obsidian weapons—black-tipped spears, black glass daggers, and a few hybrid swords that had pieces of obsidian fitted into steel blades. These last were clumsy and fragile, but Arlian thought they might be useful even so.

He concentrated on spears, some of them of prodigious size— after all, dragons were *big*, and while obsidian could presumably cut them anywhere, it had taken a thrust to the heart to actually *kill* the one he had fought beneath the Desolation. Some of these spears were of a size that would require a giant, or at least two or three men working together, to wield—but the possibility that they would be needed could not be ignored.

Arlian wished that finding the giants to wield them was as easy as constructing the spears.

While his employees were making weapons Arlian also accumulated a great deal of knowledge about Lord Enziet's past and possessions, but little of it was any use. The enciphered notebooks remained largely mysterious.

And he began the serious study of sorcery, with the occasional assistance of Lady Rime, once she had returned from inspecting her nearer estates. Although she was centuries old, her own knowledge of the magical arts was still limited; Arlian knew it would be decades before he could accomplish anything beyond the most basic level.

At one session, when he had botched a simple ensorcellment, he remarked, "Sometimes I wonder, my lady, why you bother to help me."

She looked at him oddly.

"Sometimes I wonder the same," she said. "After all, you're but a twentieth of my age, and given your habits and obsessions it seems quite unlikely you'll survive your first century. If I become too involved with you, *I* may well not survive another century. In my saner moments I avoid you, Arlian. I am here today because my inexplicable fascination with you overcame my good sense." Then she turned her attention back to the crystals they had been working with. "Shall we try it again?"

Arlian wondered, after that, whether or not she had been joking about avoiding him. He could never find a polite way to ask, and he could never decide whether the decreased frequency of their contacts was coincidental or intentional, the result of distractions or deliberation.

Caught up in his weapons and plans and sorcery, he did not take time to visit the hall of the Dragon Society again; he had no interest in another confrontation with Toribor, or perhaps the meddlesome Lord Zaner. There would be time to deal with his enemies there later; the dragons were more urgent. He did keep himself apprised of Lord Wither's whereabouts and activities; as yet Wither had not left the city, nor openly sent any hirelings southward, so Arlian did not feel particularly concerned. He also paid close attention to any reports that might indicate draconic activity of any sort, but otherwise did not trouble himself to stay current with the perpetual flow of news and gossip that swirled through Manfort.

He did continue to visit Hasty and Vanniari, and to take meals with his several houseguests and spend some time each evening chatting with them. He paid closer attention to Brook, and concluded that she and Black had indeed gotten to know each other well.

Cricket had taken an interest in cookery, and had taken a liking to Stammer, who was eager to defer to her. As a result Cricket was now unofficially in charge of the kitchen staff.

Kitten was still reading her way through the palace library, and expressed an interest in continuing on to Enziet's bookshelves when the volumes at the Old Palace were exhausted. Lily and Musk had not yet found lasting interests, but seemed content with their lot.

The weather grew warm, trees blossomed and turned green, spring flowers bloomed and faded, but Arlian did not devote much time to appreciating the progress of the seasons; he was too concerned with what a bout of dragon weather might bring.

No dragon sightings were reported. No villages ceased to communicate with their neighbors. But, Arlian told himself, the weather was not yet as hot as it would become. Toribor's dire prediction could still come true.

He heard nothing more from Lord Hardior for some time. At last, however, as spring gave way to summer, the Duke's chief adviser paid a call on Lord Obsidian.

Nominally, this was just a casual visit between friends—but Arlian knew better than to treat it as such. When he received word that Hardior hoped to find him at home the following day he dropped everything else and began preparations for a proper reception for the Duke's representative.

A year ago he wouldn't have bothered—but a year ago he had seen the Duke and his entourage as irrelevant to his own needs. He had been intent on finding and killing Lord Dragon and other human foes.

Now, though, he was preparing to fight dragons, and then to destroy the entire Dragon Society, and that was, he now realized, not something he could reasonably hope to do single-handed—or even with the help of his comrades, Black and Rime and the Aritheians.

At the very least, he did not want to find himself fighting the Duke's guards at the same time as he fought the dragons.

Accordingly, he consulted the kitchen staff to make sure a variety of delicacies were on hand, and Cricket assured him, from the high stool where she directed all matters culinary, that she would personally guarantee a fine table would be set. He arranged with Thirif for a few little illusions to create the proper atmosphere, and Black undertook, on his own initiative, to ensure that the appropriate rooms were spotless and the six palace footmen on their very best behavior.

And then they waited for Lord Hardior to arrive.

12

Lord Hardior's News

It was a good two hours past midday when Lord Hardior's coach rolled to a stop at the gate, timing that clearly meant Hardior did not care to stay for an entire meal—it was very unlikely that Arlian could stretch the visit until suppertime, and of course luncheon was past and done.

That might mean any number of things—that Hardior was too busy to spare the time, that the Duke wanted him at the Citadel for meals, that he did not yet want to bestow the consequent social status on Arlian that dining with the Duke's chief adviser would bring, or merely that he did not want to impose on Arlian's hospitality. Black suggested that Hardior was probably just wary of being poisoned, and Arlian murmured amused agreement, but in fact he knew better; Lord Hardior possessed the heart of the dragon, and those who had the heart of the dragon were immune to virtually all poisons.

Arlian, in his finest black velvet coat with layers of white lace at throat and cuffs, met Lord Hardior at the front door, and personally ushered him in. A footman stood by, ready to serve, but Hardior had not worn cloak or sword; he was attired in a light brown linen jacket, cut short in the latest fashion, over a fawn-colored silk vest and cream-colored shirt. The warmth of these colors contrasted sharply with the stark black and white of Arlian's own costume, and Obsidian's household livery.

Hardior smelled faintly of powder and perfume; Arlian had never gotten in the habit of using cosmetics, and suspected that any odor he might have was the scent of sweat. Despite the training he had received in the House of the Six Lords, he was still not entirely at home in the role of a wealthy gentleman of Manfort.

The two exchanged polite greetings and inquired after one another's health; Arlian introduced his steward, and told his guest to consider Arlian's home his own.

The formalities thus completed, Arlian showed Hardior to the small salon, where a flurry of illusory butterflies danced in the sunlight before vanishing, and where Cricket's underlings had set out assorted pastries and candied fruits. Hardior accepted a few of these, along with a glass of pear wine.

At last, though, Hardior settled into an oak-and-leather armchair, and Arlian closed the doors, leaving the two men alone in the room in apparent privacy.

"While your presence is a delight, my lord," he said, turning his back to the door, "I suspect that there is a purpose behind this visit beyond simple fellowship."

"Of course there is," Hardior acknowledged. "And I would be pleased to come directly to the point. A few words should do. You know, I had hoped to catch you somewhere else, so that we might have this conversation without putting you to any trouble, but you have been something of a recluse of late, and given me no opportunity."

"Had I known you were seeking me out, my lord, I would have been a veritable social butterfly. Could you not have invited me to one of the Duke's gatherings, rather than interrupt your busy schedule to attend me personally?"

"The problem with that, Obsidian, is that I could not be certain that you would accept, and further, that I did not know just who you do not care to share a room with. Would it have been graceless to put you in the same party as Lord Belly, for example?"

"It might, my lord, though I think I could behave myself on my host's behalf even so. Whatever the circumstances, the pleasure of your company is now mine, and I pray that you feel free to tell me whatever you sought to tell me."

"I have come not so much to tell you anything, my lord, as to ask a question—and its nature is such as to add further hesitation to any discussion of it less private than this."

"You intrigue me, my lord. Ask your question, then."

"'Tis simple enough. Why, my lord, are you stockpiling strange weapons?"

"Ah." Arlian nodded. "I thought that might be it. You refer to the obsidian blades and spearheads?"

"I do indeed. I understand you have had dozens, perhaps hundreds, of these bizarre weapons manufactured and stored."

"I have," Arlian said. "And my intention is to offer them to the Duke's soldiers, should the need for them arise."

Hardior cocked his head to one side. "Indeed," he said. "And what occasion could possibly call for blades of volcanic glass, rather than good steel?"

Arlian seated himself on a silk couch before replying, "You know I am Lord Enziet's heir."

"Indeed I do," Hardior said. "I find that as bizarre as the manufacture of stone knives, but there can be no question that Enziet did name you as such, and had the right to do so. He knew well that you meant to murder him, so a death that might otherwise invalidate his will does not interfere."

"If you will pardon me for saying so, my lord, you do not know how Lord Enziet died, and should be wary of making assumptions about the matter."

"The nature of his death is indeed unknown to me, my lord, and I did not intend to imply otherwise. Pray continue."

"Lord Enziet was the most senior member of a certain society to which we both belong, as you know, and while he did not always comply fully with that society's regulations, he did pursue its primary goal with great effect—he knew more about dragons than anyone else in Manfort. I would think you might have heard rumors—from Lord Toribor, if nowhere else—that Lord Enziet had made a pact that kept the dragons in their caverns."

"I have heard this, and dismissed it as nonsense. Do you tell me it is not? And even if this is the case, how does obsidian figure into it?"

"I tell you that I do not know what consequences Enziet's death may bring, but that a sortie by several dragons is not impossible. And Enziet's researches, which I have inherited, indicate that obsidian may be able to pierce a dragon's hide where steel cannot. While not wishing to alarm anyone, I had thought to have weapons prepared in case dragons do dare to assault the city."

He spoke as clearly and calmly as he could, and when he had finished he met Hardior's gaze openly and directly.

Hardior, for his part, leaned an elbow on the arm of his chair and rested his chin upon that hand. He contemplated Arlian's face for a long moment before replying.

"You are obsessed with the dragons, Lord Obsidian," he said at last.

"Indeed. I do not deny it."

"When last we spoke you asked what I would do if you killed one; I take it that these stone weapons are the method you meant to employ."

"Exactly."

"You cannot have *tested* this theory that obsidian will pierce a dragon's hide."

"As you say," Arlian answered. "But Enziet's research was quite thorough. He concluded that dragons are a magical manifestation of fire and darkness, while obsidian is a purely physical manifestation of fire and darkness, and thus the two interact in curious ways."

"And you cannot *know* that the dragons will come. They have been gone for seven hundred years; surely, one man's death cannot be that important to them?"

"I cannot know," Arlian agreed. "I choose, however, to be prepared."

"And that's what this is about, then?"

"What else could it be?"

"Oh, any number of things. The assumption has been that the obsidian has some sorcerous power, that perhaps you inherited Enziet's sorcery, or brought unknown magic back from Arithei, and that you plan to equip an army with magical weapons."

"For what purpose?"

"To carry out your mad schemes of vengeance, of course."

"I seek vengeance against the dragons. Surely, no one would object to that?"

"You have also sworn to kill Nail and Belly, have you not?"

Reluctantly, Arlian admitted, "I have." He was in no hurry to carry out that vow, but he could not deny having made it—he intended to kill *all* the dragonhearts in time.

"And now Nail lies ill, while you tinker with what might be hostile sorcery—surely, it's not unreasonable to suspect a connection . . ."

His voice trailed off as he saw Arlian's reaction to his words. The younger man had gone from puzzlement to surprise to extreme agitation in short order, and now leapt to his feet, interrupting Hardior.

"Nail is ill?" Arlian demanded, hesitating as if uncertain whether to grab Lord Hardior or dash for the door.

"Yes, he is," Hardior said. "These past three days. You hadn't heard?"

"*No!*" Arlian exclaimed. He stared at Hardior. "Tell me the nature of this illness."

He had a horrible suspicion that he knew its nature far better than did Hardior. Dragonhearts were never ill; no known disease could be carried in their tainted blood, any more than poison could harm them. But the draconic taint itself . . .

Lord Stiam, known as Nail, was probably the eldest surviving member of the Dragon Society, almost as ancient as Enziet had been—only Lord Wither might perhaps be his equal, now that Enziet was dead. Nail had lived almost a thousand years—the exact number was unknown.

And now his time was up, Arlian was sure of it. For perhaps a

thousand years, no dragonheart had survived to the natural end of
his life—long ago, before the Dragon Society was formed, another
secret society, the Order of the Dragon, had slain all dragonhearts
upon discovery, and only Enziet and a handful of others had survived. Enziet had betrayed and destroyed the Order of the Dragon
to save his own life, so that for centuries the dragons were able to
contaminate mortals to gestate their young, and those infected were
no longer slain.

Enziet had been the eldest of those Arlian knew, and Stiam had
been either second or third.

Enziet had staved off his own end for a few years by sorcery—
but Stiam had no idea what fate awaited him, and had done nothing
to delay it.

"He complained of chest pains, as if his heart were swelling
within him," Hardior said, hesitantly. "And of a fever in his blood,
and weakness in his limbs. And he asked me once whether I heard a
voice, when all was still."

That fit all too well. Arlian turned and strode to the door, calling back over his shoulder, "You think me mad—well, come with
me now, and we will see whether I am mad or not! I only hope we
aren't too late."

Then he swung open the door and bellowed, "Black! Fetch me
a spear at once, and one for yourself! We're going to Nail's estate!"

Behind him, almost forgotten and utterly baffled, Lord Hardior
got to his feet and followed.

13

For Want of a Nail

They all rode in Lord Hardior's coach—it was still waiting at the gate, still ready, and Lord Hardior, caught up in Arlian's obvious urgency, offered it. Black, clutching three of the obsidian-tipped spears Arlian's staff had prepared, rode atop, beside the driver, while Arlian and Hardior rode inside.

Arlian could scarcely contain himself, so overcome was he by a tangle of emotions. Anticipation and dread mingled inextricably with one another. He wanted to shout nonsense at Hardior, to tell him that he was about to face horrors and see proof that Arlian was not mad, but he forced himself to stay silent.

Nail was giving birth to a dragon—would Arlian arrive to find a man, or a monster? He had intended to kill the dragonhearts to prevent this, but he had apparently left this one until too late.

If the dragon had already emerged, then here was a chance to slay another dragon, in furtherance of his revenge, and at that a dragon burst from the heart of one of the Six Lords—but he had almost come to like Nail, who was either the most forthright dragonheart Arlian had ever met, or the subtlest.

He had the obsidian spears, but what if the dragon had been born an hour or two before? Would the volcanic glass still pierce its hide, or did that armor strengthen with time? The Enziet dragon had lived for only a few moments before Arlian stabbed it to death; would the Stiam dragon be stronger?

And that assumed the dragon had been born. If Nail were still alive and human when they arrived, what could Arlian do? He had sworn not to harm Nail within Manfort's walls, and that oath still held—though he did not think anyone would take it to apply to the dragon that Nail would become.

He could wait at Nail's bedside—but what if the wait took days? He had no idea how long a dragonheart's natural labor might be; Enziet had cut open his own chest to free the creature within, and Arlian did not imagine that Nail would do anything of the sort.

Who would be there? Who would see the emergence?

What would this do to Arlian's trove of secret knowledge? For centuries, only Enziet had known how dragons reproduced; before that the Order of the Dragon had closely guarded the information. It had never been common knowledge. Now, though, whoever was in Lord Stiam's bedchamber would see the transformation and would know the truth—servants, guests, physicians, and perhaps others. The secret, like the newborn dragon, would be out.

A dragon, loose within the walls of Manfort—that was something unknown for seven hundred years.

And really, Arlian thought, wouldn't this simplify his task? Everyone would know how dragons began, and how they could be ended; surely, everyone would be eager to aid him in his campaign to exterminate the monsters.

Everyone, that is, but the members of the Dragon Society, who would realize that they, too, had to die.

The coach pulled to a stop at Lord Nail's gate, and Arlian had the door open before Black could leap down to open it for him.

A guard stood at the gate, his hand on the hilt of his sword—a cheap guardsman's cutlass, not a gentleman's rapier, but still an effective weapon.

"We must see Lord Nail at once," Arlian said. "It is of the utmost urgency!"

"Lord Stiam is unwell, my lord," the guard began.

"We know that," Arlian snapped. "Open the gate and stand aside!"

The guard was about to speak again when he realized that Black held a spear to his throat, a spear with a jagged, glassy head. The steward had moved around behind Arlian and approached the guard from the side, unnoticed.

"Open the gate and you live," Black said.

"Open the gate," Lord Hardior said, belatedly stepping up beside Arlian and pushing Black's spear aside. "I will take full responsibility."

"My lord," the guard said, recognizing him. "I didn't see you."

"Open the gate."

The guard hurried to comply, and the three men, Arlian, Hardior, and Black, hurried across the dooryard and into the house.

A footman met them inside, and reached out to take the spears, but Hardior told him, "No."

The footman hesitated, but then decided not to argue with two powerful lords and their armed companion. He stood back and let them pass.

Hardior led the way down the central passage and up a flight of stairs, and as they strode along Black passed each of the others a spear. A moment later the three of them burst into Lord Stiam's bedchamber, weapons ready.

The clatter of boots and spears shattered the hush of the sick-room, and the several occupants turned to stare at the intruders. Even Nail, lying in his bed with his eyes closed and his thin white hair drenched in sweat, lifted his head and squinted at the newcomers.

Arlian stopped dead at the sight of the man in the bed, still outwardly entirely human; he stared intently at Nail, spear raised.

Hardior slowed to a halt and looked around at the others, lowering his weapon.

Black, almost unnoticed behind the other two, backed up against the wall of the room to one side of the door and began edging slowly around to one side, his spear pointing upward.

"Lord Hardior," Lord Wither said from the bedside, "and Lord

Obsidian. Might I ask the reason for this rather loud and abrupt entrance?"

Arlian's attention was still focused on Nail. The old man was stretched out on his bed, head and shoulders propped up on a dozen pillows, his frail body wrapped only in a thin white cotton nightshirt that was so soaked with perspiration it was almost transparent. Arlian could see that Nail's chest was swollen, bloated to almost twice its normal size—and he could see that the flesh of that enlarged bosom was rippling slightly in a horribly unnatural fashion. The skin there was feverish red, while his naked hands and feet were shrunken and bone-white. His hair and beard hung in wet strings, and as he peered at Arlian he was panting heavily.

"We are inside the city walls," Nail gasped, "if that still matters."

Arlian took a step closer, and several hands reached out for him. For the first time the fact that he and Nail were not alone in the room registered, and he looked quickly around.

"He said it was urgent that we come at once," Lord Hardior said over Arlian's shoulder. "I took him at his word, and we did not take time for explanations."

"Perhaps now you will," Wither replied angrily.

Wither, in his best green silk, was standing at Nail's bedside, on the right; on the left, in a physician's red and white, stood Lady Flute, the noted sorceress, her scarred face unmistakable even though it was well over a year since Arlian had last seen her in the hall of the Dragon Society. A woman Arlian did not recognize, richly dressed in saffron and green, fair of face but somehow less noticeable than the others, stood at Wither's shoulder. Leaning against the right-hand wall was Lord Toribor, in a maroon coat more elegant than Arlian had ever before seen him wear, his arms folded across his chest, his one eye fixed on Arlian's face.

Lady Rime was comfortably arranged in a rose silk chair behind Lady Flute, her left leg drawn up beneath a silk skirt of midnight blue so that her wooden prosthesis did not reach the floor; in her hand was the human legbone she carried as a souvenir, tapping silently against the chair's upholstered arm. She was watching silently, not moving to speak or intervene, just watching.

Three servants in the rose-and-fawn livery of the house were hovering nearby, as well, all clearly waiting for those of higher rank than themselves to take the initiative in dealing with this strange intrusion.

All of them were staring at Arlian and his raised spear.

"Obsidian?" Hardior said. "I see nothing here that would call for an armed intervention. Would you please explain yourself?"

Arlian ignored him; he lowered the spear and stepped up to Nail's bedside, pushing Lady Flute aside.

For a moment he hesitated, aware that there were others in the room who would hear, that he might be about to reveal secrets that had been held close for centuries—but then he decided that if matters had gone this far, the truth would soon be out in any case.

"Do you know what's happening to you?" he asked.

Nail's eyes widened as he stared up at Arlian. "Do you?" he asked, his voice weak, but still harsh.

"More or less," Arlian said. "I saw it happen to Lord Enziet." He glanced up at Lord Wither and, behind him, Lord Toribor. "I know you thought I killed him, but it's more complicated than that." Then he turned his gaze back to Nail. "Enziet hurried the process—he cut his own chest open well before his situation was this far advanced. If you'd prefer to end it after that fashion, I'm sure one of your servants could fetch a blade."

"My lord!" Lady Flute protested.

Arlian turned. "Do *you* have any idea what's happening to him? Has your sorcery told you?"

"No," Flute admitted. "My best spells do not show him to be ill at all, and can do nothing for him. Nail summoned me because his physicians could not help, but I've done no better."

Arlian hesitated. It might still be possible to keep the process secret after all. If all these other people could be convinced to leave the room . . .

"Would it be possible for me to have a minute alone with Lord Nail?" Arlian asked.

"No," Toribor replied, before anyone else could speak. He straightened, stepping away from the wall. "I think you may have poisoned him somehow, in your insane quest for revenge, and perhaps you've come now to finish him off."

"I didn't need to poison him," Arlian said. "He was poisoned a thousand years ago."

Several people began to reply to that, shouting protests and questions, and Arlian realized that his chances of keeping his secrets here were nonexistent. Nobody would trust him alone with Nail—and he could not leave Nail's bedside until the transformation was over. The dragon that Nail was becoming would need to be killed as quickly as possible.

And it might emerge at any moment, from the way Nail's chest was heaving. Arlian thought he could smell not merely sweat, but blood, and even a trace of the distinctive stench of dragon's venom.

He thought of perhaps requesting that at least the servants be sent away, so that only dragonhearts would hear—but surely, the news would spread in any case, and why should he try to limit it to dragonhearts? In the end, everyone would know.

He turned to Flute again.

"In a way, your spells are telling you the truth," he said. "My lord Stiam is not ill; he's in labor."

"You *are* mad!" Hardior said, staring.

Nail's eyes widened; he said nothing at first, but he stared intently at Arlian.

Arlian ignored the others for a moment as he leaned over the bed and met Nail's gaze. "Did you know?" he asked.

He listened intently as the dying man whispered a reply.

"I thought I was delirious with fever," Nail said, his voice faint. "I can *feel* it, you know. I can almost hear its thoughts. Sometimes I'm not sure which feelings are mine, and which belong to this thing inside of me."

"You know what it is, then," Arlian said.

Nail managed a single slight nod. "It wanted me to leave the city," he said. "I almost did. It wanted to go somewhere dark and hot and safe—but I wanted to live, and I feared you would follow and find me and kill me if I left Manfort. And I thought it was just a fever dream."

"It's real," Arlian said. "It's been growing in your blood for centuries, and now it's waking up, ready to come forth."

"Enziet knew, somehow," Nail said.

Arlian nodded. "He knew all along. He kept the secret for seven hundred years."

"I have been fighting to keep it in. You said Enziet cut open his own breast?"

"We were fighting," Arlian said. "He was losing. He knew he didn't have much more time either way."

"What are you two *talking* about?" Lord Wither demanded, leaning across the bed toward Arlian.

Nail waved him away. "The spears," he said to Arlian. "Are they for me, or for it?"

"For it," Arlian said. "That was Enziet's great discovery— obsidian. I learned it from him beneath the Desolation."

Nail smiled crookedly. "Then you and Enziet together will avenge me, won't you?"

"After a fashion," Arlian agreed, smiling mechanically in return. Then the smile vanished. "Does it hurt?"

"Not exactly," Nail replied. "The rest of me feels weak and cold, while it grows hotter and stronger and more impatient, but there's no real pain. My skin does feel thin and tight across my chest, which is uncomfortable, but no more than that."

"The dead gods do show some mercy, then."

"Say rather that the dragons do," Nail whispered.

"Or the power that created them."

"Do you know how long . . . ?"

Arlian shook his head. "No," he said. "Seconds, hours, days, I cannot say. You are already farther along than Enziet was when he put an end to himself."

"Lord Hardior," Wither said loudly, "will you please escort this madman out of here? He's tormenting Lord Stiam with his perverse fantasies."

"Shut up, Wither," Nail rasped, straining to be heard. "Let him stay."

Arlian glanced at Hardior, who was standing back, clearly confused and not eager to intervene, then at Wither.

Wither was glaring at him with hatred.

Behind Wither, Lord Toribor had stepped forward from the wall and was watching and listening—but Arlian was startled to see no sign of anger or hatred in his expression, but only a sort of distressed fascination.

The woman at Wither's shoulder merely looked confused. Her face seemed curiously uninteresting despite her beauty, her eyes dim, and after a moment Arlian realized that she was not a dragonheart. Because of her presence in the sickroom and her expensive attire he had at first assumed she was an unfamiliar member of the Dragon Society, but now he realized she was merely an ordinary mortal.

Lady Opal, he supposed, Wither's paramour. She was plainly out of her depth here, and aware of it.

Arlian felt a hand on his arm, and turned as Flute said, "My lords, let us not needlessly trouble Lord Stiam with our quarrels. Obsidian, put aside your weapon. Wither, our host wishes Obsidian to stay; do not gainsay him that in what may be his last hours. And my lord Nail, pray do not strain yourself. Rest."

"Thank you, my lady," Arlian said, essaying a small bow.

"My lord," she acknowledged. She hesitated, then said, "You surely realize that your words do sound quite mad."

"Sometimes I think the whole world is mad, my lady, and other times that only I am; nonetheless, I speak the truth as I know it."

"And you say something is growing in Lord Nail's chest?"

"So I believe, yes. I came here thinking it would have already burst forth—our vigorous entrance was a response to that expectation."

Flute hesitated again, glanced around the room, then asked, "And what is it you believe to be gestating here?"

Startled, Arlian in turn looked around at the gathered faces. He had thought it obvious what was about to be born, but clearly some of these people needed to hear it spoken aloud before they would permit themselves to think it.

"A dragon," he said. "It will be blood-red when it first emerges, for it is forming from Nail's own heart and blood. It will be larger than could logically be possible, larger than a grown man, too large to fit comfortably in this chamber, but still only a hatchling by dragon's standards."

Arlian heard someone, perhaps one of the servants, gasp at that; feet shuffled, and the room's other occupants glanced uneasily at one another.

"And you brought a few spears to fight it?" Wither said, sneering. "Even a madman should know better than that! No man has ever slain a dragon; what could your spears do?"

"Kill it," Arlian said. "As dragons are magical fire and darkness, obsidian is natural fire and darkness, and these spears can kill a dragon."

"You put an absurd faith in this theory of . . ." Wither began.

"It's no mere theory," Arlian said, cutting him off. "You say no man has ever slain a dragon, but that is no longer true; *I* slew one, newborn in a cave beneath the Desolation, with an obsidian dagger."

"Obsidian," Hardior said, "you are making ever more outrageous claims here. Are you sure you know what you're saying?"

"Indeed I do."

"I believe him," Nail whispered. "I feel it within me."

"This is insane," Wither said.

"I would tend to agree," Hardior said, and Flute nodded.

"The world is insane," Black said, breaking his silence. "I wish you had told me sooner, Ari."

"I may be mad," Arlian said. "I would scarcely be the best judge of that, and I freely admit I've had my doubts on occasion. Might I suggest that we simply wait, and let the passage of time settle the matter? Either Lord Nail will die a natural death, or the disease will pass, or my 'theory,' as Lord Wither calls it, will be vindicated. I am willing to wait and see which it is. I suspect we will have an answer before tomorrow's dawn."

"Sooner than that," Nail hissed. "Oh, much sooner than that."

For a moment the room was silent; then Lord Hardior shrugged and said, "We'll wait."

14

Deathwatch

Arlian had privately agreed with Nail's assessment; he had expected the new dragon to burst forth within minutes. He had misjudged either the dragon's state of development, or Nail's determination to cling to life and humanity as long as he possibly could.

Had he known how much time yet remained Arlian would probably have attempted to send away the servants, and perhaps Lady Opal as well, to try to keep what he could of the Dragon Society's secrets. As it was, he did not bother.

The sun set, and candles were lit, and still Nail lay in his bed, gasping for air as his chest swelled and writhed. Well after night had fallen Lord Hardior finally sent servants to fetch a little food to sustain the participants in the deathwatch, in lieu of the supper they had missed.

The air grew foul with smoke and sweat, and the scent of dragon venom grew ever more unmistakable.

Save for the servants no one left the room for more than a moment, and no one new entered; none of those present wanted to miss the final act of the drama.

Three times Arlian had asked, over Wither's loud objections, whether Nail wanted one of the servants to fetch a knife; each time, the old man had grimaced and refused. Each refusal had been

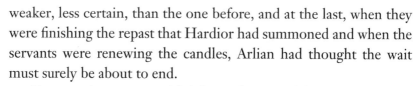

weaker, less certain, than the one before, and at the last, when they were finishing the repast that Hardior had summoned and when the servants were renewing the candles, Arlian had thought the wait must surely be about to end.

Even so, it was past midnight, and most of the company were drowsing in their chairs, when Flute screamed.

Arlian, who had been drifting in and out of uneasy sleep, jerked himself instantly upright, snatching up the spear he had let fall.

The sight he beheld through the candle smoke could have been a nightmare, and for an instant he thought he was dreaming. It *should* have been a nightmare, but was all too real.

Flute was standing by the bed, her hands over her mouth, as she stared in now-silent terror at her patient. Nail lay rigid, his head thrown back, mouth open as though screaming, though no sound emerged; if he was not yet dead, he would be in seconds.

Blood was streaming from his chest, but instead of flowing naturally it was rising upward, writhing and expanding, and the top of the rising column was shaped into a talon, the column forming a crooked leg. The gaping wound in Nail's chest was widening as the blood-thing thrust itself upward, and the flesh around the opening rippled and stretched as the creature fought to be born.

"It . . . it clawed him open from the inside," Flute gasped, as Arlian readied the spear. He was aware that Black stood beside him, his own spear raised.

And then, with a crunching of bone, the dragon burst out of Nail's corpse, struggling to stand on four unsteady legs, crowded onto the bed. Its tail whipped across Nail's unseeing eyes and its wings began to unfold as it raised its head. One foreclaw slipped from the bed, then quickly recovered its footing.

The secret of draconic reproduction was out.

"Now!" Arlian said, and he thrust his spear at the creature's flank. "Aim for the heart!"

Black's strike was scarcely an instant behind his own; both spearheads sank easily into the still-soft, blood-red scales.

The dragon screamed, a hellish shriek that seemed to shake the very walls; it thrashed wildly, trying to escape the black-tipped weapons that had pierced it through, but Arlian and Black pressed forward.

Two of the creature's clawed feet slid from the bed, one free, the other tangled in the coverlet. Its wings smashed at the bed's canopy, shattering the wooden frame and sending the bedcurtains flapping into a hopeless tangle. It spat venom that sizzled and smoked on the bedclothes and carpet but did not ignite. Its golden eyes were open, staring at Arlian and Black with hatred—and with something else, as well.

Arlian saw Nail in those eyes, and refused to look at them. He was glad he had made the spearshafts as long as he had, so that he need not go any closer to that inhuman face.

"Lord Hardior!" Black called. "Get behind it!"

"The heart," Arlian said. "We have to strike its heart!" He yanked his weapon free and thrust again, stepping forward and stabbing just behind the nearer foreleg.

This time the obsidian tip found its target; with another scream the dragon collapsed, dissolving instantly back into the blood from which it had sprung.

Blood splashed and pooled across the bed and Nail's corpse, ran steaming to the floor, dripped from the ruined canopy where the wings had caught; Arlian's hands were drenched with red where he clutched the shaft of the spear.

Impaled upon the tip of that spear was Nail's heart.

"By the dead gods!" someone muttered.

"By *all* the gods!" said another.

"I don't believe it," Wither whispered.

"You saw it with your own eyes, my lord," Black said.

"I saw *something*," Wither said. "I am not sure what."

"Sorcerous illusion," Lady Opal said, rising from her chair. "*That's* all it was!" She reached tentatively toward the still-smoking bedclothes where the venom had spattered, then drew her hand back.

"For an illusion, it seems to have left a great deal of blood," Flute remarked. The front of her gown was drenched in blood where one of the dragon's wings had collapsed across her bosom, and she looked down at herself in dismay. Then she called to one of the servants, "Fetch something to clean this up!"

The servant she addressed simply stared, stunned, but one of the others hastened out of the room. She called after him, "And take care, for it's poisonous!"

"Lord Stiam's chest burst," Opal said. "I can hardly deny *that!* But the creature we saw was merely some dire conjuration, not a true dragon."

"I smell dragon's venom," Wither said. "I haven't smelled it in seven hundred years, but that's venom." Indeed, the reek was everywhere, mingled with the odors of blood, sweat, smoke, and offal.

"Of course you do," Opal said. "From Lord Stiam's blood. But it wasn't a dragon!"

"And how do you know this?" Rime asked, still seated.

"Because the very idea that it was a dragon is arrant nonsense!" Opal said, turning angrily. "It was *red*, and are not dragons said to be green or black?"

"Enziet said that they darken as they mature," Arlian said mildly. Now that the dreaded event was over, he was able to relax again and speak calmly. "Red to gold to green to black. The adults I've seen were black, as you say."

"And do dragons pop like soap bubbles at the thrust of a spear?" Opal demanded, whirling to face him, her fists clenched. "How very strange, then, that none of our ancestors, in all the years they fought the dragons, ever managed to kill one!"

"They never stabbed them in the heart with obsidian," Arlian said, still calm. "And it may only be the newborn infants that dissolve so thoroughly; this one had scarcely finished forming, after all."

"I think it more likely a sorcerer's illusion burst than that a genuine dragon did!" Opal retorted.

"Believe as you please," Arlian said. "I came here to prevent the creation of a dragon, not to convince you of a thing. If you can reject the evidence of your own eyes, my words are scarcely likely to sway you." He looked down at the spear he held, and the grisly trophy impaled upon it. "Where shall I put this?" he asked no one in particular.

"Nail's heart belongs in his chest," Toribor said, stepping forward.

Arlian held the spear steady as Toribor carefully pulled the mutilated heart from the head, and reverently placed it in the gaping hollow that had been Lord Stiam's bosom. That done, Toribor turned and said, "You have slain five of the six lords, then, Obsidian—I alone remain."

"I slew only three," Arlian said. "Three lords, and the two dragons that killed the other two. I was sworn not to kill Lord Nail within the walls of Manfort, and I did not—but you are correct that you alone remain."

"That creature was blood of Nail's blood, and heart of his heart; are you so certain that it was not Nail himself?"

"My lord Toribor, you speak nonsense," Arlian said angrily, his brief calm shattered. He did not want to think of what he had seen in the dragon's face. "Lord Nail lies dead in his bed, butchered by that thing. Is the tapeworm that kills a man heir to his soul, then, and protected by an oath such as mine?"

"This was no mere tapeworm. I saw its eyes, Obsidian . . ."

"It was a *dragon*, Belly," Wither interrupted angrily. "Are you truly arguing that a dragon is anything more than a monster to be despised?"

Opal and Toribor both turned, startled by this outburst.

Wither glared back at them both.

"I fought the dragons for a hundred years," he said. "I stood on the ramparts of this city watching stones and arrows glance off their scales like raindrops from stone, and I saw my friends and comrades torn to pieces or blasted to bone and ash by their flaming venom. I am sworn to fight them, as is every member of the Dragon Society. I am sworn to study their ways, and seek methods to destroy them. And now, when I learn that there may be a dragon in my own body, biding its time and awaiting the moment when it might steal my heart as its own and tear me apart from within . . . when I am told that this parasite has been growing in my blood for almost a thousand years, undetected, you try to tell me that killing it is tantamount to killing *me*? That the monster did not kill Nail, but rather that Nail *became* it?" He lurched forward suddenly, reaching out with his strong left arm and grabbing Toribor by the back of the neck. Displaying a strength truly astonishing in one so old and outwardly frail, he bent the unprepared Toribor over the bed and thrust his unwilling nose within inches of Nail's torn flesh and broken ribs.

"My friend Stiam is *dead*," Wither growled. "He is not transformed or transcended, he is *gone*. He was no caterpillar becoming a butterfly; he was a *man*, and that man is *dead*. To suggest otherwise, Belly, is obscene, and I will not tolerate it!"

"My apologies, my lord," Toribor murmured.

Wither released him, and Toribor straightened up again.

For a few seconds, everyone in the room was silent. Then Wither growled. "You *knew*," he said, turning to Arlian.

"Yes," Arlian admitted.

"You knew. This was why you wouldn't fetch the venom."

"Yes."

"This was how . . . The scar on your cheek was made by Enziet's venom?"

Arlian was so startled by this phrasing, so contradictory of what Wither had said just seconds before, that he could not reply at once, but after a moment he nodded.

"Arlian," Rime asked from her chair in the corner, "why didn't you tell us?"

Arlian clenched his teeth. He closed his eyes for a moment, then asked, "Would you have believed me, if you hadn't seen it yourselves?"

"I'm not sure I believe it *now*," Lord Hardior said, his voice unsteady.

"I asked you once what you would do if I killed a dragon, my lord," Arlian said, turning to Hardior. "You said to leave such matters until such time as they moved out of the realm of fantasy. Has that time come, or do you still believe me mad?"

"Do not press me, Obsidian," Hardior said, staring at Nail's corpse. "This is a great deal to accept."

"It is too much," Wither said, to no one in particular. "I will *not* be a dragon."

"Of course not," Opal said, putting her arm around him. "It was a trick, an illusion!"

"And I wanted to curse *you*, as well," Wither said to her.

"It's a *lie*, beloved, and we *will* transform me, with the venom of a *true* dragon, to live with you forever!"

Wither looked at her with an expression that might have been horror, but said nothing more.

Arlian watched this exchange, and decided it was not his place to interfere. If her own eyes could not convince Opal, then his words surely would not—and it seemed plain that Wither *did* accept what he had seen.

He was very old himself; perhaps he could sense, as Nail had, the dragon growing within him.

Just then the door of the chamber was flung wide, and Nail's steward entered, with half a dozen other servants arrayed behind him.

"My lords," he said. "I understand my lord Stiam has left us."

"Indeed he has," Lady Flute said. "And quite spectacularly." She held up her arms, displaying her blood-soaked gown.

The steward's composure was shaken by the sight, but he quickly recovered. "Then may I ask that you all leave this room, so that we may clean the body and prepare it?" he said. "It's late, and surely you have needs of your own to attend to—we have rooms enough for you all, and you are welcome to stay as long as you choose; these will see you to your accommodations." He gestured at the other servants.

"I think he's right," Opal said. "We need to get away from this horror!"

"And clean ourselves," Flute said. "Careful, those of you with blood on your hands, that you let none pass your lips."

"We know it to be toxic, my lady," Arlian said. "We need no reminders."

"No?" Flute gestured at Black, who was staring at his own hands in bemusement, and Arlian fell silent.

"Thank you for your warning, my lady," the steward said.

"You," Lord Hardior said, "why have you not been at your master's deathbed?"

The steward looked at him, startled. "Why, he ordered me away," he said. "I sat with him through much of his illness, but yesterday he sent me away, told me to attend to his business elsewhere. I would have stayed, had he allowed it . . ."

"Just as well you did not," Arlian said. "Better to remember him as he was."

"Would that we all could!" Wither said.

"Please, gentlemen, ladies," the steward insisted, "could you leave the room?"

"There is much more that needs to be said, Obsidian," Lord Hardior said, "but perhaps it can wait until morning, when we have had time to rest, and to absorb what we have seen here."

"As you please, my lord," Arlian replied. He looked down at his own bloody hands, and the spear he still held, and then at Nail's body. He shuddered.

Toribor, standing by the bed, reached down and gently closed Lord Stiam's eyes.

15

Blood and Water

The servant stood aside as Arlian stepped into the room, then hurried to the bedside table where the pitcher and bowl waited. Without being asked he filled the bowl halfway with clean water. An oil lamp already burned dimly on a bracket above the bed.

"Thank you," Arlian said.

"Would you prefer to have your man here with you, or shall we find him a place downstairs?" the servant asked as he fetched towels from a nearby cabinet.

Arlian glanced at Black. "As he prefers," he said. "He's free to go home, if he chooses; I can attend to my own needs."

"I think a place downstairs would suit me well," Black replied.

Arlian understood that Black intended to listen to what the household servants were saying about the night's events, and perhaps guide the stories a little. It was probably too late to preserve any secrets, but it could do no harm to get a closer look at the situation. "As you please, then," he said as he accepted a towel. He reached for the bowl.

The servant stood by, and Arlian looked at him.

"You need not stay," he said. "It's late, and I'm sure you have other matters to attend to before you'll see your own bed. See to my steward, and then yourself; don't worry about me."

The servant bowed. "Thank you, my lord." He turned, and he and Black left the room, closing the door gently behind them.

Arlian watched them go, then turned to the basin, eager to finally wash Nail's blood from his hands. He put the towel down, then plunged both hands into the cool, clean water.

The water darkened and swirled, deep red spreading out from his hands; he rubbed the blood from the back of each hand, then began to clean the fingers, one by one, squeezing each between the thumb and forefinger of the other hand and brushing at the blood with his thumb.

After a moment the water was too dark to see whether he was accomplishing anything more, and he withdrew his hands and picked up the towel.

He had gotten the worst of it off, certainly—at any rate, off his hands; the cuffs of his shirt were ruined. He squinted at his knuckles and wrists, fairly sure that he would find more blood by the morning sun, though he could see nothing by the yellow lamplight. He picked up the towel, then glanced at the basin.

He froze, towel dangling from one hand.

The water in the bowl had gone unnaturally still and flat, as smooth as a mirror, even though the blood was still swirling vigorously beneath the transparent surface. This was unmistakably magic—though whether the sorcery of the Lands of Man or something more exotic, he could not yet say. Arlian stared.

The blood was not dissipating; instead it was gathering itself in the center of the bowl, where a recognizable image was forming—the image of a dragon's face.

For a moment Arlian thought that perhaps the dragon he had seen born and had slain half an hour before yet survived, in some strange and intangible form, but then he realized that the dragon's face in the bowl was fully mature, not the soft-featured visage of a hatchling, and the eyes were not Nail's.

No, this was a full-grown black dragon, one he had never seen before—dragons, Arlian had noticed long ago, had curiously distinctive and memorable faces. He could still summon up every detail of the face of the dragon that destroyed his home on the Smoking Mountain, eleven years before; he could remember exactly the face of the dragon that sprang from Enziet's chest, and likewise the beast Nail bore. Artists and sculptors almost always failed to capture this peculiar quality of draconic appearance, but the image in the bowl had it in full, and was definitely none of those three.

Arlian remembered words he had heard spoken a year before, by poor Sweet shortly after he had rescued her from Enziet's house, before she began her fatal decline.

"I didn't believe him," she had said, "so he took the bowl of water he used to wash off the blood, and showed me that he talked to the dragons."

The bowl of water he used to wash off the blood.

The image solidified, and the swirling ceased; there was no longer any movement Arlian could describe, but the image had an odd vigor to it, the same sort of indefinable something that was the visible difference between a sleeping man and a corpse. This dragon was alive.

"*We are not pleased with you.*"

No words had been spoken, the image of the dragon's mouth had not moved, but Arlian understood all the same what the dragon intended him to understand.

This was one of the oldest and most powerful dragons, and it was speaking to him as it had spoken to Enziet.

And, after all, was Arlian not Enziet's heir?

"I am not interested in pleasing you," Arlian said quietly. The possibility that a servant might be eavesdropping could not be ruled out, so he kept his voice very low. Somehow, he doubted that the dragon would have any difficulty understanding him.

"*You should be.*"

"Why? I am your sworn enemy. Your kind slaughtered my family, my entire village. I want you dead, not pleased."

"*The other understood, and told you. We had an agreement, and you are his successor. You were to keep your knowledge of our ways secret.*"

"I agreed to nothing."

"Do you understand the consequences of ending that agreement?"

Arlian felt a sudden chill, though the chamber's windows were tightly closed, and the night outside warm.

He knew what consequences the dragon meant. Enziet's bargain had ended the Man-Dragon Wars and driven the dragons into their caverns, deep beneath the earth; without it, as Toribor had warned him, there would be nothing restraining them. They might emerge at any time and destroy anything and anyone they chose. The Lands of Man might once again be plunged into war and chaos. All of Manfort might face the same fiery destruction that had befallen the village of Obsidian.

Arlian had feared this; his fears had faded when nothing happened immediately after Enziet's death, and had returned when Toribor pointed out that the weather had been cold. Arlian had still hoped, though, that Toribor was wrong, that the dragons would not venture out.

Now one of the dragons themselves was threatening him with exactly that. A sudden rush of anger swept over him.

"Do *you* understand the consequences of breaking the truce?" he demanded. "I've killed two of you! Do you think you could rule as you did before, now that we know how you can be slain?"

"You know the black stone, yes, but you will not find our elders as easily destroyed as our young. Open war would be costly to both sides, and the eventual victory uncertain—but what choice do you offer us? You are sworn to destroy us all, and we will not lie quietly in our lairs and await your attacks. An agreement must be made, your oath of vengeance forsaken, or all will suffer."

Arlian paused, startled and thoughtful.

The dragon spoke the truth—at least, Arlian thought it did. He could scarcely expect the dragons to simply let themselves be killed; of course they would fight back.

He had not really considered the possibility of carrying on Enziet's bargain—he had not known how to communicate with the dragons to arrange it. He had assumed that he would have to kill the dragons.

He had been thinking that he would go from cavern to cavern, killing them three or five or ten at a time until they were all gone or he perished in the attempt—but that had assumed that they were mere beasts, unable to communicate with one another, unable to warn one another that he was coming, so soundly asleep that they could not resist.

That was clearly not true, and he should have realized it back when he first learned that Enziet could communicate with the dragons well enough to make his pact. After all, if Enziet could communicate with the dragons, surely they could communicate with each other! And Enziet's pact could scarcely have worked if the dragons were incapable of working in concert.

Arlian's campaign to exterminate the dragons would inevitably become open warfare if he lived and continued it for any length of time. Catching them in their lairs would be ever more difficult as they warned one another and hid themselves more carefully—if they hid at all. They might post guards, as any group of humans would, so that he could never catch a group of them all asleep.

Or they might simply all come out in the open to fight, and how could he fight them then? How could anyone? Yes, obsidian could cut them, but only a thrust to the heart could kill, and the dragons were huge, they could fly, they had talons and teeth and fiery venom. Obsidian spears would be no more use against full-grown dragons than a rat's fangs were against a cat.

But there were only a few dragons, surely—dozens, yes, perhaps hundreds, but almost certainly not thousands. Humanity numbered in the millions, and in the end, wouldn't that carry the day? Enough rats could bring down a cat, and surely even a dragon could be slain by an entire army armed with obsidian. The dragons would in time be obliterated, gone forever, extinct, while mankind would survive and rebuild.

What's more, aside from the relative numbers, the dragons did not *dare* wipe out humanity—after all, if they did that, how would they reproduce? To destroy mankind would be to destroy themselves.

And once secrets were out, they could scarcely be suppressed. If it came to war, then everyone would learn how to kill dragons, and how to destroy their unborn young. Sooner or later, victory for humanity was inevitable.

Arlian opened his mouth to speak, then closed it again.

Yes, mankind would survive—but what about all those men and women and children who would *not*? What right did he have to condemn tens of thousands to the sort of gruesome death that the dragons would inflict, the same death that had taken his own family?

He needed time to think, to plan, to consider his options—but the dragon wanted an agreement *now*.

"What can I do?" he asked. "The secret is out—even if I do nothing, word will spread that obsidian can kill you."

"*You can say it was illusion, mere sorcery of your own contrivance.*"

"And how would that explain Nail's death?"

"*More sorcery.*"

"You say I should confess to killing him."

"*You swore to kill him.*"

"But I didn't kill him!"

"*You slew what he became.*"

"But . . ." Arlian began, then stopped.

The dragon didn't care about lies or oaths, or whether or not Nail and the dragon that he bore were the same being; it wanted an agreement, a restoration of the truce.

"You want me to lie," he said.

"*Yes.*"

"And in return—what? You'll stay in your caverns? You'll let me live?"

"*You have killed two of our hatchlings, and two dragons yet unborn; letting you live is generous. Lie for us, and kill no more, and we will remain in our lairs and go on as before. Fail us in this, and we will have no choice but to attempt to destroy all inhabitants of the so-called Lands of Man before you can turn them against us and arm them with the black stone.*"

"Destroy them *all*?" The idea astonished Arlian. Could even the dragons hope to wipe out *everyone*?

Perhaps they could. Perhaps a bargain would be the sensible thing—but Arlian's anger welled up, and he said, only remembering at the last instant not to shout, "You killed my family, my entire village, and now you threaten my entire race! Two of your foul offspring is not enough to begin to make up for that . . ."

The dragon's words interrupted him. *"Lie for us, and kill no more dragons, born or unborn, or face the consequences."*

And the dragon needed no more words to convey what the consequences would be.

Arlian fell silent, and stared at the inhuman face floating in the bowl.

Those golden eyes, eyes that were oddly human, eyes that had presumably once, thousands of years ago, belonged to a man or woman, stared back at him.

Arlian swallowed his rage and tried to reason with the monster. "Born or unborn?" he asked. "Do you say you would not even permit me to kill Lord Toribor? Or to kill in my own defense should a dragonheart attack me?"

For the first time the dragon hesitated.

"That one, but no other," came the reply at last. *"And in defense of your own life."*

"Fair enough," Arlian said, oddly pleased with himself. He had won a concession, however minor, from a *dragon*; he had not known that was possible.

Of course, he no longer had any particular interest in killing Toribor. Lord Belly, and all the dragonhearts, seemed insignificant compared with the dragons already born.

He would have to find some way to destroy them without permitting open warfare—though right now, exhausted as he was, he could not imagine what it might be.

And he realized, with that, that he was in no condition to deal with this just now. True, he had not been injured fighting Nail's dragon as he had been when he battled Enziet, he had not driven himself across half the Desolation in pursuit of his foe, but still, he was weary and not thinking clearly. He had been through no great physical effort, but the mental and emotional strain of the extended deathwatch at Nail's bedside, followed by this sudden apparition in his washbasin, had in its way been worse.

"Then we are agreed."

"Enough," Arlian said, and he thrust a hand into the water with a splash. The dragon's image spattered into nonexistence, and his mind was suddenly clearer. The dragon's method of communication, he realized, had imperceptibly become an oppressive weight upon his thoughts, a weight that was now lifted.

He hoped he had not been too hasty in breaking the link; he watched the bowl for a moment, to see whether the dragon would attempt to reestablish the spell.

Nothing happened. The water rippled for a moment, then stilled, the blood dispersed and slowly settling.

Apparently the monster had been satisfied, at least for the moment—but Arlian told himself that he had not actually agreed to anything. He had said the terms were reasonably fair; he had never said he accepted them.

But he had bargained with the dragons, like Enziet; he was truly Enziet's heir. He held Enziet's estates, Enziet's secrets, and now Enziet's bargains.

He stared at the water for a moment.

He did not hold Enziet's *beliefs*, he told himself. He would never sacrifice an innocent village . . .

But hadn't he, just a moment before, been considering the possibility of allowing a new Man-Dragon War, sacrificing thousands, for the sake of destroying the dragons forever?

And hadn't he been planning for months to eventually slaughter every dragonheart in the city in order to destroy the dragons they carried within?

Just where was the moral line between his quest for retribution against the dragons, and Enziet's subtle, centuries-long campaign to control them? Which side of that line was truly right and good? Enziet's blackmail had kept the dragons penned in their caverns; Arlian's actions threatened to unleash them again.

If he started a new Man-Dragon War, how could he claim to be any better than the late, unlamented Lord Dragon?

If he succeeded, the dragons would be gone forever, while Enziet had allowed them to live, had allowed them to emerge every few years to destroy a village—his *goal* was superior. Enziet had wanted his *own* long life untroubled by dragons, no more than that, while Arlian sought to free all the world of them forever. That, surely, was a better goal.

But the cost to reach it . . .

He swallowed, and looked down at his hands, and thought he could see in the lamplight a thin red film of blood still clinging to them.

"No," he said aloud. "I will think this through. I will find a way." He snatched up the towel and dried his hands thoroughly, scrubbing them until the skin was red, as he stood by the bed.

At last, when he looked down and saw the skin now as red with the blood beneath as it had been before with the blood upon it, he flung the towel aside and fell onto the bed.

Even tired as he was, it was hours before he slept.

16

A Funeral

Black's voice penetrated the crumbling wall of sleep. "The burial will be this afternoon," that voice said. "You might want to go home long enough to change clothes; while that black coat is appropriate enough, some would consider it poor form to attend the obsequies with the departed's blood still on your shirt."

Arlian reluctantly admitted he was awake; he opened his eyes and saw the canopy above the bed.

This was not his own bed. Although he had barely looked at it the night before, and seen it only by the light of a lamp with a badly trimmed wick, he recognized that canopy. He was still in Lord Nail's home.

He turned his head and saw the washbasin, still on the nightstand, and Black standing beside it.

"Is there water in the bowl?" he asked. If Black could forgo greetings and pleasantries, so could he.

Black glanced at it. "Yes, but it would appear you washed your hands in it last night."

"Does anything look strange about it?"

Black cocked his head curiously. "Other than the film of blood, no. Should it?"

Arlian waved the question aside. He would need to think about that dragon's image he had seen and spoken with, but he did not need to think about it at this very moment. He frowned, then slid his head up against the headboard, the better to see Black. "Isn't it a little soon for the funeral?" he asked. "He's been dead less than a day."

"You haven't seen the condition of the corpse," Black replied. "It's the subject of much discussion downstairs—it's decaying far faster than is normal. The steward had an embalmer in earlier this morning who took one look at the body, and refused to touch it—he allegedly said that with the entire chest torn out like that he couldn't have done much even when it was fresh, and he judged the man to be two weeks dead. When he was told Lord Nail had been alive and conscious just last night he called the steward a liar and stamped out in a huff. The staff here is all atwitter, arguing whether to attribute the phenomenon to Lord Stiam's extreme age, or his frequent use of sorcery, or to some sort of draconic curse."

"Probably all of them," Arlian said, reluctantly sitting up. "What time is it?"

"Noon, give or take a little. I've taken the liberty of summoning your coach, since Lord Hardior departed some time ago. I believe you had wanted to speak with him, but he seemed disinclined to wait, or to have you awakened."

"Oh? Well, thank you for attending to that." He did want to talk to Hardior—but right now, he was not at all sure what he wanted to say. Last night, when Hardior had suggested they talk, Arlian had thought he would tell Hardior the whole story, all Enziet's secrets, and try to enlist his aid—and the Duke's!—in a campaign to hunt down and exterminate the dragons.

But that was before his magical conversation. The dragons didn't *want* their secrets spread.

Arlian was not interested in pleasing the dragons, but he *was* interested in his own survival, and doing everything he could to protect innocents. He had not yet worked out to his own satisfaction how that might best be achieved.

He stretched, then looked down at himself.

He was still in the same white shirt and black trousers he had worn the night before, and as Black had said, blood dried to a dark and ugly brown speckled the right sleeve almost to the elbow, and a few spots showed on the lace of the left cuff. He had had the presence of mind to remove his coat and boots before going to sleep, but had simply dropped them on the floor. Glancing down, he saw that the toe of one boot was spattered, as well.

He plainly couldn't attend Nail's burial in this condition, and he very much wanted to pay his respects to the old man.

"Go see to the coach," he said, reaching for the chamber pot. "I'll be down in ten minutes."

In fact, he made it in eight.

At the Old Palace he made no pretense of a proper toilet, but simply changed into fresh garments as quickly as he could, then turned and headed quickly back to the coach.

Slightly over an hour later he stood with a few dozen others around the hastily-dug grave in the untended garden at the back of Nail's estate, close against the city's eastern wall. There he watched silently as Lord Stiam's mortal remains were consigned to the earth.

The shroud hid the mangled condition of the body, but did not entirely contain the stench of unnatural corruption. Several of the mourners held handkerchiefs to their noses and averted their faces.

Arlian kept his own hands clasped behind his back, holding his hat, and kept his eyes on the grave; unpleasant as the odor was, he felt Lord Stiam deserved to be seen to his rest with proper dignity.

When the first spadeful of earth fell on the shroud, Arlian felt he could decently turn away. He took a deep breath, then looked about at the others.

All those who had been present at Nail's deathbed, who had seen the dragon within him born and slain, were gathered here, as were several other members of the Dragon Society, the estate's entire resident staff, and a few others Arlian did not recognize. Save for the four groundskeepers acting as gravediggers, all the servants in attendance wore Nail's livery of rose and fawn; Arlian studied their faces, and thought they looked genuinely saddened by their master's death.

He wondered how many of them were slaves, and whether Nail had made any provision for them in his will—assuming he *had* a will; members of the Dragon Society generally expected to live forever, and therefore neglected such morbid concerns.

Black, who stood at Arlian's elbow, noticed the direction of his gaze. "He named his steward as his heir, when he fell ill," he said. "There are bequests to the others, as well. He appears to have been a considerate employer. I would tend to think their grief is sincere, and not merely concern over their future prospects for employment."

"He had his charms," Arlian said. "Lily tells me he was never demanding or deliberately cruel, and Musk admired his strength."

"And he had the heart of the dragon," Black said. "I think you may underestimate how much that affects mere mortals like myself."

Arlian threw Black a quick glance. "Indeed," he said.

He was curious just what Black meant to imply by that remark, whether he was hinting that Arlian's own position owed more than Arlian realized to the taint in his blood, but this was hardly the time or place to pursue the matter. Instead he looked around at the other mourners.

Lord Wither was standing close by the grave, just clear of the men shoveling earth, and Lady Opal was close behind him, peering impatiently over his shoulder. Wither still wore his green silk, but Opal had changed her gown for one of blue and gold—Arlian wondered if the other had blood on it.

Horn stood on Wither's other side, a step farther back. As Arlian's gaze reached the three of them Wither happened to look up, and their eyes met.

The two men stood, staring at one another, for a few long seconds; then Opal whispered something in Wither's ear, and the old man turned to speak with her.

Arlian watched him, noting that Wither was moving more slowly than his wont. His eyes, when they met Arlian's own, had seemed darker than before.

"They were friends for more than seven hundred years," Arlian murmured to Black. "This has hit old Wither hard."

"From what he said last night, I think it's the glimpse of his own future, as much as the loss of his friend, that troubles him," Black replied.

"You could be right," Arlian agreed. "He and Nail were the oldest surviving members of the Dragon Society, and they claimed that neither knew for certain who was the elder. If Nail's time has come, Wither's cannot be far behind." He watched Wither speculatively as the old man argued quietly with Opal; although he was not quite as forceful as usual, the old man still seemed strong and vigorous, with no sign of the weakness, fever, and swollen chest that had sent Nail to his deathbed.

"And of course," Arlian continued quietly, so no one but Black could hear, "the knowledge that a dragon is growing in one's chest is hardly a comfort." The dragons might not want their secrets made public, and perhaps they had some way to overhear his words even now, but he could not lie to Black about what they had seen last night. "I have lived with that nightmare for months, and though my own end is still centuries away, it *is* a nightmare. For Wither, it's that much more immediate."

"Everyone dies," Black said. "Some of you forgot that for a while, and he's just been reminded. As for the dragon, how much does it really matter *how* you die, when the time has come?"

"It matters," Arlian said, still watching Wither.

"The dragon will undoubtedly be slain quickly."

"I don't know if *that* matters. He's not as concerned with what the dragon might do as with what and where it *is*."

Black was silent for a moment, watching the gravediggers, then remarked, "*I* prefer to concern myself with results. A corpse is a corpse, and if the blood briefly took the form of a dragon, what of it? But then I've often been told I lack the finer sensibilities."

Arlian snorted. "They merely tell me I'm mad, never that I'm unrefined; Sweet and Rose trained me well, that winter I spent in Westguard."

Wither turned away from Opal and began to march away from

the graveside; Opal followed him, still remonstrating quietly. Arlian watched, and then realized that Wither was making his way around the grave and gravediggers, heading in his direction. He stood, waiting.

Sure enough, Wither rounded the shrinking pile of earth, then headed directly to Arlian, striding briskly, while Lady Opal trailed a few yards behind, and Horn behind her.

"My lord," Arlian said, nodding his head as Wither came within comfortable speaking distance.

"Obsidian," Wither said. "I have a favor to ask of you, and this time I don't think you'll refuse."

"Oh?" Arlian asked politely. "I am always happy to serve you, my lord, when other commitments do not intervene."

"They won't this time—and thank you, boy, for refusing me before, and saving Lady Marasa from the loathsome end I would have unknowingly inflicted upon her. If only you could have done the same for me, long ago!"

Arlian acknowledged this with a slight bow.

"You might have told me *why*, though."

Arlian hesitated.

The dragons wanted him to lie, to say that Opal had been right the night before, that Wither had seen a mere illusion. If he did not, and the dragons knew it, then he would be declaring war. He would be challenging them to come out of their caverns and attempt to kill everyone who knew their secrets.

Were they listening, even now? Arlian did not know what the dragons knew, or how they knew it; they had certainly known what befell Nail, but could they hear everything a dragonheart said, everything a dragonheart heard?

Even if they could, they couldn't listen every moment of every day. Surely Enziet could not have lived his entire life under draconic surveillance, or he would never have been permitted his studies into obsidian's properties, nor the drugs that staved off his death for a few years.

They might be listening now—or they might not.

Wither was standing there, his bad arm tucked against his side, waiting for Arlian's answer.

"My lord, to speak frankly, I did not think you would believe me," Arlian said.

Opal had caught up in time to hear this, and said, "I *still* don't believe it! It's lies and trickery; everyone knows you have Aritheian magicians in your employ!"

Wither said without turning his head, "Ignore her; she's distraught. You may be right that I would not have accepted your unsupported word, but we will never know, will we? What's done is done, Obsidian, and I would appreciate it if you could join me at my home this evening, and bring some of those stone knives and spears—I wish to purchase a few."

Arlian pursed his lips and glanced at Opal, who was obviously furious, but knew better than to argue with Wither just now. Horn, behind her, was utterly calm, unruffled by any of this.

It was not too late to lie, to tell Wither that it was all a trick. If he did not, even if the dragons were not listening now, they would surely realize soon enough what had happened when they found obsidian weapons in Wither's possession.

Wither had no doubts at all of the evidence of his own eyes; perhaps he was close enough to his own death to sense the monster within himself. Arlian might be able to convince him, all the same . . .

But that would be shameful, to lie to this man. Wither deserved better.

Besides, Wither could be an important ally against the dragons. Wither was now the senior member of the Dragon Society, a position that carried some authority. With his support, Arlian could bring most of the dragonhearts into the fight against the dragons, when it eventually came.

And it *would* come—Arlian knew that. He could not restrain himself forever. He did not have Enziet's patience, Enziet's cold-blooded acceptance of the situation—and Enziet had not had Arlian's need for vengeance.

He had to fight the dragons eventually—and when he did, he needed all the help he could get.

If he lied to Wither and the others now, why would they believe him later?

But he was not *ready* to fight an open war against the dragons.

But would he be ready later, if he tried to keep the dragons' secrets? If he spread the news now, then instead of one lord and his household preparing for war, all the city might be readying itself.

And another possibility occurred to him. What if he, himself, died? What if a dragon came and killed him, and perhaps the others who had been in Nail's bedchamber? The dragons had never killed Enziet, but Enziet had had time to prepare for such a possibility—he might well have hidden documents somewhere explaining everything.

Or he might have merely *told* the dragons he had—could they tell truth from falsehood?

And Enziet had never let the secret slip out, as Nail and Arlian had. The dragons might decide that the spread of the information had to be stopped.

They might not even need to come themselves. What if they used human representatives, as they did long ago, and hired assassins? That would make it possible to blame Arlian's death on Drisheen or Enziet or Toribor, so that no questions of *why* a dragon had sought him out would arise.

The present situation, with the secret half-in, half-out, was clearly untenable for both sides.

All that ran quickly through Arlian's mind, but in the end, what decided him was simply his respect for Lord Wither. Wither had sent Horn to his aid outside the gate, and had always behaved honorably, if not politely, toward him. It was Wither who had first told him about the Dragon Society, and encouraged him to join. Arlian owed Wither a debt, and did not want to lie to him; he wanted Wither as an ally in his impending war.

He would not lie to Wither, and he would provide Wither with weapons that could fight dragons, and if that brought a new Man-Dragon War down on them all, then so be it. At least everything would then be out in the open.

"You wish to be prepared for every eventuality, I take it?" Arlian asked. "To be armed against unpleasant possibilities?"

"Indeed. Will you come tonight, then?"

"I would be honored to come, and I will bring the weapons—but as a gift, not to sell." He bowed again, more fully this time, and added, "Let me do this much to repay your past kindnesses, and to make amends for any distress I may have caused you." He gestured in Horn's direction.

Wither snorted. "I won't argue, just so you bring them." He turned away, and called back over his shoulder, "After supper, then—your cook is surely better than mine, but I can promise you some very fine brandy."

"As you please," Arlian said, "though the pleasure of your company would surely compensate for any imagined failings in your staff's hospitality." He straightened from his bow and watched Wither march away, Horn at his heels.

Lady Opal did not follow the pair immediately; instead, as they moved out of earshot, she looked Arlian in the eye and said, "Damn you, Obsidian!" Her tone was astonishingly bitter.

A few of the other mourners overheard and turned, startled, to see who was speaking.

Arlian looked at her with mild surprise. "I am most certainly damned, my lady, but I must wonder why you say this, here and now."

"*You* did this!" She thrust a pointing finger under Arlian's nose. "You have him so upset there's no telling what he might do, and there is *no* way now that he'll give me this mysterious potion! I should have wiped the venom from the bedclothes last night, when I had the chance."

"You would have scarred your hand had you attempted it, my lady."

"It might have been worth it!"

Arlian owed Lady Marasa no debt at all, but he had determined on the truth. "My lady," he said, "you saw what became of Lord Stiam as the result of this elixir you seek."

"*You* say that was what killed him!"

She, unlike Wither, clearly *was* willing to reject the evidence of her own eyes, which amazed Arlian. "Can you really doubt it?" he asked.

Opal did not argue with that directly, but instead said, a little more calmly, "Whether I believe it or not, that elixir bought him another, what, seven hundred years? Eight hundred? Nine? I'm thirty years old, and at best I can expect twice that again before I die a drooling, shriveled imbecile. Your elixir would multiply that tenfold! Yes, you'll say it leads to a horrible death in the end, but what assurance do I have that I'll not die one equally horrible centuries sooner without it?"

"None, my lady," Arlian said. "None of us can know the manner of his death until the time for it has come. That said, I do not choose to aid in unleashing another dragon upon the Lands of Man, now or a thousand years from now."

"*You* say that was a true dragon! *I* say it was Aritheian illusion, no more real than the songbirds at that ball you held!"

"Believe me, I wish that were true." The dragon wanted him to say it was, he recalled, but he no longer cared. The secret was out, and he would not be party to the dragons' attempt to bottle it up again. "I give you my word it is not."

"Your *word*," she said, and spat.

Several murmuring voices were suddenly stilled as others saw this, and turned to observe the confrontation.

"My lady, as Lord Wither said, you are distraught," Black said, putting a hand on her shoulder. "Please . . ."

He did not finish the sentence, as she snatched his hand off her shoulder and turned. "Don't you touch me," she said, her voice cold. "Bad enough to be a scheming fraud, but the *lackey* of a scheming fraud . . . !"

Black and Arlian exchanged glances. Then Arlian looked down at the front of his shirt, damp with her spit.

"It appears I must return home to change my shirt yet again," he said. "Good day to you, Lady Marasa." He bowed, gesturing with his hat, then turned away. "Come, Black," he said.

The two men walked away, neither the first nor the last to leave the graveside.

As they approached the coach Black remarked, "She really hates you."

"I have snatched away her chance at a life so long it appears eternal to her," Arlian said thoughtfully. "Of course she hates me. I should have realized she would."

"You haven't given *me* this mysterious beverage, either, I note."

"Would you want it, knowing what you now know?" Arlian asked, staring at the ground as he walked.

Black did not answer immediately, and as the silence grew longer Arlian looked curiously at his steward. He had expected instant agreement, but instead Black was giving the matter serious thought.

But then, *Black* had not seen his home burned, his family slaughtered. *Black* had not sworn vengeance on the dragons. He did not have Arlian's visceral hatred of the creatures.

"I'm not sure," Black said at last, as they came up to the coach. "As I said, what does it matter how I die? But *when* I die is of some very great personal interest."

"Of course," Arlian said, "but would you buy that thousand years of life by creating another ravaging monster?"

"I might," Black said, "if the opportunity presented itself. Lord Wither is preparing for his fate by taking your obsidian blades; why could I not do the same?" He shook his head. "It's not an easy question you've posed."

Arlian had been thinking of Wither's interest in terms of fighting off dragons that might attack, but Arlian suddenly realized that was foolish. Wither had no reason to think dragons would attack Manfort. He wanted weapons to be on hand to slay the dragon growing in his own chest, when it emerged. Black had seen that immediately.

Black was no fool, and missed little.

"The venom does more than preserve life," Arlian pointed out.

"Oh, of course, how could I forget?" Black said sarcastically. "It bestows health and glamor and vigor, grants one the power to bend lesser wills to your own—how utterly repulsive a prospect!"

"It makes you cold and hard, robs you of any hope for a family," Arlian pointed out.

"Enziet was a coldhearted bastard, I'll give you that—but perhaps he was even before he received this elixir. Wither certainly still has his passions."

"Wither is an exception—think of Drisheen."

"Think of Rime."

Arlian stepped up into the coach, then glanced back down at Black. "Perhaps you should talk further with Lady Rime. Ask her about her great-granddaughter Rose."

"I may do that," Black said. "I very well may."

That ended the conversation, and a moment later they were rolling back toward the Old Palace.

17

Wither at Home

Arlian had not seen the inside of Lord Wither's estate before, though he had passed by it several times. The outside was a magnificent structure in the grandiose style of some five centuries before, when the Man-Dragon Wars were long over and Manfort was finally abandoning the cheerless and functional wartime architecture that still made up much of the city in favor of blatant ostentation— towering pillars supported an elaborately carved architrave, and heroic statues, twice life-size, adorned a dozen niches. The walls and pillars were still of the ubiquitous gray stone, but the statuary and ornamentation were red and white and black.

Black had served as Arlian's coachman; a stableman met them at the gate and took charge of their equipage, but no other servants were initially in evidence. Black, slightly puzzled, knocked at the massive front doors of verdigrised bronze.

A footman admitted Arlian and Black swiftly at Black's knock, and escorted them in, taking their hats and cloaks. Arlian looked around, curious about what the interior of so vast an edifice would look like.

He immediately noticed an architectural oddity. In every other great house he had seen, whether built before or after this one, the front doors opened into a small foyer, where guests could be relieved of coats and weapons, and that served to keep the chill of winter or the heat of summer out of the interior; here the doors opened directly into a series of opulent, high-ceilinged rooms— opulent, but unlit. Arlian was startled at the obvious neglect and decay in these grand rooms—even by the meager light of the oil lamp the footman carried, he saw mildewed hangings, stained carpets, and cobwebs in the fancywork on every side, gilt peeling from the carvings, and the odor of rot was unmistakable. As he followed the green-clad footman who had admitted them he remarked quietly to Black, "I would have thought Lady Opal would see to the upkeep, even if Wither no longer cares."

Black shrugged and did not reply as he accompanied his employer across a marble hall and up the grand staircase. He was carrying a bundle of obsidian weapons, intended to provide Lord Wither with a proper selection, and concentrating on not tangling the spearshafts in the balustrades rather than looking at the decor. The only light in the immense space came from the footman's lamp, and statuary seemed to leap suddenly out of the darkness at him, trying to trip him or knock the spears from his grasp, as the shadows swayed and shifted.

At the top of the stairs the footman led them down a corridor and through a door, and suddenly their surroundings changed completely, from dark, neglected formal rooms to a brightly lit little parlor, spotlessly clean, furnished with gleaming wood and brass rather than marble and alabaster. A fine fireplace took up much of one wall, and a small fire smoldered on the hearth, though the weather outside was pleasantly warm.

Clearly, *these* rooms were where Wither actually lived, and he had abandoned the rooms intended for show, turning them, in a fashion, into a gigantic equivalent of the foyer his home lacked.

Arlian noticed that half a dozen basswood chairs upholstered in green and red needlepoint were scattered about the parlor, and the footman gestured at two of them, indicating that Arlian and Black should sit.

Before Arlian could even begin to comply, however, a door at the back of the room burst open and Wither strode in. A maid was close on his heels, tugging at his hair, which had been brushed and dressed into coils in a manner Arlian had seen on many vain old men, but never before on Lord Wither. She was struggling to make sure one of the locks of hair at the back was securely tucked into its place.

Wither completely ignored her ministrations as he said, "You're here! Good. And you brought the weapons?"

"Yes, my lord," Arlian said, gesturing at Black.

"Good." He looked around, then pointed at the door from which he had just emerged. "Bring them in here."

Arlian and Black glanced at one another, then followed Wither's finger.

"You stay here," Wither said to the footman, who had been retreating toward the door. Then he turned to face the maid, who had just stepped back to admire her handiwork. "You, too. I'll need you both soon." Then he turned and followed his guests into the other room.

That room was Wither's study, and Arlian was startled to see that another guest was already present—a well-dressed man he had never seen before was seated at one side of the desk, clutching a sheaf of papers.

Horn was there as well, standing at the back of the room, but that was far less of a surprise—the man seemed to have become indispensable to Wither. He nodded a polite acknowledgment of Arlian's arrival.

The room was very fine, with numerous shelves of books and several superb drawings on the walls; the desk was large and well made, trimmed with mother-of-pearl, and the chair behind it generous and upholstered in well-worn leather. An open cabinet at one side held a decanter of amber liquid and half a dozen exquisite small glasses.

Arlian did no more than glance at most of it, though, as his attention rested on the stranger.

"Shuffler, this is Lord Obsidian," Wither said over Arlian's shoulder, as he headed for the liquor cabinet. He jerked a thumb at Black. "That's his steward."

Arlian essayed a slight bow. "Sir," he said.

"My lord," the other acknowledged. He looked about at his papers as if puzzled, and did not rise or offer his hand.

Arlian was puzzled, as well; he had expected a private meeting with Lord Wither where they could speak openly about the nature of dragons, and discuss plans to ensure that when Wither's time came, the dragon that was destined to emerge from his heart's blood would be quickly slaughtered. Wasn't that why he wanted the obsidian blades?

What killing Wither's dragon would do to the dragons' attitude toward Arlian was unknown, and Arlian did not particularly like to think about it—he did not want to see the old wars started anew, and that was the threat made the night before, that if he slew another dragon, born or unborn, the dragons would consider all agreements breached and the Man-Dragon Wars begun anew.

Arlian did not want that—but he did not want to see more dragons born, either. *He* could not kill Wither's without angering the dragons, but if he could convince Wither to leave any further dragon-slaying to others than himself, perhaps . . .

But the presence of this stranger, clearly not a dragonheart, confused matters. Perhaps Wither's plans were not quite what Arlian had thought.

"Shuffler's a clerk," Wither said, as he poured brandy. "I've had him tidying up my affairs."

Arlian glanced at Wither, hiding a twinge of uneasiness. "Is there a reason for this, my lord? Are you unwell?"

"I'm fine," Wither snapped, "but after what happened to Nail I can scarce believe I'll stay that way, so I called Shuffler in."

"Ah," Arlian said. He caught Black's eye for a moment, and thought he read a warning there, but he could not think what danger Black might have in mind.

"I promised you brandy," Wither said, handing Arlian a glass.

"Thank you, my lord," Arlian said, accepting the offered drink. He was not particularly fond of brandy, but he was not so tactless as to refuse Wither's hospitality. He was still in the man's debt—perhaps more deeply than ever, as Wither had never doubted him when Opal had tried to dismiss the dragon as an illusion.

Of course, the dragons *wanted* everyone to think it had been mere illusion. Arlian knew that his refusal to lie to Wither and Black might mean the dragons would carry out their threat of open warfare, but he still could not bring himself to deny the truth to the two men to whom he owed so much.

Wither provided Shuffler, Horn, and Black with brandy, as well, and took a final glass for himself.

"To the memory of Lord Stiam, known as Nail," Wither said, lifting his glass. "May we all learn from his fate." Shuffler looked more confused than ever, but no one spoke as the five men drank.

Arlian had to admit it was good brandy; he still didn't actually *like* it, but it was warming and not actively unpleasant. He finished his, neither hurrying nor dawdling.

When the last glass, Shuffler's, was empty, Wither collected them, saying, "That should help us face the remainder of the evening." He closed the bottle and glasses in the cabinet, then turned and said, pointing at the desk, "Now clear those papers and let's see what Obsidian's man has brought us."

Shuffler quickly snatched the remaining papers off the desk, and Black dumped his bundle onto the blotter. Wither stepped forward and opened the linen wrappings, allowing four spears and half a dozen blades of varying length and shape to spread across the white fabric. He looked them over, then picked up one of the knives in his good left hand. He studied it for a moment, then glanced at Arlian.

"They're sharp?"

"*Very* sharp, my lord, but brittle. Obsidian takes a finer edge than steel, but chips or shatters easily."

"So they're not meant for repeated use, then."

"No."

"One strike, though—that should be easy?"

"Indeed, my lord. And as you saw last night, obsidian will readily pierce hide that would turn any other blade." He did not know who Shuffler really was, or what he already knew, nor just how much Wither had told Horn, and he therefore preferred not to mention dragons unnecessarily. Perhaps it would still be possible to keep Enziet's secrets from spreading any farther.

"And if it's so very sharp, there should be little pain?"

Arlian's mouth opened, then closed again. For an instant he still thought that Wither was concerned about killing the dragon that would someday emerge from his chest, and wanted a quick demise for the creature that would still bear some connection with him.

Then he realized the truth.

For another instant he hesitated, but after all, was this not what he had planned for himself, in the end? Finally he said, "I can only guess, my lord, but yes, I would think the pain would be slight, if the blow is fast and straight."

"Good." He looked at Black. "Fetch the cloth, if you would, sir. Leave the other weapons. Then come with me, all of you." He took the knife and headed for the door.

"Ari?" Black asked quietly.

"Do as he says," Arlian said, as he followed Wither.

In the parlor he found Wither directing the maid and footman in positioning the basswood chairs in a curve along one side. When that was done Black had emerged with the linen in hand, and Wither pointed out where he wanted it laid upon the floor, at the edge of the hearth and well off the carpet. When he was satisfied with the arrangements, Wither straightened up, knife in hand, and said, "Take your seats, please." He stepped back onto the square of linen.

"My lord," Black said, still standing, "I ask you to reconsider."

"Oh, no, steward, whatever your name is. I have considered this quite enough. I have thought of nothing else since I saw my friend die last night."

"That is but a single day, my lord. Perhaps the light of another dawn will show you alternatives . . ."

"*There are no alternatives!*" Wither bellowed, pointing the stone dagger at Black's throat. "Do you think I am a fool? I say I've thought for a day, but in truth I've thought about some aspects of this for centuries, since before your grandfather's grandfather was born. Now, sit you down, steward, and hold your tongue!"

Black closed his mouth tight, glanced at Arlian, and took a seat on one of the basswood chairs.

Shuffler and Horn and Arlian and the maid sat, as well; the footman stepped back against the wall.

"You, too," Wither said, pointing the knife at the footman. "Sit."

Startled, the footman obeyed, despite the violation of normal etiquette this constituted, and the six of them sat in a semicircle on one side of the room, facing Wither, who stood on the far side on a square of linen spread across the front of the stone hearth.

"Now," Wither said, "I think some of you know what I intend, and all of you will see it—that's why you're here. I want witnesses. I want everyone to know that I do this by my own hand and my own choice; I want no questions, no ugly rumors, no lingering doubts."

"My lord . . ." Black and Horn began simultaneously.

"And no questions," Wither said quickly, cutting them off. "No questions, no protests. This is what I choose."

The two men subsided unhappily, glancing at one another.

Wither continued, "I think you all know I'm older than any man has a right to be—Shuffler, you probably know the least, but even you must know I've lived for centuries. The weight of all those years is a burden on my heart and my soul, one I bore not for any love of life, but because I would not give my enemies the satisfaction of my death. I have seen my friends die, over and over and over, and I have felt my own heart grow colder with the passing years. I thought that that coldness, the detachment, the alien thoughts so unlike the beliefs of my youth were the result of my losses over the years—that all those deaths, all that suffering, all those tears I never shed openly had eaten into my heart like rust.

"My compatriots said that my blood was tainted, and that the taint was growing with time, that the human part of me was gradually dying and being replaced by the other. I refused to believe this.

I thought it was merely the ravages of time and loss that were the rust eating away at me.

"I thought that if I could find one true companion, a soulmate who would live out the long years with me, I could clean away that rust. I thought that if I could forget the monsters that made me what I am I could remember how to be fully human once more, and that a wife as ageless as myself could make me forget them.

"And I thought I had no choice—to do otherwise than to live on, clinging to what remained of my soul, would be to surrender to the monsters I believed had meant to kill me, all those years ago, and I would not surrender, would not give them the satisfaction.

"But now, Obsidian has shown me the error of my beliefs. He and Nail demonstrated last night that my compatriots had been right all along, and the damage to my heart came not from the pain outside, but from the corruption within. I know now that it was never intended that I should die in the attack that ruined my arm, that I was flung into the pit deliberately, and that all these long years I have lived have been not for my benefit, but for the benefit of the thing growing within me. I know that I have little time remaining in any case—if Nail was my elder at all, he was no more than a year or two older than I. For me a year is nothing—when I was a child a day seemed to last forever, but now whole decades are scarcely enough time to catch my attention. I cannot delay without risking losing track of time and allowing the unspeakable culmination of my corruption. And so we are here tonight, Lord Obsidian in particular, and I hold the weapon I need." He lifted the knife. "This blade should be enough, but if perchance anything survives, the spears and knives in the study should let the five of you finish the job."

"My lord," Horn said, "doesn't Lady Opal deserve to be here?"

Wither let out a bark of bitter laughter.

"Whether she *deserves* it or not I cannot judge, but she would unquestionably interfere, in one way or another. Whether she would try to stop me or hasten me I do not know—I've named her heir to my estates, so the latter is not unlikely. What worries me, sir, is the possibility that she would attempt to drink my blood."

The maid gasped, and Shuffler said, "My lord!" in shocked tones.

"I hadn't thought of that," Arlian murmured.

"Would it work?" Black asked quietly.

Arlian threw him a quick glance, and shrugged. "I have no idea. A few months ago it would simply have killed her, but now, spilled by an obsidian blade—I don't know."

"I pray you all make certain she has no opportunity to do so," Wither said—and then, with no further warning, he plunged the black blade into his chest.

For a moment a stunned silence fell; a wisp of smoke curled up from the front of Wither's blouse where the blade had pierced it.

The maid screamed, breaking the silence and restoring the room to life.

"My lord," Horn called, leaping from his chair. Arlian and Black were close behind. As Wither crumpled to the floor Horn tried to catch him, but was only able to ease his fall; he found himself forced to his knees, his master's body sprawled face-down on his lap.

Black and Arlian knelt to either side, and Black rolled the dying man onto his back, off Horn's knees, the knife in Wither's chest protruding horribly as his hand fell away.

Blood bubbled up around the stone blade, thick and red, hissing and smoking and writhing in a thoroughly unnatural manner, but remaining merely blood; no other shape took form. Arlian saw that moving blood and knew that if the blade piercing Wither's chest had been anything but obsidian, a dragon would be rising from that wound even now.

That was why Wither had asked Arlian to bring the weapons, of course; if a steel blade would have served, he would probably have gotten the deed over with that much sooner.

And this was, of course, why he had asked about how sharp the blade was, and how painful its use would be.

"You were wrong," Wither gasped, even as Arlian thought that. "It hurts. By the dead gods, it does."

Arlian marveled that the man could still speak at all with a knife in his heart. "I'm sorry, my lord," he said.

"At least the dragon is dead," Wither said. "I can feel . . ." Then he choked, and blood trickled from the corner of his mouth, blood that smoked slightly but ran, liquid and bright red, like ordinary blood. His jaw fell open, and his eyes went blank.

Arlian looked at that trickle of blood, and the thought struck him that a few drops of that in a bowl of water would let him speak to the dragons again. He looked down at his hands and saw that one bore a smear of blood where he had held Lord Wither to turn him.

But what would he say?

Would they hold this death of one of their offspring against him? Had Wither just initiated a new Man-Dragon War?

Or had he eliminated one of the problems that might cause such a war? His death meant one less witness to Nail's demise.

"I'm sorry," Arlian repeated—but Wither was dead, and Arlian was speaking to ears that would never hear again.

"He *killed* himself!" the maid said, in a squeaky little voice that seemed completely inappropriate to the somber moment.

"Yes," Arlian said.

"I had no *idea*," Shuffler murmured, his hands clasped over his breast. "He *never* said he intended anything of the sort!"

"Of course not," Black said. "If he had, you might have stopped him."

"You tried," Arlian said, as he reached down and closed Wither's staring eyes. "You and Horn."

"You didn't help," Black said.

Arlian started to say something; then he stopped. He looked Black in the eye and said, "No, I didn't. I wasn't sure whether I *wanted* to stop him."

"*He* wasn't one of your six lords!" Black said angrily.

"No—but he had the heart of the dragon."

"So do you. Do *you* plan to thrust a glass knife into your heart someday?"

"Yes, I do," Arlian said.

Black stared silently at him for a moment, then said fiercely, "I won't help you do it, and I hope you'll have the courtesy to wait until I'm long dead."

Arlian's mouth turned up in an involuntary wry smile. "I'll try," he replied. "I do have a good many other things I intend to do first."

"I'm not sure I'll help you with those, either," Black said. "I'm beginning to have reservations about the entire matter."

"I don't blame you," Arlian said. He looked down at Wither's corpse. "I don't blame you at all."

18

Lady Opal

They had laid the body out on the linen, legs straight and arms folded across the chest; Horn had pulled the knife out and cleaned it on a rag from his pocket. Arlian was just asking the footman where a more appropriate resting place might be when the door burst open and Lady Opal stormed in, an elderly man in Wither's livery trailing ineffectually behind.

"Wither!" she called, "what are you hiding from me? Why did you have . . ."

Then she saw the five men clustered at the edge of the hearth—the maid had fled, but Shuffler and the footman had assisted Black, Horn, and Arlian in tending to Wither's remains. Opal stopped abruptly, the servant almost colliding with her, and turned to face them.

"What are *you* . . ." she began.

Then she saw the body, and fell silent, staring. The old servant gasped and stepped back, horrified, but Lady Opal simply stared.

Arlian watched her warily, expecting tears or hysteria, but when she finally broke the silence she merely asked, "He's dead?"

"I am afraid so, my lady," Arlian replied.

"Oh, *no* . . ." the old man murmured.

"You're sure?" Opal demanded.

"Quite sure, unfortunately. He was stabbed in the heart."

"By you?"

"By his own hand, my lady, as all here can attest."

She stared at the corpse for a moment, then raised her eyes to Arlian's face and said, "But it was you who drove him to this, Lord Obsidian. And it was you who snatched away my chance at a thousand-year lifespan. Do not think I will forget that, nor forgive it."

Arlian spread his empty hands. "My lady, you surely know that such a life would mean the eventual birth of another dragon, a fate scarcely to be sought."

"After a *thousand years*," Opal shouted, her calm finally breaking. "After a thousand years, and I could have done as he had when that end neared! Has *he* become a dragon?" She pointed a shaking finger at the corpse. "Were all his centuries worthless because they *might* have ended with the creation of a dragon? What harm would it do if they *had*, Obsidian? The dragons cower in their caves, troubling us not a whit!"

"The dragons killed my family and destroyed my village, my lady," Arlian said. "Furthermore, all the dragons now alive are old and tired; a young and vigorous one would not be content to sleep the years away in the caverns."

"You don't know that!"

Arlian started to answer, then bit off his reply. Opal was clearly not willing to listen to reason.

And she certainly wouldn't want to hear him talk about a dragon's image warning him of dire consequences if their wishes weren't heeded.

"Why do *you* care so much?" Opal demanded. "What harm would it do *you* to let one more woman join your secret society?"

From the corner of his eye Arlian saw Black looking at Horn, at the footman, the clerk, and the old man—this last, who Arlian thought was Wither's steward, had retreated to the door. They were hearing discussion of matters that should theoretically be kept secret—but really, how much could stay secret anymore? And were the secrets justified at all?

If it was truly too late to renew Enziet's bargain, then what further harm would it do for the truth to be known throughout Manfort and the Lands of Man? In fact, in open warfare, that knowledge should be spread as widely as possible, so that the dragons could not stamp it out.

But if open warfare could still be avoided, then the secrets might yet be better kept quiet—but Opal was clearly not concerned with that.

"The dragons destroyed my home, my lady," Arlian said. "I want them exterminated, not increased."

"So are you going to hunt down and slay every dragonheart in the *world?*"

Arlian quietly replied, "Such is my intention, my lady, yes."

That caught Opal off-guard; for a moment she stared silently at him; then she said, in a voice dripping disdain, "You're mad."

"So I'm told."

She turned away from Arlian and demanded, "Horn, is he truly dead?"

Horn glanced at Arlian, then replied, "By his own hand, as Lord Obsidian said. Yes, he is."

"He had you here to witness it, I suppose?" She jerked a thumb at the old man. "He had this fool keep me away, but he had *you* here to see?"

"Yes, my lady. I was here at his request, without explanation—you know how he liked to have me on hand in case he wanted some errand run on short notice. He had summoned Shuffler to complete his will, and to attend to some other matters—and as a witness. He summoned Lord Obsidian and his man here to provide the weapon, and required them and Dovliril . . ." he gestured at the footman ". . . to stay on as witnesses. She's gone now, but he had also asked Orlietta to dress his hair, as he wanted to look his best—he said to impress Lord Obsidian, but I think now he was concerned with his funeral, instead. She was also a witness."

"And I was not."

"No, my lady. I said you should be here, and he refused."

"And you did not see fit to ignore that refusal?"

"There was no time, my lady. He acted very suddenly. I knew he thought he would die soon, my lady, but by all the dead gods I did not guess he intended *this!* I'm so very sorry."

"He *chose* this, Horn. He got what he wanted. I won't cry for him."

"Cold," Black murmured in Arlian's ear. "She'd have been right at home with your friends in the Street of the Black Spire."

"Indeed," Horn said to Opal, his voice curiously strained. "As you say."

"I must inform the staff," the old man said, and Arlian thought he saw tears in the servant's eyes. "Your pardon, gentlemen and lady." He turned and vanished.

Opal ignored his departure; her attention turned to Shuffler.

"You drew up his will?"

"Yes, my lady."

"And I suppose he's left everything to Obsidian, to use in his grand crusade against the dragons?" she said.

"Oh, no, my lady!" Shuffler said. "He left a few little bequests here and there, and freed all his slaves, but the bulk of the estate goes to *you*."

For a moment Opal stared silently at the clerk, who stared uneasily back. Black, Arlian, and the others waited.

"You mean I own this house?" Opal said at last.

Shuffler nodded vigorously. "Yes, my lady!"

Opal considered that for a moment, then turned her attention back to Arlian. He met her gaze.

"You're trespassing," she said. "Get out of my house!"

He bowed. "As you please, my lady."

"Shall I get the spears?" Black asked, pointing at the door to the study. As he did the footman was looking from face to face, clearly confused.

"Yes, please," Arlian said. He asked the footman, "Would you be so kind as to see us out, sir?"

"I . . ." The footman looked at Opal as Black slipped away toward the study.

"Do it," she said. "Make sure he and his lackey are off my property as soon as humanly possible, and that they take nothing with them they didn't bring!"

"Lord Wither did leave Lord Obsidian certain papers . . ." Shuffler began.

"*He can get them later!* I want him out of here *now!*" She stamped her foot and pointed at the exit. "And you will not be welcome at my lord's funeral—do not trouble yourself to attempt to attend!"

That last hurt. Arlian bowed again, and strode toward the door. "For anything I have done that troubled you, my lady, I do apologize," he said. "I have but acted in accord with the dictates of my conscience."

The footman stumbled, then snatched up his lamp and headed after Arlian.

"I can't afford a conscience," Opal retorted, as Black emerged from the study with the bundle of weapons. "I don't have time."

"You have a lifetime, my lady," Arlian said.

"And you have a dozen! Get out!"

With that, Arlian left the room, the footman close behind, and Black a step behind the footman, leaving Horn and Shuffler with Lady Opal. Silently they made their way along the corridor and down the grand staircase. They saw no sign of the steward or anyone else as they made their way through the vast dark rooms; Arlian had half expected the house to be bustling already with news of the master's death.

When they reached the echoing entryway, as he was fetching Arlian's hat, the footman hesitated and then asked, "My lord, are there perhaps any openings on your staff?"

It was the first complete sentence Arlian had heard the man speak, and it caught him by surprise.

"Black?" he said. "Are there?"

"Not as such, my lord," Black said, "not unless you intend to restore the Grey House to a full establishment. But with the baby an extra hand could be of use."

Arlian absorbed that, remembering that he had been planning to sell one house and dismiss several servants. He had hardly intended to hire anyone new.

Then he looked at the footman, who stood awaiting a reply, still holding Arlian's hat. "I take it you do not expect to stay on in Lady Marasa's employ?"

"I would prefer not to, my lord, even if she would have me."

Arlian nodded. "Black, even if we cannot use him, surely we could find this man a position more to his liking?"

"Surely," Black said, a trifle sourly. "However, might I suggest, my lord, that we not do so immediately? Lady Marasa is irked with us as it is; if we abscond with one of her servants, and furthermore one of the witnesses to Lord Wither's death, I suspect she would take it ill and find it evidence of some sort of dire conspiracy."

"A good point," Arlian admitted. "A very good point. Perhaps, sir, you might give your new employer ten days' notice—I'm sure you can find a way to phrase that to give no offense, and ten days cannot be too much to bear. By then I'm sure my steward will have found some position more to your liking, though perhaps not in my own establishments—come to the Old Palace and ask for Black."

"Thank you, my lord," the footman said, bowing and almost crushing Arlian's hat against his belly as he did. At the last moment he remembered the hat was there and held it to one side, and when he straightened again he handed it to Arlian, who clapped it onto his head.

"Let us be off, then," he said. "And I wish you well, sir—you and all within these walls."

A few minutes later, in the coach, the impact of everything that had happened in the preceding twenty-four hours seemed to strike Arlian all at once; he fell back in his seat, trembling.

"Oh, gods and powers," he said.

Nail and Wither were dead, both their human selves and their draconic descendants, and Arlian knew that he ought to be pleased, that the number of potential dragons in the world had just been reduced by two, but somehow just now he could not see past the fact that two old men had died, two old men he had, despite his oaths of vengeance, rather liked.

He looked at his hands, but saw no blood in the uncertain light of the coach's interior.

He had not killed them, not the human portions at any rate, but their blood had been literally on his hands. And he had slain the dragon that had been all that remained of Nail—he didn't really know how much of the human parent survived in the new dragon. It could be that a new dragon was a mere parasite, bearing nothing of its ancestor's spirit or intelligence, or it could be that a new dragon was a fresh incarnation of the departed—Arlian had no way of knowing. He had seen something of Enziet in that dragon's eyes, and something of Stiam in the other, but what did that *mean*?

Had he truly slain Nail?

The dragon that had addressed him in the bloody bowl had clearly held Arlian responsible for a death, but was it Lord Stiam's?

Lady Opal certainly thought Arlian was responsible for Wither's death. And Lady Opal, who had until now been a lady by courtesy but of no great significance or power, had just inherited one of the city's great estates, and had clearly come to blame Arlian for her own mortality. That might have unfortunate consequences.

She still wanted to extend her life, to become a dragonheart—*that* might have unfortunate consequences, as well.

And Black, whom Arlian had thought completely on his side and always to be trusted, seemed to think such a fate might be worth pursuing, as well. That was startling and upsetting—but now that he thought about it, Arlian could see how Black would think so. He had had no direct dealings with dragons other than aiding in Nail's death, and had far less contact with other dragonhearts than Arlian had. A thousand years of life, a quick suicide in the fashion of Wither's—wasn't that better than an ordinary lifetime?

Arlian had not thought so; his own life had hardly struck him as enviable, and the other members of the Dragon Society had all seemed, right from the outset, to be damaged both inwardly and outwardly. Black saw it differently, though—and perhaps he was right.

Nobody ever called *Black* a madman.

Until Nail's final illness, Nail and Wither had still thought their lives worth living; Nail had fought death right up to the end, refusing the offer of a quick demise, and only Wither's hatred of the dragons had driven him to his own death. Two long lives had ended, two minds snuffed out and gone, all their memories lost forever.

Two hatchling dragons removed, but at a cost that Arlian was suddenly finding hard to bear—and there were more than three dozen members remaining in the Dragon Society altogether, all of whom he theoretically intended to see dead. He saw their faces in the darkness around him, imagined them all awash in blood . . .

And what would the dragons do if he began to slaughter their unborn offspring? Plainly they could somehow sense what happened in Manfort, at least as it related to themselves; he could not hope to keep a campaign of extermination secret from them, and they had said they would retaliate.

They might *already* be preparing to retaliate for his refusal to lie to Black and Wither, and for his allowing Wither's suicide. They might be emerging from their caves even now.

Since the day Enziet's men pulled him from the cellar of his ruined home, Arlian had dedicated his life to vengeance on the dragons that had wiped out his village, and vengeance on the people who had wronged him and those around him. More than half his lifetime had been devoted to revenge. He had never, in all those years, seriously doubted the righteousness of that revenge. He had been willing to die in pursuit of it.

Dying, it appeared, was only a fraction of the cost. Now, for the first time, he began to wonder whether that cost might be more than he could stand to pay.

And he also wondered whether it might be too late to avoid it.

When he washed his hands that night he studied the basin carefully, wondering whether the image of a dragon might appear, wondering whether he would have a chance to address his foes again and learn, one way or the other, whether they would remain in their caverns.

No image appeared, and at last he dried his hands and tried to sleep.

Revelations

19

Summoned by the Dragon Society

Arlian slept poorly the night of Wither's death, and likewise the night of Wither's funeral—which, at Lady Opal's insistence, he did not attend.

On the following morning, during his regular visit to Hasty and Vanniari, he found himself impatient with the baby's cries.

"What do you suppose troubles her?" he asked Hasty, as Vanniari refused the proffered breast and continued to wail.

"Oh, it could be anything," Hasty said, cuddling the infant. "Sometimes babies just cry. I remember my mother telling me that when my brother was behaving like this."

"You have a brother?" Arlian asked, startled.

"I had three of them once, two older and one younger, and an elder sister, as well. They're all dead, along with my parents." She did not look at Arlian as she spoke; her eyes were fixed on Vanniari. "There, there, Vanni," she cooed, "it's not *that* bad."

The baby apparently agreed, as she changed her mind about nursing and fell abruptly silent.

"What happened to them all?" Arlian asked.

"Plague," Hasty said, gazing lovingly at her daughter. "I was the lucky one—I survived and made my way to the next village, where slavers caught me. I was nine."

"Lucky?" Arlian's gaze fell to the stumps of Hasty's legs.

"Well, I lived, didn't I?" Hasty said, looking up at Arlian. "And you rescued me eventually, even if you did kill Vanni's father doing it, and here I am." She lowered her eyes again. "Isn't she beautiful?"

"Like her mother," Arlian said.

Hasty's smile broadened.

"Some might say that your family was more fortunate," Arlian said. "Their trials are over, their suffering was brief."

"But they're *dead*," Hasty said, looking up. "Their joys are gone as well, and aren't those more important?"

"Are they?" Arlian asked.

"Well, *I* think so!" Hasty said. "What else is life for? We have our friends and our families, however large or small they might be, and we have sunlight and wine and song, and handsome men and good food, and those are always there, sooner or later, when the pain ends. I lost one family to the plague, but now I have another, and my memories of the first, and I'm happy."

"I'm glad you are," Arlian said sincerely.

She looked up at him. "Aren't you happy, Triv?" she asked. "You have all the money you could want, and this fine big home, and your friend Black, and Lily and Kitten and Musk and Cricket and Brook and me—you know you could have any of us any time you want, though you've been too sweet to ask. And you have all your secrets, and you've slain your enemies, and the Aritheian magicians will do whatever you want them to. Aren't you happy?"

Arlian looked at the mother and child, both content, both with their needs of the moment met and little thought for anything more, and for a moment he wished his own life could be so simple for just a day or two.

And then he thought about Hasty's question and answered honestly, "I don't really know."

"How can you not know?" Hasty asked. "You were a slave, and now you're a great lord—isn't that enough?"

"No," Arlian said. "I never cared much about the money, save as a means to an end, or about having people bow to me and call me 'lord.' And my parents' little house on the Smoking Mountain was more than enough; living in this palace makes me no happier."

"Then what *do* you want, Triv?" She smiled curiously at him, her head tilted to one side.

"Justice," he said. "I want wrongdoers to be punished. I want the deserving to be rewarded."

"Well, you're a lord," she said. "You can punish anyone who disobeys you, can't you? And you can give money to anyone who you think deserves it."

Arlian grimaced. "I can't punish other lords as freely as you suggest," he said. "And I can't find a way to punish the dragons that killed my parents without starting a new Man-Dragon War."

"Oh, dragons," Hasty said with a shrug that almost dislodged Vanniari. "You can't punish them at *all*, any more than you could punish a storm, or the plague that killed *my* parents. They're just a part of the world."

"No." Arlian shook his head. "I know how to punish them. I don't know whether I can kill the adult dragons, but I know how to kill their young."

Hasty's gaze had slipped back to her baby, but now her head snapped up and she stared at Arlian.

"You know how to kill their *babies*?" she said. "But the *babies* haven't done anything!"

"It's not so simple as all that," Arlian said, raising a hand. "Each newborn dragon *has* killed a man or woman—and it's a *dragon*, Hasty."

"But it's just a baby!"

"Not really, it . . . it's complicated."

She frowned at him. "How complicated can it be? You wouldn't *really* kill a baby, would you, Triv? Not even a baby dragon?"

"I have," he said. "Twice, in fact. But the first was trying to kill me, and the second would have had it lived a moment longer."

"Oh, don't be silly. No one has ever killed a dragon."

"I have," Arlian said quietly. "Enziet taught me how."

Hasty started to say something, stopped, and shook her head. "I don't know what to say," she said. "Killing babies to punish their parents is just *wrong*."

"Of course it is," Arlian agreed. "But these were dragons."

"And you said they were trying to kill you, so I suppose it's not so terrible," she said. "But it's still not right to use *that* to punish the dragons that killed your parents! The *babies* didn't kill your parents!"

"But they would have grown up to kill other innocent people, Hasty. That's what dragons *do*."

"I thought they mostly stayed in deep caves, and only came out when the weather was right."

Arlian hesitated. The thought that the dragons might be emerging haunted him, but he did not want to tell Hasty that. It might still be possible to avert that disaster.

Still, Hasty seemed to have missed a crucial point. "But when the weather *is* right, they kill innocent people, and burn entire villages," Arlian said.

"And if you want to punish them for *that*, why, that's fine," Hasty said. "But the babies haven't *done* that yet."

"But they *will*, if they live long enough."

"Then it's not punishment," Hasty said. "It's prevention."

"True,' Arlian conceded.

"So you aren't really avenging anything," Hasty said. "You aren't hurting the dragons that killed your family, you're just trying to make it harder for dragons to hurt anyone *else*."

"Well, so far," Arlian agreed.

"Well, then," Hasty said. "So is that why you aren't happy? Because you haven't found the dragons that killed your parents and made them pay for their crimes?"

"I suppose so," Arlian said, startled. He had never thought of Hasty as capable of that much insight.

"So you're still trying to hunt them down? And if you find them and kill them, *then* you'll be happy?"

"If it doesn't cause open warfare between humans and dragons, I think so, yes."

"Why would it start a war? Are those particular dragons especially important?"

Arlian sighed. "Hasty, up until very recently, no one had ever killed a dragon. No one knew *how* until Enziet figured it out. We were no threat to them, so they were content to leave us alone while they slept underground. But if we start killing dragons, *any* dragons, then they'll fight back."

"And start a war?" She made a face. "I hate politics. I used to hear the lords talking about it sometimes, back in Westguard, and I always hated it. All that fighting."

"That's the way things are."

"Well, it . . ." She stopped suddenly, staring at nothing, clearly thinking hard, then said, "But then you can't ever be happy!"

"What?"

"Well, you *can't* kill those dragons if it would start a war! You can't do that. So you'll never have your revenge, and you'll never be happy."

"It might be *worth* starting a war," Arlian said. "We could put an end to the dragons *forever*, so that no more innocents would *ever* die from their attacks."

Hasty shook her head. "Oh, no," she said. "If there were a war, *Vanni* might be killed. There mustn't be a war."

Vanniari had finished her meal and fallen asleep as they spoke, but now as Hasty made her vigorous protest the motion sent Vanniari's head flopping backward, awakening her. She let out a small wail, and Hasty quickly snatched the child back to her breast.

"I'm sorry," Arlian said. "I may not . . ."

"I don't want to talk about this any more," Hasty said, cuddling her baby. "There *won't* be any war. The dragons have been in their caves for seven hundred years, and they'll *stay* there, won't they, Vanni?"

"Of course," Arlian said.

He left just a moment later, sooner than he had intended, and much sooner than his wont.

He wished he were as sure as Hasty that there would be no war. He wished he could even be certain that the war had not already begun.

And he also wished he were as sure as he said he was that humanity would win such a war.

They would win only if people *fought* the dragons—and people like Hasty probably wouldn't. They would hide, or they would allow the dragons to enslave them as mankind had been enslaved long ago.

And the people who did so would probably be happier, and live longer, than the people who fought—yet the dragons *must* be fought.

Though he had to admit he found it hard to imagine how anyone, even someone armed with obsidian spears, could fight an attacking dragon. Catching them asleep was one thing, but fighting them openly . . .

He decided he didn't want to think about it. He busied himself with his household affairs for a time, reviewing expenditures and employment, but quickly tired of that as well. It was almost a relief when a footman, the young man named Wolt, informed him that he had visitors.

"Show them in," he said. "I'll meet them in the small salon."

"They asked that you meet them at the front door, my lord," the footman said.

Puzzled, Arlian said, "Oh? Who are they, then?"

"I do not know, my lord; they gave no names."

"You didn't recognize them?"

The footman hesitated. "I thought one might be Lord Hardior, perhaps."

"Hardior?" That was interesting. The Duke's adviser had said, at Nail's bedside, that he and Arlian should have a long talk, but as yet they had not spoken since then; perhaps he intended to pursue that now.

But if he wanted a long conversation, why not come inside and be comfortable? Meeting at the front door implied either that a quick exchange of some sort was desired, or that they wanted Arlian to accompany them elsewhere—did Hardior want to take Arlian to the Duke, perhaps?

And who were the other visitors?

"How many guests do I have, then?"

"Three gentlemen, my lord."

All male—that meant, at least, that Lady Opal was not among them.

"I'll come at once," Arlian said.

A moment later he stepped out the front door into the bright sun of early summer, and immediately recognized his three callers.

"Lord Door," he said. "Lord Hardior, Lord Zaner. I had not expected to see you today."

In fact, he had never really expected to see Door outside the hall of the Dragon Society at all; Door seemed to always be there, watching everyone who went in or out and making sure that only members were admitted.

Door cleared his throat as the other two looked at him expectantly. "Arlian of the Smoking Mountain, known as Lord Obsidian, sometimes called Lord Lanair or Triv of Westguard, you are summoned, under oaths you swore, to explain your actions to your peers," he announced.

Arlian stood silently for a moment, absorbing this.

He supposed he shouldn't have been surprised; he knew that the Dragon Society could summon a member to a hearing if there was some suspicion that that member had broken some portion of the Society's oath. He had himself tried to summon Lord Enziet on a charge of conspiring with the dragons, but Enziet had already left the city at the time.

He had never expected to be on this end of such a summons, though.

"Who accuses me?" he asked at last. "And in what manner am I alleged to have broken the Society's rules?"

"Lord Toribor has accused you of concealing information about the dragons, and of plotting the death of another member within Manfort's walls," Hardior replied. "I agreed to oversee a hearing on this matter."

Well, Arlian thought, so much for his attempt to mend fences with Toribor.

And concealing information—he could not really truthfully deny that. This hearing should prove interesting, to say the least.

He had some idea how it would work, from Enziet's never-held hearing. Rime had been the overseer for that, and Arlian had been the accuser, required to wait at the Society's meeting hall. Door had been the Society's herald in both matters—he had, Arlian had once been told, been the Society's herald in everything of the sort for at least the past hundred years.

There was a great deal he did *not* know, however. "Forgive me, my lords, but might I ask how long this hearing is likely to take, and what preparation I am allowed, if any?"

"It will take as long as necessary to determine the facts of the case, and the appropriate response to them," Hardior said. "Minutes, hours, or days, I cannot say. As for preparation, you may have a moment to fetch any evidence you feel necessary, but no more than that. We do not care to risk your escape."

"I cannot think of any relevant evidence, my lords, but I pray you allow me to inform my staff that I will be absent for an indeterminate time."

"'Indeterminate,' he says," Lord Zaner said. "That's one way of putting it."

Hardior hesitated. "Obsidian, you do realize that the penalties for breaking the Society's oath may include death?"

"Oh, certainly," Arlian said. "I understand that. I have faith in the common sense of my fellows, though, and do not expect any such verdict."

Zaner and Hardior exchanged glances. Arlian smiled.

Toribor wanted him dead, and presumably some of the other dragonhearts did as well, but Arlian thought, despite the obvious misgivings of his escort, that he would be able to convince a solid majority not to do anything so foolish as imposing a death sentence.

And he already knew much of what he would say. This hearing settled the question that had troubled him ever since he spoke to the dragon's image in the bowl. If the Dragon Society was going to demand the truth of him, they would have it—he would not be forsworn of the oath he had made upon joining.

That might bring the dragons down on Manfort—but at this point, Arlian thought that *anything* he could do might bring such an attack. It might well be on its way even now. Better to go ahead and have it all out.

"Come on," Zaner said. "Let's get on with it."

"A moment, please." Arlian turned and leaned back into the Old Palace, where Wolt was waiting. He took his second-best hat from the hook there.

"Tell my steward I have been summoned to a hearing," he said.

"A hearing, my lord? Before the Duke?"

"No. Before a far more dangerous court than that."

Then, before the man could respond, he stepped back out onto the path, closing the door behind him.

"I am at your service, my lords," he said.

20

Accusations Made

Arlian did not remember ever seeing the Dragon Society's hall so full before. He could not think of a single member who was not present. Of course, with fewer than two score surviving members, and the room as large as it was, it was still far from actually being crowded.

Toribor had taken a seat near the center of the room, facing the door, ready to confront his foe; his head was turned slightly, so that his good eye was forward and the patch over the one he had lost to a dragon's attack so very long ago was slightly back. A small group was gathered about him.

Rime sat close by Toribor's right elbow, her legbone in her hand, tapping quietly on the tabletop. Flute stood just behind Rime, her hands clutching the back of Rime's chair. Lord Shatter sat to Toribor's left, and Lord Spider just beyond, with his wife, Lady Shard, beside him. Lord Ticker, whom Arlian had seen but never spoken to, was standing by Shard's shoulder.

The other members were scattered about, all watching intently as Arlian confronted his accuser.

Once Arlian and his three escorts were inside, Door resumed his accustomed place by the entrance, while Hardior and Zaner remained at Arlian's sides, but pulled up chairs and seated themselves facing Toribor's party. Arlian had no idea what the proper procedure was, but he suspected this affair might take a considerable length of time, so he grabbed a chair as well, tossing his hat onto a small table nearby.

He could not see any particular pattern in the seating arrangements; Toribor was his chief accuser, certainly, but Zaner was Toribor's friend, while Arlian thought Rime preferred his own company to Belly's. Shatter had never taken a side, so far as Arlian could recall, while Spider, Shard, and Ticker were almost strangers.

"I am here, as summoned," Arlian said.

"And I must ask you, my lord, to speak when addressed, and not to interrupt," Lord Hardior said.

"I did not interrupt," Arlian said mildly. "No one was speaking."

"Yes, but in the future," Hardior said, slightly discomfited. "Now, Belly, you are the accuser. State your charges."

Toribor rose from his chair and looked over the assembled Society with his one good eye.

"Friends and comrades," he said, "you all know the terms of the oath that each of us swore upon joining this organization. We are united in our support for one another, and in our efforts to ensure that the dragons never again ravage the Lands of Man. We are sworn to share our knowledge of the dragons, to keep no secrets from the other members of the Society. Yet two nights ago, Lord Obsidian arrived at our late friend Nail's bedside armed with obsidian-tipped spears, clearly aware of what fate awaited him.

"I assume all of you have heard what happened. *Something* burst from Nail's chest, formed of his heart's blood, something that took the form of a dragon, and Obsidian and his steward slew it with their spears.

"Whether this was truly a dragon I do not know—but I do know that Obsidian *expected* this apparition to appear, and came prepared to deal with it.

"I think it plain that he has kept secrets about dragons from this Society, in violation of his oath. Furthermore, while I do not know exactly what happened, I believe we need to consider the possibility that Obsidian somehow *planned* Nail's death, in further contravention of his oath.

"And as if this were not sufficient, last night Obsidian took more stone weapons to Wither's home, and today Wither is dead, as well.

"I think we are entitled to a full explanation, and that at the very least Obsidian must pay some penalty for failing to reveal his knowledge."

Upon completing this speech Toribor looked around the room again, and then sat down.

Hardior nodded. "Does anyone else have further accusations to make?"

To Arlian's surprise, Lord Ticker stood up. He pointed at an ornate cabinet against one wall where a row of skulls filled one shelf.

Arlian had seen the skulls before, of course, but now, for the first time, he noticed that more had been added.

"My lords and ladies, I ask that you count the skulls upon that shelf," Ticker said. "There are eleven. Soon, when we have retrieved Lord Wither's skull from his paramour, there will be an even dozen. Lord Enziet's would be a thirteenth, had we been able to retrieve it. I am sure you all remember, though, that two years ago there were only eight. In seven hundred years, only eight members of this Society had died."

Arlian stared. Those added skulls had belonged to Horim and Drisheen and Nail?

Rime coughed.

Ticker raised his hands. "Yes, there are members who vanished and who may have died—fourteen in all, I believe. Even granting all those, though, that brings the total for seven centuries to twenty-two; usually we will go for decades without a single loss, yet since Obsidian's arrival we have lost no fewer than *five*."

Arlian frowned and glanced at Hardior, who said, "While this unfortunate circumstance is true, I fail to see just what accusation you are directing at Obsidian."

"I am saying that he is a menace, a bringer of disaster. He killed Horim and Drisheen himself, and while he may not have laid a hand directly upon Ilruth or Stiam or Enziet, he was present at *all three* deaths. Whatever the details, Obsidian is a creature of ill omen, and I think we should exile him from Manfort for our own safety. Let him return to Arithei, whence he came."

Arlian cleared his throat, and Hardior nodded. "You may speak."

"I am not from Arithei," Arlian said. "I was born and raised on the Smoking Mountain, and then spent seven years in Deep Delving before relocating to Manfort; my stay in Arithei was no more than a month."

"Then let him return to the Smoking Mountain," Ticker said. "I just want him out of the city." Then he sat down.

Arlian considered this rather vague position with interest. He had never before thought about how rare death was in the Dragon Society, and how disruptive his activities had been; death had been commonplace on the caravan to Arithei, and among the slaves in the mines of Deep Delving, and he had not realized just how rare it was among dragonhearts.

For those who had not been directly involved in his activities, it must indeed have seemed as if he had brought Death Incarnate with him.

And in a way, he had—but if these people thought the carnage already inflicted was bad, they were likely to see far worse soon, when the Society and the dragons fought.

He was also interested to note that Lord Ticker had referred to Wither by his true name, Ilruth—Arlian had only ever heard it spoken once before, at his own initiation into the Society.

"Anyone else?" Hardior asked.

"I want to hear his response," Lady Shard said.

"I would be happy to give it," Arlian said.

"Very well, then," Hardior said. "The accused may speak."

"Thank you, my lord," Arlian said, rising to his feet.

While he had spoken with Hardior and Door and Zaner at the door of the Old Palace, and then while walking to the Street of the Black Spire, Arlian had thought carefully about what he would say, and had decided on telling the complete truth. He was sure that none of these people were in league with the dragons, as Enziet had been. Only Toribor was his sworn enemy, and even he was not utterly blind to the possibility of making common cause with Arlian. These people were all sworn foes of dragonkind, and he had sworn an oath not to conceal knowledge of the dragons from them.

Those dragons would emerge soon enough, Arlian was certain—if he had not already antagonized them sufficiently to trigger a new war, he surely would some day not too far in the future, either deliberately or inadvertently. He was no Enziet, able to plan his every word and action and keep secrets to himself for centuries. He knew that open conflict was inevitable.

And he would not be forsworn for the dragons' benefit. If it would save innocent lives, then he might have abandoned his oath and lied, told them all a slew of comforting stories about Aritheian illusions—but he could not convince himself that lies or silence would save anyone, in the long run.

Therefore, Arlian would explain the situation, give up his legacy of secrets, and let the Society's common sense guide it. In this room were the secret rulers of the Lands of Man; if he could convince them that the Man-Dragon Wars were beginning anew, they could organize defenses, prepare Manfort for a siege, help devise some way of striking at the dragons' hearts with blades of obsidian.

These were surely the people who would aid him in destroying the dragons once and for all. He had merely to tell them all he knew, as he had sworn he would.

Accordingly, he began to speak.

21

Secrets Revealed

"I must immediately confess that there is some element of truth in these accusations," Arlian began, "but I hope I can justify my actions and show you that I have not violated the spirit of my oath. I have always acted with the goal of destroying the dragons forever in mind."

"The dragons and half the Society," Toribor muttered.

"Not just half," Arlian said to Toribor before continuing his speech.

"As you all know, I came to Manfort determined to find and destroy Lord Enziet and others who had worked with him in harming me and my friends and family. Only incidentally did I learn of the Dragon Society's existence, and my qualification for membership, and I joined primarily for aid in my pursuit of justice—or vengeance, if you prefer to call it that, and I will not argue if you do. That said, I took my vow seriously. At the time I knew no secrets about dragons I did not reveal, and I felt myself bound by the precise phrasing of the oath not to attempt to kill Enziet or the others *within Manfort's walls*. That Horim, Drisheen, and Enziet left the city meant I could pursue them, and I did; I do not deny killing Horim and Drisheen, and pursuing Enziet intent upon his death. This was no violation of my oath, though it perhaps may have

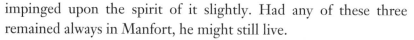

impinged upon the spirit of it slightly. Had any of these three remained always in Manfort, he might still live.

"However, as you may recall, in this very room I accused Lord Enziet of the very crime with which I am now charged—withholding information about the dragons. It was the threat of a hearing such as this that caused him to flee the city.

"I did not pursue him immediately, but when other matters had been settled, yes, I set out with the intent of seeking him out and killing him. I slew Drisheen along the way, and followed Enziet into the Desolation.

"I fought my present accuser, Lord Belly, in the streets of Cork Tree, and although I defeated him I let him live—an act of generosity I do not regret, though it allowed him to demand this hearing." Toribor stirred uncomfortably at this. "He told me that yes, Enziet knew secrets about those dragons, and that if I slew Enziet there would be dire consequences indeed. Has he, then, told you all everything that Enziet told him about the dragons, or is my accuser as guilty as I am?"

"I told anyone who asked!" Toribor protested.

"No one *asked* me directly what I had learned," Arlian replied. "At least, no one in this Society. Lady Rime did make plain an interest, but even she did not ask me directly."

"All I knew was hints and rumors, Obsidian," Toribor protested. "You clearly knew more."

"Indeed I did, my lords and ladies—once Enziet was dead. Until that hour I knew no more than Lord Belly. I followed Enziet into the Desolation, as I said, and caught up with him as he entered a cave in the wilderness. There we fought, with swords and words; it was a more even match than you might imagine, as he was old, feeling his age, and I now realize he was beginning to sicken as Nail did. He told me some of his secrets, at first in hopes of discouraging me from trying to kill him, and later to distract me, but without success. One secret he said he possessed, the most important, he would not tell me. When at last he made a careless attack I broke his sword, and had him at my mercy."

"And did you spare *him*, as you did me?" Toribor demanded, sneering.

"No," Arlian said calmly. "I did not have that choice, nor would I have done so. Instead he plunged his own knife into his chest, freeing what had been growing there for so long, and showing me the secret he had withheld."

"A dragon," Rime said.

"An infant dragon, yes, formed of Enziet's heart and blood. I was almost helpless against it, until I found an obsidian knife hidden in Enziet's clothing. Enziet had told me that he had searched for six hundred years for a means of killing dragons, and had thought he was very close; he also had told me that he had looted my village to obtain obsidian. When I found that knife I realized that these facts were related, and I stabbed the dragon with the stone knife, and killed it, though I was injured in the process."

"You were badly injured," Rime said. "I'm not sure an ordinary man would have survived."

"But I, of course, am not an ordinary man," Arlian said. "None of us here are. We are dragonhearts—and that name is far more literal than we had realized."

"I don't understand," Lord Ticker said.

"Don't you?" Arlian said. "The secret Enziet had kept all those years, had withheld from this Society, was how the dragons reproduce. They do not breed as natural beasts do; instead they contaminate men and women and the dragons' young grow within them, like a disease, until they are ready to emerge, killing their hosts. This development takes centuries, so our lives are unnaturally extended, and to ensure we survive long enough to 'hatch,' as it were, we are made immune to other poisons and lesser diseases. Perhaps to keep us from ties that would hold us back, we are made sterile—or perhaps it is merely that once pregnant, we cannot breed again until the offspring is born."

"Then you claim *all* of us here are going to . . . to die horribly, when these baby dragons burst from our chests?" Ticker demanded.

"Yes, exactly," Arlian said.

"And why did you not *tell* us this when you first returned to Manfort?" Toribor asked angrily. "Why did you wait until that ghastly scene at Nail's bedside?"

"Well, firstly," Arlian said, "I doubted you would believe me. I had no evidence beyond my word, after all, and many of you mistrusted me then—and mistrust me now. I can hardly blame you, under the circumstances."

"You apparently expect us to believe you *now*, though," Lady Shard said.

"Now, my lady, you have *asked* me. Perhaps you'll believe, and perhaps not, but I will not lie about it further."

"Go on," Lord Hardior said. "That was your first reason; are there others?"

"Of course." Arlian spread his hands. "Secondly," he said, "I was not at all sure how you would react to the news, so I hesitated. I was still struggling with the question of what should be done about it myself; you may recall that I have sworn to destroy the dragons or die in the attempt, and I had to consider the question of whether that included dragons yet unborn."

"You mean whether you should try to slaughter the lot of us," Toribor said.

"Yes," Arlian said.

"Have you decided upon your answer to this question?" Rime asked.

"No," Arlian said, "I have not."

"So you might just try to kill us all?" Zaner said, astonished. "And you *admit* it?"

"My lord Zaner," Arlian said, "I am still bound by my oath not to harm you within the city walls. You need have no fear that I will snatch up a sword and try to skewer you here and now."

"No, you'll wait until I go to visit my businesses in Lorigol, and waylay me on the road!"

"Possibly. That remains to be seen. Because there is a third reason I did not speak, my lords and ladies—the same reason that Lord Enziet did not speak in all those years." He paused dramatically.

"You're enjoying this, aren't you?" Rime asked, smiling.

Startled, Arlian said, "What?"

"Drawing this out, teasing us—you're enjoying it."

"I just want to keep everything clear," Arlian protested, disconcerted, and suddenly wondering whether he *was* enjoying himself. It certainly didn't seem reasonable to take pleasure in being put on trial for his life, though it was true that he was not at all nervous, but rather enthusiastic. . . .

"Well, get on with it, then," Rime said with a dismissive wave.

"Yes, of course," Arlian said. "The other reason is that Enziet told me why the dragons gave up their war against humanity and withdrew to their caverns—he made a bargain with them, promising to keep their secrets in exchange for their withdrawal. He told me that he had gone so far as to destroy the covert organization known as the Order of the Dragon that had been hunting down and killing dragonhearts; he had been a member of the Order, but changed sides—I suppose when he became a dragonheart himself—and betrayed and murdered his former comrades to keep the dragons' secret."

"I don't see . . ." Ticker began, but he stopped as others around him reacted.

"By the dead gods," Hardior said.

"I knew it," Toribor muttered. "That's what he meant, then? That with him dead, the bargain would be ended and the dragons could emerge again?"

"Yes," Arlian said. "If the secret was lost, they would be free to do as they pleased."

"That's why you were making those spears," Hardior said.

"Yes," Arlian said. "And that's a reason why I did not tell anyone of the dragons' method of reproduction—I thought I might perhaps somehow take up Enziet's end of the bargain. But then Nail remained in Manfort, for fear of me, instead of leaving the city as the dragons wished, and the secret could not be kept when so many people saw the beast emerge from his chest, and here I am."

"You're a fool," Toribor said. "You could have brought your Aritheians to his bedside and told us it was all some illusion they had conjured! Lady Opal said it was a sorcerous trick, and you *denied* it! You could have told us it was a final trap Enziet laid for you! Drisheen hired an assassin—Enziet might have devised something sorcerous."

Arlian gazed at him. "I didn't think of any of that at the time," he said. "It seemed the secret was out, and pretense had become pointless; do you mean to say that you would have believed me, had I told you those lies?"

"*I* wouldn't," Rime said, "but you might have convinced us to keep the matter quiet."

"And what of the servants?" Arlian asked. "What of Lady Opal herself? And Flute, here—why would she join in such a deception?"

"To keep the dragons in their caves," Flute replied. "If it was not yet too late then. I would have kept silent, had I known."

Arlian stared at her, astonished, then turned to Toribor and demanded, "Belly, would *you* have joined in a lie *I* requested?"

"If you'd told us why, that it was to keep the dragons away, yes. You saw in Cork Tree that I was still willing to listen to you."

"No," Arlian corrected him, "I saw that you would still ask *me* to listen to *you*. It's hardly the same thing." Then a thought struck him, and he looked around the room.

"You realize," he said, "that I am here accused of keeping secrets, and now you say I have not kept them well enough!"

"*I* don't say that!" Ticker objected. "How would the dragons ever know what's happened? How could Lord Enziet make a bargain with them in the first place?"

"Enziet could speak with them, through sorcery," Arlian said. "I thought that was already generally known among the members of the Society. They have ways of knowing things—they spoke to *me*, after Nail's death."

"And how are we to know this was not merely a hallucination?" Rime asked. "I have often heard you say you may be mad, after all."

"Very well, then," Arlian said, "I *thought* they spoke to me. When I washed Nail's blood from my hands an image appeared to me in the basin, and I heard the dragon's thoughts—or so I believed; if you prefer to think this the delusions of a lunatic, I cannot prove you wrong."

"What did they *say* to you?" Spider asked, speaking for the first time.

"They told me not to kill any more of their young, nor to reveal their secrets, else they would resume their war against humanity. They asked me to lie for them, and say that what we saw at Nail's bedside was mere illusion—as it would seem many of you would have preferred."

"And did you agree to these terms?"

"Have I told you, my lord, that the dragon sprung from Nail's death was an illusion?"

"So you challenged them to come out and fight," Toribor said, disgusted. "You doomed us all."

"No," Arlian said. "I am not quite *that* mad. I tried to mislead the dragon—I only spoke with one. I attempted to make it believe that I had acquiesced, without actually lying about it—though truly, I am unsure why I bothered; I am under no obligation to speak the truth to dragons. I was very tired, my lords."

"It would seem," Rime said, "that *everyone*—young Marasa, Flute, our friend Belly, the dragons themselves—wanted you to keep the truth hidden, and tell us that we had been fooled by a magical illusion. Yet you didn't. Is that just the perversity of your nature asserting itself, Arlian?"

"My lady Rime, I was brought here today accused of keeping secrets from the Society, and warned that a conviction could mean death. Would it be wise to attempt to keep secrets from the Society under such circumstances? You have brought this, albeit unknowingly, upon yourselves. There would have been some who did not believe my lies, and the truth would eventually have come out in any case; I prefer to have it out *now*, with all of us here, so that we can plan our collective response."

"Collective response?" Hardior said.

"Indeed," Arlian said. "I have refused my end of the dragons' bargain. I gave Wither the weapon he needed for his suicide, and I have revealed the dragons' secrets here, at this meeting. I think that if the dragons were sincere in their threats—as I hope they were not—then we can expect open warfare between Man and Dragon to resume. I assume that we will collectively respond to that."

"And what do you think that response should be, Lord Obsidian?" Spider asked.

Arlian smiled crookedly. "Although I have been a member of this group only briefly, I have observed that agreement among the Society's members is scarce. I don't really expect an entirely unified response; I expect thirty-eight individual, sometimes contradictory, reactions. I note that Lord Wither has made his own irreversible response to the news, one that I think honorable, if extreme."

He did not say that he *hoped* they would start planning ways to exterminate the dragons; he feared that if he pushed too hard, he would only strengthen resistance to his ideas. Toribor and Ticker were already inclined to favor the opposite of whatever he proposed.

"But what of your *own* response? What would you *prefer* as our response?"

And there he had been asked directly. Before he could reply, though, Lord Hardior observed, "His response was making obsidian weapons, and killing the dragon that Nail bore."

"Yes, but beyond that," Spider said.

"He probably meant to kill all of us," Toribor growled.

"In fact, I did," Arlian said. "I swore long ago to destroy the dragons by any means I might discover, and killing their unborn young would seem to fit that purpose. But on the other hand, I am sworn not to encompass the death of any of you within the city's walls, and I am fully bound by that—and I am glad of it. I do not enjoy killing; some of you are my friends, and others acquaintances, while only you, Belly, do I consider in any way an enemy, and even in your case I respect you and would prefer to make peace. Better in the long term that you all die before you can add new dragons to the world, but in the short term, I would much prefer not to harm any of you."

"So what *do* you plan to do?" Ticker demanded.

"And what do you expect *us* to do?" Zaner asked.

Arlian spread his empty hands.

"I don't know," he said. "I assume that you will all want to use the knowledge I have brought you against the dragons and work toward their eventual extermination, but I have reached no decision as to the best time or place or method to fight the dragons—and it may be that the dragons will not leave those decisions entirely up to us. I believe they can somehow sense what befalls their kin—perhaps including the unborn kin we all carry. How else could they have known what befell Nail? They may well be hearing every word we say here. They may even now be leaving their caves and making their way toward Manfort, leaving us no choice but to fight them here, and soon."

There was a frightened murmur in response.

"But do we need to fight?" someone said.

Heads turned to see who had spoken. Arlian did not recognize her at first, a pale woman missing three fingers from her left hand, then placed her—Lady Pulzera.

"After all," she continued, "we are, in effect, pregnant with their children; they will have no wish to harm us. Quite the contrary, they would surely want to protect us and ensure that we each live out the full term granted us."

"But they're *dragons*," Toribor protested. "We're *sworn* to oppose them; if we don't, they'll enslave humanity again."

"But they won't harm *us*," Pulzera insisted.

Hardior said sarcastically, "Are you suggesting that we should betray humanity and side with the dragons in the coming war?"

Pulzera looked around uncertainly, then said, "Well . . . yes, I suppose I am."

22

The Society Divided

When the hubbub had subsided somewhat and Lord Hardior had restored a semblance of order, he said sternly, "I think it's clear that we can't take seriously any proposal that we should side with the dragons against our own kind."

"It's not clear to *me*," Pulzera said, a little more confidently.

Arlian studied her curiously. This was something he had feared might happen someday—he had realized during the long ride back to Manfort that in fact the Dragon Society was, despite its avowed purpose, a natural ally of the dragons. Enziet had implied, during their final conversation, that he had deliberately created it that way after he betrayed the old Order of the Dragon.

But Arlian had not expected the others to realize it so quickly.

Oh, it was obvious that anyone who wanted to exterminate the dragons—as Arlian did—must eventually destroy the Society and all its members, as well, but Arlian had hoped that the others would either fail to see this, or fail to admit it, or not draw the conclusion that this meant that, in a new war between the dragons and humankind, the human side would want to wipe out the Dragon Society to prevent the eventual reinforcement of their foes. That reinforcement was centuries away, in most cases, but still, it would happen someday.

All the same, the members of the Dragon Society thought of themselves as human. They had all survived dragon attacks, and all knew how monstrous the creatures were; they had all been exposed to centuries of propaganda intended to convince them that the Society was unalterably opposed to the continued existence of dragons. Arlian had thought that the desire to avenge their long-dead friends and family would ensure that they would help him in fighting the dragons.

He had assumed all that would keep them on the human side, at least initially—that it would take time to see through the superficial appearances.

Lady Pulzera, though, had seen through to the truth almost immediately. Now, as the others stared at her in varying degrees of astonishment and shock, she explained, and she seemed to grow steadily more certain of her position as she spoke.

"What we are, the dragons made us," Pulzera said. "We are no longer entirely human, whether you want to admit it or not—the blood that flows in our veins is as poisonous as the dragon venom that transformed us. We can no longer breed with humankind; instead, we are all gravid with the dragons' young, and the dragons will surely therefore want to protect us, while ordinary humans will surely want us dead, so that those young will never be added to the foes they confront. Our interests lie with the dragons, in the long term. Our older members have often remarked on how we grow colder as we age, and more like dragons ourselves—of course we do. Whatever our outward appearance, we *are* half-dragon, half-human, and that means that we are free to choose the side we prefer—and I would choose the side that has a very good reason not to kill us."

"And would you choose the side that slaughtered your natural family?" Toribor asked angrily. "The side that took my eye and half your hand?"

"I would choose the side that gave us a thousand-year lifespan and freedom from disease," Pulzera retorted, "the side to which my only possible surviving offspring will turn when I die."

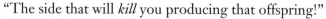

"The side that will *kill* you producing that offspring!"

"Belly, I am almost two hundred years old; if not for the dragons I would be long dead. The dragons have given me centuries I would never have seen; should I loathe them that their gift is finite?"

"*Yes*, damn you!" Toribor shouted. "You should hate them with all your heart for polluting you thus!" Then he whirled back to face Arlian. "*You* did this!" he said. "You have ruined everything! You have perverted this Society, divided it against itself, with your secrets and your murders!"

"I have merely revealed the truth, and removed a traitor and his allies from our midst," Arlian said calmly.

"You call Enziet a traitor?" Toribor demanded.

"Of course," Arlian said, genuinely startled. "He withheld crucial information and bargained with the dragons, in violation of the Society's oaths."

"He kept us from one another's throats by keeping his mouth shut!"

Arlian could not think of any sensible reply to that; he merely shrugged. Around them, he could hear other members arguing with one another—it appeared that while a majority of the Society still found the idea of siding with the dragons intolerable, Pulzera was by no means alone in her opinions.

"Pulzera," Hardior said loudly. "Stop and think what you're saying."

"I *have*," she replied. "The dragons will not harm us if we do not fight them ourselves; they want us to survive. If we take up those magic spears Obsidian has reportedly made, then perhaps they will kill us in self-defense—after all, they can make more dragonhearts. But if we say and do nothing to oppose them, they won't bother us!"

"They may slaughter thousands of innocents," Hardior said. "They may enslave us all, as they did our ancestors."

"For some of us, *we* were enslaved, not our ancestors," Shatter said. "We have been free for seven centuries; I have lived for eight. I still remember."

"We can bargain with them, as Enziet did," Pulzera said. "We need not be enslaved. We know their secrets."

"And so do others," Arlian said. "What can you offer the dragons? Enziet offered his silence, but isn't it too late for that?"

"Well, who does know about it?" Spider asked. "All of us here, but who else?"

"Marasa," Rime said.

"And the servants," Arlian added.

"We could kill them," Pulzera said. "They're just servants, after all. We could accuse them of poisoning poor Nail."

"And Wither," Ticker added.

"They stabbed poor Wither, didn't they?" Pulzera said. "This Marasa probably arranged it so that she could inherit the estate; we can have her tried and hanged."

"Wait a minute," Arlian said, holding up his hands. "Wait. Are you seriously proposing to kill two entire households in order to keep the dragons' secrets from spreading further?"

"Yes," Pulzera said. "Why not?"

For a moment the room fell silent, and Arlian looked at the faces before him.

Ticker merely looked confused; Toribor was angry and uncertain. Rime's face bore a wry smile, while Spider was deep in thought. Shard was frowning, Shatter uneasy. To one side, Hardior was clearly very unhappy indeed; to the other, Door appeared determined while Zaner was, like Arlian himself, looking at other faces to judge his companion's moods.

It was clear that while not everyone liked it, this proposal was meeting no more resistance, and perhaps much less, than Pulzera's initial suggestion of siding with the dragons in the anticipated war.

Arlian hid his own disgust.

He should have known, he told himself. Most of these people were slave owners. Many had fought duels to the death. None of them had protested when Enziet and his five partners had maimed slaves to prevent them from running away. None of them had objected when the Six Lords killed five women in closing down their brothel in Westguard. None had thought the Society had any reason to meddle when Enziet and Drisheen and others killed or tortured people. None of them had seriously objected, for that matter, when Arlian had, in turn, killed Horim and Drisheen and Enziet. They attached no great value to human lives. The only lives they seemed to care about, and the only rules, were their own.

As Pulzera said, they were half-dragon—their hearts were cold. They were far more concerned with their own convenience than with anything like fairness, justice, or mercy. Arlian was appalled. He debated whether to point out that his own steward, Black, had been a witness to both deaths, or to mention that Shuffler might not be on Wither's staff at all, but decided that far from deterring anyone, he would merely be adding more names to the death list.

He could keep at least one name off, he thought. "Lady Opal wants to be a dragonheart," he said. "It might be better to arrange that than to kill her, if we start bargaining with the dragons—a little blood and venom and she would be happy to join you, leaving no need to risk upsetting her relatives or allowing a trial where she might say something unfortunate."

Even as he finished speaking, he realized he might have just made a serious mistake. Saving Lady Opal might be a generous gesture, but it would also mean empowering a woman who already hated him, and perhaps creating a new dragonheart.

Furthermore, it would set an unfortunate precedent. If the Dragon Society began "rewarding" others with the elixir that spawned new dragons Manfort, far from being a refuge from the dragons, would become their breeding farm.

He silently thanked the dead gods that the Society had no ready source of venom. His own interests and intentions still included exterminating the dragons, not breeding more of them. Pulzera was probably a lost cause, but he still hoped to convince most of the Society's members to join him in that fight.

"Listen," he said, "if a war with the dragons begins, what makes you think the dragons will deal with you? Might they not just destroy all of Manfort, and create new dragonhearts to replace us all?"

"They won't want to do that," Pulzera said. "That would set them back centuries."

"Dragons are patient," Lord Spider said.

"But they can trust humans, when it suits them," Pulzera said. "They've done it before. Ask Lord Shatter—in the old days, before they retreated to their caverns, the dragons had their human servants who served them willingly and ruled over the rest of humanity. Those servants lived like kings. *We* could be their new servants!"

"I would rather be a free man, and a lord in my own right," Spider said.

"But will we really be free if war comes? We will serve either the Duke or the dragons," Hardior said.

Several voices spoke at once in reply. Arlian realized as he looked around and listened to the deepening hum of conversation that the meeting was breaking apart into smaller discussions—or arguments.

He could not prevent that, but there were matters he felt needed to be addressed before anything got out of hand. He arose from his chair.

"Excuse me," he said loudly, raising his hands, "but I would like to warn you all that if you attempt to kill everyone on Nail's staff, or Wither's, I will take it very badly indeed. There are people there I think deserve better, and furthermore I think it likely that rumors have already spread from household to household, and that any such slaughter would simply draw attention and lend interest to these tales."

"He's right," Shard said, but before she could say more Arlian continued.

"I was summoned here for a hearing regarding secrets I had withheld from this Society. I have now revealed those secrets, and explained why I withheld them. Am I to take it that the charges against me have been answered?"

"Ah," Hardior said. He looked around the room. "*I* am satisfied, and see no need to pursue this; I think you've given us all much more important concerns to think about."

"It's not for you to decide, Hardior," Toribor said. "It's the *Society* that decides."

"Then should we vote?"

"The senior members usually speak," Ticker said.

"What senior members?" Toribor demanded, turning in his chair. "He's killed them all! Enziet, Wither, Nail, Drisheen—all dead!"

"Who *is* senior, then?" Hardior asked. "I hadn't thought about that . . ."

Door cleared his throat, and Hardior turned.

"My lords," Door said, "the senior surviving member is now Lord Illis, known as Shatter."

"Me?" Shatter said, startled.

"Door's the archivist and herald," Rime said. "He should know."

"Yes, but . . . I suppose I am the senior now, but I hardly know what we should do about this! Young Obsidian has upset everything we thought we knew. He's telling us the dragons *wanted* us to survive, to bear their young—that our survival wasn't due to oversights and accidents. That's . . . well, it's different. And we can't live forever, but only a thousand years?" He snorted a quick laugh. "*Only* a thousand! But to end as mere eggshells for dragons—it's undignified."

"*Undignified?* It's *horrific!*" Toribor said.

"Yes," Shatter agreed, "it is. But Pulzera here proposes that it's still a better fate than we would otherwise face, and that we should be grateful to the dragons, and serve them. Some of us remember the dragons' servants from before, the ones who ruled over us in the old times, that Pulzera spoke of, and I don't think we remember them fondly—do we *want* to become their successors?"

"Do we have a choice?" Pulzera said.

"We *always* have choices," Rime said. "Wither made his choice."

"That's not one *I'd* take!" Pulzera retorted.

"Excuse me," Arlian said, "but I insist we return to the original subject—decide my fate, please, before you debate these far weightier and more complex matters I had sought to spare you."

"Let him go," Shard said. "He doesn't matter anymore."

"Kill him," Toribor said. "For the murder of Lord Drisheen, if nothing else."

"Exile him," Ticker said. "Make him leave Manfort."

"Take away all those stone weapons," Pulzera said. "If they really *can* kill dragons, then aren't we better served if they're destroyed?"

"We might need them," Spider objected. "What if the dragons can't be trusted? What if they decide we'd be safer locked away in their caverns?"

"I don't see how we can justify killing him," Shatter said. "He killed Drisheen outside the walls, apparently in his own defense, and don't we owe him something for finally showing us the truth?"

"He broke his oath!" Toribor insisted.

"I have now revealed what I withheld," Arlian said. "I don't recall that the oath specified how quickly I must share my knowledge with the Society. I seem to recall you, Belly, telling me that when Enziet withheld secrets from the Society that he had his reasons, and this somehow mitigated his treachery; well, I had those same reasons."

"Punishing Arlian would be foolish," Lord Voriam said from one side. "He's brought us vital information, and what does it matter if he dawdled a month or two? All here possess the heart of the dragon, and a life expectancy measured in centuries; this delay is of no moment."

"I would tend to agree," Spider said.

"And I," Shatter added.

Hardior looked uncertain, but said nothing.

"Who present yet opposes a dismissal of the charge?" Door bellowed.

"I do!" Toribor shouted.

"I'm not sure," Ticker said. He looked around at the others.

No one else spoke; silence settled over the room like a cloud of dust.

At last Hardior reluctantly spoke. "It would seem the charges are dismissed."

"No!" Toribor bellowed, rising.

Arlian considered swiftly. He had tried to make peace with Toribor when they had spoken before, and Toribor had refused; indeed, he had had Arlian summoned before this hearing, clearly hoping to see Arlian destroyed. Now that that had failed, Toribor still would not accept it.

He clearly didn't want peace. He didn't even want to be assured that he was safe from Arlian's revenge.

He wanted Arlian dead.

And after all, why would he not? Arlian was responsible for the deaths of five of his friends, and had wounded and arguably disgraced him in a previous duel. Toribor wanted revenge.

Arlian understood revenge.

"My lord," Arlian said quietly, "it is not for you to say whether the charges are dismissed. It is for the Society as a whole."

"I don't accept that!" Toribor said angrily.

"My lord, I think you are acting from personal motives now, not in defense of the Society's interests."

"I hardly think it is in the Society's interest to keep a liar, a traitor, and a murderer alive in our midst!"

Arlian would have preferred to make peace with Toribor, but if that was not possible, then he wanted to get the entire affair over with now, rather than later. He did not think the Dragon Society could ever be united while both he and Toribor lived—Toribor would not stand for it.

"I think that is for the Society to decide," he said. "If you will not accept the decision of this body, and insist that matters between us be settled by blood, I am ready to meet you outside the gate, with swords, at a time of your choosing, to end this once and for all."

"That would resolve everything nicely," Spider said, sitting back in his chair. "If Belly kills Obsidian we'll be rid of someone given to making trouble, and if Obsidian kills Belly he'll have completed his vaunted vengeance and can behave like a civilized man thereafter."

Arlian did not say anything further, but he knew that killing Toribor would hardly complete his quest for revenge. The dragons were far more important. Disposing of the last of the Six Lords would merely end the overture, and allow him to raise the curtain on the main action.

Toribor stared at Arlian for a moment, and for a few seconds Arlian thought he was going to refuse—but that hardly seemed possible. A simple refusal would brand Toribor a coward and make a mockery of his accusations; only an apology and a genuine attempt at reconciliation could avoid both duel and disgrace, and Arlian did not think Toribor would do that.

For a few seconds, though, he *hoped* Toribor would make peace.

But then Toribor threw up his hands.

"Fine!" he said. "Fine. I think it's mad, but the whole *world* has turned mad since you first appeared, Obsidian. You should be hanged, but if I can't arrange that, then I will kill you myself. Tomorrow at midday, Obsidian, I'll gut you before a hundred witnesses."

"Tomorrow at midday, then," Arlian agreed, "in the plaza beyond the gates."

"Then I must ask one of you gentlemen to leave this hall," Door said. "It is not appropriate for you to debate by any means other than cold steel prior to your arranged meeting."

"I left last time," Toribor said. "It's your turn. Besides, you challenged me, not I you, and that makes the responsibility yours."

That caught Arlian by surprise, and he hesitated. He had not thought about that before offering to fight, but Toribor was quite correct, according to the customs of dueling—the burden of any inconvenience was on the challenger, not the challenged.

But Arlian wanted to hear what the Society's members had to say! He wanted to take part in the debates . . .

"My lord Obsidian?" Door said.

Arlian looked around, and saw three dozen people watching

him intently—three dozen people he hoped to convince to join him in his crusade against the dragons. He would not convince them of anything if he ignored the proprieties and customs of Manfort's nobility.

"As you wish," he said, picking his hat up from the table. "Tomorrow at midday, Belly, we will see who is the better swordsman." He turned and headed for the door, donning his hat on the way.

As he stepped through the little vestibule he grimaced. He was fairly sure who was the better swordsman, actually. They had fought before, and while they were closely matched, Arlian thought he knew who was the superior fencer.

Toribor.

When they had fought before Arlian had won, but he had relied on trickery and darkness, and Toribor had been distracted and unprepared, not fighting his best. Tomorrow Arlian would not have those advantages.

He would therefore have to find others.

He had fought swordsmen better than himself before—Toribor, and Enziet, and Horim had all been more practiced with a blade. He had won all three bouts, through cleverness and good fortune rather than swordsmanship.

He hoped that cleverness and good fortune would be enough once again, tomorrow at midday.

23

Crossed Swords

You really are mad," Black said, as he handed Arlian the wooden practice blade. "You haven't used a sword seriously in months, not since Enziet's death! An hour's practice isn't going to make up for that."

"I doubt Belly has had any more practice than I," Arlian replied, hefting the mock weapon—but even as he spoke, a memory tickled at the back of his mind. Hadn't Lord Hardior said that Toribor spent all his time practicing swordplay?

"I wouldn't be any too sure of that," Black said. "How do you know he hasn't been planning this ever since he got back to Manfort?"

"Black, I challenged him," Arlian said. "He could have issued his own challenge and met me outside the gates at any time, if he so chose. He did not."

Even as he spoke, though, Arlian wondered if perhaps Toribor had deliberately goaded him into issuing a challenge, to avoid alienating other members of the Society. It did not seem in character for him, but Toribor was a dragonheart, centuries older than Arlian—it could well be that he had depths Arlian had not perceived.

"And what if he thought you'd been practicing day and night, preparing for exactly such a meeting as this?" Black asked.

"Wouldn't he have tried to stay in form against the day when he found it necessary to leave the city?"

Lord Hardior *had* said that Toribor had been practicing, Arlian was sure of it now—but there was little he could do about it. "Then he's more prepared than I," Arlian said with a shrug. "I'll just need to find some way to handle him. I'm younger and lighter than he is, and not *that* much less skilled; I have no intention of dying today."

"What we intend and what we accomplish often don't match," Black said, raising his own wooden sword. Then, without warning, he lunged.

Arlian parried clumsily, and the practice bout was on.

At the end of the one-hour limit Arlian had set both men were tired and sweating, and Arlian was worried.

"You're not as rusty as I feared," Black remarked as he placed the swords back on their rack.

"I'm worse than I thought," Arlian said. "You would have killed me in seconds had these blades been steel."

"But I'm a better swordsman than Lord Toribor," Black said. "It's my job."

"No, your job is overseeing my household," Arlian said. "You haven't worked as a guard in over a year."

"I'm still better with a blade than he is."

"Well, that's true," Arlian admitted—and he did not add aloud, but thought, "though not by much." He had fought Black in practice, and he had fought Toribor in earnest, so he knew both men's abilities; Black had no such direct knowledge, and Arlian thought Black was underestimating Toribor.

Either that, or Black was trying to be encouraging, to keep Arlian's fighting spirit up.

"And you were doing better toward the end," Black added.

Black was being encouraging. Arlian made a noise but did not reply in words. For his own part, though, while he knew he had indeed done better toward the end, he was fairly sure that his recovery was due more to Black's tiring than his own improvement—

dragonhearts tended to have somewhat more stamina than ordinary men. That was not an advantage he would have against Toribor.

Furthermore, he now doubted he would last long enough for stamina to matter. He would need to find a stratagem of some sort; in a straight and fair duel, he could expect Toribor to defeat him in fairly short order.

Of course, he shouldn't have been a match for Horim, and he had won that fight. Fate had often seemed to be on his side.

Relying too much on Fate would be foolish, though. Fate might have had a purpose for him—but if that purpose was accomplishing Enziet's death, or killing Nail's dragon, or revealing secrets to the Dragon Society, then it had now been fulfilled and Fate was done with him. It was entirely possible he was about to go to his death.

He had lived with the possibility of sudden death much of the time since he was a boy of eleven, but just now, when the Dragon Society was debating its allegiances and dragons might be about to attack, did not seem a very convenient time to die.

When he had issued his challenge he had not been very concerned with the possibility of dying, but now he had reconsidered, and was beginning to regret his decision to fight Toribor. It had seemed an obvious way to dispose of the last of the Six Lords he had sworn to kill, to remove his greatest opponent in the Dragon Society, to reduce the number of gestating dragons, and generally to settle several old matters so that he could devote his entire attention to the likelihood of open war with the dragons, but all those purposes assumed he survived the encounter.

And right now, that seemed unlikely.

Everything seemed to be going wrong for him of late. He had had an extraordinary run of good fortune for a time, from the moment he saved Bloody Hand's life until the moment he slew the dragon that Enziet had become; he had risen from being a slave to being one of the wealthiest men in the world, and had found and defeated most of his foes. He had learned secrets that had been kept for centuries. Oh, there had certainly been setbacks and tragedies along the way, but in general, all had gone well for him. He had known what he wanted, and had worked steadily toward achieving it.

Since his return to Manfort, though, events had slid out of his control. He had not expected Drisheen's assassin, had not anticipated Nail's death, had misjudged Wither's intentions, and now it appeared he had perhaps condemned himself to death by issuing a challenge he was unprepared to back up.

If Fate had indeed abandoned him, and he was about to die, there were matters he did not want to leave unattended.

"Listen," he said as he toweled the sweat from his neck, "you know I've named you my heir. I trust you to handle everything properly and see that the women are all treated well if I die today. However, I'd also like to be sure you will make at least some attempt to carry on my work, and make sure that the dragons' secrets do not remain secret, and that any attempt to restore their rule is resisted. I have told the Dragon Society what I know, but I am not convinced any of them have the stomach to carry on in my place. If the dragons come, I want the Duke's men to have obsidian weapons available. I do not want the Dragon Society to make some costly peace for the sake of their own lives. I do not want more dragons to be born and survive. I think you can trust Rime, and perhaps Shatter and Hardior and Door, but Lady Pulzera would rather see you dead and the dragons triumphant than give up any of her own privileges."

"Are you asking me to take over your madness?"

Arlian smiled crookedly.

"I know better than that," he said. "You're far too sensible to waste your life in such a fashion. I'm merely asking you to stay alert, and to always know which side you're on—the side of humanity. The dragons may make promises, they may even fulfill some of them, but they remain a blot upon the face of the world, a blot that should be expunged."

"I'm hardly likely to forget *that*," Black replied.

"Of course," Arlian said. "But you may forget that appearances notwithstanding, the members of the Dragon Society, and anyone else with the heart of the dragon, are not truly human. They're part dragon, and they cannot be trusted in any conflict between human and dragon. Remember that. Don't be swayed by their words."

"I'll remember," Black said quietly, with a sideways glance at Arlian.

They ate a light luncheon, then separated. Arlian dressed quickly, choosing a blouse with loose shoulders that would not impede his arms, and wrapping a silk scarf around his throat despite the day's warmth, in hopes it might turn a thrust.

When he arrived at the gate, sword and sword belt in hand, he found Black waiting beside the coach—and Brook and Kitten waiting inside. When he saw the women he glanced at Black.

"Stammer is already walking down to the gate," Black said, "and I believe a few of the other servants, as well. Hasty chose to stay behind with Vanniari—a baby has no business at such an affair. Lily wanted to come, but Musk couldn't bear the thought of possibly seeing you die and begged Lily to stay behind with her. Cricket couldn't make up her mind, and finally I told her there wouldn't be room in the coach."

"Oh," Arlian said.

He had not thought about how any of this might affect the others in his household; he had been far too concerned with himself and his own plans. Naturally, though, the women would take an interest in a threat to their host's life.

Arlian looked at the two faces peering out the coach window at him, Kitten openly worried and Brook's expression unreadable. Riding down to the gate with those two sitting across from him was not an appealing prospect, but he had little choice; they could hardly be expected to walk, and he had no intention of tiring himself by walking, and to order them back into the Old Palace would be unkind.

He sighed, climbed into the coach, and settled onto the bench with his sword across his lap. Black closed the door, and climbed up to the driver's seat.

"Are you going to kill him this time?" Kitten asked, as the coach began to move.

"I certainly hope so," Arlian said. "The alternative would be for him to kill me, and I can scarcely consider that a desirable outcome."

"You can't just leave one another wounded?"

"I don't think so," Arlian said. "I doubt Belly would stand for it. I think it's time to settle the matter."

Kitten nodded.

"Just how good a swordsman is Lord Belly?" Brook asked. "The subject never came up during the time he owned me."

Arlian hesitated. He could reassure them with false bravado, but would that be a kindness? Wouldn't it be better to tell them the truth and begin to prepare them for what was likely to happen?

"Better than I," he said, "though not by much."

"You beat him once," Brook said. "In Cork Tree."

"In the dark, taking advantage of his missing eye," Arlian said. "He chose midday for a reason."

"Then how do you expect to win?"

Arlian shrugged, and Kitten glanced from him to Brook and back, her expression going from worried to frightened.

"He wasn't particularly unkind to Cricket and me," Brook said. "Couldn't you settle this short of death?"

"He was one of the six who owned the House of Carnal Society," Arlian said, as much to himself as to Brook. "He let you all be maimed. He let Rose and Silk and Amber and Velvet be murdered. He helped Enziet flee." He wanted to work himself into a rage, to get his heart pumping, to give him the strength and speed and determination he would need.

"But he didn't kill or maim anyone himself. He let Enziet tell him what to do, that's all—he's weak-willed, not evil. And you say he's a better swordsman than you—is it worth risking your life against him?"

Arlian tried not to glare at her—she was undoing his efforts to prepare himself. "I think so," he said. "I tried to make peace once, and he refused. It's my life to risk, and I swore to avenge Rose and the others."

Even now, years later, he remembered how he had last seen Rose—sprawled lifelessly across her bed, her throat cut at Enziet's command, in a room rapidly filling with smoke. Silk had lain on the floor a few rooms away, where she had been dropped in a pool of her own blood. He hadn't found Amber or Velvet, though they had died at the same time; the flame and smoke had been too thick to look further.

He had sworn to avenge them, and rescue as many of the others as he could—which hadn't been enough.

Enziet had later killed Dove, simply for his amusement, and had poisoned Sweet—and he was dead now, though whether it was truly Arlian who had killed him was debatable.

Horim had killed Daub and Sandalwood when he grew bored with them, and Arlian had killed Horim. That had been fitting.

Drisheen had hanged Sparkle and Ferret to spite Arlian, and Arlian had killed Drisheen, not in a duel, but simply murdering him in an inn in Cork Tree; that, too, had been fitting.

Kuruvan hadn't harmed Hasty or Kitten, but Arlian had fought him anyway, wounding him in a duel; he had died of his wounds.

Stiam had freed Lily and Musk when asked, and Arlian had allowed him to live out his few remaining days.

That left just Toribor, who had freed Brook and Cricket only at swordpoint, and had opposed Arlian at every turn. He was not a monster on the order of Drisheen, but it was time to finish the matter, and today's combat would do that. Arlian hoped that if he survived this duel he would never again see that image of Rose's corpse.

Apparently his expression, as he considered the matter, was forbidding; Brook looked at his face, then turned away and made no further argument.

24

The Duel Begins

None of the party in the coach spoke again for the remainder of the journey down through the winding city streets, and as they neared the gates Arlian rose and thrust his head out the window, ostensibly to study the situation but partly to forestall any renewed conversation.

The gates were wide open, as always, and half a dozen of the Duke's guards were watching the coach's approach. The center of the plaza beyond the gate was clear, but the sides were lined with spectators, as they had been when he fought Lord Horim a year before. Most of these observers were strangers, merely people who had heard that two great lords were staging a duel, but Arlian spotted Stammer and Wolt and a few other familiar faces in the crowd.

Several members of the Dragon Society were there, as well. As the coach passed through the gate Arlian noticed Zaner close by, leaning against a wall; Flute and Shatter were near him, while Spider and Shard stood together on the far side of the plaza.

Neither Lady Rime nor Lord Hardior was anywhere in sight, which disappointed Arlian. He had hoped that the Duke's right-hand man would take an interest in this unpleasant business, and Rime . . . well, he had thought Rime would take an interest in his own fate. He wondered what business had kept her away.

He was fighting this duel largely in an attempt to unify the Dragon Society, so that the dragonhearts would act together against the dragons; it did not bode well that two of the Society's most influential members were not present.

Of course, Lady Pulzera's words might be a more significant wedge than his own dispute with Toribor. He wondered what more had been said in the Society's hall after he left the night before; had Pulzera been silenced, her ideas rejected?

Arlian hoped so; otherwise, this entire duel might well be a waste of his time, and perhaps his life.

Arlian tried to push that possibility out of his head as he looked around at the crowd, and saw that Toribor was already there, waiting; Arlian had not noticed him at first, but now the big bald man stepped out of the crowd into the open plaza.

He had removed his eyepatch, revealing the ruined socket where his left eye had been burned out by dragon venom centuries before; he wore a blouse of a sort Arlian had never seen before except in old pictures, with sleeves that narrowed just above the elbow and stayed almost skintight from elbow to wrist.

Those sleeves were clearly designed for dueling—a blade would never catch in those tight cuffs, but the looser upper portion would allow free arm movement, and the shoulders appeared to be padded, for added protection.

The coach stopped, and Arlian opened the door before Black could reach the latch. He sprang out, pulled his sword and swordbreaker from their sheaths, then tossed the belt aside—he did not expect to have any use for it until this fight was over and done, and it would merely be in the way.

He turned, both blades ready, and faced his opponent across the plaza.

Toribor stood, waiting.

Without taking his eyes off his foe, Arlian asked Black, "Any last-minute advice?"

"Don't get killed," Black said.

"I had worked that much out for myself," Arlian said.

"He's still blind on his left side, then. Maybe you can use that."

Arlian nodded.

"Ari, one more thing . . ."

Arlian waited, expecting some parting sentiment—gratitude or affection, perhaps. Instead, Black said, "There are archers on the ramparts."

Startled, Arlian risked a glance at the city walls, and quickly saw that Black was right—there were half a dozen archers in the Duke of Manfort's livery posted atop the battlements, their weapons held ready but not aimed at anything in particular.

"What are *they* up there for?" Arlian muttered.

It occurred to him that these might be another of Drisheen's relics, but surely Drisheen had only had time to hire the two brothers, not this half-dozen—and would Drisheen's assassins dare to wear the Duke's uniforms? Men entitled to those uniforms might perhaps be hired as assassins, Arlian supposed, but would Drisheen have done that?

Of course, there were other people who might hire assassins. Arlian had not thought anyone still lived who would resort to such measures to kill him, but perhaps he had misjudged Lady Opal, or Lord Zaner, or Lord Ticker, or some other person.

Surely not Toribor, though. Arlian would never expect such treachery from Toribor.

But the Duke's livery . . . they were probably *not* assassins. The Duke would surely disapprove of his men acting in the pay of others while in his uniform, especially in so public a fashion.

Of course, the Duke himself had the authority to order the death of anyone he chose—but what the Duke did not have, in Arlian's opinion, was the wit to involve himself in this affair. Perhaps Lord Hardior, as the Duke's chief adviser, had decided to take an interest in the outcome of the duel and given these men orders—but what orders, and what interest, and why? Who were the archers intended to kill, and under what circumstances? Why wasn't Lord Hardior anywhere to be seen?

What had happened in the hall of the Dragon Society yesterday after Arlian left?

He realized that he was letting his sword fall out of line, and decided he really didn't need this sort of distraction right now. He forced himself to ignore the archers and focus on his opponent.

Toribor was still standing in the plaza, waiting. Arlian stepped forward warily, away from the coach.

Toribor raised his sword to guard position, and Arlian brought his own blades up. The two men were still more than twenty feet apart, but Arlian knew they could close that distance in a heartbeat. He kept his gaze focused tightly on Toribor—but he couldn't help wondering who, if anyone, the archers were aiming at.

Toribor had stayed at the meeting hall the day before, and presumably heard the entire discussion. He might know what Hardior was up to, and what had become of Lady Pulzera's obscene suggestions.

"Satisfy my curiosity, my lord," Arlian said, as he stepped forward and to his right. He was now closer to Toribor than to any of the audience, and thought he could converse with his opponent without being overheard. "What did our comrades decide after my departure yesterday?"

"Nothing," Toribor said, his tone disgusted, as he turned to keep his good eye toward Arlian. "They argue endlessly and get nothing done. They can't agree on anything. They have no leaders, thanks to you!"

"*You* were there," Arlian said.

"I have never claimed to be a leader, and I am scarcely senior enough to matter. I merely listened. Now, are we going to talk, or fight?"

"Why not both?" Arlian asked, as he made a sudden feint to the left. Toribor scarcely bothered to react; his swordbreaker came up in a halfhearted block, but he had clearly recognized the feint for what it was.

"What about Shatter?" Arlian asked, moving closer. "He's senior."

"Can't make up his mind."

"And Hardior? I noticed the archers." He jerked his head toward the ramparts.

"Archers?" Toribor's gaze did not waver. "Are there archers on the walls?"

"In the Duke's livery," Arlian said.

Toribor made a quick thrust, which Arlian easily turned aside.

"I assume Hardior sent them," Arlian said after the blades had disengaged. "Would you know why?"

"Hardior didn't say much after you left," Toribor said. "I have no idea what he has planned."

"Then who *did* speak?" Arlian asked, lunging.

Steel clashed, and for a moment both men were far too busy to say anything as they thrust and cut at one another. Toribor's sword blade slashed through Arlian's right sleeve, but no blood had been drawn when they separated again.

"Pulzera spoke," Toribor said. "And Ticker wouldn't shut up. Rime and Spider—everyone had a few words, it seemed, but most of them might as well have saved their breath."

"And nothing was decided?" The mention of Pulzera was not encouraging.

"Not by the time I left," Toribor replied. "They were still chattering, but I needed my sleep before facing you." He made a quick little attack that Arlian took for a feint until it was almost too late; the tip of Toribor's sword missed his cheek by no more than an inch before Arlian's swordbreaker turned it aside. Arlian countered, but Toribor's swordbreaker was ready, and Arlian barely escaped seeing that shorter blade live up to its name.

He was allowing himself to be distracted, Arlian thought. Talking was not a good idea after all; he could satisfy his curiosity later, if he lived through this. Even with Toribor dead, surely Rime would be able to tell him what had happened. He could attend to that later.

First he had to live through the duel.

25

Bloodied Blades

Although the duel had only just begun it was already clear to both participants that despite his missing eye, despite the outcome of their previous nighttime meeting, Toribor in daylight was the more experienced, better-trained swordsman. Furthermore, he had kept up his skills better than had Arlian, which compensated for his heavier frame and greater age, factors that might have been expected to slow his responses. His reach was slightly less than Arlian's, but his sword slightly longer, so that there was no advantage to be had there.

Arlian would need to find some stratagem, some device that would give him an edge, if he was to win this fight.

There were no shadows to exploit, and Toribor had no old wounds other than his missing eye. There was nothing irregular about his style save the way he kept his head turned to make up for his limited vision. While heavy and far from young, he was not weak or sick. Arlian had not noticed any weaknesses in his swordsmanship.

He had to find *something*, though. Arlian ducked and tried a low attack—in Cork Tree he had cut open Toribor's thigh with that approach.

This time he had his sword knocked roughly out of line by the swordbreaker, while Toribor's own sword came overhand for a slash at Arlian's shoulder, drawing the first blood.

It was only the merest scratch, but it stung—and it was not a good sign. Arlian pivoted back, attempting to disengage, but Toribor pursued him, forcing him backward three steps before he was able to stand his ground once again.

This would not do.

Arlian told himself that he was in the right, that justice demanded Toribor's death; he remembered Rose and Silk and the others, and remembered how Toribor had tried to delay or kill him in Cork Tree . . .

And he remembered how even when Toribor was at his mercy, he had begged not for his own life, but for Enziet's, to keep the dragons restrained. The man had courage—and he hated and feared the dragons. He had treated the slaves in the House of Carnal Society as tools rather than people, but he had not been deliberately cruel. Perhaps he had been under Enziet's thumb. Enziet could be very persuasive.

All the same, he had been one of the Six Lords, and he constantly opposed Arlian. He must die for it. Arlian attacked again, moving first toward Toribor's left, as if to try for his blind side, then abruptly shifting direction and striking at Toribor's right.

That did catch Toribor off-guard—for perhaps half a second. Arlian was able to slash diagonally across his foe's right wrist, drawing a widening line of red blood across the tight white sleeve, but did not manage the crippling blow at the inside of the elbow that he had hoped for.

Toribor countered with a jab at Arlian's chest that speared through the silk scarf tucked into his breast. When Arlian brought up his swordbreaker, hoping to snap the sword's blade before Toribor could free it from its silken entanglement, Toribor slashed upward, cutting free of the scarf and drawing a line of blood upward from Arlian's right eyebrow to his hairline.

Neither man could spare a single breath for speech now; they were much too busy with their blades. Steel clashed against steel as both moved in to the attack.

Arlian fought automatically, the long, hard training Black had given him returning now that his life depended on it; he sensed what Toribor intended and reacted before the blows could strike.

Unfortunately, Toribor could do the same, just as effectively.

Around them, the watching crowd cheered and whistled and applauded as the swordsmen fought; each attack, each retreat, elicited gasps and shouted comments and encouragement. Arlian and Toribor ignored it all, and focused only on each other.

The two men maneuvered around one another, and at one point, as Arlian ducked under a high attack and sent his own blade stabbing toward Toribor's sizeable belly, Arlian found himself looking directly over Toribor's shoulder at the archers atop the city wall.

Someone not in uniform was speaking to two of them, and each archer had an arrow in his hand, ready to nock and draw.

But then Toribor turned to dodge Arlian's lunge and brought his own sword down toward Arlian's neck, and Arlian was too busy bringing up his swordbreaker to turn the attack to see any more of whatever might be transpiring on the battlements.

Even in the midst of combat, Arlian found himself wondering once again who had sent the archers there, and why.

Perhaps that distraction was why he misjudged a parry—or perhaps Toribor's greater skill simply caught up with him. Toribor's sword slashed across the inside of Arlian's wrist, and Arlian's hand spasmed slightly—enough to loosen his grip on the hilt of his own sword, and cost him a fraction of a second of control. Toribor reversed his blade's motion abruptly and thrust, and the point jabbed into Arlian's arm.

Arlian's fingers twitched, and Toribor brought his swordbreaker slamming down on Arlian's blade.

The sword did not break, but flew from Arlian's grasp and bounced, ringing, on the stone pavement.

The audience suddenly fell still.

Arlian quickly brought up his swordbreaker and countered Toribor's first thrust, but he knew then that he was doomed. He would die with his vengeance incomplete; the dragons that had slaughtered his family would survive, and breed new dragons in the hearts of unsuspecting humans . . .

Or perhaps not so unsuspecting.

"Belly," he said, as Toribor disengaged from the swordbreaker and prepared to strike again, "don't let them side with the dragons."

Toribor paused.

"What?"

"The others. The Society. Don't let them side with the dragons. Don't listen to Pulzera. You can destroy them if you'll just stay together, and use the obsidian weapons."

"Don't talk to me about that!"

"But it's important! You're going to kill me before I can deal with the dragons, so someone else has to do it, and only the Society . . ."

"*Shut up!*" Toribor bellowed, thrusting the tip of his blade past the swordbreaker and up against Arlian's throat.

"But you mustn't let the dragons win! Don't you see . . ."

"I *do* see!" Toribor shouted. "You let me live last year in Cork Tree because I was more concerned for Enziet than for myself, so now you're trying to save your *own* miserable life by pretending you care about the Society!"

"I care about the *dragons*, and what they may do to mankind if the Society sides with them! I know you're going to kill me . . ."

"Beg for your life, damn you!"

Arlian blinked at him, startled. "You know me better than that, don't you?"

Toribor's face was purple with rage, and the tip of the sword had pierced Arlian's scarf and dug into the skin of his throat; a drop of red appeared on the white silk.

"*Damn* you, Obsidian!" Toribor said. "If I kill you now, in front of all these people—they *know* you spared my life last time we fought. If I kill you, you'll be the better man forever!"

Arlian could think of no intelligent reply to that, and stared silently at Toribor.

"I'd almost think you dropped your sword on purpose!"

The corner of Arlian's mouth quirked upward.

"Unless I thought you as good a man as myself, that would simply be suicide," Arlian said. "And if I thought you as good as myself, why would we be fighting?"

"A sword at your throat, and still you chatter and argue and bait me? You're *mad*, Obsidian!" The sword moved half an inch to the left, cutting the skin of Arlian's throat.

"Then go ahead and rid the world of a madman, Belly, but just remember that mad or not, I do know I'm a man and not yet a dragon or the slave of dragons. You make certain that the others all know it!"

For a moment Toribor stared silently at him; then he said through gritted teeth, "Pick up your sword."

Arlian stared back.

Toribor was not going to simply kill him. By ancient tradition, Toribor had every right to finish him off here and now—but Toribor was not doing it.

Enziet wouldn't have hesitated for an instant. He wouldn't have cared what anyone thought of him. Drisheen would have relished every second, and found a way to kill Arlian slowly. But Toribor was giving him another chance.

Arlian was not at all sure whether he would have done as much were the roles reversed. After all, he had killed Drisheen in cold blood, and Shamble—he had had Shamble at swordpoint, as Toribor now had him, and he had cut open the man's throat.

But Toribor was not going to kill him. Toribor did not even want to march back into the city and leave matters unsettled—he wanted a resolution.

"If you care so much about your reputation, my lord," Arlian said, "you could withdraw your blade for a moment, and then strike me down and say I'd lunged with my swordbreaker. I might even do it. I'm not defenseless, not unarmed."

"I care about my *honor*, Obsidian, not my reputation."

"And if there were no audience here, would you still tell me to pick up my sword?"

Toribor hesitated, his anger fading.

"I *hope* so," he said at last.

"An honest and honorable answer," Arlian said. "Tell me, then, what will you do if I choose not to retrieve my blade?"

"I don't know. I might yet kill you. Why should you risk it?"

"Because if I do retrieve my weapon, and we resume our duel, one of us will die, and I think the odds better than even that it would be me. If I do not, and we speak, either I will die, or neither of us will—and I think I've come to prefer the latter. I tried to make peace with you once before, and you refused—but I wish I had tried again, rather than challenged you. Now I *do* try again. Can we not end this without a death?"

"And what of your famous oath, to kill me or die trying?"

"I think the time may have come to withdraw that oath, my lord. I made that vow to myself, and I can therefore release myself from it."

"And you'd do this to save your own life? You think so little of your own promise to die rather than forgo your vengeance?"

"I would do this to spare *your* life, my lord. You have *mine* in your hand, and can take it if you choose."

"I will take it *honorably*, Obsidian, if at all. Pick up your sword. You spared my life, I have spared yours—we are even. Now let us conclude the matter properly."

"I will oblige you if you insist, but I would be far more willing to conclude our quarrel peaceably. You have shown yourself to be a better man than I thought you."

"And *you* have . . . I don't know what you've done. Pick up your sword!"

Reluctantly, Arlian stepped back, away from Toribor's sword, and stooped, keeping his eyes always on his opponent's right hand as he groped for his own blade.

The crowd, which had been cheering and chattering so constantly until Arlian lost his sword, watched in utter silence.

26

A New Vow

Toribor stood back as Arlian picked up his sword; he waited until Arlian was upright once more, sword ready, before he attacked.

Arlian defended himself, but did not attempt a riposte; he no longer felt any desire to kill Toribor. He would do it if he had to to defend his own life, but he no longer believed that justice required it.

Toribor had been one of the men who owned the brothel in Westguard; he had allowed the mutilation of the sixteen slaves imprisoned there, and the murder of four of them. He had taken two of the women as his share of the business when Lord Enziet shut it down.

But he had not harmed the two he took. He had not harmed anyone else, so far as Arlian knew. He had allied himself with Enziet and Drisheen and the others, but he had not instigated their evil.

And he had argued, in Cork Tree, not for his own life but for the greater good of humanity. He had spared Arlian's life here and now. He was prone to anger and thoughtlessness, but he also maintained a sense of honor, something Enziet, Drisheen, and Horim had considered unnecessary.

And he opposed the dragons. That was certainly a point in his favor. At one time Arlian would have taken that for granted, but now he knew better—Lady Pulzera had shown him that much.

Toribor deserved punishment for his crimes, certainly. He

owed the surviving maimed women a debt he could never pay. Arlian no longer believed, though, that he deserved death.

Around them the crowd was cheering again, but with less enthusiasm than before; they seemed subdued. Steel clashed, and Arlian saw an opening, but he did not strike; instead he stepped back, his blades on guard. It might be that there was no way to end this fight short of death, but Arlian was not yet convinced of that.

Of course, Toribor was a dragonheart, his blood toxic, a monster growing in his heart. He might still be human enough for mercy and honor now, but he was centuries younger than Enziet had been. What would he be like in time, if Arlian let him live?

And what would become of that dragon in his heart?

Perhaps it was best if Toribor died, after all. Arlian parried a thrust, and this time he struck back, catching Toribor off-guard and scraping the tip of his sword across Toribor's right shoulder before Toribor could turn the attack.

But there were dragons in so many hearts—thirty-eight, counting Arlian's own.

And killing them would not end the threat; the dragons would pollute more, unless the dragons were destroyed *first*.

And the people best equipped to destroy the dragons were the dragonhearts. Killing Toribor would not help. Killing Toribor would make it that much more likely that the other dragonhearts would distrust Arlian, and would listen to Pulzera and side with the dragons against him.

Toribor made a low, sweeping attack, and Arlian was forced to concentrate on his swordplay. Steel flickered and clashed, the four blades locked together for a moment; then both men sprang back, disengaging. They stood, just out of each other's reach, staring warily at one another. The crowd's noise was only a murmur.

Toribor would have to die eventually, but the dragons had to die first.

"Belly," Arlian said, "I would swear a new oath, in your hearing, by all the dead gods and whatever else you ask. I cannot until we end this fight, but if you allow it, I will swear not to kill you, in

Manfort or anywhere else, so long as we know a single dragon to survive."

"What?" Toribor stared at him as if he were mad—and of course, Arlian remembered, Toribor thought he *was* mad.

"I want the dragons dead far more than I want to harm *you*," Arlian said. "Can we not end this duel in a truce, and turn our whole attention to destroying the beasts we both agree deserve to die?"

"With what, your stone knives? No one's ever slain a dragon— not a grown one."

"Yes, with obsidian—or whatever else we can find. And if we never find a way to kill them, then I will never again try to kill *you*."

"Unless you change your mind again." Toribor made a quick feint.

"I do not change my mind so easily."

"You change your *name*, Triv, and your appearance, and every-thing else."

"Not everything. Never everything. I stand by my word."

"Oh, of course you do." Toribor's blade flicked out, and Arlian turned it aside.

Words alone would not end this fight, he saw—but he knew what would. He launched a sudden quick attack, a lightning series of jabs, none really meant to kill or seriously injure, but enough to keep Toribor very busy for a moment.

Toribor fell back a step, and as he did Arlian leapt backward himself, out of reach.

And once the two men were too far apart to reach one another with their swords, Arlian flung aside both his sword and sword-breaker. Steel jangled on the pavement, and the murmur of the crowd suddenly stilled again.

"Our quarrel is ended," he said. "Kill me if you must, but I will fight no more."

"Oh, now you're doing it deliberately?" Toribor shouted. "You think because I spared you once, I'll do it again?" He stepped for-ward and raised his sword, but did not strike.

"Yes," Arlian said, spreading his empty hands. "You have shown me that you're a better man than I had thought, that I was wrong to seek your death. I swear, Lord Toribor, that I will not fight you again today, that I will not try to kill you while a single dragon yet lives. My vengeance oath was to myself, and I have released myself from it; *this* oath I give to *you*."

Toribor hesitated.

"You can still prove me wrong," Arlian said. "Plunge your blade through my heart, and we'll both see that you are less honorable, less worthy, than I thought. I don't think either of us wants that."

Toribor growled, then said, "Confound you, Obsidian!" He lowered his sword.

Then, for the first time since Arlian had stepped out of his coach, Toribor took his eyes off his opponent and looked around at the crowd of spectators. He glanced up at the city wall.

"No archers," he said. "The ruse was hardly a clever one."

Startled, Arlian turned. Sure enough, the archers were gone.

"They were there," he said.

Toribor snorted.

"I never know where I stand with you," he said. "You lie as easily as most men breathe, and you're loyal to no one but yourself. I would not put it past you to pick up your blades and strike at me, despite your new oath."

Wounded, Arlian said, "The archers were there, and I will not break my oath." He stepped back, away from his discarded weapons.

"You won't resume the fight, and put an end to the matter?"

"You heard my vow. I consider the matter ended."

"And I must accept that?"

"You have your sword, my lord; I am at your mercy."

"No, you aren't. I don't think you even understand the concept. Are you afraid of nothing, Arlian?"

Arlian blinked in surprise. "I am no more fearless than you," he said.

"You lie as easily as others breathe. You claimed to be pursuing sworn vengeance, unappeasable, yet now you say it's over, and that means our quarrel is resolved. Forgive me if I do not immediately agree—let me remind you that while I may have abused women you came to care for, you have slain three of my comrades, two of them men I had known for hundreds of years. Horim and Kuruvan died in honest duels, but you murdered Drisheen. The circumstances of Enziet's death remain unclear, despite your claims, and I might reasonably believe you had slain him as well. You did not kill Wither, but you encouraged him in his suicide. Am I to simply forget all these, all my friends? Have I no right to seek vengeance upon their slayer?"

"I am here, unarmed," Arlian said. "If you think Drisheen deserving of such revenge, strike me down—but remember first what kind of man Drisheen was. Do you know what he did to Ferret and Sparkle? And what Horim did to Daub and Sandalwood?"

"The women? You know all their names? And what became of them?" Toribor sounded genuinely surprised.

"Of course I do," Arlian said, startled. "Did you think I simply wanted an excuse? I loved them all. They deserved far better than they received. You and Nail and Kuruvan treated the ones you held no worse than any other slaves might be treated, but the others—do you know what Enziet did to Dove? Did you know he cut Madam Ril's throat in the street? She was a free woman!"

Arlian did not mention Sweet, whom Enziet had poisoned; that particular death was somehow not something to be shared.

"I knew," Toribor said.

For a moment the two stood silently, facing each other; then Toribor said, "You say you will swear not to kill me so long as the dragons live—do you *seriously* believe you can slay them?"

"Yes," Arlian said simply.

"I don't," Toribor said. "I believe you are an amazing man, Obsidian, but not *that* amazing. Killing a soft-skinned infant is not the same as slaying an armored sixty-foot adult."

"I know," Arlian said.

"I am not so foolish and selfish as to listen to Pulzera's nonsense—but I cannot believe yours, either. I find Pulzera's arguments much easier to believe, but I find yours far more appealing. If you really *could* slay the dragons . . ."

His voice trailed off; then, suddenly, he jammed his sword-breaker into its sheath.

"Very well, then," he said. "Our fight is ended until you tell me otherwise, but you'll forgive me if I decline to sheathe my other blade, or to turn my back on you until we are safely inside the walls."

Arlian bowed. "I'll have my steward retrieve my own blades, then."

"That would suit me."

Toribor stood where he was on the plaza and watched as Arlian retreated to his coach.

"Where did the archers go?" Arlian whispered to Black as he neared the vehicle.

"They received new orders a few moments ago, and withdrew," Black said. "Is there any point in asking what happened out there?"

"You couldn't hear?"

"Only when Belly shouted."

"I'll tell you later, then." He waved at Brook and Kitten, who were leaning out the coach windows. "When everyone can hear. For now, would you be so kind as to recover my sword and sword-breaker? Lord Toribor does not trust me with them just yet."

"I don't blame him," Black said. "I don't blame him at all." He strode forward to retrieve the blades.

Arlian turned as he stepped up into the coach's door, and saw that Toribor had finally sheathed his own sword and was walking away, toward the city's gate.

Toribor's final words nagged at Arlian. Toribor did not believe the dragons could be killed?

Toribor was far older than he, and probably had seen more of the dragons—Arlian had been trapped in a cellar during most of the attack on his village. If Toribor believed, even after hearing what had become of the dragons born of Enziet and Stiam, that an adult dragon could not be killed, then how could Arlian be sure he was wrong?

Did the rest of the Society also still believe any attempt to fight the dragons was futile, despite the obsidian blades? If so, no wonder they had taken Pulzera's words seriously.

Arlian looked thoughtfully out at the plaza.

The crowd that had watched the fight was dissipating, many of them clearly disappointed to see no deaths, no crippling injuries. As Arlian stood in the door of the coach, Lord Zaner pushed forward through the throng, clearly wishing to speak a few words with him.

Perhaps, Arlian thought, Lord Zaner could tell him something more of what had been said yesterday on the Street of the Black Spire.

Stammer had been moving hesitantly toward the coach as well, but when Zaner pushed past her she stopped, frowned, waved, and then turned toward the gate, leaving Arlian and his party to those more important than herself.

Politely, Arlian waited as Zaner approached. Several other spectators turned and fell silent, eagerly waiting to hear what one lord had to say to the other.

Zaner stepped up to stand a few feet from the coach and said, without preamble, "Lord Obsidian, I had not realized you were a coward, to fling down your sword when bested!"

That had not been what Arlian expected. He knew Zaner considered Toribor a friend, and had thought perhaps Zaner intended to thank Arlian for not fighting to the death. Apparently, Zaner did not see anything to be grateful for; presumably he was quite certain that it was Arlian's death, not Toribor's, that had been avoided here. All the same, his remark seemed unreasonable.

"You think it cowardice to stand unarmed before a foe?" Arlian asked mildly.

"You knew Belly would not kill you! Had I faced you out there, I wouldn't have killed you, but by the dead gods, I'd have at least slashed that pretty face of yours!"

Arlian dabbed at the blood running down his cheek from the cut above his eye and said calmly, "I will keep that in mind should we ever meet at swordspoint, my lord."

Black had come up behind Zaner as they spoke, and now he pushed past the dragonheart, interrupting Zaner as he was about to say more.

"Your pardon, my lord," he said, as he extended Arlian's sword, hilt-first. "You'll want to clean the blood off before you sheathe it," he said.

"Thank you," Arlian said, accepting the weapon. He was grateful for both the reminder and the interruption; the exchange with Lord Zaner did not seem to be going anywhere profitable. He pulled out a handkerchief and began ostentatiously wiping Toribor's blood from the steel.

Zaner looked from Arlian to Black and back, then snorted and turned away, to Arlian's relief.

A moment later the blades were clean and back in their scabbards, and Arlian was aboard the coach, the door closed and ready to go. Before he could give the command, though, he heard a woman's voice call, "Lord Arlian!" He turned and leaned out the window.

The plaza had been transformed from a cleared stone circle surrounded by an audience to its more usual existence as a thoroughfare and meeting place; the duel was definitely over, and its traces fading—at least, those traces outside the coach; Arlian's handkerchief was bloody, his shirt and scarf slashed and bloodied in several places, and the wounds on his arm, shoulder, forehead, and throat all stung.

Making her way through the milling crowd was Lady Rime, stumping along on her wooden leg, brandishing the bone she carried everywhere she went.

"Arlian!" she called again.

"My lady," he called back. "Would you care to join me? It's a long walk back to the Upper City."

"Of course I would," she said. "And you can tell me how it happens that you and Belly are both still alive."

Arlian opened the coach door and waited, and a moment later

he helped her up, into the coach and onto the seat, where she set-tled beside Brook, facing Arlian and Kitten. Black watched from the driver's seat, and when the door was closed again he shook the reins, setting the horses in motion.

Kitten was already dabbing at Arlian's wounds with her own delicate little handkerchief, cleaning away blood and fibers.

"Now," Rime said, "I seem to have missed the entire thing, so pray tell me, Ari, just what happened."

"Black wanted to hear, as well," Brook said, before Arlian could reply.

"Indeed he did," Arlian said, "and I'm sure that several others will want to know the details as soon as we're home, so he can hear it all then. For now, rather than keep Lady Rime in suspense, I will say that we fought, and Lord Toribor had the best of me at one point, having knocked the sword from my hand. He declined to slay me on the spot—I believe the parallel to our previous meeting in Cork Tree, when I left him wounded but alive, was responsible for this, as he did not care to be seen as less merciful than myself. Once I had recovered my sword he intended to continue to a fatal conclu-sion, but I thought better of it. Belly is a braver and more honorable man than I had believed him to be, and I therefore decided to aban-don my pursuit of his death; I flung aside my weapons, and offered him a choice between killing me, or ending our quarrel peacefully. I am pleased to say he chose the latter course."

"Lord Zaner called you a coward," Brook remarked. "I thought he meant to challenge you on the spot."

Arlian opened his mouth, then closed it again. He hesitated, then said, "You know, I believe he did."

He had honestly not considered that when speaking to Zaner; he had been tired and bloody and eager to sit down and rest, and had not considered the implications of allowing Zaner to insult him. Zaner had probably expected him to take umbrage, if not at the blunt accusation of cowardice then at the remark about slashing his face, so that the exchange of words would escalate into something irretrievable. He had not risen to the bait, and Black had interrupted before Zaner could try again.

Arlian had simply not thought about the significance of the exchange. He had unjustly been called a coward often enough in the mines of Deep Delving that although he knew it was considered a deadly insult among noblemen, the word carried no special sting for him; he had been a slave in the mines, not a lord, and a slave had no honor to defend from such accusations, so dire insults were often directed at him.

In his days in Manfort he had been called mad often enough that it had become merely tedious, but no one here had ever before called him a coward. After all, he had crossed the Dreaming Mountains to Arithei alone. He had dueled Lord Kuruvan and Lord Horim, called Iron, men older and more practiced than himself, and had killed them both. He had openly challenged the dreaded Lord Enziet, and had pursued him into the Desolation and fought him to the death. He had faced *dragons*. While his sanity might be called into question, his bravery had never been.

Until now.

Had Zaner truly thought him a coward, or had he merely intended to provoke him? Did Zaner want him dead? He knew Zaner didn't much like him, but he had thought that was due to the bad blood between himself and Toribor, which would hardly account for a challenge when he and Toribor had just made peace. He had never wronged Zaner; he had scarcely *met* the man . . .

"Zaner?" Rime asked. "I wonder, was that Hardior's doing?"

Now Arlian was not merely puzzled, but baffled. "Hardior?" he asked.

"Yes, Hardior," Rime said.

"He wasn't even here, so far as I could see," Arlian said. "No more than you were."

"And that was because we were both at the Citadel with the Duke, arguing our respective positions. I'm afraid that Lord Hardior may have a bone to pick with me." She tapped her legbone against the windowframe and smiled crookedly. "It's entirely possible I have displaced him, at least for the moment, in the Duke's favor."

"Indeed?" Arlian asked. "Might I ask how?"

"Because the Duke likes you, Arlian, or at least likes hearing about your adventures, and Lord Hardior wanted you killed."

27

The Duke's Favor

Arlian stroked his beard with his left hand and stared at Rime's unreadable face; Kitten held his right hand as she swabbed at the cuts on his wrist and forearm.

"Why would Lord Hardior want me dead?" he asked.

"I don't know for certain, but I would suppose it is because he understands that if you live, one way or another you'll almost certainly destroy the Dragon Society."

Kitten looked up, startled, and exchanged a glance with Brook. Arlian eyed Rime thoughtfully.

"You phrase that in a way that implies you believe it, too," Arlian said.

"Oh, of course I do," Rime said. "You may say you have not yet decided, but I think I know what your decision must be, given your rightful hatred of dragons, and that in the end you intend to systematically murder us all. Even if you don't, you've certainly divided the Society against itself in a way I find it hard to believe can be mended."

"Have I? I had hoped to rally the Society to action, not divide it."

"Arlian, you've pitted hatred of the dragons against the desire to live. Pulzera is not the only one to choose life—but not all of us can stomach her answer. The Society is split."

"You seem surprisingly untroubled by this," Arlian remarked.

"There are two reasons for this," Rime said. "The first is that I believe the damage has been done, and the rift cannot be mended, regardless of whether you live or die; given that, I'd prefer to have you alive."

The coach jerked suddenly as a wheel bumped over an obstruction, and Arlian grabbed at the windowframe. "Thank you," he said. "And the second?"

"I think you're right to destroy us," Rime replied. "I think we deserve it. We can hardly complain that our deaths would be untimely; I have lived more than four hundred years, five times what any ordinary woman could expect, and at least half the Society is senior to me. If our deaths are necessary to eliminate the threat of the dragons, then let us die. Wither believed that, and acted upon it. I am not so noble as he, and have no intention of taking my own life, but I have another five centuries or so in which to change my mind. If you cut my throat one day, I'll try not to resist."

Arlian stared at her, then smiled crookedly.

"And here I had decided that I could not in good conscience murder the entire Society," Arlian said. "When I threw down my weapons it was no stratagem to prolong my own life; I genuinely no longer wanted to kill Toribor. And if I cannot bring myself to kill him, how could I slay you, or the others?"

"I had wondered why you did that," she said. "Have you, then, chosen to side with the dragons, after all? Has Pulzera won you over?"

"*No!*" Arlian was genuinely shocked at the suggestion. "The dragons must be destroyed—but killing the people who unwillingly bear their young is unjust. There must be another alternative—keeping a careful watch and killing each new dragon as it's born, perhaps."

"Ah," Rime said. "And who would undertake this task? It will be a thousand years before the last dragonheart—you, that is—will die, and even that assumes the dragons do not contrive to create more. How can you hope to arrange this watch over such a span of time?"

"As the youngest of the dragonhearts, I would say the onus falls upon me."

"So you would devote the rest of your life to this?"

"There are only thirty-eight of us, my lady. Spread that over a thousand years, and it's no great hardship."

"If you have no opposition, perhaps."

Before Arlian could reply he noticed Kitten's expression; she was staring at him with her eyes wide and her mouth hanging open, her ministrations to his wounds forgotten. Brook had managed to keep her face under better control, but she, too, was staring, clearly astonished by what she heard.

"I see that neither of us is much concerned with secrecy," he said. "It would seem we've just revealed things to these two that they had not known."

"Indeed," Rime said, glancing at the astonished women. "I had assumed that you had told your entire household all about the situation, and nothing remained to conceal; it would seem I misjudged."

"I have not been profligate in such matters," Arlian said.

"You'll live a *thousand years*?" Kitten asked.

"More or less, if I am not killed," Arlian said.

"And you're four hundred years old?" Brook asked Rime.

"Four hundred and some, yes. I no longer recall the exact number." She met Brook's gaze evenly.

Brook shifted away from Rime on the seat.

"And that brings us back to your meeting with the Duke," Arlian said. "I'm sure that you and Hardior were not as open with His Grace as we have been here."

"Indeed we were not."

"And just what *did* you tell him? How did Hardior argue for my death, and you for my life?"

"Oh, that was simple," Rime said. "Hardior argued that you had murdered Drisheen and Enziet, that you intended to kill Belly by fair means or foul, and that you had threatened him, Hardior, as well. He accused you of conspiring to remove all the Duke's advisers, and other powerful figures that threatened unspecified plans you had made. This was all nonsense, of course, as I'm sure Hardior knew as well as we do, but he made it quite convincing—Hardior can be persuasive when he chooses. He told the Duke that he had taken the liberty of placing archers on the city wall, and at a signal he would have them remove you, once and for all, and end the threat to the peace and welfare of Manfort."

"Ah," Arlian said. "That explains the archers."

"The Duke hesitated," Rime said. "In fact, I received the distinct impression that he was relieved to have Enziet and Drisheen gone, though of course he would never admit it. I spoke on your behalf, explaining that you were a headstrong young man with a personal grudge against six lords, of whom Toribor was the last survivor, and that you had no mysterious scheme to disrupt the city. The only threat you posed to Hardior, I said, was that he feared you might prove more popular than himself—which was a lie, of course."

"Of course," Arlian agreed.

"I also mentioned what a great benefit you had provided by bringing your Aritheian magicians and all their spells to Manfort. I said that if you died, they would almost certainly return to their distant homeland. I carefully did *not* say what they might do to Manfort before their departure, but I made sure His Grace considered the possibilities."

Arlian had not himself considered those possibilities; now he stroked his beard again as he did. Shibiel, Isein, and Qulu had no magic left to them—but he was unsure what Thirif or Hlur might yet be capable of, and of course the entire Aritheian House of Deri had professed to be in his debt. The magicians might have no magic available in Manfort, but they could always bring more.

"And of course, I pointed out that intervening in an affair of honor was hardly going to help the Duke's own reputation," Rime added.

"But why couldn't the Duke just kill Arlian after the duel?" Brook asked.

"He could," Rime said, "but Lord Hardior could not propose

it—that would violate the Society's oath, to arrange the killing of a fellow member that might take place inside the city's walls. And Hardior could not insist that it happen outside the city without telling His Grace things that he did not care to reveal."

"The Duke could still . . ." Brook began.

"The Duke doesn't *want* to," Rime interrupted. "He likes Lord Obsidian. He thinks Obsidian is a dashing young rogue who makes Manfort more interesting by his presence. I could argue for sparing Arlian's life, and Lord Hardior, bound by his oath, could *not* argue for killing him other than during the duel. Quite aside from anything else, that made the Duke's decision easy; with no one arguing otherwise he could do what he wanted, and spare Obsidian's life."

"He didn't seem very impressed with me when we first met," Arlian remarked.

"That was before you fought two spectacular duels and went roaming across the countryside in pursuit of your foes, before there were rumors about strange stone weapons and sorcerous images of dragons. You're much more interesting now."

"And besides, there really are the magicians to think about," Kitten said, releasing Arlian's arm. "We really *don't* know what they would do if Triv were killed."

"I should give them instructions," Arlian said. "I hadn't thought about it." He flexed the fingers of his right hand, winced at the resulting pain, then told Kitten, "Thank you."

He was not entirely sure what instructions he should give the Aritheians, though, nor whether they would obey him. He had no hold on them; they had come to Manfort with him freely, for their own benefit. If they once returned home, they might not want to risk coming north again.

And what did he *want* to happen after his death? He could ask Thirif and the others to avenge him, and one way or another they would probably do as he asked, killing those responsible—but what good would it do? He would be dead. Did he want to leave a legacy of vengeance, or of mercy?

He wouldn't be around to see it in any case, so he was not at all sure he cared. He preferred to live, rather than leave a legacy—at least, until he had accomplished everything he wanted to accomplish.

And at this point, that meant the destruction of the dragons. He had had enough of revenge against humans, and had rescued everyone he had wanted to rescue.

But the dragons still lived, and therefore he wanted to live, too. He might take risks, such as defying the man who held a blade at his throat, but he did not *want* to die—he simply didn't fear it.

"So you convinced the Duke to spare me," he said. "Thank you, my lady."

"You're quite welcome, my lord," Rime replied. "Like the Duke, I find the world more interesting with you still in it. It's a more violent and less predictable place, but there's a certain promise to it. I think it far more likely that we will see the dragons exterminated if you survive."

"You flatter me."

"I speak the truth, no more than that. And to speak further, my lord, I would remind you that while I may have won today's debate with Lord Hardior, my opponent has not given up. He wants you dead, or at least gone. If he can't convince the Duke to eliminate you, he'll probably look for other means—which is why I wonder whether he was behind Zaner's accusation of cowardice."

"Would he have had time to devise that?"

Rime shrugged. "As to that, I can't say. It may be that Lord Zaner acted on his own."

"He really thought Triv was scared of Lord Belly?" Kitten asked. "But that's silly."

No one had a useful response to that, and the conversation died. A few minutes later they arrived at the gates of the Old Palace; Rime had declined Arlian's offer to deliver her to her own doorstep.

To Arlian's surprise, most of the household was waiting for them—Venlin, several of the cooks and maids and footmen, even Ferrezin and one or two others in Enziet's livery who appeared to have just arrived. Hasty and Lily and Musk and Cricket had been carried out, and now sat on the benches in the forecourt; Vanniari was asleep in Hasty's arms. The Aritheian magicians in his employ, Shibiel and Qulu and Isein, were clustered to one side, watching solemnly; Thirif, who was technically Arlian's guest rather than an employee, was close by the gate.

Stammer and Wolt were not yet back, and a few other faces were missing, but clearly word had run ahead of the coach.

"I see everyone else—where's Hlur?" Rime asked sardonically, as she stepped to the door of the coach. Black had leapt from the driver's seat and was reaching for the latch.

"Presumably still at the Citadel, where she belongs," Arlian retorted from behind her. Hlur was the Aritheian ambassador to Manfort, and although she and her husband, Kthelik, had originally been brought to the city by Arlian they had long since taken up residence in the Duke's establishment, as befitted Hlur's station.

Arlian waited until Rime, with a little assistance from Black, had climbed down and gotten herself steady on the ground, and then he scooped up Kitten and handed her to Black.

Black promptly passed her along to a waiting footman, and turned back for Brook.

When all three women were out of the coach Arlian was finally able to disembark himself and demand, "What are all of you doing out here?"

Thirif cleared his throat, but before he could speak Hasty called, "It was my idea, Triv! We wanted to let you know that we're all on your side."

Arlian stared at her for a second, then turned to Thirif.

"My apologies, my lord," Thirif said, "but she has the gist of it. We felt a show of . . . community? No, solidarity. We felt a show of solidarity was in order."

Arlian was impressed that Thirif had found the right word in a language other than his own. He stared at the Aritheian for a moment, idly stroking his left hand over the wounds on his right arm as he did, then asked, "And *why* is this display in order? Simply because I've survived my duel?"

"No. Because the Duke's guards tried to force their way into the Old Palace, and we drove them away."

"They came to the Grey House, as well," Ferrezin said. "We turned them away, and then came here to report."

"The Duke's guards?" Arlian was still trying to absorb this.

"You're hurt!" Hasty called, seeing the blood on Arlian's sleeve and scarf. Arlian held up a hand to silence her.

"The Duke's guards came here? What did they want?"

"The glass weapons," Thirif said.

Arlian turned to Rime, who shrugged.

"I have no idea what this is about," she said. "This must have happened after I left."

"Tell me what happened," Arlian said to Thirif.

Thirif nodded, and began. "Chiril was at the gate," he explained, gesturing at one of the footmen, "waiting for news of the duel. He saw the guards coming and ran to tell others. I was nearby and heard, and I came out to see."

"The Duke's guards?" Arlian asked. "You're certain?" Chiril was one of his more reliable footmen, but not the brightest of them.

"Yes, the Duke's guards," Thirif said, visibly annoyed at the interruption. "An officer spoke to us and said that they had come to take the obsidian weapons. He told Chiril and Venlin to bring the weapons, and Venlin said he could not do that without his lord's permission."

Venlin pointedly did not meet Arlian's glance at him. This was Thirif's story.

"The officer said that the Duke had ordered it, and that if we did not give him the weapons he would come in and take them. I said he would not. Then he and his men tried to force their way in, and I used a spell I had saved for an emergency and drove them away."

"It was a big fiery monster, Triv!" Hasty called.

"An illusion," Thirif said with a shrug. "My last."

"We had no magicians at the Grey House," Ferrezin said. "We told the officer we could not admit him without your consent, and barred the door."

Arlian nodded; he could see how that would be sufficient. The Grey House was built like a fortress, with massive stone walls and heavy bars and shutters on the few ground-floor windows.

"I left by the postern and came to fetch you, my lord," Ferrezin continued. "The Duke's men may well still be there."

"This is bizarre," Arlian said. "Why would he try to confiscate those weapons? And why would he do it when he *knew* I wasn't home?"

"I suspect Hardior's hand in this," Rime said. "Perhaps he doubled back after we left the Citadel."

"It seems to me that the Duke might have intended this as a precaution," Black said. "Suppose you had lost your duel, and died— who would then own those weapons, which are rumored to be magical?"

"*You* would," Arlian said.

"Does His Grace know that?"

"No." Arlian frowned. "I think it's time I spoke to His Grace myself. And a word with Lord Hardior, as well, might not be amiss."

28

Secrets Revealed Anew

Speaking with His Grace the Duke of Manfort was not simply a matter of walking up to the Citadel and sending in a message, Arlian knew; he had to petition for an audience. Accordingly, he composed an appropriate note and sent a messenger to deliver it. He did that immediately, while still wearing the slashed, sweaty, and bloody blouse he had fought in; only when the messenger, one of the two men who had accompanied Ferrezin from the Grey House, was on the way did he allow himself to relax and tend to his own needs.

It was plain that Ferrezin wanted instructions, that Black wanted to know what he and Toribor had said to one another, that several people wanted detailed descriptions of the duel, but Arlian did not feel himself ready to deal with any of that. He retired to his chamber, pleading the need to get out of the clothes he had fought in.

When he had removed his ruined clothing and donned a robe he closed the door of his chamber and lay down for a rest, intending merely to close his eyes for a moment before speaking further with his staff and guests.

He was awakened by Venlin's announcement that dinner would be served shortly.

Embarrassed, he dressed, and came downstairs to find that Stammer and the others had returned, and the household had regained the appearance of normality. The servants were bustling about, preparing for the coming meal; Rime was in the small salon, chatting with Kitten, Brook, and Cricket. Ferrezin and the others in Enziet's livery were nowhere to be seen.

No more soldiers had appeared at the gate, but somehow, Arlian doubted that this appearance of normalcy was reliable. The afternoon's events surely could not be dismissed as easily as that.

He greeted Rime and the others, and took Rime into dinner on his arm. As they ate he described the duel in some detail, repeating as much of his conversations with Toribor as he could remember; several of the servants stood close by, much more closely than usual, and Arlian was careful to speak loudly enough that they, as well as all his guests, could hear him.

When the meal was over, and most of the questions answered, Arlian sat back in his chair, a glass of sherry in his hand, and listened to the women arguing about Toribor's motives in not killing him. He had drunk only half the wine when Venlin bent down and whispered, "Your messenger has returned from the Citadel." Arlian looked up, then set his glass aside and rose.

The messenger was waiting in the servants' corridor. He bowed as Arlian approached.

"You delivered my note?" Arlian asked.

"Yes, my lord."

"Who did you give it to?"

"To His Grace's chamberlain," the messenger said.

"Is there a reply? Did he say anything?"

"He asked who it was from, my lord, and when I told him he said, 'Oh, the Duke will want to see *this* one!' I asked whether there would be a response, and he said to wait, so I waited, but then he came back and told me to go, that the Duke would not read it tonight."

That was reasonably promising, at any rate. "Fine," Arlian said. "Have you had anything to eat?"

"No, my lord."

Arlian turned. "Venlin, see that he's well fed before you send him home, would you?" Then he turned back to the messenger. "If there's any trouble at the Grey House, come and tell me at once, and thank you." He clapped the man on the back, then watched as he marched down the corridor to the kitchens.

Venlin hesitated for a moment, then hurried after the messenger. He seemed uncomfortable with the messenger's presence, and Arlian realized that he probably wasn't sure how to treat the man. After all, the messenger worked for the same master, but was not part of the same household, and Venlin was unsure of their relative status. For a man like Venlin that was awkward.

This business of maintaining two households and two separate staffs was absurd, Arlian told himself—especially if he might need to defend them against the Duke's guards. One would have to go.

And after today's events he knew which he intended to keep. The Grey House was the smaller, the more practical, the more defensible—and that was why he intended to sell it. He had no desire to barricade himself into a fortress, to shut out the outside world; if he were to live in the Grey House it would be all too easy to cut himself off from humanity as Enziet had.

Furthermore, Sweet and Dove were buried in the garden here at the Old Palace. The Grey House had no gardens at all; instead there was the room on the top floor where Dove had been murdered and Sweet held prisoner. Arlian did not care to live in the same building as that ill-omened room.

Arlian stepped back through the door into the dining hall and signaled to Black.

"When you have a moment, could you have a few words with Coin? I think it's time we sold Enziet's house. Also, I'll want all the furnishings—the books, trunks, all of it—transferred here, at least initially. There should be room in the north wing. I'll want to keep Ferrezin on; we'll determine his exact position later."

Black did not reply at first, but simply stared at Arlian.

Arlian stared back, then realized the situation.

Black wanted an explanation, not just orders. He was no born servant, like Venlin, but his own man, who stayed in Arlian's employ because he had taken a fancy to Arlian, not because he had ever aspired to be the steward of a great house.

And for months, Arlian had told Black far too little of what was going on. It was time to end that.

"Ah," Arlian said. "The Duke's chamberlain accepted my message, but His Grace was not disposed to read it as yet. Seeing the messenger in Enziet's livery was what reminded me about the house."

Black nodded. "I was beginning to think that keeping secrets had become a habit."

Arlian smiled crookedly. "I believe it has," he said. "I depend on you to help me break it. If you think I'm concealing something you deserve to know, please do speak up—I don't want to keep secrets from you any longer, Black. I've had enough of secrets. It's time to let them all out."

Black smiled in return. "In that case, I think you should expect a late night tonight—there are several questions I intend to ask."

"As you please—but do send word to Coin first, and to Ferrezin."

Black bowed mockingly.

Arlian returned to his guests, and made polite conversation for another hour or so before seeing Rime to the door and calling the coach for her. Hasty had already gone to put Vanniari to bed, with Wolt carrying Hasty and Stammer carrying the baby, but the other women continued to talk.

Arlian did not join them; when Rime had departed he turned to find Black waiting for him. The two men retired to Arlian's study, where Arlian finally told Black, in detail, what had happened to Enziet beneath the Desolation; what had happened when Arlian washed his hands after Nail's death; what had been said at the hearing in the hall of the Dragon Society.

Black took it all in, then asked, "What happens now?"

"I don't know," Arlian said. "I don't know what the dragons are planning, or what the Dragon Society is planning. I don't know what *anyone* is planning, not even myself! I don't know whether the dragons will attack this summer, or cower in their caverns. All I know is that sooner or later, the dragons and I will meet—and when we do, I want to be ready."

"So you want those spears."

"Yes."

"Why do you think the Duke tried to take them—so he would have them, or so you or your heir would not?"

"I don't know. That's the major reason I want to speak to him."

Black nodded. "Ari," he asked, "how big is a dragon? A full-grown one, I mean, not like the one we killed in Nail's bedchamber."

"Big," Arlian said. "I couldn't say for certain. I haven't seen one since I was a boy of eleven, and the circumstances at the time did not allow for a very accurate estimate."

"Fifty feet from snout to tail-tip, perhaps?"

"More," Arlian replied. "A dragon's face filled almost the entire pantry door, top to bottom and side to side, and their proportions are roughly those of a winged serpent."

"And to kill one, you need to drive an obsidian blade into its heart."

"Yes."

For a moment both men were silent, but then Black asked the question both of them knew he would ask.

"Ari, your best spears are perhaps eight feet long. If you stood at a dragon's flank and drove one that full eight feet into the beast's flesh, would it *reach* the creature's heart? And how do you ever expect to get close enough to do anything of the sort?"

"I think it would reach, from the right angle," Arlian said slowly. "Dragons are very long, but slender."

"And how would you get close enough?"

"I don't know," Arlian admitted.

"And you don't even know whether obsidian *can* kill an adult. Belly didn't think so."

"The dragon that spoke to me seemed to think it could."

"Did it *say* so?"

"Would it matter if it did? We can't believe anything the dragons tell us."

"And how many dragons still survive?"

"I don't know. I can't really even guess."

Black said nothing, just looked at him, and Arlian continued, "Although it may well be overtaken by events, my original plan was to creep up on the dragons in their caves and plunge the spears into them while they slept."

"Drive a spear *several feet* into a monster while it sleeps? While its companions are in the same chamber?"

"There will undoubtedly be difficulties," Arlian said.

Black stared silently at him for a moment. Arlian let out a sigh. "Yes, I'm probably mad," he said. "It may well be impossible."

"It would seem to require rather more than human abilities, yes," Black said dryly.

Arlian blinked.

"Yes, it would, wouldn't it?" he said. He had somehow managed to not think very much about this until now, much as he had not thought about how he would defeat Toribor before the duel. While he still thought it might be possible to kill sleeping dragons, it now seemed obvious that getting at a dragon while it was awake *would* take more than human abilities—and he no longer thought it very likely that he could catch the dragons asleep.

Fortunately, more-than-human abilities were available. "I suppose it would take magic," he said.

Black's eyes narrowed.

"Is there magic that could help?"

"I don't know," Arlian admitted. "But I think that it's past time that Isein and the others made a buying trip to Arithei. I put it off because I had thought it might be better to cross the Desolation in cooler weather, but I think now that no more time should be wasted." He frowned. "Tell Isein to start planning what she will need for the journey."

29

Lord Hardior's Logic

Arlian awoke the next day to news that His Grace the Duke of Manfort would expect him at the Citadel the following day, at two hours past noon.

"I didn't expect it so soon!" he told Black at breakfast. "I had heard that it could take a fortnight to see the Duke."

"It would seem Lady Rime was right," Black said. "His Grace *does* like you."

"Or he wants to confront me directly and demand I turn over the obsidian," Arlian said.

"Also a possibility," Black admitted. "Will Lord Hardior be present at your audience?"

"I don't know," Arlian said. He grew thoughtful. "I think I had best pay a call on Lord Hardior *today*, before I see the Duke, so that I know where I stand."

"I think it wise, if it can be arranged," Black agreed.

"I'll arrange it," Arlian said. He beckoned to Wolt, who was standing nearby, and told him, "Fetch me pen and ink—I have a letter to write. And when it's ready, you will deliver it forthwith to Lord Hardior's estate, where you will see it delivered either into Hardior's own hand or, if he is not there, his steward's. If neither is there, you will wait, and make yourself obnoxious about it."

"My lord?" Wolt was plainly startled by this last directive.

"I don't want them to be able to ignore you. Don't let yourself be pushed into a corner and forgotten."

"Yes, my lord." Wolt bowed, then turned and left to fetch writing supplies.

A moment later Arlian began composing his note. He kept it short:

"Inasmuch as I have recently been taken to task for keeping secrets, I think it urgent that we discuss certain matters before I speak to His Grace the Duke tomorrow. I would not care to inconvenience you by remaining silent when I should not, nor by revealing matters you would prefer to keep private. I will be delighted to wait upon you at your earliest convenience."

He signed it "Obsidian," then folded and sealed it, and handed it to Wolt.

"Off with you," he said. Wolt bowed, and turned to go.

"And hurry!" Arlian called after him. Wolt hastened his footsteps, though he did not actually run. Arlian watched him go, then sighed and headed for his regular morning visit to Hasty and Vanniari.

Hasty was as cheerful as ever, and Vanniari growing at a healthy pace—she focused on Arlian's face when he bent over her, and when she did she stopped waving her hands about and stared at him in wonder and awe. Of course, she stared at *any* human face with that same fascination.

Arlian spoke gently to her, and allowed her to grab an extended finger. He listened to Hasty chatter about the baby, and about how foolish Arlian had been to fight a duel with Lord Belly, and how brave it had been to throw down his sword, and how she didn't believe those people who said Arlian had begged for his life.

Arlian glanced at Hasty. "Who said that?" he asked, genuinely curious.

"Oh, you know, people who don't know any better. I heard Stammer and Cricket talking about it. *They* don't believe it, of course, any more than I do."

"Of course." Arlian shook his head, amazed. Beg for his life? Why would he do that?

He had left Hasty and her daughter and was striding along the east gallery on his way to speak to Isein when Wolt came running up to him.

"My lord!" he called, out of breath.

Arlian turned. "Sir," he said. "You delivered my note?"

"He's here!" Wolt gasped.

"Your pardon, Wolt . . ."

"Lord Hardior is here, my lord, in the Old Palace," Wolt said. "He insisted on coming back with me. He's waiting for you in the foyer."

"Indeed!" Arlian had not expected quite so prompt a response to his threats. "Take him to the small salon, and I will be there presently."

Wolt bowed, and hurried away.

Arlian watched him go, considering whether there was anything that he should do before meeting Lord Hardior. Nothing came to mind; accordingly, he was already standing in the salon when Wolt showed Hardior in a moment later.

"My lord," Arlian said, holding out a hand. "Welcome to my home, and my thanks for so prompt and unexpected a response to my missive!"

Hardior ignored the outstretched hand. "Unexpected, Obsidian? I doubt that."

"Unexpected in truth, my lord—while I expected you to agree to a meeting, I had thought it would be I who was the guest, and you the host, and that we would meet later in the day."

"I don't have time for that," Hardior said. He glanced at Wolt. "Might we speak privately?"

"Of course," Arlian said. He gestured to the footman, who quickly left the room, closing the door securely behind him.

"Might I offer you a seat, my lord?" Arlian asked, gesturing at the silk couches.

"I think not," Hardior snapped. "You have an audience with the Duke?"

"Tomorrow afternoon, my lord."

"And just what do you intend to tell him? Are you planning to babble all your supposed secrets?"

Arlian frowned. "My lord, I think your manner is inappropriate. I asked to meet you so that we might avoid any unnecessary conflicts."

"I suppose you mean to make sure that I won't again try to arrange your assassination."

Arlian closed his eyes and let his breath out slowly, then opened them again before speaking.

"Lord Hardior, I am far more interested in learning *why* you sought my death than in preventing a recurrence. I know I am safe from you as long as I remain within Manfort's walls, so my safety is not a significant concern—but I had thought we were on the same side, and the archers on the ramparts were disturbing. What is it I have done that prompted you to place them there, and to petition the Duke for permission to have me slain?"

Hardior stared at him for a moment, then said, "I had forgotten—you truly are mad. I had thought it would be plain to you."

"It is not."

"You threaten to bring the dragons down on us all."

Arlian blinked. "Threaten? My lord, the mere fact that you know this means that in all probability I have *already* brought the dragons down upon us, and they wait only for the weather's cooperation before striking. I hardly see what my death will accomplish *now*."

"It may not be too late to stave them off, Obsidian—but not if you continue to live, to threaten them, to goad them to action with your profligate revelations of their nature, and your distribution of obsidian weapons, and your plans to slaughter their young. I know you better than to think you will abandon your mad schemes of vengeance while you still draw breath—and therefore, I hoped to stop that breath."

Arlian gazed at him in silence for a moment, then said, "I am honestly disappointed, my lord. I had hoped for better from you."

"Better? I am attempting to shield all the Lands of Man from the consequences of your folly—what else would you have of me?"

"My lord Hardior, you told me not so very long ago that if I could slay a dragon, or better yet, exterminate their entire race, then I would be a great hero. You saw me slay the dragon that rose from Lord Stiam's heart, yet now you seem determined to reward that heroism with death, rather than aiding me in achieving the second, greater goal."

"You slew a newborn thing that was no more a true dragon than a newborn babe is a man. Yes, you killed it, and yes, it would have become a dragon, but you cannot kill a *dragon*, any more than a babe in arms can kill a trained warrior."

"You seem very certain of that."

"I *am* certain of that! I have *seen* the dragons, Obsidian—I have *fought* the dragons. I was not a boy hiding in a cellar when they destroyed my hometown; I was a grown man, and I saw my sword shatter on a dragon's scales." He drew a shuddering breath, and said, "We thought they were gone, you know—they had not been seen in fifty years, not since my grandfather's day, when the wars mysteriously ended, when the dragons withdrew to their caves. We didn't realize they still lived. And then one day when the skies were hot and dark we saw them coming.

"We had heard the old stories about how warriors defied the dragons on the ramparts of Manfort, and how our weapons would be useless, but the dragons had *gone*, hadn't they? We thought they must be old and weak, that the weapons had hurt them and they had merely concealed their injuries. So we did not run and hide; instead we gathered, swords in our hands, to face them.

"At the last minute I was sent to chase a few children who had disobeyed their parents and come to watch the battle to what we thought was safety. I had done that, sent them into the guildhall, and had turned to rejoin the others, when the dragons arrived.

"That was how I survived. I saw what they did, saw it all—saw them spit flaming venom at the gathered warriors, then systematically tear apart each and every building and butcher the women and children hiding within. I heard the screams . . ."

He shuddered. Arlian said nothing for a moment; then Hardior continued.

"There were four. When the biggest one came to the guildhall I ran at it with my sword, screaming with rage, trying to drive it away. It did not bother to kill me, or even knock me aside—it simply *ignored* me as it ripped away the roof. I was hit by falling stones and burning thatch, my head was cut and my face covered in blood, but the dragon itself never deigned to touch me as I hacked at it.

"My sword broke, and I picked up stones and flung them, and it looked at me, and a dribble of venom from its jaw struck the stone in my hand and burned my fingers. I dropped the stone and put my fingers in my mouth—which is why I am here today, instead of six hundred years dead.

"And then it turned away again, and set about burning out the interior of the guildhall, making certain it killed each of the children I had sent there, but it did not trouble itself any further with *me*.

"And now you say you can kill these monsters with your magic glass spears?" Hardior snorted. "I say you are a madman. They can't be killed."

"So you propose to appease them, instead? To serve as a mere incubator? To become one of their servants?"

"I intend to communicate with them, if I can. Blood and water in a bowl is simple enough; *you* spoke to one, and you're no sorcerer. We will offer them peace—if they continue as they have, then the Society will keep silent about their young. After all, as Pulzera said, they want us to live—and we want to live."

"Pulzera," Arlian said. "You are siding with Pulzera?"

"Because she is *right*, my lord," Hardior said. "I did not like it at first, either—I remember the screams of my brothers, and those children in the guildhall. I remember the utter disdain on that dragon's face, and the savage cruelty they displayed. I hate the dragons as much as you, my lord—but I know better than to think we can defeat them. If there is war, there will be many, many more screaming children, slaughtered by the great beasts; if we bargain with them . . ."

"Then there will be fewer at any one time," Arlian said, "but the dragons will survive forever, preying on our people. If we fight them, and kill them, yes, many will die, but in the end we will win, we will destroy them."

"We will not!" Hardior shouted. "You can't kill them! No one has ever killed a grown dragon, in all the thousands of years that men and dragons have existed."

"No one else ever thought to use obsidian!" Arlian shouted back. "Lord Enziet spent six hundred years studying the dragons and sorcery in order to learn what could harm them, and he *succeeded*! You have seen me kill a dragon—how can you deny it?"

"I saw you kill an animated cloud of blood," Hardior said. "Not a dragon! An ordinary sword could probably have done as well as your silly stone knives."

"No, I tried that," Arlian said. "In the cave beneath the Desolation, where Enziet died. My sword could not cut that newborn dragon any more than you could cut the one you fought. When I ran my blade down its throat, it simply bit it off."

Hardior stared at him.

"You lie," he said at last.

"I do not," Arlian said.

"So obsidian can cut where steel cannot—still, do you think you could *kill* a grown dragon?"

"Yes!"

"I do not," Hardior said, "and I believe that your schemes are going to enrage them all and bring them down upon us. Further, you have said that you considered killing all the dragonhearts in Manfort—should I trust you? You showed what your vows are worth when you threw down your sword fighting Belly—so much for your oath to kill him or die trying! Should I put any more faith in your vows to the Society? You are a madman, and a danger to us all, and I had hoped the Duke would have you killed. He did not, and I cannot try again while you remain in Manfort, but by the dead gods, Obsidian, I will do what I can to keep you from antagonizing the dragons and endangering this city."

"So they are already your masters, even while they lurk in their caverns," Arlian said in disgust. "You will not help me in my campaign to destroy them?"

"*Help* you? I will do my best to *stop* you!"

"Then I think we have no more to say to one another, my lord." Arlian gestured toward the door.

"Oh, no," Hardior said. "You brought me here to discuss what you will tell the Duke tomorrow, and we will discuss that before I depart."

"Will we? You have just reminded me that you are sworn not to harm me, so why should I not tell His Grace whatever I please, regardless of your wishes?"

"Two reasons, my lord. First, I doubt you intend to spend your entire life inside the ramparts of Manfort, and while I may not have your obsessive concern with revenge, I can hold a grudge as long as may be necessary. Second, I am not sworn to leave the Duke himself unharmed. The old warlords' blood of Roioch's line has grown very thin in these modern generations, my lord, and it would be little loss to the Lands of Man if the present line died out completely. His Grace has no heir; were he to die there would be an end to the Dukes of Manfort, and a new system of governance would arise—a council of lords, perhaps, as some towns have. And can you doubt who would control such a council? I do not kill the Duke because I prefer not to deal with the consequences, and because I like the old fool—but if I am confronted with the possibility of even *worse* consequences if I let him live, if he falls under your sway, listens to your tales about weapons that can kill dragons . . ."

He did not bother to complete the threat.

"Then you would have me keep silent on the manner of draconic reproduction, and on the uses of obsidian," Arlian said.

"Of course. I suppose you will have to discuss your silly spears with him, but I trust you will be discreet as to their actual purpose."

"I will not promise that, my lord."

Hardior sighed. "Obsidian, I probably won't be there tomorrow, but do not think that means I won't know what you say. I have eyes and ears in the Citadel besides my own, and there are sorcerous methods for hearing what is said elsewhere. I cannot prevent you from saying what you will—but I will know what you have said, and I will respond accordingly. Do not sign the Duke's death warrant with careless words—nor your own!"

Arlian stared at him for a moment, then said, "I thank you for your advice, Lord Hardior, and I think we have now said all that we need say."

"Indeed, I think we now have," Hardior said. He turned.

Arlian was scarcely in time to open the door for him.

30

An Audience with the Duke of Manfort

On the morrow, after the midday meal, Arlian dressed in his best clothes and allowed Cricket and Lily to comb and trim his hair. He donned his best white silk shirt and a black linen coat, with a red silk scarf to add a touch of color—and hide the cut Toribor had made on his throat. The slash on his forehead was not so readily concealed, and remained visible.

When his preparations were complete he made his way up to the Citadel. He did not bother with the coach, but walked the one-mile distance and arrived perhaps a quarter-hour before the appointed time.

He used this extra time to look over those portions of the Citadel open to the public. Unlike most visitors, though, he looked not so much at the paintings, tapestries, gardens, and statuary, but at the defenses—after all, the original Citadel had once lived up to its name.

That time was long past. The moat had been mostly filled in, becoming a garden and a series of ornamental fishponds. The battlements had been widened into verandahs and terraces. Openings clearly originally intended for dumping large objects or hot liquids on unwelcome visitors now had glass-paned doors in them and opened on ornate balconies.

And that was the outer defenses. The inner structure had never been defensible at all.

The original Citadel had been built well after the end of the war against the dragons, during an unsettled period, and had been designed to fend off rioters and rebellious lords, not dragons. When peace came the Citadel had been abandoned in favor of the Old Palace—then simply the Ducal Palace—but after a century or two the present Duke's grandfather had decided the palace was too much trouble to maintain and had had the ruins of the inner Citadel torn down and a new palace built on the site. The old walls, outerworks, and tunnels provided plenty of space for the bureaucracy necessary to run Manfort, and if that stone-walled space was less pleasant than the plaster and gilt rooms in the Old Palace, that bothered the Dukes not at all.

The new palace, the inner Citadel, was the Duke's home, and it was as luxurious as anyone could ask.

Arlian could not help thinking, though, that if the dragons ever did return the Citadel would be about the most unsafe place in the city. Most of Manfort was built of gray stone, unbroken by trees or gardens; every street and alley was paved. That was so the dragons would have little to burn; flaming venom would simply run harmlessly off the stone.

Of course, draconic talons could break stone if necessary, but at least the solid walls and pavements would slow them down.

The one part of the city that was *not* built of stone was the Upper City, where several great lords had, over the centuries, built themselves mansions and palaces, complete with broad windows, spacious gardens, and wooden structures as well as stone. For at least five hundred years now no one had thought the dragons would ever return to Manfort, and the architecture reflected that.

And as long as Enziet had lived, the dragons would indeed not return—but Enziet was dead, and Arlian estimated that a dragon could reduce most of the Citadel to burning ruins in a matter of minutes.

Of course, his own home in the Old Palace was no better. The

Grey House would be safe—but Arlian still intended to sell it. If the dragons came he did not want to cower behind stone walls, but to face them openly.

He was standing on a path in what had once been the moat, watching butterflies dance above the flowers, when a footman came hurrying up.

"Lord Obsidian?" he asked.

Arlian turned. "Yes?"

"His Grace will see you now. If you would follow me?"

Arlian followed.

He discovered, however, that "now" actually meant after roughly a quarter hour of sitting in an antechamber staring at a painting of the present Duke's grandmother when she was a young woman. Arlian could not decide whether she had been the most vapid-looking woman he had ever seen, or the artist had simply been exceptionally unflattering.

At last, though, he was shown into the Duke's audience chamber, where His Grace sat upon a great red cushion beneath a silken canopy. Arlian went down on one knee, as Black had instructed him, ignoring the half-dozen courtiers and guards standing to either side.

He had seen some of the courtiers before, at the auction of Drisheen's estate; he was pleased to see that none of those present were dragonhearts.

At least one was probably a spy for Lord Hardior, though.

"Lord Obsidian," the Duke said, smiling. "A pleasure to see you again!" The smile appeared genuine.

"The pleasure and honor is all mine, Your Grace," Arlian replied, rising.

"I understand you wanted to see me," the Duke said, still smiling.

"Yes, Your Grace," Arlian said. "I wanted to ask you why your guards attempted to enter my estate the other day. If there's something I have that you need, surely I can find it for you more easily than your soldiers."

"Ah, that!" The smile dimmed somewhat. "Your people must

have told you what I'd sent my men for—to fetch out those sorcerous weapons of yours."

Arlian feigned puzzlement. "So they said, Your Grace, but I *have* no sorcerous weapons."

"Oh, come now! You don't claim you haven't been making strange weapons, do you?"

The appearance of sudden understanding transformed Arlian's features. "I have been making *obsidian* weapons, Your Grace," he said. "An affectation to accompany my name." He had devised this lie the night before, but he had not decided until this very moment whether he would use it. Now, looking at the Duke, he believed that Lord Hardior would live up to his threats, and he did not see any reason to condemn this harmless old fool to death.

"I assure you," he concluded, "there is nothing sorcerous about them."

"Indeed? I am told one of these spears dispelled a sorcerous illusion when poor Lord Stiam died of a curse someone had put upon him."

Arlian waved the idea away. "Any spear would have done as well against the sorcery there. I brought obsidian merely because I had them on hand."

"That was not the impression Lord Hardior received."

"Oh, now, Your Grace, please don't hold me responsible for Lord Hardior's errors and misinterpretations! I have enough trouble coping with my own."

The Duke chuckled. "Of course," he said.

For a moment the two men simply looked at one another; then Arlian cleared his throat and said, "Your Grace has not told me why the order to confiscate my weapons was given."

"Oh, well, it was just a precaution," the Duke said, waving a hand dismissively. "When I heard that you had challenged Lord Belly, I was uncertain as to just what you might be planning. The possibility that you might die, and the weapons fall into the wrong hands, had to be considered; likewise the possibility that you had gone mad. Lord

Hardior *assured* me that the spears were sorcerous. I am no sorcerer myself, and it seemed wise to take *precautions*, as I said."

"And were the archers on the wall another precaution?"

The Duke's smile vanished completely.

"You saw them."

"Yes, Your Grace."

"That was Hardior's doing. I ordered them removed. I do not use assassins. I think Lord Enziet did, on my behalf or my father's, but I never liked the idea. If I want you removed, my lord, I will have you arrested and properly tried, not shot from ambush."

"I am reassured, Your Grace," Arlian said, trying not to sound sarcastic.

"I'm sure you are," the Duke said. He studied Arlian seriously for a moment, then said, "You're a strange man, Obsidian."

"I do not mean to be," Arlian replied, honestly.

"Yet you are. I don't understand you, and that means I need to be careful. Lord Hardior says you're dangerous, and he may well be right."

Arlian could think of no safe response to this.

"You've killed several of my lords," the Duke continued. "The gossip would have it that you were pursuing some personal vengeance, but all the same, you've cut an impressive swath through Manfort. The Aritheian ambassador, and Lord Enziet, and Lord Drisheen . . ."

Arlian opened his mouth to protest, but remembered at the last instant that one did not interrupt the Duke of Manfort.

". . . Lord Iron and Lord Kuruvan, Lord Stiam, Lord Wither . . ."

The strain of not responding was plainly visible on his face, but Arlian kept his tongue still.

". . . and then it appeared you meant to kill Lord Belly, as well. When you had disposed of Enziet I had thought you were finished, but then there were three more, and Hardior said he did not think you would ever stop killing. I can't have *that*—I need to know that my advisers will live long enough to advise me!"

"Your Grace, I did not kill all those people!" Arlian said, when the Duke finally paused. "I did not kill Stiam or Wither or Enziet, nor the Aritheian ambassador."

"Then do they still live?"

"Ah . . . no. I don't know what became of the ambassador; that was an internal matter among the Aritheians and I thought it best not to ask. Lord Stiam died of a fever, and both Wither and Enziet took their own lives."

"*Enziet* a suicide? I did not know Lord Wither well enough to say whether he might consider such an act, but *Enziet*?"

"We fought, and his sword broke, Your Grace; he stabbed himself in the heart rather than yield to me."

The Duke's expression made it plain he still didn't believe Arlian's account.

"Your Grace, I admit to killing Lord Drisheen; why then would I deny killing Enziet, had I done so?"

"I have already said I do not understand you, Obsidian." He waved the matter aside. "In any case, you certainly *attempted* to kill him, yes?"

"Yes," Arlian admitted.

"Then the details don't matter. You're responsible for the deaths of half a dozen lords, not to mention at least two of my guards and, rumor would have it, a shopkeeper or two."

"That was Enziet!"

"The details, *as I said*, do not matter," the Duke said angrily. "Whatever the exact circumstances, you have killed several men in my service. You have let it be known that you had personal reasons for each killing—but all the same, the result has been to remove several of my supporters. Furthermore, sorcerous or not, you've been making weapons—and by all accounts not just a handful for the guards at your gate, but enough to equip a small army. And what is there in Manfort to turn an army against, my lord? What else, but myself?"

Arlian's mouth opened, then closed again.

"This is what Hardior suggested to me, at any rate, and he advised me to remove you once and for all. Lady Rime argued for your life, and I agreed, because I had no proof that you meant me any harm—but still, why did you need all those spears? So I sent my men to retrieve them until we could discuss the matter—and *your* men refused them, going so far as to use *magic* against them!"

"They acted without orders, Your Grace," Arlian said.

Of course, if he had suspected the occasion might arise, he would have ordered them to do exactly what they had, in fact, done.

"I thought that might be the case," the Duke said, sitting back. "And you spared Belly's life, even letting him think he had beaten you, so that suggested you were perhaps not the bloodthirsty lunatic Hardior believed you to be. In fact, it suggested you haven't the *courage* to plot against me!"

Arlian blinked at that—had Zaner spoken to the Duke, perhaps?

Before he could say anything, the Duke continued. "I decided to think matters over before pursuing the matter of the spears further—and then you requested this audience, and here we are, able to discuss it like the men of good sense we are."

"I assure you, Your Grace, the notion that those spears might be turned against your guards had never even occurred to me," Arlian said, deciding to ignore the implication of cowardice. "I have no designs on you or Manfort at all."

The Duke nodded. "Then what *did* you want so many spears for?"

For once, Arlian's knack for quick lies failed him, and the idea of speaking the truth, and risking Hardior's retaliation, did not appeal to him. Telling the Duke of Manfort that those weapons were intended to fight dragons did not seem like a good idea at all. He stood awkwardly silent for a moment, then said, "I wanted to have enough for my entire staff."

"Why?"

"I . . . I don't know; just a whim."

The Duke's expression was plain; he thought Arlian a liar, a madman, or both.

Before he could speak, though, inspiration struck, and Arlian said, "Your Grace, I confess, it was more than a whim. I do have a use for those weapons, but it's a trade secret. Must I reveal it?"

That clearly intrigued the Duke. "I'm afraid you must," he said.

Arlian sighed theatrically. "Of course you know, Your Grace, that my fortune is built upon trading in Aritheian magic. Have you ever wondered what I trade to the Aritheians for their magic?"

"Weapons?" The Duke was obviously delighted by his own perspicacity in producing this answer.

Arlian nodded. "I give them the weapons they need to defend themselves against the wild magic in those unholy lands beyond the border."

"And you've been preparing your trading stock? Is *that* what these spears are for?"

"Exactly. Your Grace is very quick."

"I see! And you've kept this secret so that no one else could share in your profits."

"Exactly," Arlian repeated.

The Duke considered this for a moment, staring at Arlian. Then he said, "You know, there are other rumors about you, besides Hardior's theory that you meant to take the city from me by force or sorcery."

"Oh?"

"It's rumored that you used sorcery to kill Stiam, and then destroyed the sorcerous aftereffects to remove any evidence that another sorcerer could use against you."

"Your Grace, I had no part in causing Lord Stiam's death. I swear it by the dead gods."

"And it's said that Lord Wither caught you somehow, and you slew him to cover your tracks, and bribed his clerk and his servants to lie, and say he killed himself."

"Your Grace, Lord Wither believed that he had contracted the same ailment that killed Lord Stiam, and he chose to die quickly rather than suffer as Stiam had."

The Duke leaned forward now and spoke quietly, apparently not wishing his courtiers to hear. "Some people claim that you and

Lord Enziet knew how to make an elixir of immortality, and fought over who would control it—that that was the root of your conflict."

That one caught Arlian off-guard, and he hesitated.

"We all knew that Enziet had some sort of elixir," the Duke added. "After all, he advised my father and grandfather, and looked no older when I last saw him than he did when I was a child. He claimed the formula was lost, though, no matter what threats were made, or what payment offered."

"I cannot say anything about that," Arlian said. "I know of no elixir of immortality."

That was the truth. After all, dragon venom did not provide immortality, but only a millennium of incubation for a new dragon.

"That's unfortunate. I would pay almost any price for such a thing."

"I cannot help you, Your Grace." He suppressed a shudder at the idea of this fool of a Duke living and reigning for a thousand years, becoming ever more draconic—not to mention the question of the succession when he did eventually die, since as a dragonheart he would be sterile.

The Duke sat back again and said, "I see. Ah, well. And you swear that you planned no treason, and did not intend to use those stone-tipped weapons against me?"

"I swear it, Your Grace, by all the gods, alive or dead."

"Nonetheless, I think it might be best if you were to remove them from the city."

That startled him. "Your Grace?"

"I want those obsidian weapons removed from Manfort. You say they are not sorcerous, and that you did not intend to turn them against me, but nonetheless, my lord, they do cause *rumors*. I do not insist they be destroyed, but I will be happier when they are no longer within the walls."

Reluctantly, Arlian decided he had no choice in this. The Duke had plainly made up his mind.

Arlian had put off any travel, in case the dragons came sweeping down upon Manfort, but there were matters to attend to in Deep Delving, and magic to be brought from Arithei, and really, what could he hope to do if the dragons *did* come, if he had no aid from either the Dragon Society or the Duke? It was time to go.

Taking the weapons on his postponed journey would be an inconvenience, since they would take up space in the wagons, and it would mean that there would be no weapons ready should the dragons attack Manfort—but then, why would they attack, if Arlian was not in the city? *He* was the one who had revealed their secrets and otherwise angered them.

And the Duke appeared quite determined in his desire to have the weapons removed. Arlian bowed. "As you wish, Your Grace. I had been planning a trip to the south, to trade; I will take the obsidian weapons with me."

Of course, this expedition would also give Hardior a chance to kill him once he was outside the city—but that did not trouble him. He was fairly sure he could handle an assassin or two, and if Hardior sent a larger force against him word would get back to the Duke, which would probably not have pleasant consequences.

"I do not require that *you* leave the city, my lord," the Duke said, startled. "Only that you remove the weapons."

"Of course, Your Grace—but in fact, I do have business to attend to outside Manfort, and this will permit me to make absolutely certain that the weapons are not stolen or mishandled."

"I see. And you know, I think you are wise in this," the Duke said. "Your presence has unsettled Manfort, and I think the city needs a rest. For that matter, *I* need a rest. Very good, then. I would suggest you depart as soon as possible."

Arlian said again, "As you wish, Your Grace."

It began to appear as if the Duke had said all he intended to say, but Arlian was not content to stop here; before the Duke could conclude the audience, Arlian quickly said, "Your Grace, if I might ask a question?"

"Yes?"

"Your Grace, let us suppose that I discovered a means of killing dragons. The Aritheians have much astonishing magic, and I think there may be such a possibility."

"I thought dragons couldn't be killed," the Duke said, cocking his head to the side.

"So it has long been believed," Arlian said. "But you know I am Lord Enziet's heir, and Enziet had spent much time and effort studying dragons, in hopes of finding a way to kill them. I believe he might have been on the right path."

"That would be *wonderful*, of course—but do you really think such a thing exists?"

"I do, Your Grace."

"Ah, you fascinate me. Do tell me more!"

"Alas, I cannot—I am bound not to. You understand that magic has certain peculiar properties. I am taking a very considerable risk even mentioning it."

"Then why do you bring it up at all?" The Duke was visibly annoyed.

"To ask, Your Grace, whether your aid might be forthcoming in attempts to use Enziet's knowledge."

The Duke frowned.

"It might be," he said. "But I think that I would first need *proof* that dragons can indeed be killed."

Arlian blinked. "Forgive me, Your Grace, but what would constitute such proof?"

"A dead dragon, of course. You show me that your magic can kill a dragon, and by the dead gods and the spirits of my ancestors, Obsidian, I promise you you shall have all the assistance you need in killing more."

"But . . . Your Grace, what if I need your help to kill even one?"

"Then I am afraid that you are on your own, my lord. I am not going to help you stir up those monsters unless I am *certain* of success. You know, they destroyed a village just ten or twelve years ago, burnt it all to the ground . . ." He paused, and blinked stupidly. "In fact, I believe the village was called Obsidian. How curious!"

"Very curious, my lord. As it happens, I own that village, and it is because of that attack that I had thought to seek a way to kill dragons."

"Oh, really? How very interesting! You are very fortunate, my lord, that you were not in the village at the time!"

"Very fortunate, Your Grace," Arlian said dryly.

"At any rate, my lord, I would not have you provoke the dragons into burning any *other* villages. Show me that you can kill them, and you can have whatever you need—but until then, I will not help. Now, I am tired—you go off to Arithei, or wherever you're going, and let me rest."

Then he signaled that the audience was at an end, and Arlian was escorted from the room.

Consequences

31

Discussions Before Departure

It took several days to prepare Lord Obsidian's caravan for departure. Arlian realized that this gave Lord Hardior, and anyone else who thought the world might be improved by Arlian's death, plenty of time to hire assassins, but he saw no alternative. This was not a simple pursuit, but a full-fledged trading mission to Arithei.

During those days Arlian, with Black's extensive aid, gathered eight wagons and hired appropriate personnel, including twenty guards. No ordinary caravan that size would have hired so many guards, since they would eat into the profits to a level a serious trader would never allow, but Arlian wanted to be absolutely sure that the bandits on the southern slopes of the Desolation would not bother his friends and employees.

And besides, ordinary caravans did not cross the magic-haunted, monster-infested Dreaming Mountains.

Arlian had not decided yet whether *he* would be crossing the mountains. The caravan would initially be bound not for Arithei, but for Deep Delving, to collect silver and amethysts, and Arlian thought he might well turn back to Manfort there, and let the Aritheians and the rest of the caravan proceed on their own. It would depend on what the exact situation was at Deep Delving, and what news he heard along the way. He thought that such an absence would be sufficient to give the Duke the rest he wanted—especially since Arlian had no plans to stir up further trouble upon his return.

He had had quite enough trouble, in fact. It seemed as if everything he had done lately had made matters worse—now not only Toribor, but Pulzera, Hardior, and perhaps others in the Dragon Society were his foes. The Duke had spared his life, but then sent him into exile, at least briefly.

And nobody wanted to help him fight the dragons. If and when they did come, Manfort would be defenseless, and he himself, while properly armed, would be almost alone.

It seemed to him that the best thing he could do would be to stay out of the way, prepare himself for the worst, and see what happened. Taking this trip to Deep Delving was as good a way to do that as any—but going all the way to Arithei would probably leave Manfort undefended for too long.

He would be back, if he thought he could return without creating any more difficulties for himself, and when he returned he intended to focus entirely on the practicalities of dragon-slaying, not on antagonizing anyone further.

Disposing of anything that might complicate his life and distract him from the tasks he faced seemed advisable; accordingly, when not directly involved with preparing the caravan, he spoke with the broker known as Coin, who had sold him the Old Palace. Coin had agreed to sell the Grey House, and had begun to advertise it, but there were no immediate takers.

"We've had several properties come on the market of late," Coin said slyly, when Arlian stopped in to discuss the matter. "Lord Drisheen's estate, and Lord Horim's, and Lord Stiam's."

"I see," Arlian said. "Well, do your best."

He set Ferrezin to overseeing the transfer of the contents of the Grey House to the Old Palace, while he and Black concentrated on the caravan.

These preparations for departure occupied most of his time, but Arlian did hear some of the news and gossip that was making the rounds of Manfort. While all the servants picked up the occasional tidbit of information and shared it with the guests, Arlian discovered, when talking to Cricket and Hasty one morning, that Stammer had an extensive network of informants. She had developed this from her old contacts among the city's poor and displaced, as well as the servants on other estates, largely to please Cricket and Lily, who were eager to keep up with the goings-on elsewhere.

Hasty, both Cricket and Hasty herself told him, was too busy with her baby to worry about what anyone was doing elsewhere.

That afternoon Arlian found Stammer in the kitchen, and called her aside.

"I understand you keep up with the news of the city," he said.

She stared at him in terror. "I . . . I . . ."

Arlian held up a reassuring hand. "Calm down, please, my dear! This is not an accusation. I don't own you, and you're free to do as you please when your work is done. I'm pleased to know you take an interest in the world; my guests find it most generous of you to share with them, since they cannot go out and about freely themselves."

Stammer curtsied awkwardly in response, unable to speak. She had not been given her name lightly.

"It's come to my attention that there are rumors about me abroad in Manfort, and I wondered whether you had heard any of them."

"My lord, I . . . I . . . don't know . . ." She seemed to stick at that point, unable to continue.

"Would it be easier to write them down, perhaps?" Arlian suggested.

Stammer shook her head violently, and it occurred to Arlian that she might be illiterate. His mother and grandfather had taught him to read and write when he was a child, but Stammer might not have been so fortunate.

"I would be glad to hear anything that's being said," Arlian said, "no matter how dreadful. I assure you, no harm will come to you if you speak freely."

"I . . . I cannot, my lord." She looked down at her hands, her fingers rubbing at the front of her apron.

Arlian was curious about what rumors might be circulating, but it was not an urgent matter. "Very well, then," he said. "If you change your mind, let me know."

He dismissed her with a wave, and watched as she hurried back to the table where she had been kneading dough for tomorrow's bread. She returned to her work, but glanced up nervously every so often, seeing he was still there but not meeting his eyes. At last Arlian took pity on her, and left.

That evening he was alone in his study, going over the costs of assembling his caravan, when someone knocked timidly on the door.

"Come in," he called.

The door opened and Stammer stepped in. She closed the door behind her, took a deep breath, and then said, "They say you're a madman, my lord, that you meant to slaughter all who would oppose you and then overthrow the Duke himself, but that when Toribor challenged you to prevent you from taking over all the Lands of Man you lost your nerve, and when he offered you a last chance you flung down your weapons and abandoned your schemes, at least for now, and now you're said to be hiding here in the palace, and when word got out that you were preparing to travel everyone said you were fleeing in disgrace, that you spoke to the Duke and were so frightened by him that you're leaving the city forever. It's all over the streets, my lord, and when I tell any-one it's not true they don't believe me, they think you've put a spell on me or seduced me or tricked me somehow, but it's *not* true, is it?"

Arlian stared at her for a moment, absorbing what she had just said, then said calmly, "It's not true. None of it."

She gasped, hands clutched over her heart, then said, "I knew it."

"What else?" Arlian asked.

"Wha . . . what . . ."

She had clearly reached the end of her prepared speech.

"Are there any other rumors abroad in the city?" he asked.

She nodded, gulped, composed herself for a moment, then said, "They say you poisoned Lord Stiam or put him under a curse you learned from Lord Drisheen before you killed him, or from the books in Lord Enziet's house, and you went to his deathbed to make sure it worked, and the sorcery went wrong and became visible and you had to dispel it to hide the evidence of your crime, and Lord Wither found some trace you had missed and told you so at the funeral, so you went to his house and stabbed him to death and bribed his servants and his clerk to say he had died by his own hand, but after all, it was your black stone knife that killed him, and . . . and . . . and . . ." She took another deep, gasping breath, blinking helplessly at him.

The long, fast sentences were obviously a way to avoid stammering, so Arlian did not suggest she slow down and speak clearly, or ask her to untangle the pronouns; instead he said, "Take your time."

She stared silently at him.

"Do you know who's been spreading these tales?" he asked.

That drew a burst of stammered names Arlian didn't recognize—Thumb and Trot and Korri and Werrin and several she couldn't get out clearly. Attempts at explaining who they were quickly became hopelessly garbled, but Arlian thought he puzzled out part of it.

"They work for Lady Pulzera?" he asked. "Or Lady Opal?"

"And . . . and . . . and . . ." She swallowed hard, and said, "Har . . . Hardior. And Zaner. Or T . . . Ticker."

All of them.

For a moment Arlian considered canceling his expedition to stay and refute these calumnies, but he quickly discarded the idea. His denials would mean nothing, and he needed to attend to matters in Deep Delving so he could send his Aritheian employees for more magic—in particular, magic that might be useful against dragons.

And what harm could such rumors do him? All would blow over soon enough.

"Thank you," he said. Stammer curtsied, and hesitated.

"You may go now," Arlian said, "or stay, if you've more to tell me. And feel free to come to me as you have tonight should you learn or remember anything else you think might interest me."

Stammer said, "Thank you, my lord," then snatched open the door and vanished.

Arlian stared after her, thinking.

The rumors were harmless in themselves, but he wondered whether a conspiracy might be forming in opposition to him. Opal hated him for refusing to bring her dragon venom, and could be expected to speak ill of him; Pulzera had chosen to side with the dragons Arlian had sworn to destroy, so her enmity was also unsurprising. Hardior thought that if Arlian were gone, the dragons would leave Manfort alone. Arlian had thought he and Hardior were natural allies, but it had become very plain that Hardior did not agree.

As for Zaner and Ticker, their motives were less clear, but Arlian supposed they were in agreement with either Pulzera or Hardior.

And one name was, he realized, conspicuous by its absence; Stammer had not mentioned Toribor's household as a source of rumors. Had this been an oversight? Or did her web of informants perhaps not extend into that particular domicile?

Arlian frowned, and stepped out into the corridor. He spotted a footman, and beckoned to him; the youth trotted quickly over to his master.

"Send word to Lady Rime that I wish to speak to her at her earliest convenience," he said. "I would be glad to wait upon her at her home, or to have her as my guest, whichever would please her more."

The footman bowed. "Yes, my lord," he said. He hesitated for an instant, then turned and hurried away. Arlian watched him go, and frowned.

Rime was the only living member of the Dragon Society he trusted—and *that* was a sorry commentary on his situation.

It was hardly a surprise, though. He had come to Manfort seeking revenge, not companionship, and had not gone out of his way to make the acquaintance of his fellow dragonhearts—and that was quite aside from having killed some of them, and planning to kill the rest.

He could have gone to the Society's hall and talked to whoever he found there, but somehow he suspected that would produce anger and evasion, rather than honesty—and really, he supposed he could not blame anyone for such hostility when he had openly admitted that he had considered slaughtering the lot of them.

But he did not want to kill them *now*.

Rime did not seem troubled by his murderous intent, in any case, and perhaps she would be able to shed some light on what was happening among the members of the Dragon Society.

32

Lady Rime's Report

The following morning Rime arrived in time to share Arlian's midday meal, hobbling on her wooden leg, her legbone clutched tight in her right hand.

At table they discussed Arlian's upcoming journey, and Arlian made it plain that Rime was welcome to accompany him, if she chose, as she had in his pursuit of Enziet.

"No, thank you," she said. "Last time you were pursuing business that directly concerned us all." She glanced at the servants, and did not specify which "us" she referred to, but Arlian understood her to mean the Dragon Society. "This time you are traveling on your own business, and matters of considerable interest are being discussed here in Manfort."

"True enough," Arlian said. "And these matters you mention are of some interest to me, as well. I would be glad to hear you speak of them."

"Perhaps later," Rime replied, with another glance at the footmen bringing in platters of meat.

Arlian nodded.

After they had eaten, Rime, Arlian, and Black retired to the study, where Rime settled quickly into a chair and Black leaned against a wall. Arlian sent the servants away and closed the doors securely.

"Now," he said, turning to face his guest, "tell me, if you would, what is happening among the dragonhearts."

Rime glanced at Black, who stared back impassively.

"I have promised Black I would keep no more secrets from him," Arlian said, crossing to his desk.

"I see," Rime said, tapping her bone against the palm of her left hand. "*I* have made no such promise."

"Indeed you have not—but anything you might tell me I would share with Black in any case, so I have chosen to eliminate a step in the process. If there is anything you cannot bear revealing to him, then do not tell it to me, now or ever." He pulled out his own chair and sat down. "But surely there must be *something* you can tell us."

"Fair enough. Arlian, you have thrown the Society into chaos such as I have never seen before."

"I had that impression," Arlian said.

"They argue constantly. In the past I could walk into the hall at almost any time and find it quiet, no matter what might be happening in the world outside; now the city is calm, but I cannot set foot through the door there without hearing voices raised in anger. When you first came to us I found your presence a break in the tedium; with your open avowal of vengeance against five of us, I thought you'd brought a little life to a virtual tomb. Your honesty was refreshing. You stirred up Belly and Nail, and I thought it was all quite amusing—to see Belly stamping about angrily, or others recoiling in horror from your intentions toward Enziet." She sighed. "I'm afraid the novelty has worn off. Now I'm weary of anger and horror and constant bickering."

"I'm sorry," Arlian said.

She waggled her bone at him. "Don't be. They dragged the truth out of you by calling that hearing."

"I am not claiming responsibility for the dispute, my lady, merely expressing regret that it troubles you."

She shrugged. "I can handle trouble."

"I'm sure you can," Arlian said. "As can I—but it is always easier if I know what trouble to expect. I have heard some of the rumors circulating in the city, blaming me for every dragonheart's death for the past two years and accusing me of plotting treason against the Duke, but I have not heard the nature of the arguments within the Society, nor who is on which side."

"There are certainly plenty of sides to choose from," Rime said. Arlian waited for her to continue, but she merely tapped her bone against her palm.

"I take it Pulzera still thinks we should pledge ourselves to serve the dragons, and side with them in the event of renewed war?" he asked at last.

"Oh, yes," Rime said. "And at least a dozen others agree with her. Alas, they would appear to be the largest single faction, and Shatter, the eldest, is one of them, and has therefore become their leader."

Arlian grimaced. "Shatter? He *fought* the dragons and their servants, centuries ago, didn't he?"

"Indeed. But he is hardly the first person to ever reconsider his previous actions, Arlian."

"I see. And the others?"

"Hardior has taken a 'wait-and-see' attitude toward the dragons, or at least so he claims, but he has come out strongly in favor of removing you from the city," Rime continued. "He seems to feel you are too unpredictable and uncontrollable; your refusal to finish the duel convinced him that you cannot be trusted at all. He also points out that any grudge the dragons may hold would be against *you*, rather than the Society as a whole, and that therefore you are a threat—if the dragons do come to Manfort, it will be to kill *you*, but the rest of us may well suffer as a result. He and Lady Pulzera are substantially in agreement on that."

"So I suspected," Arlian said.

Rime nodded. "He further argues that we need to settle our differences and act as a unified group if we are to maintain our position of power in the Lands of Man, and that that will never be possible while you live. I have the impression that he doesn't really believe the dragons will ever threaten Manfort, and expects the whole affair to blow over once you are eliminated."

"I'm disappointed," Arlian said. "I had hoped for better from him."

"He and Pulzera disagree on some things—Pulzera and Shatter and their party believe that you have indeed ended the peace, and we should resign ourselves to serving the dragons, which makes you, personally, largely irrelevant. Hardior, on the other hand, believes that if you are removed, then the dragons will have no cause to attack us, and will be content to return to the behavior they have displayed these past several centuries. Ticker and Zaner both support Hardior in this—but I don't think anyone else does."

Arlian nodded. That was not particularly surprising, really.

"Perhaps seven or eight people, led by Lord Voriam, think we should name you master of the Dragon Society and do whatever you say," Rime said. "They maintain that as Enziet's heir and the only one of us to communicate directly with the dragons, you are clearly the chosen of Fate. They argue about what happened when you and Belly fought, whether you decided to spare Belly's life, or that your own could not be thrown away so lightly before your great task is complete. They have spoken of sending you an emissary, but when last I listened they had not yet agreed on how best to approach you, or whether they should wait until they have won over more of the membership."

"That's . . . um."

Arlian had started to say the idea of naming him master was ridiculous, but in fact it would certainly simplify matters in many ways. Instead he asked, "What about Toribor? I suppose he's sided with Hardior?"

"Belly? No. His faction, like Shatter's, maintains that you are simply irrelevant, now that your secrets are known. However, they maintain that Shatter and Pulzera are traitors, and that we should be preparing to fight the dragons by whatever means come to hand.

He has spoken of buying obsidian weapons from you, or making his own, and of seeking out the caverns where the dragons sleep—but as yet he has not acted. I think he can't quite bring himself to speak to you."

"Oh," Arlian said.

"He's been speaking to the Duke, though," Rime continued. "I believe he's trying to convince His Grace to restore the city's fortifications to their proper condition and prepare for war with the dragons. Really, Arlian, it's quite amazing—for centuries Belly took no interest in politics, but now he's spending every moment he can at the Citadel." She smiled crookedly. "I don't know what will happen if the dragons don't come. I suppose that would discredit Belly, and make a prophet of Hardior."

"Is Belly trying to displace Hardior at the Duke's ear, then?"

"Not replace, but supplement," Rime said. "Belly takes no interest in anything *but* defense against the dragons, and that's a subject Hardior avoids."

"Does he?" Arlian asked, startled.

"Oh, yes. As I said, Hardior doesn't seem to believe the dragons will ever come, and he does not care to choose sides between dragon and human—he doesn't think he'll ever need to make a firm decision, and he knows that if he does he will estrange himself from half the Society. You and Pulzera have split it down the middle, Ari—I don't think the rift will ever heal."

For a moment Rime and Arlian gazed silently at one another; then Arlian said, "Well, one way or another, the Dragon Society must be destroyed eventually, if we are to avoid inflicting dozens of eager young dragons upon the world. Splitting it now may be a start."

"Oh, absolutely. It's a cancer at the heart of the Lands of Man, and it's past time it was cut out. We have been manipulating humanity for centuries, and look at the world we've built—a world of cruelty and slavery, where women like your guests, like my Rose, are treated as playthings or less, to be discarded at a whim. We live in a city of hard stone, as hard as our poisoned hearts."

Black shifted uneasily. He cleared his throat. Rime looked at him inquiringly.

"Your Rose?" Black asked.

"My several-times-great granddaughter," Rime explained. "She was one of the women in the House of the Six Lords. Lord Enziet had killed most of her family and enslaved her, and eventually had her murdered because sixteen was not evenly divisible by six."

Black stared at her for a moment, then said, "Oh."

"I explained this to Arlian in the wagon, on the way to Cork Tree," Rime said. "You were driving; I had thought you would have overheard."

"My attention was elsewhere," Black replied.

"And you never asked Enziet for her life?" Arlian asked, although he already knew the answer. "Or made any attempt to help her, or punish Enziet?"

"No," Rime said.

Arlian exchanged a glance with Black, then said, "So you feel that the Dragon Society deserves to die."

"Yes, I do," Rime said.

"And if I were to ask you and Lord Voriam and his faction to turn on the others and kill them all, would you?"

Rime smiled coldly at him.

"No," she said, "I wouldn't—but I think some of Voriam's friends would, and I would watch the slaughter without making any move to stop you. I would lift my own chin to the knife when the time came for you to slit my throat, but I cannot bring myself to wield the blade."

Arlian looked at her, this woman who had lived many times her apparent age, her grey streaked hair pulled back tightly, exposing every line of her weathered face. Her dark, unwavering eyes returned his gaze.

The bone in her hand tapped idly on one arm of her chair. Half of one of her legs was missing, severed just below the knee in a long-ago mishap—and that bone was her own shinbone. Although she had told him the story of how she lost her leg, and how she came to have the bone, he had never asked her why she had held on to it all these years, why she carried it with her everywhere she went.

She had kept track of her surviving family for several generations after the encounter with a dragon that had transformed her from an ordinary woman to what she was now, but had never told them who she was, that she still lived.

Holding on to things she knew she should discard was simply part of what she was, he decided—and her life was no different to her than the bone or her granddaughters, something she had no need of any longer, but could not let go.

Those members of the Society who agreed with him would be the easiest to kill. Those who opposed him would fight fiercely for their lives, he was certain—as Toribor had.

But Toribor did, in fact, agree with him in intending to fight the dragons, unlike Pulzera and Shatter . . .

It was all too confusing.

"I think perhaps it's time for some fresh air," he said. "Shall we take a walk in the garden?" He rose, and held out a hand to help Rime from her chair.

33

On the Road to Deep Delving

At last, eleven days after his audience with the Duke, Arlian led his caravan southward, bound for Deep Delving. Only after he had collected silver and amethysts and dealt with the miners there would the caravan continue onward, across the Desolation and the Borderlands into the magical realms of the south.

The wagons left the suburbs of Manfort without incident, rolling between lush fields just starting to fade from green to yellow as the crops ripened. If Lord Hardior had hired any assassins, they had not shown themselves.

Arlian had refused to take the traditional caravan master's position at the rear; instead he had put the Aritheian magicians there, while he and Black took the lead. He wanted to look at the open road and the countryside, not the dusty back of the wagon ahead.

Arlian had hired a man called Quickhand, whom he had traveled with before, as his chief guard; Black, who had earned his keep commanding caravan guards for years, was instead assistant master and driver of the lead wagon, so that he and Arlian sat side by side at the head of the caravan, Black holding the reins and Arlian simply watching their surroundings.

The obsidian weapons, all of them, were in the two wagons at the front of the procession, which left little room for anything else.

Arlian glanced back over his shoulder as the wagon rattled along the road, hoping that the brittle edges wouldn't be too badly chipped by the bumps.

Black noticed his gaze, and said, "You aren't really sending those to Arithei, are you?"

"No," Arlian said.

"You'll need to keep them hidden when we return, then. That would seem to complicate their distribution and use."

"We'll keep them hidden until they're needed," Arlian agreed. "If and when the dragons come, we'll distribute them then."

"And what about your fellow dragonhearts? When do you intend to murder them?"

Arlian looked at Black, startled.

In fact, he had just been thinking about that, trying to determine what the best thing to do would be. None of them had chosen to gestate dragons, after all, and killing them would not be just.

Allowing new dragons to be born would be unwise, though.

He had thought that he would let each dragonheart live out his thousand years, and would then dispose of each new dragon as it was born, but if the Dragon Society was broken and its members scattered, tracking them all down when the times came could be difficult. It might be better to kill them all before they could disperse. . . .

But it would still not be just.

"I don't know," he said. "I'm not sure I intend to murder them at all."

"That would disappoint Lady Rime, if you did not."

"I'm sure she'll bear up under such a disappointment."

"The two of you seemed quite determined to see the Dragon Society destroyed the other day."

"Well, we don't want them to hatch into dragons," Arlian said uneasily.

"It seemed more than that for Lady Rime," Black said. "She called the Society 'a cancer at the heart of the Lands of Man.'"

"She exaggerates."

"Rather, she understates," Black said. "Ari, the Dragon Society isn't a cancer—it's the heart itself. Have you ever thought about just what the Society controls?"

Arlian looked at Black, clearly puzzled. "Well, the Duke's advisers are mostly dragonhearts . . ." he said uncertainly.

"Besides that," Black said. "Haven't you ever looked at who the other lords are? You haven't told me all their names, but I can guess. You did mention Lord Voriam, who owns most of the lands and mills from Norva to Kariathi, and there's Lord Zaner, who owns half the trading vessels and warehouses in Lorigol. Lady Flute operates the pumps and aqueducts that supply Manfort's water, and owns most of Clearpool. Lady Rime herself owns salt mines, tanneries, and dye works. You started out dealing in magic, which is not of any great importance, but have you ever considered that list of holdings you inherited from Enziet? As your steward I went over it with Ferrezin. You control perhaps two-thirds of the tin mines in the western mountains and thousands of acres of barley to the north, and your employees in Westguard coin the silver the Duke uses to pay his troops, to name just a few of the largest holdings."

"Hmm," Arlian said. He had not thought about any of this, and did not see yet what Black was getting at. "But even if we do own all you say, what of it? We don't personally grow those crops or mine those metals; if we die, the businesses will go on."

"Will they? Most of you have no heirs, as I understand it—do you want the Duke to inherit it all? Imagine that man as not merely the hereditary lord of Manfort, but the master of most of the enterprises in the Lands of Man. Or what if, without killing anyone, you divide the Society so that its members will no longer deal with one another? What if Lord Zaner will no longer carry your tin and barley on his ships? What if the Duke's men no longer trust the silver you send? Or perhaps worst of all, what if the dragons *do* come, and you fight them? Manfort could be destroyed, and even you must agree that would cut the heart out of the Lands of Man."

"That's why the dragons must die," Arlian said. "So that they can't destroy what men have built."

"So you're willing to risk destroying everything we have to protect what our descendants might build."

"Yes, I am," Arlian said.

"And what gives you the right to decide this?"

Arlian blinked and turned to look at Black again. "The right?" he said. "There's no 'right.' I have the *ability* to destroy the dragons—or at least, I hope I do—and I have chosen to do it."

"And the thousands of other people who may be affected by this have no say in it?"

"Each can choose for himself what to do," Arlian said. "They can join me, oppose me, or simply hide until it's all over."

"But you believe they can't tell you, 'No, leave well enough alone.'"

"No, they cannot. This is no special circumstance. The Duke's decisions affect other people every day; every lord's decisions affect his employees. We are forever at the mercy of others."

"But everyone *knows* the Duke reigns over them. Every employee has *chosen* to work for his lord. The only people who have *no* choices are slaves, yet you propose to give no choice to all of Manfort."

Arlian frowned. "Now, are you comparing me to a slave owner to enrage me, or do you really think I might accept this specious line of argument? No one chooses to live at the whim of dragons. No one chose the present Duke. No one can tell Lord Zaner what cargoes to load in his ships, though that may mean the difference between wealth and starvation for everyone in Lorigol. Black, do you really think that I could stop at this point, and that matters would simply return to what they were? Enziet is dead and his secrets are out, and I am caught up in the result, as we all are. Lord Hardior is a fool to think my death would restore things to what they were."

"You could dump these weapons and tell the dragons you will keep their secrets if they stay in their caves. You could stay in Deep Delving and never return to Manfort. You could work to reconcile the factions in the Society."

"It's too late to keep the dragons' secrets."

"Is it? You heard the lies Stammer collected about you; rumor and gossip spread through the city like mushrooms after a rain, and vanish as swiftly. A year from now no one but the dragonhearts will remember how Nail died."

Arlian did not answer immediately. The wagon rolled on down the ruts in the road, the oxen plodding steadily.

"You can't be sure of that," he said at last. "It may be too late. The dragons may already be out of their caverns—and they do deserve to die, all of them."

"So you're going to go on with your revenge even if it destroys Manfort and ruins the Lands of Man."

"I am."

It was Black's turn to pause before replying, but at last he said, "So you will let the Dragon Society destroy itself."

"I don't believe I can prevent it."

"That will tear the heart out of Manfort. Have you given any thought to what might replace it?"

Arlian started as the wagon hit a bump. "What?"

"The Dragon Society may be a bunch of coldhearted bastards, Ari, but they have kept Manfort peaceful and whole for six hundred years. If you destroy it, or it destroys itself, who will rule Manfort? Do you expect the Duke to actually do the job he was born to, with no Enziet or Hardior to direct him? And if the dragonhearts die without heirs and leave the Duke a hundred times as wealthy as he is now, do you think that would be a good thing?"

"Do you expect me to lead a *real* insurrection against him?" Arlian asked. "He's the Duke of Manfort, warlord of the Lands of Man."

"He's an idiot."

"Well, yes. But he's the Duke. I'm sure he'll find advisers, as he always has—they just won't be dragonhearts."

"So you would replace dragon-hearted sorcerers possessing the wisdom of centuries with ordinary men."

"Indeed I would," Arlian said.

"You have a higher opinion of my fellow men than I do."

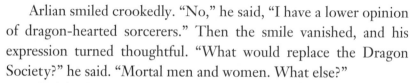

Arlian smiled crookedly. "No," he said, "I have a lower opinion of dragon-hearted sorcerers." Then the smile vanished, and his expression turned thoughtful. "What would replace the Dragon Society?" he said. "Mortal men and women. What else?"

Black looked at him, but said no more. The conversation died, and no new one rose to take its place—Arlian was distracted, plainly thinking hard about something.

In fact, he was thinking about what might become of the Dragon Society—not the organization as a whole, but its individual members. They could become dragons, if their tainted blood was allowed to mature, or corpses, if that blood was spilled—but was there no third possibility?

Black had asked what would replace the Dragon Society at Manfort's heart. Surely, ordinary mortals could fill the gap, and the Lands of Man would live on. Could something similar be done on a more personal scale?

He had wondered before whether there might be some way to remove the taint that made a dragonheart something other than an ordinary human. He knew sorcery could not do it. Could the wild magic of the south?

Could Aritheian magic replace a dragon heart with a human one?

That night, in the street before an inn in a village called Grandfather Elm, as soon as the caravan was secured for the night, Arlian spoke to the Aritheians.

"When you come back," he said, "I want you to bring certain things."

"Love potions?" Thirif asked, smiling.

"No." Arlian shook his head. "I don't mean the things to sell. You know better than I what will bring the best profits, now that you've had all these months in Manfort, and I trust you to invest wisely. There are two matters I need to attend to, though, that will require magic—if they can be done at all."

"What are they?" Isein asked.

"First, I need some way to drive a spear into a dragon's heart."

The Aritheians exchanged glances.

"You spoke of that in Manfort," Thirif said. "We have spoken among ourselves. We think it can be done, but must speak with the elders of the House of Deri."

Arlian nodded. "That's fine," he said. "The other—I think I need a physician."

"You are ill?" Isein asked worriedly.

"No, I . . . well, perhaps I am. But I need a magician who can drain a man's blood, perhaps even stop his heart, yet keep him alive. If there is some way to *replace* tainted blood with clean . . ."

For a long moment the magicians were silent; at last Thirif spoke.

"I have never heard of such a thing," he said.

"Is it impossible?"

"I do not know."

"Find out," Arlian said. "Please. Speak to whoever might know in Arithei—not just the House of Deri, but all the eleven houses, even the House of Slihar. I will pay for this magic in silver and amethysts and whatever else you might want; it's worth more to me than everything else put together."

"We will ask," Isein said.

Arlian nodded. "Good," he said. Then he added, "If you do find such a magic, bring it to me at once, even if it means abandoning everything else. And bring enough to do it many times over, if that is possible."

"As you say," Isein said, bowing her head.

"Good!" Arlian looked up at the night sky, the stars hidden by clouds, then at the inn. "Then let us find ourselves some supper, and rest while we can."

He led the way inside.

In the morning they set out again, beneath an overcast sky, and rolled onward through an uneventful day of oppressive heat.

34

At the Mine

Arlian was startled to realize, as his caravan rolled down the dusty main street of Deep Delving, that he had never seen the place before. He had spent seven years in the mines, but he had never set foot in the town, half a mile away.

Now, though, he saw a crowded tangle of narrow streets lined with half-timbered buildings, nestled into a steep-sided valley. There was no open market, no plaza—but there was an inn, of course. A town that relied on the sale of what its mines produced could hardly fail to provide accommodations for the people who came to buy. Arlian guided the weary oxen toward the inn, and when the wagon had creaked to a stop by the door he dismounted, sweat sticking his shirt to his back.

He left his hat in the wagon, and left the caravan waiting in the street while he and Black went inside. He stood by the door, looking impatient, with Black beside him, until the landlord deigned to notice them.

"May I help you, my lord?" the proprietor asked, brushing crumbs from his apron.

"I'm looking for an old man named Lithuil who operates a mine near here," Arlian said.

The innkeeper glanced over the customers in the taproom, then shrugged. "I know him, but he's not in here."

"Where might we find him, then?"

"He has offices in Brown Street—the second street on the left, that way." He pointed.

"Thank you." Arlian turned away.

Fifteen minutes later Arlian found himself face-to-face with the Old Man for the first time in almost a decade—across a cluttered desk in a dusty office, this time, rather than in stone tunnels. For a moment he had an irrational fear that the Old Man would recognize him and fling him back down into the mine, but he fought it down—after all, how could Lithuil recognize that ragged eleven-year-old boy in the elegant young lord who stood before him?

Arlian recognized the Old Man, however, though he was even older and had lost weight. He had the same wrinkled face and long beard, but the wrinkles had deepened and he was no longer so impressively fat.

Either that, Arlian thought, or his memory had exaggerated the Old Man's girth.

Once upon a time this man had carried him down into the darkness of the mine and had left him there, to slave away breaking the galena ore from the tunnel walls and carting it to the shaft.

Now that same old man said, "It is a great honor to meet you, Lord Obsidian. How fortunate that I was here in town today! Usually I would be out at the mine, but urgent matters . . ."

"Yes, I'm sure," Arlian said, interrupting. He could not bear to hear that voice wheedling like this, when he remembered it bullying. "I have my own urgent business to attend to here. I assume you know that I now own four of the five shares in your mine?"

"I had heard . . ." Lithuil began.

Arlian cut him off. "That means you work for me," he said. "I sent instructions to gather amethysts, like this one." He displayed the silver pendant that held the largest of the stones he had taken from poor Hathet so long ago. "Do you have them ready?"

Lithuil spread empty palms. "Oh, well, my lord, we had not yet determined a price for the stones, and the miners report that they have had no luck in finding them . . ." He shrugged, and smiled apologetically.

Arlian stared at him for a moment.

"Was my message not clear?" he snapped.

Lithuil's smile vanished. "I don't . . ."

"I said I needed them, and you were to start mining them immediately," Arlian said angrily. "Are you telling me that you have found *none?*"

"My lord, I never even heard of these stones before you sent your messages," Lithuil said defensively. "I had no idea that these purple crystals could be found in the ore. I did as you instructed and told the miners to look for them and send them up with the ore, but as yet none have been delivered."

"And what did you offer the miners in exchange?"

Lithuil blinked. "Offer them? My lord, they are slaves—I *told* them to send up the purple stones."

Arlian stared at him for a moment, remembering his own years in the tunnels. None of the miners would have done anything to please their masters simply because they were *told* to—or rather, almost none, and those who might try would be reminded of the folly of their actions. If someone had fetched a few amethysts to the ore lift, one of the others would certainly have made sure the stones did not make it up the pitshaft.

In fact, the demonstration of folly might have permanent results.

"Have there been more deaths than usual since you told them to fetch the stones?" he asked.

Lithuil cocked his head to one side. "More than usual? Not really. There have been deaths, of course. Two men were killed in fights. Why? Are these stones supposed to bring bad luck, then?"

Arlian shook his head. "No," he said. "Quite the contrary. They can protect the bearer from certain sorts of magic."

"Then why did . . ."

"We'll go to the mine," Arlian said, interrupting again; he

found he had very little patience with this unpleasant old man. "I want to speak to your slaves."

In fact, he intended to do considerably more than speak to them.

"It's late, my lord, not long until suppertime," Lithuil protested. "Let us look at the books tonight, so you can see how things stand, and wait until tomorrow to . . ."

"We'll go to the mine *now*," Arlian said, not loudly, but in a tone that brooked no argument.

Lithuil looked at Arlian's face, and said nothing more.

Half an hour or so later Arlian, Lithuil, Black, and four carefully chosen caravan guards arrived at the entrance to the mine. Arlian stared at the heavy wooden door in the shadowy opening, remembering when he had last seen it.

He had been coming out into sunlight after seven years in darkness, wearing rags, carrying a bag of amethysts, and with nothing else to his name but his freedom, newly restored to him by a pair of brothers named Enir and Linnas in gratitude for saving Enir's life.

Enir, also known as Bloody Hand, had been one of the mine's overseers; Linnas had been a guard.

Lithuil opened the door and stood aside so that Lord Obsidian could enter; Arlian hesitated, thinking for a moment that the Old Man would slam the door behind him once he was inside—but Black and the guards would see that no harm came to him. He was not a half-starved boy anymore; he was Lord Obsidian. He stepped in.

Lithuil followed, then Black, then the guards.

The stone passageway was lit by widely spaced torches mounted on the walls, providing light but filling the air with smoke. Even with the torches, though, the air inside was cooler than the raging heat of summer outside.

Arlian remembered the system—farther down the tunnel the torches gave way to oil lamps, and both the torches and the lamps were lit before each shift change for the convenience of the guards, overseers, and ore-haulers, but mostly because the mules that hauled the ore wagons didn't like the dark. The guards would light the torches and lamps as they went down the passage ahead of the empty carts, and would replace any torches or wicks that had burned down too far, and refill the lamps that needed it.

A shift change must be in progress, as it had been all those years ago when he was first carried down to the pitshaft.

"How many people work for you here?" he asked Lithuil as the party started down the tunnel.

"We employ two overseers, two guards, and six teamsters," the Old Man replied.

Naturally, he didn't mention the slaves. "Very efficient," Arlian said. "And you trust these men?"

"Well enough."

"Have the present overseers worked here long?"

Startled, the Old Man glanced at him. "Why do you ask?"

Arlian shrugged. "Simple curiosity. I take an interest in how men live their lives, and a job like that, spending the day down in the dark with slaves . . . well, I'm curious whether it's something men do for their entire lives, or whether they find it unbearable after a time."

He was not about to explain that he wanted to know whether Lampspiller, the sadist who had made his life as a slave even more miserable than it should have been, was still there, and available as a target for revenge.

"It can be either one, my lord," the Old Man said. "We've had men who lived out their lives as overseers, and others who quit quickly."

"And the current pair? Have they been here long, then?"

He knew that Bloody Hand had begun working in the mine about ten years ago, and Lampspiller about six—but he didn't know whether they were still there.

And he couldn't ask about both of them by name; Bloody Hand and Lampspiller had been the slaves' names for them, and Lithuil presumably knew them by other names. Arlian knew that Bloody Hand's true name was Enir, but he had no idea who Lampspiller might be outside the mine.

Lithuil grimaced. "No," he said. "We had an unfortunate incident last year—one of the overseers was murdered by the slaves, and the other resigned, so we had to hire new men. One of the new ones didn't work out, so . . . well, one of our overseers has been here just over a year, and the other seven or eight months."

Arlian had to remember to keep his expression calm. "Murdered?"

Lithuil shrugged. "Apparently. We don't really know."

"What happened?"

"The other overseer, a man named Enir, arrived for his shift, and the dead one didn't come up out of the mine when he should have." Arlian smothered a sigh of relief—Bloody Hand had lived. "Enir went down to see what had happened, and found Klorikor's body. The slaves tried to tell him there had been an accident, but Enir said Klorikor appeared to have been beaten, and then strangled with his own whip."

"Unpleasant," Arlian said—but he could not help thinking that Lampspiller had deserved it.

It also resolved any question of whether to seek vengeance on Lampspiller; the other miners had beaten him to it.

That assumed, of course, that it was indeed Lampspiller who had been killed. "How long had the dead man worked here?" he asked.

"Oh, five or six years, I think."

That was Lampspiller. "And what became of the slaves responsible?" Arlian asked.

Lithuil did not answer immediately, and Arlian glanced at him, feeling a sudden chill. Had all the slaves been killed in retaliation?

"We never determined which men were responsible," the Old Man said at last. "Enir came back up, and we left them unsupervised and unfed, telling them that they would get no more food or water until they turned over those responsible for Klorikor's death. But they never admitted his death had been anything but an accident, and we couldn't afford to let them *all* die, so after a few days we gave in. That was when Enir resigned, rather than risk his life down there."

"But you found new overseers?"

Lithuil nodded. "We didn't tell them what had happened to Klorikor."

Arlian suspected that the new overseers would have found out by now. The miners would have told them, if no one else did. That might be why the one "didn't work out."

Black cleared his throat. "Pardon me, sir," he said. "You said Enir described the injuries Klorikor sustained. Did no one else see the body? Didn't *you* see it?"

"Uh . . ." Lithuil glanced uneasily at Arlian.

"Speak up, man," Arlian said. "Surely you don't think you can keep secrets from me?" He met Lithuil's eyes with his own intense gaze.

"Well, Enir left a little hurriedly after seeing the body," Lithuil explained. "He didn't bring it up with him. He left it down there. And then—well, as I said, we decided not to feed the slaves."

Arlian missed a step, stumbling on the smooth stone of the floor. He remembered what it was like down there, how they had all been perpetually hungry, all slightly underfed. Missing a single meal could be agonizing.

He knew what had happened to Lampspiller's body.

"They ate him," Black said.

Lithuil nodded unhappily. One of the guards gagged.

"*Very* unpleasant," Arlian said mildly, though in fact it seemed oddly fitting. He wondered whether he would have eaten any, had he still been in the mine, or whether he would have preferred to stay hungry.

"We hadn't thought them so depraved," Lithuil said defensively. "It didn't occur to us at all!"

Arlian had no reply to that, and conversation was becoming more difficult in any case, as the ore wagons were coming up the tunnel just ahead. The rattle of harness and the creak of heavily laden wheels echoed from the stone walls.

The six men stepped to one side of the tunnel to let the wagons pass. The drivers glanced at them in surprise, but said nothing.

A few minutes later they reached the lip of the pitshaft, where a heavy wood and metal framework supported ropes and pulleys that would haul ore up from below, tons at a time. A lone guard in leather had been leaning against one of the support beams; he stepped aside at the arrival of this unexpected party of visitors. He recognized Lithuil, and did not question the presence of strangers; his job was to make sure the slaves stayed down where they belonged, not to interfere with any guests his employer might bring.

Arlian breathed in; the air down here was cool and still, and smelled of dust and stone. It might have been pleasant and restful, a welcome change from the heat outside, if not for what he knew lay at the foot of the pitshaft. This was the end of the world of free men, Arlian thought as he looked down past the beams and ropes at the flickering light of oil lamps at the bottom. Down there, fifteen feet below, was the dark and tiny world of the mining slaves.

And if the ore had just been hauled away, then the slaves would be eating the food that they received in exchange. Most of them, maybe all of them, would still be nearby.

Arlian stepped to the edge and bellowed, "You miners! Listen to me!"

"My lord!" a shocked Lithuil protested.

From somewhere below another voice called, "Who in hell is that?"

"I am Lord Obsidian," Arlian called, ignoring Lithuil. "I am the majority owner of this mine, and I want all of you miners to listen closely to my proposal."

"My lord, this is . . ."

"Shut up," Arlian told Lithuil, without looking. "Black, keep him quiet. Cut his throat if you must."

Arlian heard the hiss of steel sliding on leather, and Lithuil made no further protest. A glance showed that the caravan guards had cowed the mine guard, as well—one of the caravan guards, a man called Stabber, whom Arlian had fought beside two years before in the Desolation, held a blade at the mine guard's throat.

"You men," Arlian shouted, "you heard a month ago that you were to collect the purple stones called amethysts, and send them up with the ore. You didn't deliver any. I don't think I blame you— what were you offered in exchange?"

"Nothing!" a braver-than-usual miner called back.

"Exactly. But those stones are very precious to me, and I'm going to offer you something precious in exchange. I know what men everywhere are like, and I assume you've all been saving the amethysts, and just not delivering them. That's fine—but deliver them *now*, and if you *collectively* deliver one hundred suitable stones, each large enough for my purposes, then you'll *all* go free."

When the echoes of this speech faded away there was a moment of stunned silence; then Lithuil protested, "You can't *do* that!"

Arlian turned, his hand on the hilt of his own sword.

"Yes," he said, "I can."

"But they're not your slaves! They're mine!"

"I'll pay you for them," Arlian said, smiling an unpleasant, tight little smile. This was his revenge on the Old Man. Then he turned back to the pit and called, "One more thing—if any one of you dies before the full hundred has been delivered, the total goes up to one hundred and ten! Each additional death will add ten. If you steal from one another, you had better make sure your victim survives— and it won't buy you anything more; nobody wants these but me, and I will not pay you with anything but your freedom. I don't care who found how many—it's all of you or none. The sooner you can find the hundred, the sooner you can go! Now, how many do you have?"

There was a murmur from below, but no clear answer.

"All right, you aren't ready to say," Arlian said. "I'll be back here at the end of the shift with a bucket, and you can put the amethysts in the bucket, and we'll see what we have."

The thought of a mere bucket brought a wry, uncomfortable smile; ordinarily the miners filled a gigantic ore hopper twice a day, but to him, the contents of that one ordinary bucket would be worth far more than a dozen of the hoppers.

Then he turned away, and found he was trembling. Being back in this place did not frighten him in the usual sense of the word, but it made him feel as if his mind were stretched tight and plucked, as if his identity were oscillating between Arlian the mine slave and Lord Obsidian the mine owner.

"We'll go now," he said to the others, pointing up the tunnel.

Lithuil started to protest further, then thought better of it and closed his mouth before a word had emerged. The mine guard hesitated.

"You stay here," Black told him.

He stayed, and the other six men trudged back up the passage to the surface.

35

A Deception Discovered

Arlian and his crew ate a late supper at the inn in Deep Delving. Lithuil did not offer to feed them at his home, as might ordinarily have been expected, and Arlian did not ask; he knew that his treatment of the Old Man at the mine, satisfying as it was, had swept aside the customary etiquette. A lord who had held a subordinate at swordpoint and arbitrarily claimed the right to free the subordinate's slaves had clearly given up any claim on the usual hospitality.

This bothered Arlian not at all; he had seen quite enough of Lithuil, and preferred to eat with his own people.

The four Aritheian magicians, Thirif, Shibiel, Qulu, and Isein, sat together at one table, chattering in their own language. The guards were clustered around another three tables, while Black, Arlian, and Quickhand ate at a small one in the back corner.

As lord and master Arlian could have had his meal brought to a private room, but he preferred to eat in the main room, with the others. He did however indulge himself to the point of ordering pork chops, rather than the greasy sausage that was the inn's common fare.

As he speared a piece of pork and lifted it to his mouth he recalled the conversation in the mine, and what had become of Lampspiller; the pork suddenly seemed much less appealing.

He stuck it in his mouth anyway, chewing dutifully, and then to distract himself he glanced around the room, his gaze falling on the tables full of cheerful, talkative guards. He asked Quickhand, "How are the men we hired working out? Is it a good crew?"

Quickhand looked over his shoulder at the others, then shrugged. "They're good enough," he said. "They think you're mad, hiring so many guards for just eight wagons."

"I probably am," Arlian said reflexively.

"You've worked with these men before?" Black asked.

"Not all of them," Quickhand said. "Twenty is a big company. We have four or five I'd never met before."

"Think they'll fight, or run?" Black gulped ale after asking his question, but kept his eyes on Quickhand's face.

"Oh, fight, most of them," Quickhand said, lifting his own mug. "There's one I'm not sure about—he's the sort with a little too much imagination. He might get thinking about just how much a sword in the belly would hurt, and decide not to risk it." He sipped his own beer, and made a face. "I think this is watered."

"Probably," Arlian agreed. "This guard you think might run— what makes you think he's over-imaginative?"

"Oh, because he's always asking questions, my lord. That's a sure sign of someone who thinks more than most. And the questions he asks aren't the practical ones that Black or I would worry about."

"Really? What sort of questions did he ask?"

"Well, any number of questions about where we were going— were we really going all the way to Arithei? Would we stop anywhere along the way? Are there dragons in Arithei? Not bandits, mind you, or anything else—I'd already told the men when Black and I hired them that we might run into southern magic, but he didn't ask about that, he specifically asked about dragons."

"It would seem you've become associated with dragons in the popular mind, somehow," Black remarked.

"Mmm." Arlian took another bite of pork.

"I don't know about anyone else, Lord Ari, but *this* fellow certainly associates you with dragons! Or maybe he's just obsessed with them. He even asked whether there were dragons sleeping in the mines here in Deep Delving."

Arlian blinked and put down his knife. There was something strange going on here—that question felt wrong, somehow. Why would anyone think there might be dragons in Deep Delving? Oh, Arlian had sometimes worried, down in the mine, that he and the other miners might break through into one of the caverns in which the dragons slept, but in truth there was no evidence at all that there were any such caverns in the area.

And why would a caravan guard ask that? Neither mines nor dragons were his concern.

For that matter, why would *anyone* be displaying such an unhealthy interest in dragons? Usually people tried to *avoid* speaking of them, since too much mention of them was believed to attract, if not dragons themselves, then at least lesser forms of misfortune.

"Who is this man?" Arlian asked.

"He calls himself Post," Quickhand said, pointing at one of the guards two tables over.

Black snorted. "Post? I suppose that's meant to impress women, but the first thing it brings to *my* mind is whether he's commenting on his own wits."

"At least he doesn't call himself Dragon," Arlian said. "That seems to be what he prefers to worry about."

"That, and sorcery," Quickhand agreed. "I tried to explain that southern magic isn't sorcery, but he didn't seem to understand or care, and he didn't want to hear anything about the Borderlands or the Dreaming Mountains except whether there were dragons there. *I* wanted to hear everything the Aritheians could tell us about the route, but Post wasn't concerned with that. He seems interested in the strangest things! He asked how old you really were, my lord, as if it mattered—and as if he couldn't see for himself as much as I can."

Arlian stared at Quickhand for a moment, a suspicion forming. These odd questions were beginning to make a pattern. He turned to look at Post again. "Which one is he?" he asked.

"There," Quickhand said. "In the blue."

Arlian studied Post as best he could from this angle, and decided that no, he didn't know the man.

"I want to talk to him," Arlian said. "Bring him to my wagon after supper."

"As you wish," Quickhand said.

Black did not speak, but cocked an eyebrow at Arlian.

"I suspect," Arlian said quietly, "that this Post may have another employer, in addition to myself."

"An interesting possibility," Black said.

After they had eaten Arlian returned to his wagon—but he paused in the door of the inn to see that Quickhand was indeed speaking to Post.

Then he turned and stepped out into the street.

The inside of the inn had been hot and damp and slightly smoky, and Arlian had expected to cool off in the night air, but he found that the weather outside was still hot and sticky, as well, despite the late hour. The sun was long since down, but no moon or stars could be seen—the sky was heavily overcast.

Nasty weather, Arlian thought as he trudged to the waiting caravan. Hot and dark . . .

Dragon weather.

He stopped and looked up at the sky.

Maybe he would have thought of it anyway, he told himself, or maybe Post's questions about dragons had reminded him, but yes, this *was* dragon weather.

He turned and looked back at the inn; men were emerging, but he could not tell who through the gloom. He clambered up onto the driver's seat of the lead wagon and waited in the dark, not lighting the lantern that hung near his head.

He looked back at the wagon's interior, at the waiting spears and blades. In this weather they might be needed soon, he thought—and they were all *here*, but they might be needed in Manfort.

There was a disturbance in the street; he turned again, and saw men struggling. One man was holding another, trying to keep him from fleeing; others were standing close by, watching. The light all came from the inn behind them, so he could not see anything but black outlines; still, he thought the captor might be Quickhand, which would mean the other was probably Post. He could hear shuffling and grunting. Someone called, "Give me a hand!"

Arlian reached down and picked up his sword from its place behind the seat. He laid the scabbard across his lap, then loosened the blade in its sheath.

Three men were holding the one now, dragging him forward.

Arlian found his firekit and lit the lantern as the men approached. Then he stood up and called, "Post, I'm not going to hurt you. Come and talk to me."

The captive looked up, and his struggles weakened. He allowed himself to be led, rather than dragged, the rest of the way, until he stood beside the wagon. Arlian could finally see his face in the light of the lantern, and see that yes, this was Post, held by Quickhand, Stabber, and two guards Arlian didn't know by name.

"Climb up here," Arlian said, sliding over to make room. He kept the sword on his lap, his hand on the hilt.

Reluctantly, Post obeyed.

"Thank you, Quickhand," Arlian called. "You can go."

Quickhand gave Post a doubtful look. "You're sure, Lord Ari?"

"I'm sure," Arlian said, shifting the sword.

The guards departed, leaving Arlian and Post alone. Arlian looked at Post thoughtfully. He was a fair-sized man but not really large, and appeared to be getting rather old to work as a caravan guard.

But then, he wasn't really there as a guard.

"You know," Arlian said, "if you hadn't resisted coming here, you might yet have convinced me your peculiar questions were just harmless curiosity. Now, though, I'm afraid it's too late."

"What questions?" Post blustered.

"Your questions about dragons, and sorcery, and my age," Arlian said. "I take it someone's sent you to accompany me in hopes of learning something about the sorcerous uses of dragon venom."

"No one sent me," Post said resentfully.

His right hand remained on the sword hilt, but Arlian's left hand flashed out and closed on Post's throat. He rammed the man's head back against the wagon's frame.

"I told you it's too late for that," Arlian growled. "I am not in a forgiving mood tonight, sir—my trip to the mine was unsettling, and I don't like this weather, so the discovery of your deceit, which I will generously not yet call treachery, has aggravated me a great deal. Do not lie to me again."

He released the pressure on Post's throat.

"I didn't lie!" Post protested, when he could breathe again. "Not really." He rubbed at his neck and looked resentfully at Arlian.

"You claim no one sent you—then why are you here? Don't tell me you just wanted honest caravan work."

"No," Post said, still rubbing his neck. "You were right that I wanted to find out where you got your dragon venom, and how to use it."

"And why are you interested in dragon venom? It's poisonous stuff, you know."

"Lady Opal told me that you use it to make yourself young again."

"Lady Opal sent you?"

"Not exactly. She agreed to pay me if I bring back a sample, or even just knowledge of where you get it, but she didn't *send* me. I volunteered."

"Lady Opal." Arlian relaxed somewhat.

"Yes, Lady Opal," Post said. "She had wanted to send Horn, but you would have recognized him, so he suggested me."

That was nowhere near as bad a piece of news as Arlian had feared. He had worried that Post might have been a hired assassin in Lord Hardior's employ, waiting until he knew where to find the dragons before he struck, or that he might have been spying for the Duke as part of some court intrigue. He had thought that Lady Pulzera might have sent Post as her emissary to the dragons, using Arlian to find them, or that some other faction in the Dragon Society might have hired him for some esoteric reason.

It had even occurred to Arlian that someone within his own household might have betrayed him, and planted this spy among his hirelings. He had also considered the possibility that the dragons themselves had sent this man.

All in all, Lady Opal was perhaps the least frightening explanation that made sense—though of course, she might be working in concert with Pulzera or Hardior.

"And did she want you to kill me when you had learned my secrets?" Arlian asked.

"No," Post said. "I know better than to fight *you*, my lord, or to try to ambush a sorcerer. Even if you were no sorcerer, and not a famous swordsman, just killing a caravan master surrounded by a score of honest guards—well, I wouldn't live to see my family again if I tried that. If Lady Opal wants you dead she'll have to hire someone else; I wouldn't attempt it for all the gold in Manfort."

"You show *some* sense, I see," Arlian said.

Post made a wordless noise.

"She lied to you, you know," Arlian said conversationally. "Or at least misled you. Dragon venom doesn't make one younger. I really *am* as young as I appear."

"Then why does Opal want it so badly?" Post asked, apparently over the worst of his fear.

"Because it extends life," Arlian explained. "I'm only in my early twenties, yes, but there are men and women in Manfort who have lived for centuries, thanks to the dragon elixir. They age only very, very slowly—but they do age, they never grow any younger."

"*Centuries?*" Post's eyes widened.

Arlian nodded. "Lord Enziet was the oldest," he said. "And Lord Wither was almost as old. Lady Opal learned about it from him."

"Lord Wither? I heard . . . well, I heard you killed him, but I also heard he killed himself."

"Lord Wither took his own life," Arlian said. "The elixir has other effects besides extending life, and he feared the consequences were catching up with him."

Post did not appear convinced. "How often do you take it?" he asked. "I mean, if you're still so young, but you're going to get more . . ."

"I'm not," Arlian interrupted. "I told you she lied to you. This journey has nothing to do with fetching dragon venom. Drink the elixir *once*, and the damage is done—I will never need it again. Though I'm not sure Opal believes that."

"I don't think she does," Post said. His expression seemed to add, *And neither do I.*

Arlian gazed at him for a moment, then asked, "Have you spoken with the men who accompanied me to the mine today?"

"I . . ." Post stopped, but Arlian could read the answer in his face.

"Did they tell you what I wanted from the mine? Did they say anything about dragons?"

"They said you offered the slaves their freedom in exchange for amethysts," Post admitted. "No one said anything about dragons." He hesitated, then added, "They said the miners ate an overseer."

Arlian sighed. He hadn't told the guards to keep anything secret from their fellows, since he had assumed that they would all be traveling through the Dreaming Mountains together, and would see for themselves what the amethysts were for. Now, though, he feared that this fool would carry word back to Manfort that Lord Obsidian prized amethysts even more than his glassy namesake, and new rumors would spread.

"Did the slaves really eat him, or did they feed him to the dragons?" Post asked.

"There aren't any dragons in the mine," Arlian said wearily.

Again, Post's disbelief was obvious. The man really was a fool.

"Why do you want the amethysts? Do you need them for the elixir?"

"No. We need them to . . ." In midsentence, Arlian decided against telling the exact truth. ". . . trade with the Aritheians. They prize the amethysts highly." A sudden spirit of mischief caught him, and he added, "They believe amethysts keep dragons away, and that that's why the dragons have never ventured into Arithei—they think they're guarded by their jewelry." He smiled as if deriding this silly fantasy. "The stones are the only thing they'll accept in trade for their magic—what else could we have that they need, after all, when half of them are wizards? And for myself, I don't care *why* they want them—if that's what they want, that's what they'll get."

"*Do* amethysts keep dragons away?" Post asked, marveling.

Arlian shrugged. "How would I know?" Then, in another burst of whimsy, he added, "But no one's ever seen any sign of dragons in the mine, even though it goes deep enough to reach their caverns."

Post's eyes were wide as he absorbed this nonsense.

Arlian sat back and slapped his thighs. "So, you came here because Lady Opal thought I was fetching dragon venom. I'm not. I'd suggest you go on home to Manfort and tell her so."

"Um," Post said.

"I'm afraid that under the circumstances, I cannot employ you as a caravan guard," Arlian said. "I'm sure you understand. I'll tell Quickhand to settle your pay. You can take your belongings and leave in the morning."

"Um," Post said again. "You aren't going . . ." His voice trailed off.

"I'm not going to punish you, or withhold your pay," Arlian said wearily. "You have committed a deception, but no actual crime, and you have carried out your duties heretofore. You are free to go." He had a horrible thought, and added, "But I would really very strongly recommend that you not attempt to follow the caravan to Arithei. I don't think you could make it across the Desolation."

"Then you really are going to Arithei again?" Post asked, startled.

"No," Arlian said, the matter suddenly settled beyond question. Up until this very moment he had still thought it might be possible, but now he was sure he could not afford to be away from Manfort for so long. "My caravan will be going to Arithei, but I will be staying a few days here in Deep Delving, settling matters."

"Of course," Post said—but his now familiar look of disbelief was back, more obvious than ever, and more than Arlian's fraying temper could bear.

"Go, sir," Arlian said, his hand closing on the hilt of his sword. "I have had a bellyful of you. Go back to Opal, and may both of you be damned!"

Post hastily backed away, and almost fell as he quickly clambered out of the wagon.

36

The Price of Freedom

Arlian arose the next morning just after dawn, so that he might reach the mine before the shift change without undue hurry. When he first opened his eyes he thought that he had awoken *before* dawn, so dark was the sky, but then he realized that was due to thick, low-hanging clouds, and the sun was indeed up.

And the air was sweltering hot.

At least, he thought, this gloomy weather would be easy on the miners' eyes if they had collected the hundred amethysts he had demanded, and earned their freedom. He remembered well how he had been blinded by the sun when he first fled the mine.

He rose from his bed, dressed himself, and gathered together the various things he needed to carry out his promises.

Just over an hour later he stood at the mouth of the pitshaft, leaning against the heavy framework, lowering the promised bucket down to the waiting miners.

He could hear them muttering, talking among themselves. He supposed they were exchanging suspicions, wondering how their masters would betray and abuse them this time.

The others at his own level—Black, Qulu, half the caravan's guards, and the drivers of the ore wagons—were utterly silent; the guards stood half-hidden in the shadows. The waiting day-shift overseer, a young man who had said the miners called him Whip, was standing back, as well; the night-shift overseer was still down in the pit. Arlian had interrupted the regular loading of ore into the big hopper.

The bucket reached the bottom and the line went slack as Arlian paid out a little extra. Then he called, "All the amethysts, in the bucket, right now."

The muttering grew louder, and he heard feet stamping and shuffling; then came a rattle, and a voice called up, "They're in."

Almost trembling with anticipation, Arlian began hauling the line up, hand over hand. A moment later he had the bucket in his hands. He tipped it toward the light.

Purple stones glittered in the bottom.

He took the bucket to where Qulu waited, and the two squatted down on the stone and began inspecting and counting his haul.

"What now?" Whip called.

"You might as well go on loading the ore," Arlian called back. "This will take a moment." The possibility that the miners might have tried to pass off bits of purple glass or other detritus as amethysts had occured to him—but of course, such things would be almost impossible to obtain down here.

And in fact, so far as he could tell by lamplight, the stones in the bucket were indeed amethysts, ranging from chips the size of an ant to a hexagonal chunk the size of a pigeon's egg.

Behind them, Arlian could hear the rattle of ore being dumped into the hopper, a sound that brought back a great many memories, most of them unpleasant. It was more distant than he remembered, of course, since he was up here instead of down below, but it was unmistakably the same sound. He shivered slightly, then concentrated on counting.

The final total was seventy-one stones—more than Arlian had expected. Hathet had saved amethysts for decades and only accumulated a hundred and sixty-eight; someone must have made a lucky find.

"It is not a hundred," Qulu said.

"Is it enough?" Arlian asked.

"Oh, more than enough, my lord," Qulu said. "Some are much larger than I expected."

"Then it will do," he said. He turned to the men in the shadows. "As soon as the ore is loaded in the wagons, lower the ladder."

"You're really going to free them?" the overseer asked, as the guards slid the ladder toward the edge.

"Yes, I am," Arlian replied. He got to his feet, leaving Qulu to collect the amethysts, and walked over toward the pitshaft.

He had intended to shout down to the miners, but he realized he wouldn't be heard over the clattering and banging of ore being loaded into the hopper. He grimaced, then stepped back and waited.

The overseer below signaled the waiting teamsters, and they in turn set their mules to hauling on the ropes. The hopper was pulled up and the support arms pivoted, with much creaking, to sway it over to the waiting wagons. The ore was loaded into the wagons, which took several minutes.

And then the hopper was empty, ready to be lowered again. Sacks of food and kegs of water and lamp oil had been set by the rim of the pit, ready to be lowered down as the miners' payment, but the workers hesitated.

"Go ahead and send the supplies down," Arlian said. "Then lower the ladder."

"What about me?" Whip asked. "Should I go down with the food?"

"I think so," Arlian said. "Keep order while the ladder is readied."

He watched with interest as the supplies were loaded into the hopper, and then as Whip clambered in—he didn't stand on the rim holding a rope as Bloody Hand and Lampspiller always had, but instead sat inside.

The arms swung out over the pit, the teamsters hauling on the ropes alongside their beasts.

Arlian had never seen the operation from this side before. He hadn't realized just how much work the teamsters did, or just how complex the machinery was.

Then the hopper began to descend, and Arlian stepped to the edge to watch. He could see the glow of the miners' lamps in the radiating tunnels, but not the miners themselves—they were forbidden to enter the pitshaft itself while the hopper was in use.

The hopper came to rest on the heap of rags used as a buffer, and Whip climbed out, beckoning.

"Listen, you!" he bellowed, his voice oddly faint from above. "Lord Obsidian says he's going to free you." He lifted out the bags of food.

"But that wasn't a hundred!" someone called, as the miners emerged from their tunnels.

"I know it wasn't, you useless fool, but Lord Obsidian's crazed with generosity! Now, shut up, and come get the last meal you won't have to pay for." He gestured for the nearest miners to lift the first water barrel out of the hopper.

For a moment the shaft was silent; then the miners surged forward, rushing for the food. Arlian could see the other overseer coming to whisper to Whip, and a faint memory stirred—was that the man they had called Loudmouth, who had served as a temporary replacement for Bloody Hand when Hand was injured?

Wood clattered on stone, and Arlian turned to see the end of the ladder sliding over the rim as the caravan guards lowered it.

A sudden hush fell below as the miners saw and heard the ladder.

Arlian stepped to the edge and called down, "Listen to me, all of you!"

He could see dirty, long-bearded faces turned up toward him.

"I am Lord Obsidian. I have bought this mine, and freed you, because I believe every human being who wants freedom should have it. My men are lowering a ladder, and you are all free to climb it and leave the mine any time you choose. The ladder will not be removed. However, you are also free to stay here, and to work for me here, if you are not ready to face the outside world. You will be paid two ducats a month if you stay, and will be free to come and go as you please. The quality and quantity of meals will improve—but probably not very much. Overseers will still have the authority to use their whips, but not to kill or cripple.

"If you leave my employ at any time you will be paid ten ducats apiece for the work you have done, and after that you're on your own. Choose carefully."

That said, he stepped back. Voices sounded below, a dozen conversations starting at once.

The ladder touched bottom.

Arlian waited.

A minute or so later he heard the first awkward feet clambering up, and then a face appeared above the stone rim, looking around in wonder.

Arlian recognized him immediately—Bitter.

Bitter clearly did not recognize his former comrade Arlian in the finely dressed, well-groomed Lord Obsidian. He climbed slowly up the ladder and then stepped out onto the stone, where he hesitated, staring at his surroundings.

The ten caravan guards, the Aritheian magician, the lord and his steward, and the half-dozen teamsters all stared back at him.

"Can I ride one of the wagons up, or do I have to walk?" Bitter asked.

The teamsters looked at Arlian, who shrugged.

"As you please," he said. He glanced at the ladder; no one else was climbing up. "You might want to reassure your fellows that it's not a trick."

Bitter turned and called back, "I'm fine so far!" Then he turned and headed for the lead wagon.

More feet sounded.

Arlian waited and watched as more than a dozen men climbed the ladder to freedom. He recognized Stain and Rumind and Swamp and Elbows and Verino and a few others; some faces were new, and several old ones were missing.

None of them showed even the faintest glimmer of recognition when they saw their deliverer.

That was oddly distressing. Arlian had lived and worked with these men for seven years; had he really changed so completely?

Of course, he remembered, they probably thought he was dead. Bloody Hand had tried to convince them that he had flogged Arlian to death, when he had actually helped Arlian escape; it would never occur to anyone here that Arlian was still alive and free, let alone that he was this mysterious madman, Lord Obsidian.

Still, he couldn't resist calling to Verino, and beckoning him to a quiet corner.

Puzzled, Verino obeyed. "Yes, m . . . my lord?" he said, stumbling over the unfamiliar formality.

"I spoke with a man who escaped from this mine once," Arlian said.

Verino frowned. "No one ever escaped," he said. "At least, not in my time here."

Arlian realized his mistake, and said, "Not a slave—an overseer. I believe you called him Bloody Hand."

Verino's face tightened.

"On the basis of what he told me, I would like to inquire after certain slaves," Arlian said.

"If the Hand wants me to help you punish . . ."

Arlian held up a hand. "Verino, I've just had you freed—why do you think I would seek to punish anyone?"

Verino blinked. "How did you know my name?"

"I asked. Now, Verino—is Wark here?"

"He's still down there."

"Olneor?"

"Dead, weeks ago—maybe years. Broke his hip and died."

"Rat?"

"Didn't he come up?"

Arlian hesitated, trying to think who else he could remember. He was sure there were more . . .

But really, what did it matter?

"Why is Wark still down there?" he asked.

Verino shrugged. "I don't know," he said. "He went back down Number Twenty-Eight." He hesitated, then said, "May I ask a question, my lord?"

"Go ahead."

"Why are you doing this? I mean, why are you freeing us?"

Arlian stared at him for a moment.

"Because I can," he said at last. "I'm trying to make the world a better place, Verino, and this is part of that."

"So you're spending all your money buying slaves, and freeing them?"

"No," Arlian said. "I can't free everyone. You miners were just lucky. I needed amethysts, so you got my attention."

"It really was the amethysts?"

"It really was."

"We didn't have a hundred, though."

"You had enough."

"Rat has some more, I think. He started saving them *years* ago, because a crazy old man named Hathet said they were valuable. We made him give us some, but I think he had more hidden."

"Thank you," Arlian said. "I'll look into that."

Verino hesitated a moment longer, then asked, "Is it night or day out?"

"It's morning—but it's very cloudy. You'll have time to adjust to the sunlight, I think. It's dark and hot."

An odd look came over Verino's face, as if he were remembering something that troubled him, and he said, "Dragon weather?"

"Dragon weather," Arlian agreed.

Verino shuddered, hesitated—then bowed, turned away, and started marching up the tunnel.

37

The Bloody Bowl

Even the dim light of the heavily overcast day was too much for some of the miners. Three of them burst into tears at the sight of the sky; a fourth lost his nerve and retreated back down the tunnel, babbling, "No, no, too much, I can't, it's not right."

Most of them, however, stepped out through the heavy door with arms shielding their eyes against the daylight, but with broad smiles on their faces. One man laughed nervously. Arlian felt his own mouth turning up at the sight. They were filthy, ragged, half-blind from so many years of darkness—but they were free.

It was a pleasure to do good things for people. This felt better, more satisfying, than killing anyone—except possibly, Arlian had to admit, Lord Drisheen, but monsters of his ilk were scarce.

Perhaps, Arlian thought, he should completely abandon his obsessive pursuit of vengeance and devote himself to improving the world in other ways. He had already decided that Lord Toribor could be forgiven; Tooth and Dagger were nowhere to be found; all his other human foes, even Lampspiller, were dead, unless he extended the definition to include people like Lithuil, Opal, Hardior, and Zaner, who had not, to his knowledge, personally killed or enslaved anyone, though he supposed they had probably been complicit in deaths and enslavements.

He did not think his vengeance should stretch that far.

That left the dragons. They certainly deserved to die, but if he tried to kill them they had told him they would fight back, and innocents would suffer.

Of course, over time, if the dragons were permitted to live, innocents would suffer anyway. He tried to tell himself that fighting them really wasn't so much vengeance anymore as survival. In the long run, he thought, he probably couldn't avoid fighting them even if he wanted to.

He looked up at the sky, and his smile vanished. The dragons might well be out even now. They might be on their way to Manfort, or they might be destroying some unsuspecting village.

But if they weren't . . .

"That way," someone called. "Half a mile."

Arlian, distracted by the interruption, looked again at the miners, who were milling about in confusion. One of the caravan guards was counting out the payment Arlian had promised them, while another was directing them to Deep Delving, pointing out the road. The ore wagons were already rolling down the slope toward the smelters.

"Come on," he said, beckoning, leading the party toward town.

As they walked he glanced at Qulu, who was keeping the precious bag of amethysts in his hands, not trusting it to hang on his belt or be stuffed in his shirt. Amethysts and the silver in the vault on Brown Street would be enough to fetch a caravan of new magic back from Arithei—but what sort of magic? The love charms and illusions he could sell, or magic that would drive a spear into a dragon's heart, and replace tainted blood with clean?

If he could kill a single dragon, to prove it was possible, the Duke would help him continue the fight—or at least, so he had said. Could the Aritheians provide the magic to make that first kill?

And if he could restore a dragonheart to full humanity, he would have no reason to kill any more of his fellows in the Dragon Society.

He glanced up at the sky again.

It would take months for a load of magic to be brought from Arithei, and in those months, how much damage could the dragons do?

Perhaps he should find another way to handle the dragons. Perhaps he could still come to an agreement with them, as Enziet had, even though he had already revealed their secrets. After all, he had a thousand years to deal with them. If he could stall, could keep them from attacking anyone . . .

He pushed away the thought that Enziet had had a thousand years, and had not been able to destroy the dragons or prevent his own transformation. Enziet had not had anyone to tell him the secret of obsidian; he had needed centuries of research to learn that, while Arlian had had the information handed to him, ready to use.

Arlian needed to contact the dragons. He needed to negotiate a truce. It could not be coincidence that this dragon weather had come now, after years without it. The dragons must have some way of causing it.

He had to communicate with them, stop them from attacking—if it was not too late.

With that in mind, upon reaching Deep Delving Arlian went directly to the inn and demanded three things: a room, a basin of water, and complete privacy.

The innkeeper grumbled, casting uneasy glances at the ragged, dazed-looking miners who had followed Arlian to town, but when Arlian showed him gold he complied quickly enough.

"Do you want these men with you?" he asked, pointing at the miners.

"Of course not," Arlian said. "I told you, I want complete privacy."

The innkeeper bowed and retreated.

The room was on the ground floor, a small storeroom at the back; Arlian closed the room's shutters and latched them, checked to be sure the door was securely bolted, then settled into a chair, the basin before him on the table. He drew his swordbreaker.

He had no assurance this would work, of course; he did not know how the sorcery actually operated, only that it was possible to speak to the dragons in this manner. All the same, he could see little choice. He took the swordbreaker in his right hand, pressed the tip of the blade against the inside of his left forearm, and drew a line of blood on his flesh.

He remembered that before, when he had spoken with the dragon, he had washed blood from his hands into the bowl; further, when Sweet had seen Enziet conjure a dragon's image, he had just washed blood from his hands. Therefore, Arlian did not just drip blood into the water; instead he smeared it on his fingers, then spread the blood on both hands, rubbing palm on palm and twining his fingers together.

Only then did he wash his hands, soaking and scrubbing until his skin was clean and pink, the water dark and bloody.

That done, he stared at the water.

At first nothing happened. Arlian was not much of a sorcerer, but he tried to re-create the calm focus that Rime had taught him was the beginning of controlling sorcery, and to direct his energies toward the polluted water.

The water stilled, becoming as flat as a mirror, while the blood gathered below the surface. An image took shape—the same image he had seen before, the same dragon he had communicated with in Nail's home.

The dragon was amused. Arlian could sense that before anything that could be put into words was conveyed.

"Why do you trouble us?"

"I want to discuss an agreement," Arlian said.

"It is late for that." Arlian noticed that it did not say *too* late. *"You have revealed our secrets."*

"I know," Arlian said—though he had still hoped the dragons did not yet know. "But is there no bargain we can make?"

"Oh, there are no doubt many possible bargains. To make a bargain, one party must state a desire, and the other must set a price for its fulfill-ment—what do you desire of us?"

"I want you to stay in your caverns, and harm no one."

The amusement was much clearer now. *"It is* much *too late for that."*

A cold sense of foreboding swept over Arlian. "Why?" he asked.

"Because we are already a-wing," the dragon replied. *"A fishing village is aflame, and soon another will be, as well."*

"Another? A second, so soon? But I thought ... you never before ..."

"We were bound," the dragon said, before Arlian could bring his thoughts to order. *"By our bargain with the other."*

Arlian knew it meant Enziet's bargain, the agreement that had ended the ancient Man-Dragon Wars and driven the dragons into the caverns. "Then you're on your way to Manfort? You mean to rule the Lands of Man, as you did long ago?"

"There is no hurry," the dragon replied. *"We are unbound, but we are few and old. First we must rebuild our strength, which you have depleted."*

"Rebuild?" Arlian was baffled.

"We think one survived in the first village—perhaps more than one. There will be more in time."

And then Arlian understood. "You're making more dragon-hearts."

"Of course. You slew many, you and the other. We must make many."

Arlian was too distraught to notice the confirmation that Enziet had, indeed, killed dragonhearts. "But they won't be dragons for a thousand years!"

"We are patient."

"And if I hunt down these new ones, and kill them?"

"We will make more. We are old, but we will yet outlive you, little one. We are few, but we will make more than you can kill."

"Not if I kill *you!*"

The amusement became even plainer and more derisive—the dragon was laughing at him. *"With your black spears? Kill us all?"*

"Do you think I can't?"

"We think you can't."

"I'll find a way! I'll make you tell me how."

"You cannot compel us."

"No? Then why are you talking to me?"

"Because it pleases us to do so. You are no sorcerer, little one. We speak to you at our pleasure, not your own—if you attempt another summoning, it will fail. We have no more to say to each other."

"But you haven't heard what I have to say!"

"You can have nothing more to say that will matter to us."

And with that, the image abruptly broke up into a swirl of blood.

"No!" Arlian shouted. "Come back!"

The dragon was gone.

Arlian stared at the bowl for a moment, his mind struggling with too many concerns at once. He thought of emptying the bowl and trying again, but he did not really doubt what the dragon had said, that the summoning was at the dragon's whim, and not his own—if a binding sorcery had been so simple as that, the real sorcerers in the Dragon Society would all have learned it long ago.

And even now, the dragons were out of their caves, and burning villages on the coast, and there was nothing he could do about it.

Or almost nothing. There would be survivors, their homes destroyed, their friends and families dead. If he could send help, bring them to Manfort, keep them under watch, maybe someday use Aritheian magic to cleanse their blood . . .

But he didn't know *where* on the coast the dragons were attacking, which villages they were burning, where the survivors would be. Most would flee and take shelter elsewhere—he couldn't expect them to be trapped in cellars as he had been. By the time he could reach the coast and find the destroyed villages, the survivors would be long gone, scattered across the land.

Perhaps he could do *something* for them, though.

And most importantly, perhaps he could find a way to kill the dragons and stop the killing before it spread much further. The truce he had hoped for was out of the question now.

He rose from his chair, opened the shutters to let in the dim light of the overcast day, and poured the bloody water out the window; then he crossed to the door and left the private room.

A few minutes later he was in the street, calling "Thirif! Isein!" as he strode purposefully toward the caravan. The freed mine slaves who were still milling around the street—perhaps half the party that had accompanied him from the mine—stopped and stared at him as he passed; Arlian ignored them.

At the sound of his voice the Aritheians emerged from their wagons to stare at him, as well.

When all four of the magicians—Thirif, Shibiel, Isein, and Qulu—had gathered, he announced, "You have the amethysts and silver now. I have business elsewhere and cannot accompany you, but you must head for Arithei at all possible speed, and you must bring me back the two things I asked for—physicians who can keep a man alive with his blood drained away, and a way to drive a spear into a dragon's heart."

"We will try," Isein said.

"You *must* find them," Arlian said. "The weapon against the dragons most of all. And you must *hurry*. The dragons have come out of their caverns. Waste no time! Leave at once!"

"I . . ." Thirif began.

"*Go!*" Arlian shouted, turning away.

Half an hour later Arlian's caravan had been split in two. Six wagons were headed south, toward the Desolation, the Borderlands, and Arithei, under the command of Quickhand, since none of the Aritheians was qualified to lead. Two wagons, loaded with obsidian weapons, were bound north, toward Manfort, driven by Stabber and a man named Firiol.

Two of the freed miners had begged to ride with one group or the other, to get away from Deep Delving, but Arlian refused them; he did not trust them. After so long in the mines, they would need time before they were again able to function normally in the outside world.

Three of the men who had accompanied the wagons from Manfort did not accompany either party. Post, like the miners, had been sent to find his own way, while at Deep Delving's only livery stable Arlian stood impatiently aside and let Black negotiate for mounts.

"I keep mares for breeding stock," the proprietor explained, "not to sell. I sell mules."

"Can your mares be ridden?" Black asked.

"Oh, they're broken to the saddle, of course—they earn their keep between foals. But I don't want to sell them."

Arlian poured gold on a barrelhead; at the sound of rattling coins both Black and the stableman turned.

"How much?" Arlian asked. "You can buy more horses elsewhere with this."

"Ah . . ."

"Eight ducats," Black suggested.

"Oh, no, I couldn't possibly take less than fifty!"

Black could have driven a harder bargain had not Arlian been there, visibly impatient and willing to overspend; Black said as much as the pair rode northward under thick clouds and oppressive heat.

Arlian shrugged.

"And why is it so urgent that we return to Manfort?" he asked. "Why could we not ride the wagons?"

"Because *you* aren't going to Manfort," Arlian said. "You're turning east at the next crossroads, and heading for the coast to see what's happened there."

"Am I?"

"Well, I hope so," Arlian said. "It's your own choice, of course." He explained what the dragon had told him.

Black absorbed it; by the time Arlian had finished they had caught up with the two northbound wagons. Stabber waved at them as they passed; Black waved back, then said, "You're right, I'll turn east. And what about you?"

"I don't know," Arlian admitted. "I'll come with you, if you think it best, if you think two men would serve better than one at the job."

"If the job is merely to see what the dragons have done, I think one should be sufficient."

"You must also find as many of the new dragonhearts as you can, and bring them to Manfort."

"I can do that, as well."

"Then I'll return to Manfort and try to rally the Dragon Society to prepare to fight." He did not mention that most of the Society would almost certainly refuse.

"Then the dragons are now on their way to Manfort?" Black asked.

"Yes," Arlian said.

But then he remembered what he had actually been told. Yes, the dragons intended to restore their interrupted rule—but only when their depleted ranks had been restored.

In a thousand years.

"Eventually," he added.

Black cast him a sideways glance.

"Keeping secrets again?"

Arlian hesitated in replying, and Black waved the matter away. "You'll have to explain that when next I see you," he said.

Then he spurred his mount to a trot, and Arlian watched as he turned at the signpost ahead, bound for the coast.

38

A Place of Refuge

Arlian's entrance into Manfort, alone and on horseback, was hurried and without ceremony. He rode through the stony streets without stopping, weaving through the crowds of everyday pedestrians.

He did not think anyone would have set assassins in wait for him, but he kept moving and breathed a sigh of relief once he was inside the walls.

The people he passed seemed to stare at him a little more than usual, but Arlian assumed that this was merely because he was riding a single horse, without entourage. The great lords usually traveled on foot or in coaches.

He found his way to the Upper City, and made his way to the Old Palace without incident. It was odd to be returning there without Black there to see that everything was made ready, but the rest of the staff was still in place, and they were quick to take care of his mount and see that food and water were waiting by the time Arlian had changed out of his sweat-stained and dusty clothes.

The footman who admitted him had seemed startled to see him, but tried not to show it; Arlian attributed that to his unexpectedly quick return, without the wagons.

Venlin took over Arlian's care the moment he learned that his master had returned, appearing at his dressing room door while

Arlian was still stripping off his blouse, but Arlian thought there was something odd in his manner, as well. The possibility that something had gone wrong in his absence could not be ignored, but he put the thought aside until he was dressed and had made his way down to the small dining room.

When he had eaten enough to take the edge off his appetite and drunk enough to wet his throat properly, Arlian leaned back in his chair, trying to soothe the aches his ride had produced, and asked, "What troubles you, Venlin? Is everyone well?"

"I would ask you the same, my lord," Venlin said. "Is everything in order? You have returned without your steward, without any of the wagons with which you departed, riding an unfamiliar and wholly unsuitable mare—has there been some disaster?"

Arlian started to say no, then caught himself. The people of those seaside villages undoubtedly would say there had been a disaster, could any of them still speak.

"I am well enough," Arlian said. "The caravan is on its way to Arithei, save two wagons I have sent to Westguard, whence their contents will be properly disposed." He did not mention just what that contents might be; he trusted Venlin well enough, but the possibility that someone less reliable was eavesdropping could not be ignored. His encounter with Post had made him cautious. "I have sent Black on an errand to the east, and hope he will return here safely in a month or so."

"And all are safe?"

"So far as I am aware, they are," Arlian replied. "Why do you ask? While I can understand that my return may have come as a surprise, surely I have surprised you in the past without evoking such concern."

"There is word in the streets, my lord, that you are involved in treason and vile sorcery, and that your caravan was merely an excuse to flee the city. We have heard threats. Some have taken action to express their distaste for you—or at least, for what you are rumored to be."

"Action?" Arlian was puzzled. "What sort of action?"

"Stones have been flung at the gate and house, my lord. Stones and dung."

"Oh," Arlian said. He grimaced. "How very unpleasant. I hope no one has been injured?"

"No one, my lord. A window was broken, and has been repaired."

Arlian waved that away. "A window is nothing. I am pleased to hear that no one was hurt."

"I had feared, my lord, that *Black* had been hurt."

"No, he was in fine health when last I saw him, and I have no reason to believe that has changed. I simply asked him to make certain investigations for me. I'm sure that when he returns he will be gratified by your concern."

Venlin hesitated, then asked a further question—an action that astonished Arlian, as the old man had never before been so inquisitive. Venlin had always made plain that he thought a servant should be as unobtrusive as possible, and not trouble his employer with unnecessary comments or inquiries; this exchange was, Arlian realized, the longest conversation he and Venlin had ever had.

"May I ask the nature of those investigations, my lord? I believe the household would find your steward's presence reassuring; might his return be expedited?"

Arlian stared at his chief footman for a moment, then decided there was no point in hiding the truth.

"The dragons have come out of their caverns," Arlian said. "Sorcery told me this, and told me that they have destroyed a fishing village on the coast. I have sent Black to see if he can locate and aid any survivors."

"Survivors of a *dragon* attack, my lord?" There was pained disbelief in Venlin's tone.

Arlian sighed. "My sorcery indicates there is at least one," he said.

Venlin's expression was still troubled.

"My lord," he said, "one among the rumors in the streets is an accusation that you have somehow, presumably by sorcerous means, disturbed the dragons, and that they may emerge from their underground lairs. What you tell me is dismayingly similar to these tales, and will undoubtedly lead to further speculation and further hostility . . ."

"I'm afraid that one's true," Arlian interrupted, toying with his goblet. "I *did* disturb the dragons, albeit unintentionally."

Venlin swallowed, more ruffled than Arlian had ever before seen him. Arlian studied him silently for a moment, then added, "That's why I made those obsidian weapons. Because I knew I might have disturbed the dragons."

"My lord," Venlin said.

"It's taken them some time to emerge," Arlian said. "In all likelihood it will take them considerably more time to reach Manfort. I hurried home, though, in part because I feared they might be here soon, and I did not want to leave you to face them without me."

Venlin said nothing, but his stricken expression was not suppressed quickly enough—Arlian saw it clearly.

What could he say, though, to undo the harm his words had caused? All he could do was try to find something else to speak of.

"Are my guests well?" he asked. "Vanniari?"

"Oh, mother and babe continue to thrive, my lord; all your guests are well, though I believe the rumors and unrest have troubled them."

That was not the cheerful subject Arlian had hoped for. "And is there any word from Coin regarding the sale of the Grey House?"

"Ah, my lord, there have been messages sent, but Ferrezin has been responsible for that, and I have not inquired into the matter. Shall I summon Ferrezin, or Coin?"

Arlian waved wearily. "Let it wait until morning." He suddenly realized that he was exhausted—he was not much of a horseman, and the ride had been long and strenuous. "Let it *all* wait until morning." He set his goblet back on the table, then settled back in his chair and folded his hands upon his chest. He closed his eyes, just for a moment's rest.

He was only vaguely aware of Venlin helping him to bed, but once he realized where he was, he sighed gratefully and settled to sleep for the night.

In the morning Arlian looked in on Hasty and Vanniari, breakfasted with Lily and Brook, and made sure that Kitten, Cricket, Musk, and Stammer were all well and had no urgent news to relay. Lily complained of the hot, cloudy, rainless weather at length, but had nothing more to report; Hasty had numerous details of Vanniari's accomplishments; the others had only minor items of gossip.

No word of any draconic activity had reached Manfort as yet, and Stammer did not offer any detailed reports on just what new rumors were drifting through the city, though she acknowledged that Venlin's account had been accurate, so far as it went. Arlian did not press her on the matter, not yet, nor did he tell any of the women that the dragons were out of their subterranean refuge.

That done, he met with Ferrezin to discuss both the Grey House and methods for smuggling the obsidian weapons from Westguard back into Manfort—he was fairly certain that Ferrezin had had some experience of such things while in Enziet's employ, and Ferrezin did nothing to convince him otherwise.

Coin had indeed received offers for Enziet's home, but none that he and Ferrezin considered serious. Arlian accepted their counsel and sent a polite note to Coin to the effect that he was dismayed Coin had even bothered to inform him of such absurd offers; Coin could then show this letter, as if betraying a confidence, to the prospective buyers, who might be encouraged to reconsider and offer more.

That afternoon Arlian and Ferrezin set out for Westguard, to make preparations for the returning wagons. Halfway from the Old Palace to the city gate Arlian was startled by the thump of a rock striking the side of his coach. He looked out quickly, and saw a fist-sized paving stone tumbling down the steeply sloping street, but he could not see who had thrown it. After a quick look at the hostile faces of passing pedestrians he urged the coachman to move on.

That encounter dismayed him; clearly, the rumors of his alleged treason were having an effect on the people of Manfort. Later, when he disembarked in Westguard, he discovered that the stone had chipped the gilding on the door; it had clearly been flung with some force.

Events in Westguard proceeded as planned, however, and no one there seemed to notice him particularly; Stabber and Firiol arrived on schedule, and the process of smuggling the obsidian weapons back into the city piecemeal was begun.

That done, as Arlian rode back toward the Old Palace he could see little to do but wait—wait for the weapons to be back within the walls, wait for Black, wait for the Aritheians, and wait for the dragons. He did intend to arm those members of the Dragon Society who would stand against the dragons, but he was not ready to do that—not when word of the dragons' emergence had not yet reached the city, not when his obsidian weapons were still in Westguard.

He wished he could arm the Duke's guards, but the Duke would not have it—not unless Arlian could first show him a dead dragon.

The oppressive hot weather—dragon weather—continued unbroken, wearing on everyone's nerves. Several times over the course of the next few days Arlian drew blood and washed his hands, attempting to communicate with the dragons and learn more of their plans, but as the dragon had promised in Deep Delving, his attempts failed.

He could only wait.

39

A Visit from Lady Opal

The first interruption of Arlian's wait was unexpected. He had been in the garden, meditating by the graves beneath the ash tree where Sweet and Dove lay buried, when Venlin appeared.

Venlin never set foot in the garden without good reason; Arlian turned and asked, "What is it?"

"Lady Marasa, my lord."

Arlian blinked. "What of her?"

"She awaits your pleasure in the small salon."

"She's here? She came here?" Arlian stared at Venlin. What did Opal want here? She hated him, and had made no secret of it; there could be no pretense of a mere social call.

"Yes, my lord."

"You let her in?"

"Yes, my lord. Lady Marasa can be very forceful."

That was true, Arlian knew—she did not have the supernatural presence of a dragonheart, but she was not shy about asking for what she wanted. Arlian suspected that that was why Wither had liked her. "Did you leave her unattended?"

"No, my lord. Wolt is with her."

An unpleasant thought struck Arlian. "She didn't see Dovliril, did she?" That was the footman who had witnessed Lord Wither's death; he had left Opal's employ some time ago, and been hired by Arlian to help transfer goods from the Grey House to the Old Palace. Seeing him would not do anything to endear Arlian to Lady Opal.

"I do not believe so, my lord."

"See that she doesn't," Arlian said, as he brushed pollen from his breeches and strode toward the door.

A moment later he stepped into the small salon and bowed.

"Lady Opal," he said.

She was arrayed on one of the blue silk couches, the full skirt of her white dress tucked provocatively high on her hip, raising the hem to reveal a trim ankle. She leaned toward Arlian, displaying her low-cut bodice. Her black hair was elaborately coiffed, ringlets framing her face, and her eyes were dark with kohl.

"My lord," she said, her voice lower than Arlian had ever before heard it.

"Wolt," Arlian said, without taking his eyes off her, "thank you. You may go."

Wolt bowed, and vanished through the other door. Arlian heard the latch click behind him.

"My lord Obsidian," Opal said. "What a pleasure to see you!"

Arlian gazed silently at her for a moment, then said, "Must you be so blatant, my lady?"

She stared at him for a moment, then forced a laugh. "My informants have reported that you have not responded to less obvious overtures," she replied.

In the back of his mind Arlian wondered just who these informants might be, but he only said, "That would probably be because I do not care to respond, my lady, not because I was unaware of the possibilities."

Opal frowned slightly, an expression Arlian was sure was carefully cultivated to appear charming and girlish. "But I *know* you like women!" she said. The frown vanished, and she shrugged. "I suppose that your harem of half a dozen whores is enough for you."

Arlian had known for weeks that he and Opal were not friends, that they were on opposite sides of a dispute, but only now did he realize he actively disliked her on a personal level. "What brings you here, my lady?" he asked. "What is it you want from me?"

"Post told you," Opal said, straightening up. "And you knew, anyway. Poor Ilruth told you."

"And he agreed you should not have it," Arlian said. "He made certain you would not be present at his death to ensure you would not attempt to drink his blood to obtain it."

Opal feigned shock—or perhaps it was not entirely feigned. "Was *that* why? I would never have drunk his blood!" Her expression turned thoughtful. "Would that have worked?"

"Probably not," Arlian said, disgusted. "Certainly it would not have worked before he thrust the knife into his heart and killed the dragon that was growing there, but after the thrust, who knows?"

"I know his blood was poison when he was still alive," Opal agreed. "He told me about that stupid Vorina he killed that way. It hadn't occurred to me that his death might alter it." She eyed Arlian curiously.

"My blood would not suffice," Arlian said, "no matter when or how you took it—I have not been tainted long enough."

"There are others who have," she said.

"Possibly. Or possibly you would simply poison yourself. My lady, why do you not abandon this perverse quest of yours, and live out the life the gods have given you?"

"Because the gods were miserly about it, and the dragons can be far more generous!" she said. "It's easy enough for *you* to speak of how horrible it is, to be beholden to the dragons and to have one of their young spawning in your heart, but *you* face another thousand years of life, while *I* can expect perhaps half a century, much of it spent withered and gray."

"That's the natural lot of humanity, my lady."

"The natural lot of humanity—look about you, my lord. Is it natural to sit on silken cushions, beneath gilded fretwork? No, our natural lot is to huddle naked in caves, like the barbarians beyond the mountains. We have improved our surroundings in any number of ways; why should we not improve upon ourselves, as well?"

"Because in so doing, we unleash more dragons upon the future."

"Dragons can be killed, my lord, before they do any harm." She leaned eagerly over the arm of the couch toward him. "You showed us that yourself, with Stiam and Enziet!"

Arlian sighed.

"My lady," he said, "I have told you I will not help you. Why do you not accept my decision?"

"Because *you know where they are!*" she replied. "None of the others do. I've asked them—Lady Pulzera went through the Society's records for me, and swears she cannot find the location of a single one of their lairs, but Enziet *showed* you where one is!"

"You have spoken with Pulzera?"

"Of course," Opal said. "She said you suggested it; that was why I thought you might have relented of your cruelty, and could be cozened into helping me."

"I spoke only to discourage her from killing you, my lady," Arlian said.

"Well, thank you for that much, at any rate. But Obsidian, you could have much more than that! I will do *anything* for you, if you will but show me where that cave is. I will give you all Wither's estate; I will do your bidding in every way I can. I am still young, but Wither taught me things he had learned over the years—I can please you in ways that your whores cannot, I am sure of it! And I will help you to kill the dragons, if that's really what you want—Pulzera may try to stop us, but I will betray her to you, so you can kill her, if you like. *Anything*, my lord!" She stared up at him pleadingly.

Arlian stared back, appalled.

"Lord Wither was more of a fool than I thought, to tell you what he sought," he said.

"He didn't know what you did!" she said. "He was lonely, and he thought he was immortal—where's the folly in seeking a companion? I can be *your* companion, my lord—I can be your *slave*, if you wish!"

"I wish no such thing!" Arlian said, shaken. "I will not help you damn yourself, no matter how much you want it!"

"Damn me, please!" she said.

When he did not reply, and the horrified expression on his face lingered, she straightened up again.

"Obsidian," she said, "if you do not want anything I can give you, then perhaps you will be more interested in what I can withhold. You know there are rumors abroad about you."

"I have heard so," Arlian admitted warily.

"I have helped spread those, at Pulzera's bidding," Opal said. "She and Lord Hardior have been waging a campaign to disgrace you, to convince the Duke to have you put to death, or at least to drive you from the city, and I have been helping them in this. Pulzera promised to help me—but now she says she cannot find the dragons' lairs. She says that the dragons will come back soon, and when they do she will give herself into their service and coax from them the venom I crave, but can I believe her? What if the dragons refuse her service? So I would prefer to deal with *you*, my lord. I sent Post with you, to see whether you might lead him to the cave beneath the Desolation, but you and he came back without going farther than Deep Delving, and now you are warned, so I cannot hope to do better with another spy; I must have your willing aid. If you give it, then I will gladly betray Pulzera; my people will deny the rumors she spreads, contradict whatever she says. I could not seduce *you*, but perhaps I could seduce the Duke, and assure him of your loyalty, your courage, your importance to the city. I could counteract Hardior's lies. They call you a coward, and say you threw down your sword out of fear; I could tell him I know it was mercy. Please, my lord!"

Arlian began to pity her, but he still despised her, as well. This woman dared call his guests whores, yet spoke openly of giving herself to Arlian or the Duke to get the elixir she craved.

"No," he said.

"Please!"

"Lady Opal, you embarrass yourself," he said. "Please, go

home, reconsider your situation. You have a long life ahead of you without this corruption you seek."

"Not long enough!" she said. "Nowhere *near* long enough!"

"I will not help you."

She stared at him silently for a moment, then said, "I will not accept that as final. You may reconsider someday. Until you do, I will do what I can to help Pulzera and Hardior, and maybe someday they will find me the venom I need. If you change your mind, you know I will give you anything you ask for it—but only until the others find a source."

"I do not think I will change my mind," Arlian said.

"Then you're . . ." She caught herself. "You may," she said. "We will see."

"Indeed we will. Now, is there anything else, or shall I have Wolt see you to the door?"

"I'll go," she said, rising to her feet. Arlian opened the door for her.

As she stepped through she turned and spoke over her shoulder.

"I hope to hear from you soon, my lord."

"May you always have hope, my lady," he replied.

40

A Visit with Lady Rime

Opal's visit nagged at Arlian; he did not like the idea that she, Pulzera, and Hardior were conspiring against him. Pulzera and Hardior could not try to kill him, but there was no such restriction on Opal; Arlian knew that the only thing restraining her was the hope that he would one day change his mind and give her a drop of venom. As long as he was the only man in Manfort who knew where to find a dragon's lair, she would not seek his death—but if anyone else ever revealed such knowledge, or obtained dragon venom anywhere else, then Arlian suspected Opal would be quite happy to hire an assassin to dispose of the inconvenient Lord Obsidian.

And with no need to hurry, and Lord Hardior advising her, she would probably do a better job of it than Drisheen had.

He wished Black were back, so that he might have someone he could talk to freely, but there was no sign of his steward's imminent return.

To distract himself, and to learn a little of what current sentiment among the other dragonhearts might be, Arlian visited Lady Rime a few days after Opal's visit.

He had thought that perhaps he could speak openly with her, as he might with Black, but he found her oddly detached, not her usual frank and friendly self at all, and he held back, growing steadily more uneasy.

Finally, at supper, he asked her directly, "Have I offended you in some way, my lady? I had thought we were friends, but you have not spoken to me today as a friend."

She looked at him, then put down her fork and reached for the familiar legbone.

"Why are you back here?" she asked.

He blinked at her in surprise. "Where else should I be?" he replied.

"Arithei, perhaps. Or the Desolation. Or the caves beneath it. Or lurking in the streets, hoping to waylay Hardior or Belly. Or in the Citadel, seducing the Duke into aiding you in your schemes."

"I do not understand your point, my lady. Would you do me the favor of explaining this?"

She sighed. "Arlian," she said, "I thought you were sworn to vengeance, dedicated to destroying the dragons once and for all. You came back from disposing of Enziet and Drisheen and set about elaborate preparations, you slew the dragon Nail became and showed us all what fate awaits us, you not merely allowed that knowledge to destroy the Dragon Society but encouraged it, you witnessed Wither's suicide and dueled Toribor and went to speak to the Duke himself.

"And then you threw aside your preparations and fled the city, and I thought it was to further your vengeance, that you would be gone for months or years and return carrying a dragon's head, or at the head of an army, to proceed to the next step in your campaign.

"But instead you have returned alone, far too soon to have visited Arithei in pursuit of new magic, too soon to have reached the dragons' cave beneath the Desolation, too soon to have done anything of importance, and you have not spoken to the Duke, nor to the Society, though Opal visited you, and gossip would have it she wore her most attractive gown on that occasion. True, you sent her home soon enough, but you did nothing to stop her from spreading lies. Instead you come here and waste the day in polite small talk, telling me nothing of importance, saying not a word about revenge or dragons. I look at you from the corner of my eye, wondering whether you have decided that I should be the next dragonheart to die to prevent a dragon's birth, wondering whether I'm *ready* to die when I would otherwise face another five hundred years of life in my present form—and wondering whether something has happened to put out the fire in your heart and extinguish that flame of vengeance. Has the venom in your blood acted more swiftly than usual, to turn your heart cold? Or do you have some deep and subtle scheme in progress that you're hiding from me?"

"Ah," Arlian said. He sat back in his chair and considered her, then continued, "I have no intention of killing you any time soon, my lady; rest assured on that point. Nor have I abandoned my plans to destroy the dragons. I did not *flee* the city; I had matters to attend to in Deep Delving, and having dealt with them, I have returned to my home. I was not on my way to the caves beneath the Desolation. I had thought perhaps I might accompany my friends and employees to Arithei, but reconsidered. They are on their way now, and should return in the spring with magic I need for my planned revenge."

"You didn't go with them? You came back here?"

"That's right."

"Why?"

Arlian stared blankly at her for a second, at a loss for words.

"You sent Black and the Aritheians southward without you? Arlian, you have always, in the brief time I have known you, been one to attend to your own affairs, and not to leave them to others. Why did you not accompany the caravan to Arithei?"

"I didn't send Black south," Arlian said. "He's on another errand entirely."

"But you did not attend to that yourself, whatever it might be?"

"He thought he could do better without me," Arlian said. "And I thought I might be of more use here. I did not feel I could afford the time for the journey to Arithei."

"*What* use? Why couldn't you afford the time?"

Arlian hesitated, then said, "It has sometimes seemed to me, my lady, that since Enziet's death everything I have done in attempting to further my campaign against the dragons has made matters worse. It almost seems as if I would be best advised to simply do nothing—yet now, when it appears that I am doing just that, you take me to task."

"Of course I do! I want you to finish the job you started, and to clean up the mess you've made."

Arlian met her gaze. She was telling the truth, he was certain— she *did* want him to destroy the dragons, and wanted to know why he was doing nothing toward that end. She deserved the truth in return.

"The mess is worse than you know," he said. "The dragons are out of their caves."

Rime stared at him for a moment, then demanded, "What, *all* of them?"

"I don't know how many," he admitted. "Some of them, certainly."

"How do you know? Why haven't we heard anything?"

"I learned Enziet's sorcerous trick for talking to them, as you'll recall . . ."

"You told us," Rime interrupted. "Half the sorcerers in the Society have attempted it, but if any have succeeded, they have kept that success to themselves."

"Nonetheless, I have used it successfully twice—and attempted it unsuccessfully several times, as well. It works only when the dragons deign to allow it. I used it in Deep Delving, and one of the dragons spoke to me so that it might taunt me with their freedom. They are destroying villages on the coast, and deliberately attempting to leave envenomed survivors to replace the dragonhearts I've slain. The news has not yet reached Manfort—but I expect it will soon."

"And when it does, you want to be here?" Rime asked. "*Why?* If the dragons are raiding the coast, shouldn't you be *there*, in Lorigol or Sarkan-Mendoth, to meet them?"

"And what would I do, even with an obsidian spear?" Arlian

demanded. "One man against a dragon, in a burning city? But Manfort was built to be proof against dragonfire . . ."

"Seven hundred years ago," Rime interrupted. "How much of it cannot burn *now*? Look around you—are these walls stone?"

Her dining hall was paneled in rich dark wood, the ceiling crossed by carved and gilded wooden beams. Through the wood-mullioned windows lay a vista of fretwork and fruit trees—an ornate wooden promenade, and her lower garden beyond.

"Still," Arlian said, "there are the city walls and the Duke's guards . . ."

Rime snorted derisively.

"Better here than any other habitation," Arlian insisted. "And more importantly, Lady Rime, sooner or later I feel certain that the dragons will come here, while they may well pass Lorigol and Sarkan-Mendoth by. If I went to the coast, how could I find them? How could I fight them? They could flee into the air if I posed any threat, as if I were a dog set on pigeons. Here they may find themselves confined by the walls and towers, encircled by men with obsidian spears. Here, at least, there is a *chance* we might slay one or two of them!"

"Yet you sent *Black* to the coast . . ."

"To gather news, and to see to any survivors he might find, not to fight dragons."

Rime considered this carefully. Then she said, "You said encircled by men with spears—what men did you have in mind? The Duke's guards?"

"Actually, I had hoped to rally the Dragon Society to the cause—at least, those who have not given themselves over to Pulzera's theories or Hardior's stupidities. We have seen dragons before, and lived; none of the Duke's guards can claim as much." He did not mention that the Duke had said that he would not help until after a dragon had been slain.

"Ha!" Rime said.

"My lady?"

"Ari, most of the Dragon Society hates you." Despite her harsh words, Arlian was relieved to hear her use the familiar nickname for the first time that day. "Even Voriam has begun to doubt you. Pulzera and Opal and Hardior have spread their poison well, and you have played into their hands with your recent actions—meekly leaving the city with your weapons at the Duke's order, sneaking back in unattended . . ."

"*Sneaking*? I rode in openly!"

"Without entourage."

"I need no entourage!"

She shrugged. "You let Belly live."

"Lord Toribor has surprised me with his courage and honor," Arlian protested. "And in truth, he let *me* live."

"You had sworn to kill him. We thought you meant to kill the entire Society, or die in the attempt."

"I am seeking alternatives; would you prefer I kill you here and now?"

"No. Although I will not yield to the dragons or Pulzera's treason, I yet want to live—as, I think, we all do."

"It is the dragons who are my enemies, my lady," Arlian said. "I have no ill intent toward the Society, save to make certain that no dragons are born therefrom."

"And how can you do that? And what of the survivors you say Black seeks? If they exist, you may no longer be the youngest dragonheart in the Lands of Man—what will that do to your plans?"

"I don't know," Arlian said. "I am still awaiting developments."

"That hardly seems your style."

"Matters are in motion, my lady, and I must see where that motion leads before I act further."

"I hope you have the chance," Rime said. "You do have human enemies, you know."

"And I will cope with them as the need arises." Arlian lifted his cup. "I thank you for your explanation, my lady, and I hope we are friends once more."

"So do I," Rime said, putting down the bone and picking up her fork. "So do I."

41

On the Nature of Slavery

Three days after Arlian's supper with Rime word reached Manfort of the destruction of a fishing village a few leagues south of Benthin, a place known as Kirial's Rocks. Witnesses—and to everyone's surprise, there *were* living witnesses, from surrounding cottages—reported that three dragons had dropped down out of the clouds and swept the town's fishing fleet from the seas with their flaming venom, then set the docks and houses ablaze.

Two fishermen, father and son, had been washed ashore on the rocks, badly burned but alive.

That was the full extent of the actual news, but rumors were rife, as Arlian heard from Stammer. Some of the rumors accused him of complicity in the dragons' reappearance, though the exact connection seemed vague.

Vague or not, it was presumably the impetus for a fresh round of rock-throwing and vandalism; two more windows were broken, and the glyph of a sorcerous curse was painted on one gatepost in what appeared to be blood. Arlian decided that venturing out or inviting guests would be unwise, and stayed indoors, going over the household accounts and otherwise taking care of his everyday business. Roughly two-thirds of the weapons had been smuggled in from Westguard; he considered sending word to delay transferring the rest, but decided to leave it up to Stabber's judgment.

That day's delivery was late, but arrived safely.

The following morning word arrived of the destruction of Tiapol.

Tiapol was a larger town, midway between Kirial's Rocks and Benthin, but the dragons destroyed it as thoroughly as any lesser community—and again, they left witnesses alive in the surrounding countryside, and allowed the survivors of shattered boats to swim safely to shore.

The stones were more numerous than ever; Arlian ordered the shutters kept closed so that any further breakage would not spread glass inside. He wondered whether Opal and Pulzera were openly provoking these attacks, or whether the stone throwers were acting spontaneously.

He thought he glimpsed Horn in the crowd, but the man disappeared before Arlian could confirm his identity.

Arlian heard further ghastly details of Tiapol's destruction from Stammer just before taking his midday meal, which left him in a somber mood. He had just finished eating when Wolt brought him a note. Curious, Arlian opened it at the table.

The vellum was adorned with Lord Toribor's crest and read, "I will wait on you at your home this afternoon. I believe there are matters we must discuss."

Arlian hurried to his study and wrote a hasty response, which read, "I regret that I cannot guarantee your safety, but you will be quite welcome should you come. If you choose not to I will think none the worse of you, and hope that further arrangements can be made." He sent Wolt out the postern with that message.

There was no reply, but around midafternoon Toribor's coach rolled up to the gate.

Arlian met him in the gallery, which had the advantage of facing the garden, rather than the forecourt or street, so that they would not be interrupted by further breakage. Neither man offered to shake hands, but they greeted one another civilly, and walked side by side as they spoke.

"While I wish it were otherwise," Arlian said, "I believe you must find it uncomfortable to be here, so let us dispense with pleasantries and proceed directly to these matters you felt we must discuss. What are they?"

Toribor seemed relieved by this direct approach. "I assume you are aware of the destruction of Kirial's Rocks and Tiapol," he said.

"Of course."

"Do you have any knowledge of these attacks beyond what has been widely reported? You have the closest ties to the dragons of any of us—do you know anything more than we?"

Arlian frowned. "I know no more details of the attacks themselves than do you," he said, "but I have known for some time that at least some of the dragons had emerged from their long retreat."

Toribor frowned angrily. "And *how* did you know this, my lord?"

Arlian sighed. "A few weeks ago I was in Deep Delving on business, and was troubled by the weather—it was then, as it still is now, what my grandfather called 'dragon weather.' I remembered that the last time I saw such weather, the dragons came, destroyed my home, and slaughtered my family. I feared that they might arise again, and so I attempted to contact them with the bowl of blood and water."

"We have all tried that," Toribor said. "It doesn't work."

Arlian smiled crookedly. "I know," he said. "Or rather, I know that whether it works or not is entirely at the dragons' discretion, rather than our own. I have tried and failed repeatedly since then, but there in Deep Delving it amused the dragons to reply. Their spokesman told me that yes, they had come out of their caves and destroyed a fishing village, and would destroy more; their bargain with Enziet is ended, and they intend to make up for all the dragonhearts that he and I slew, killing hundreds of innocents in order to contaminate a handful of others with their foul venom."

"Then they let those fishermen live deliberately?"

"So it would seem."

"They burned two towns; will they burn more?"

"They did not say so explicitly, but I assume so."

Toribor stared at him for a long moment, then said, "And this is what comes of your mad vengeance."

Arlian stared back. "It might be. Believe me, I regret the deaths of those villagers profoundly."

"And all for the sake of a few slaves!"

Arlian did not reply immediately, but they came to the end of the gallery, and rather than turn around he beckoned. "Come this way, my lord." He led the way into an adjoining passage, and thence to the sitting room, where some of his guests were passing the time.

On the way, he said, "I was one of those slaves, my lord."

"A mistake, I grant you," Toribor said. "You are clearly no born slave. Enziet should not have taken a freeborn youth and sold him. But that had nothing to do with Drisheen, who might have been Enziet's heir and kept his secrets better than you have, nor with Iron, nor Nail, nor Kuruvan."

"No?" They stepped into the sitting room; the women looked up, startled. Brook was seated by the window, where she had been staring out at the gloomy sky; Hasty and Cricket were on the floor, playing with Vanniari. Hasty seemed undisturbed by Toribor's presence, but Brook's expression went blank, and Cricket's smile turned to a hostile frown.

"You recognize these women, my lord?" Arlian asked.

"Two of them," Toribor said. "I owned them for two years, after all. The third I assume was another resident of the House of Carnal Society, though I can't place her."

"And do you think they were born slaves?"

Startled, Toribor looked at Arlian. "Weren't they?"

"Did you never think to ask, in the two years you held them?"

Toribor blinked. "No," he admitted. "It never occurred to me. Enziet and Drisheen supplied the women for the House, and I had assumed the women had been born to their role."

"Let us start with the stranger, Hasty," Arlian said. "Who, I might add, was held and impregnated by the late Lord Kuruvan. Hasty, were you born a slave?"

"No, of course not, Triv," Hasty said. "You know that. My family died of plague when I was nine, and slavers caught me."

"Unfortunate . . ." Toribor began, but Arlian cut him off.

"Cricket?"

Cricket looked from one man to the other, then said, "My father died when I was ten—his heart gave out. My mother tried to go on, but there were too many mouths to feed—I had three brothers and a sister—so she sold me for food when I was eleven. She picked me first because I brought the best price; I was older and prettier than my sister, and more obedient than my brothers. She had to sell my sister later, though. I think she and my brothers stayed free."

Toribor stared at her in surprise.

"I was fourteen," Brook said from the window, without prompting. "I was madly in love with a boy named Sarcheyon, who was a few years older. I wanted to marry him, but my father wouldn't hear of it, so we ran off together. Sarcheyon had always talked of running away to sea, so to fool everyone we headed inland instead."

"Inland?" Toribor asked, startled.

"I'm from Siribel, my lord, a league north of Sarkan-Mendoth."

"You didn't even know that?" Arlian asked.

Toribor shook his head. "I thought they were all from Manfort," he said. "Slaves born and bred."

"Raising slaves is too expensive, my lord," Brook said. "Hardly anyone takes the trouble. There are always enough unfortunates to prey on."

Toribor stared silently at her, and after a pause she continued, "We made it as far as Gan Pethrin before our food and money ran out, and we stayed there for a time, begging and working at whatever jobs we could find, and I thought it was a marvelous adventure, because I was young and with the man I loved. My father was right about Sarcheyon, though; he grew tired of me, and hungry, and about four months after we ran away he sold me to a slave trader. He told the trader he was heading for Coldstream, but I don't know whether that was the truth or another lie."

Toribor stared at her, then asked, "Why haven't you gone home to Siribel?"

Brook stared back.

"Why should I?" she said. "They didn't come after me. We were in Gan Pethrin for months, and they never sent an inquiry. And what would I do there?" She gestured at the stumps of her ankles. "You and the others made certain I could never be an ordinary man's wife, nor a fit mother for active children, and the only special skills I learned in my youth are of no use outside a brothel. Here I have friends, and Triv's staff to care for me when I cannot care for myself."

"I don't know where my mother and brothers are," Cricket volunteered. "They didn't stay in Lassir."

"Triv and Vanni are all the family I have," Hasty said, reaching out to tickle the baby, who gurgled appreciatively.

Arlian smiled, and put a hand on Toribor's arm to turn him and guide him away. When they were in the passageway, walking toward the gallery, Arlian said, "You see, my lord, I think of them as *people*, not slaves—perhaps because, as you say, I was one of them. As people, I think they deserve vengeance for the wrongs inflicted upon them."

"Perhaps they do," Toribor replied. "I'll leave that to the gods to decide, if any gods survive. Whether they deserve it or not, Obsidian, your vengeance has unleashed the dragons upon us all."

"Perhaps it has," Arlian said, "but perhaps that would have happened anyway. You surely know that Enziet did not have long to live, in any case, and who would have taken up his bargain? Might we not be facing just the same fate we do now?"

"Not quite," Toribor said. "Drisheen might have been Enziet's heir. And the Dragon Society would be united in opposing the monsters, instead of fractured as it is."

"Would it? And would that matter?"

"Oh, I don't know," he said unhappily. "Damn you, Obsidian!"

They emerged into the gallery and continued walking.

"My lord," Arlian said, "you think me the cause of all your miseries, but it may be that Fate sent me to end them, not to cause them. You would prefer to see the dragons destroyed, would you not?"

"Of course I would! I'm no traitor like Pulzera."

"And is anyone but me working toward that goal?"

"We're trying, blast it, but what can we do? Voriam and his little group expect you to appear in a blaze of glory and lead them to victory, and most of the others have been swayed by Pulzera, to one degree or another. She and Hardior and that odious Lady Opal have all been exchanging schemes not to defeat the dragons, not to destroy or confine them, but only to ensure that they do not attack Manfort itself. They would sacrifice all the Lands of Man to protect themselves—and Opal would give her entire fortune for a few drops of venom; she's been flattering and cajoling Pulzera and Hardior in hopes of learning from them just how she might obtain some." He snorted. "At least, that's what she does when they allow it. When they can stomach no more of her, she devotes her time to spreading lies about you."

"Does she?" Arlian found this oddly amusing.

"Lies and truth, mixed together," Toribor said. "She knows altogether too many of the Society's secrets, and I'm not sure how much she learned from Wither and how much from Pulzera." He glanced sideways at Arlian. "She says you've turned your coat, and intend to rule Manfort as the dragons' viceroy. At least, so she says when she isn't saying you've sunk into utter despair and abandoned yourself to debauchery, here with your six whores."

Arlian frowned. "They are no longer whores, and I do not trouble them."

"You know, Obsidian, I believe you." He glanced back at the passage toward the sitting room.

They walked in silence for a moment. Then Arlian said, "Belly, I wish I could tell you that there is a way to drive the dragons back into their caves, and save us all from their flame, but I can't. I know very little more than you about what to expect. I do have plans—I have hopes for a magical solution to at least some of our problems, and I do have weapons that can, in theory, slay dragons. If the dragons do come to Manfort, come to me and I will give you a spear, so at least you can die fighting them."

"That would be something, at any rate," Toribor replied. He glanced at Arlian again. "You say you have plans?"

"Hopes, really. I have asked the Aritheians to see what they can provide to help us. After all, the dragons have never dared cross the Dreaming Mountains; perhaps something can be found there to defeat them."

"Perhaps." Toribor considered that, then said, "You know, Obsidian, I'm glad now that I didn't kill you. As you say, the dragons would be free anyway."

The corner of Arlian's mouth quirked upward.

"I'm pleased you let me live, as well. And furthermore, I'm pleased I let *you* live, in Cork Tree last year."

"It would seem we've found grounds for agreement after all."

And on that note, Toribor took his leave.

42

The Long End of Summer

Stones and mud and dung were flung at the Old Palace with depressing regularity for the next few days, breaking several more windows, but the assaults began to taper off eventually.

Then word came of the destruction of Cork Tree, and the barrage was renewed, heavier than ever.

On the second day of this assault Arlian sat in the small salon, staring at the shuttered window and listening to the shouted insults beyond the broken glass. He had glimpsed outside earlier, and seen the angry faces of the mob, and wondered who these people were, and why they had the time and energy and anger to come and harass him. He thought he might have seen faces he recognized in the crowd—Post and Horn.

He was not certain of it, however, and he retreated back out of sight before his appearance could provoke a new barrage.

He wondered whether the dragons had chosen Cork Tree deliberately, to taunt him—or to intercept the caravan to Arithei. Did they know what the magicians were after? Had they read the information from his thoughts? Had someone who knew of Arlian's plans somehow sent them a message?

He could not think who might have done so; he had not spoken freely of his intentions. Some of the servants might know, but he knew how rarely the lords and ladies of the Dragon Society listened to their household employees.

He had told Toribor that the caravan sought dragon-fighting magic—had Belly told the wrong person, perhaps?

It was possible. Anything was possible. He would probably never know whether Cork Tree had been deliberately targeted with the caravan in mind.

He would know, sooner or later, whether the caravan had survived, though.

Just then someone knocked on the door of the salon. "Come in," he called.

The door opened and Black stepped in.

Arlian leapt up from his chair, his despondency vanished, a grin stretching from ear to ear. "Beron!" he said. "You've returned safely!"

"Ari," Black acknowledged, somewhat less enthusiastically. "Yes, I'm home."

Arlian embraced him, then stepped back, studying his face. Black's expression was weary and somber, his beard untrimmed, a few strands of hair escaping the tight knot at the back of his neck.

"Was it very bad?" Arlian asked.

"Bad enough," Black replied. "And my homecoming hasn't been what I might have hoped for."

Arlian glanced at the shutters, just as a heavy object thumped against them—mud, by the sound of it, rather than a stone.

"They blame me for the dragons' depredations," Arlian said. "Lady Pulzera and Lady Opal and Lord Hardior have been spreading lies."

"Hm," Black said noncommittally.

"Did any of them trouble you?" Arlian asked, concerned.

"I came in the postern, and they took me for a servant," Black explained. "No one troubles servants over such matters—except, of course, that someone has to repair the damage and clean off the stains, and it's not the lord and master who dirties his hands."

"I'm sorry I couldn't give you a better welcome," Arlian said.

"Have you eaten? Have you had anything to drink?" He reached for the doorknob.

"I had a bite when I came in," Black said. "And I left my charges in the kitchens, eating."

"Survivors? The two fishermen?" Arlian opened the door wide, and the two men left the salon and turned their steps toward the kitchens.

"*Five* fisherfolk," Black said. "Two from Kirial's Rocks and three from Tiapol."

"And are they . . ."

"Dragonhearts?" Black said. "Three of the five, I believe." He glanced sideways at Arlian. "Do you intend to kill them? I could have done that easily, if that's what you had in mind."

Arlian shook his head. "No," he said. "Primarily, I want to know who and where they are. I want to talk to them, help them find new lives—and let them know what awaits them. Perhaps eventually it will become necessary to kill them, but I am in no hurry to put more innocent blood on my hands, and I can still hope to find some alternative in the coming centuries."

"Centuries," Black said, a trace of bitterness in his voice.

Arlian thought better of replying, and the two men said no more before reaching the kitchens.

There Black introduced Lord Obsidian to his new guests— Splash and his father, Rope, of Kirial's Rocks, and from Tiapol a man called Shell-Edge, his wife, Demdva, and her brother Dinan. All were tired and dirty, wearing clothes little better than rags; they had lost most of their possessions when their homes were destroyed, and Arlian had not thought to provide Black with sufficient funds to compensate for that.

Rope, Demdva, and Dinan believed they had swallowed blood and venom in the chaos of sinking, burning boats; Splash and Shell-Edge had not. That certain something, that forcefulness that was the heart of the dragon, was not really discernable yet in any of them, but after all, they had only drunk the elixir a few weeks ago, Arlian thought, and it took time for the contagion to do its work.

Demdva had lost her right hand, trapped and crushed in twisting debris as her family's boat came apart around her, smashed beneath a dragon's claws—but the stump had healed quickly, without infection. That loss had provided the blood necessary for the elixir, spurting on herself and her brother; Shell-Edge had been at the far end of the boat, trying to keep the little craft steady, and he was still whole. Demdva and Dinan both bore half-healed venom burns on their faces and arms—burns that Arlian knew would never heal completely, any more than would the scar on his own cheek.

Splash had lost the skin of one hand when a rope tore from his grasp, an injury that might well have healed cleanly if not for the venom that later fell in the torn flesh. His father had already fallen overboard by then, clear of the fray, and it was when Splash followed and put an arm around Rope's neck to help him to shore that the older man swallowed the blood and venom from his son's wound.

"I told them you would pay well for their story," Black said.

"As I shall," Arlian promptly agreed. "Enough to make a fresh start, in Manfort or on the coast, as they choose."

His guests were visibly relieved by these words, and Demdva, emboldened, asked, "My lord, why were those people outside shouting and throwing things?" She spoke with a broad accent Arlian did not recall hearing before.

"They believe I am responsible for the dragons' attacks," Arlian explained.

The five exchanged glances, and Rope asked, "Are you?"

"I don't *think* so," Arlian said. "And if I did in some measure contribute inadvertently, still, is it not the dragons themselves that deserve whatever blame there may be? They chose to destroy your homes; I certainly did not desire anything of the sort."

"Are we safe here?" Shell-Edge asked. "What if that mob outside sets this place aflame?"

Arlian started to say that Manfort had been built to withstand flame, but then he remembered what Rime had said, and looked around at the room in which they sat.

The great hearth and ovens were of stone, with black iron fittings, but the doors and doorposts were of wood, and elsewhere much of the Old Palace and its furnishings were wood and plaster and cloth.

"If it worries you," he said, "I have another house you can use, a stone one."

"The Grey House still hasn't sold?" Black asked.

Arlian gestured at the window. "I suspect the potential buyers are hoping to acquire it more cheaply at an estate auction. I hope to disappoint them." He turned back to his guests. "In the meantime, though, surely you can risk one night here, to tell me of your adventures?"

They agreed to one night, and Arlian listened intently to everything they could remember of the dragons' actions. He took careful note of how low the dragons flew when attacking, how they sometimes landed and approached on foot to strike more easily at walls and doors, rather than rooftops—that would clearly be the time to strike at them, as they strode toward their targets.

He said as much to Black, after their guests had retired for the night. "That's the sort of thing I wanted to know when I sent you east."

"Killing a dragon with a spear still does not strike me as an easy task," Black remarked. "It requires getting much too close for comfort."

"Well, unless the Aritheians find some suitable magic, I can't very well hope to kill them from a distance," Arlian said. "An arrow, even one with an obsidian head, would never reach a dragon's heart."

"Not unless it was a very big arrow," Black said, smiling wryly.

Arlian laughed, but then stopped.

A very big arrow, as big as a spear, or even larger . . . why not? An ordinary archer could never loose an arrow long enough to pierce a dragon to the heart, but perhaps something could be constructed. An ordinary man could never lift a bucket the size of the ore hopper in the mine, but with pulleys and ropes and mules that hopper was lifted twice every day—or at least, it had been until he freed the slaves who filled it.

Aiming such a giant arrow-throwing device would be difficult, of course, and it wouldn't be something he could take with him into the dragon's caves, but still . . .

He found himself wondering why he had not thought of this sooner.

In the morning Arlian escorted the fisherfolk to the Grey House and saw them settled comfortably into their new residence. He arranged for some of Enziet's furnishings to be returned to their former places, and took the opportunity to talk with Ferrezin about various matters, as well.

It was late evening when he finally returned to the Old Palace to find that the front gate had been smashed down. The crowd that had haunted the street for weeks was gone, the entire vicinity apparently deserted.

Horrified, he ran to the door and knocked loudly. When the door did not open at once he feared the worst, but after a moment Venlin admitted him, his face ashen—and a spear in his hand, the long obsidian head gleaming in the lamplight. The shutters had hidden the light, so that Arlian had not seen it before the door opened.

He had also not seen that the door's lock was broken, the door and frame splintered several places; to open it Venlin had had to remove a hastily erected barricade.

"My lord," the footman said. "Are you all right?"

"I'm fine," Arlian said. "What happened?"

"Word of another village destroyed," Venlin said. "The mob went mad when they heard, and broke through the gates and stormed the house. I had feared the worst and armed the staff, so that when they broke in the door we were ready. They might have fought us, even so, but we told them you were not at home, and they turned aside."

"Where did they go?" Arlian asked. "They didn't come to the Grey House."

"No," Venlin said. "But I'm afraid they found the garden. I'm surprised they didn't break in the windows there—we couldn't have held them all off if they had."

"The garden?" Arlian turned his steps toward the gallery.

A few moments later he made his way carefully through the wreckage, Venlin at his side with the lamp held high.

The mob had torn up the vines, trampled the herb garden into the dirt, and snapped the branches of a dozen carefully cultivated trees. Flowers had been ripped apart and scattered everywhere. The paths were strewn with debris.

Arlian looked around in silent astonishment. Why would anyone have done this?

"Was anyone hurt?" he asked.

"I don't think so," Venlin said.

Just then Arlian came to the gravesite, where Sweet and Dove had been buried side by side, their graves marked by white stones at the corners. Arlian had never known their true names, so the stones were blank save for one that bore Sweet's epitaph, "She was loved."

That stone was gone, and a hole had been dug in the center of Sweet's grave, a hole a foot or so deep and two feet across. Clearly, the marauders had deliberately defiled the site.

The hole was not empty, and the image of someone squatting there on Sweet's grave, breeches pulled down, laughing, came unbidden into Arlian's mind. He stared down at the foul mess and said, "I'm sorry, Sweet."

Then he could no longer speak, and he turned away.

The bright side to the whole affair—though it was no brighter than the overcast skies of the hideously prolonged dragon weather—was that the mob had apparently spent its wrath, and no more stones were thrown, no more attacks made, for the next few weeks.

During this period of peace Arlian had the damage to the Old Palace repaired, and also began preparing plans and conducting experiments in his pursuit of a device that could fling a spear into a dragon's heart.

And during that time the long drought finally broke—cold rain drenched the streets and buildings of Manfort, washing away the traces of mud that had not already been cleaned from the walls and paths. The summer, the dragon weather, and the dragons' attacks were all at an end for the year.

All in all, the dragons had destroyed five towns—Kirial's Rocks, Tiapol, Cork Tree, Shardin, and Blackwater. Almost a thousand innocents had perished.

It all appeared to be done, though, and Arlian thought the winter would be a time of healing, a time when he might reconcile Manfort to his presence, when the city's people might realize that he was not responsible for what the dragons did.

Then he made the mistake of not merely replacing a broken window, but leaving the shutters open, and again a stone flew.

As he and Black inspected the damage, feeling the cool autumn breeze blowing through the broken glass, Arlian said, "I wish there were a single foe I could strike down, rather than this great nameless mob."

"There are names," Black said.

"Oh, of course there are," Arlian said, "but I can no longer be certain which name belongs on which side. Consider Lord Toribor, whom I swore to kill—he and I are now in agreement on everything of any importance. And Lord Hardior, whom I once thought my best ally against the dragons, conspires to see me discredited or dead. I don't know who my enemies are."

"Well, those fools throwing stones are clearly not your friends. Lady Opal incites them; you could deal with *her*."

"And that would give Lord Hardior an excuse to send the Duke's guards to fetch me to trial," Arlian said. "And Lady Pulzera would use it as proof of my perfidy. If I strike at one human enemy, it will only strengthen the others. I need to destroy the roots from which this tree grows."

"And what roots are those?"

"The dragons, of course. I need to kill the dragons. If I could kill even *one*, it would prove me to most of the city."

Black stared at him silently for a moment, then turned away without another word.

43

The Aritheians Return

The winter was cold and hard. Stores were low because of the extended drought. No one was inclined to wander the streets unnecessarily.

This undoubtedly saved the Old Palace from further indignities.

The fisherfolk lived in the Grey House, but were not happy; the city was strange to them, a harsh and alien environment where they never felt welcome, despite Arlian's best efforts. The first snow had not yet fallen when Arlian reluctantly agreed to send them back to the coast and buy them two fine new fishing boats in exchange for their promise to remain always where he could find them.

Snow had not fallen, but the weather was unsettled, and the journey east a long one. It was decided that they should wait until spring before departing.

While they waited Arlian found work for them, using their knowledge of nets and rigging and boatbuilding to help guide the construction of his experimental weapons, the spear-throwing devices he hoped to turn against the dragons.

He let them know that their experience with the dragons might have changed them forever, but he did not call them dragonhearts, nor did he tell them that the Dragon Society existed, or that they might be eligible to join such an organization.

For his own part, Arlian discovered, well after the Society's decision had been made, that he was no longer welcome in the Dragon Society's hall; when he did finally venture thither he was turned away by Lord Door.

"The rules have changed," Door said. "You have no place here, by command of Lord Shatter."

Startled, he spoke to Rime and Toribor—and found that they, too, had been shut out. The Dragon Society no longer welcomed every dragonheart.

This seemed a fundamental change in the Society's very reason for existence. Curious, Arlian attempted to contact Lord Voriam, to learn whether he, too, had been banned, and instead learned, some four days after the fact, that Lord Voriam had hanged himself.

The Dragon Society, it appeared, had re-formed itself around the leadership of Shatter, Hardior, and Pulzera.

Re-formed itself to what purpose, Arlian was not sure—but he feared it was to serve the dragons, rather than oppose them.

He still had a few friends among the dragonhearts—Rime and Toribor, and oddly, Spider and Shard; he had scarcely known Spider and Shard before the breaking of the Society, but now he encountered them every so often in the streets, or when visiting Rime, and spoke warmly with them.

By the time the weather began to warm again, and the snow on the palace roof began to melt, Arlian realized that this new friendship was because the five of them were the only dragonhearts still excluded from the Society. Voriam's death had destroyed the little faction that had believed Arlian was fated to lead them in defeating the dragons, and the survivors had fled back to the larger group. Toribor's party, which continued to oppose any peace with the dragons but held no special place for Arlian, had dwindled down to just three members: Spider, Shard, and Toribor.

All the others, some thirty-two dragonhearts, had eventually acquiesced to Pulzera's arguments that their own survival meant siding with the dragons in the current conflict.

Arlian was disgusted, but he took little time to concern himself with the matter; he was instead spending as much time as he could spare from the everyday matters of household and business to work on his machines.

Since the scale of these devices made it impossible to keep his activities hidden, Arlian was careful never to use any obsidian in any of his tests; the obsidian weapons stayed safely out of sight, and his various machines were all tested with simple wooden poles. The Duke had never forbidden him the making of weapons, after all—only *obsidian* weapons. If His Grace had any objection to these new devices, Arlian was sure he would hear of it soon enough, and until he *did* hear, he intended to continue his experimentation.

The most promising approach seemed to be to use massive counterweights to swing a long wooden arm, which would then slam against a padded crossbar, releasing a spear—or several spears, as Rope pointed out that fishermen often used more than one line when trawling, and Black pointed out that the vagaries of aiming arrows over a distance were traditionally compensated by using a volley, rather than a single shaft—from the arm's outer end. Such a mechanism could fling half a dozen eight-foot spears for several hundred yards with very satisfactory force.

Unfortunately, the first working model was huge, towering some three stories high. Arlian could not see any practical way to transport it swiftly from one place to another to meet an attacking dragon. He had it mounted on wheels, but it would require a large team of oxen to move it from Manfort to whatever town might be threatened, and the journey would take several days.

Even if the dragons came to Manfort, they would need to come to a small area in the Upper City for the weapon to be effective, and Arlian could not see any way to arrange that. Dragons were not stupid.

He had once assumed they were, when he had plotted to hunt them down in their caverns and kill them as they slept, but now he knew better. They were not human, and did not think like men; but they were not mere beasts, and they were not stupid. Luring them into range would not be easy.

He contemplated schemes for mounting a dozen of the devices on the city walls, with guardsmen trained to use them—but that would require the Duke's active cooperation, and His Grace was still listening to Hardior's advice. Quiet inquiries had determined that the Duke was not interested in granting Arlian another audience; the Duke's position was not entirely immune to popular sentiment, and the mob's opinion of Arlian was plain enough.

Indirect replies from the Citadel said that the Duke felt nothing of importance had changed. Arlian interpreted that to mean that the Duke would aid him in killing dragons only when Arlian had demonstrated that it was *possible* to kill a full-grown dragon.

When he thought about it, Arlian was somewhat startled that Hardior and the Duke had not interfered with his experiments; surely, Hardior must realize that these machines were intended to kill dragons, and Hardior would surely consider their construction a further provocation, something that would stir the dragons anew. Convincing the Duke that these huge weapons could be used against the Citadel should have been easy.

At supper that night Arlian asked Stammer, who was his conduit for news from the Citadel staff, what she had heard about the matter.

"Th . . . they think you're . . . you're mad," she said. "Lord Har . . . Hardior wanted to smash them, said they were dangerous, but the D . . . D . . . *Duke* says he thinks they're harmless and . . . and funny. And everyone else thinks so, too."

"I see," Arlian said.

"Except the Duke said one mo . . . mo . . . more thing, my lord," Stammer said. "He said that if they ever *did* work, they might be useful. After what the dragons did last summer, he would be ha . . . happy to have a weapon to use against dragons, and he wouldn't let Hardior smash *any* chance, no matter how mad it seemed."

That, Arlian thought, was interesting; perhaps the Duke was

neither as stupid nor as completely in Hardior's sway as Arlian had thought.

If he could somehow kill a single dragon, that might well pry the Duke free of Hardior entirely.

"Thank you," he said. He ate the rest of the meal in contemplative silence.

The winter dragged on, but at last the snow melted away and the breezes began to blow warm. Arlian began to hope for word from the south—from Arithei.

Even when the weather turned from warm to hot the days remained sunny and bright, not dragon weather, which he took as a good sign. Perhaps the dragons had exhausted themselves during the previous summer.

When it was clear that winter was truly gone for good, he reluctantly sent the fisherfolk home to the coast—though obviously not to their now-vanished villages of Tiapol and Kirial's Rocks—with money for two new boats. They seemed very glad to go.

That left the Grey House empty again, and Arlian reminded Coin that it was still for sale.

The days and weeks passed, and it was late spring, almost a new summer, when the caravan finally rolled into Manfort. The news ran well ahead of the wagons, and Arlian's coach hurried down through the streets at word of their approach. He met them scarcely a hundred yards inside the gates.

Only five of the six wagons had returned, he saw, all of them somewhat the worse for wear, but Quickhand was smiling from the driver's seat of the lead vehicle, and Arlian could see Isein and Qulu aboard the next two. Arlian called to Quickhand, "What word?"

"It went well, my lord," Quickhand replied. "For the most part, at any rate."

Arlian grinned.

At last the magicians had returned, and they had, he hoped, brought magic he could use to replace the tainted blood of a dragonheart, and magic that would help him drive a spear into a true dragon's heart.

He might yet prove himself to the Duke and the city.

"I'll meet you at the Old Palace," he called, as he climbed back into the coach and signaled the driver.

He allowed them time to eat and drink, and to bathe and dress in clean attire, so it was not until mid-evening that Arlian finally found himself face-to-face with Isein, Qulu, and Quickhand in the small salon.

"What became of the other wagon?" Arlian asked. "Did you leave it in Arithei?"

"A wheel broke in the Desolation," Quickhand explained. "We loaded what we could into the other wagons and abandoned it."

"You had no spare wheels?"

"An unfortunate oversight, my lord. I am a driver and guard by profession, not a caravan master . . ."

"Of course," Arlian said hastily. "That's fine. Now, where are Thirif and Shibiel? Are they not well?"

"They chose to stay in Arithei, my lord," Isein explained. "As was their right."

Arlian blinked. "Oh," he said. "Of course." Thirif was not his employee, and had long since discharged any obligations; he and Shibiel had intended to return home more than a year before, when they pursued Lord Enziet into the Desolation.

"We have brought three young magicians with us," Qulu said, "to see the northern lands for themselves. Naturally, they will be glad to earn their keep in your service."

"Very good," Arlian said. "And what else have you brought me?"

"A fine assortment of philtres and illusions," Isein said, "and various talismans. We noted what had sold well before, and bought accordingly."

A horrible suspicion was beginning to grow in the back of Arlian's mind. "I asked about two magicks in particular," he said. "Did you obtain them?"

Isein looked uncomfortably at Qulu, who bit his lip and said nothing. Finally, as the silence grew seriously uncomfortable, Isein said, "We did *try*, my lord. We brought you a physician who may be able to do what you asked, but as for the other—we could not find anything that would do it."

"But surely, that was the easier of the two!" Arlian protested. "Just something that would drive a spear . . ."

"I am sorry, my lord," Isein said, eyes downcast.

Arlian began to form another objection, but then caught a glimpse out the window, where the shadow of his spear-throwing device could be seen across the forecourt. His dismay faded.

The spear-throwing machine certainly still had problems, but now that the magicians were back, he thought they might be able to find some way to make it work. That could wait.

"You did find a physician?" he said.

Isein nodded. "Her name is Oeshir," she said. "She has worked for many years to find a way to counteract the venom of the creatures of the Dreaming Mountains, and we think her methods may do what you want."

"Excellent! That's excellent."

"My lord, about the other . . . no magic we know would serve, and we could find no one . . ."

Arlian glanced out the window at the machine again, and held up a hand to silence her. "It doesn't matter after all," he said. "I think I may have built my *own* magic."

44

The Cleansing of the Blood

Oeshir was a thin old woman who spoke only a few words of Man's Tongue, and who wasn't interested in wasting them. She listened to Arlian's questions and conversational remarks and answered them all with, "Doesn't matter."

A few words from Isein, on the other hand, could elicit a twenty-minute speech in rapid Aritheian. Arlian had learned a few words of Aritheian—fewer than Oeshir had of Man's Tongue—but he could not make out anything at all in the torrents Oeshir spouted.

When Oeshir had finished one such tirade, Isein turned to Arlian and said simply, "She is ready at any time. Bring her the patient."

And that brought Arlian to a question he had given some thought, but had not completely decided. Who would be the subject of this experiment in magic?

He would have volunteered himself, but Black had argued strongly against the idea. "Suppose the process leaves you weak and sick," he said, "and that mob comes back—or a dragon—before you've recovered."

That had been persuasive, and Arlian's next step had been to ask the fisherfolk, who had been unenthusiastic about the idea—Arlian had never really told them what the dragon venom had done to them, so his request was of necessity vague. They saw nothing about their situation to justify meddling with dangerous magic.

And in any case, by the time the Aritheians arrived they were gone, having left for the coast a month before.

That left four other possibilities—Toribor, Rime, Spider, and Shard.

Somehow, Arlian did not think Toribor would yet trust him sufficiently to undergo the procedure. He still knew Rime far better than he knew Spider or Shard, and Rime alone had spoken of deliberately allowing her own death to prevent the birth of another dragon.

It would have to be Rime—but he had not yet actually *asked* her. He had not wanted to raise false hopes, in case the Aritheians had returned empty-handed.

They had not. They had brought Oeshir.

Accordingly, the moment Oeshir and Isein were gone, he sent Rime a message asking if he could call upon her at her earliest convenience. The reply arrived a little over an hour later, assuring him that Lady Rime would be at home by midmorning.

He debated bringing Oeshir and her magical apparatus with him, but quickly decided that would be impolitic. He went to bed early, so as to be well rested for his meeting with Rime, but the excitement of finally being able to *do* something about the dragons growing within himself and his friends kept him awake and staring at the canopy over his bed until almost midnight.

Naturally, he slept late; since he had retired early he had left no instructions to wake him. That meant a later start than he hoped, but at last, clad in a black velvet coat and a silver-gray blouse trimmed with the finest white lace, he clambered into his coach and waved to Black, who held the reins.

He had considered just slipping out the postern in working-man's attire, but had dismissed the idea; for a proposal as momentous as the one he was making today, some formality was appropriate.

He had also considered walking openly as himself, but he had not dared show his face on the streets unguarded in more than half a year. The last of the mobs had been driven away when the snows began and they had not yet returned, but Arlian still did not think it wise to offer them too tempting a target.

That meant the coach, even though the distance hardly justified it.

Walking would have been faster, he thought, as he jounced impatiently through the streets of the Upper City. When the vehicle finally came to a stop at the entry to Rime's elegant little mansion he did not wait for Black to climb down from the driver's seat, but flung the door open for himself and leapt to the ground.

He left Black to tend to the coach and hurried to the door, where Rime's doorman bowed deeply to welcome him. The servant led him without comment to the sitting room where his hostess waited, sprawled comfortably on a pink silk divan, her wooden leg nowhere in sight, her ancient bone resting on an end table. She wore a lavender gown that complemented the divan nicely, and her grey streaked hair, usually pulled back in a tight ponytail, hung loose.

"Lord Obsidian," she said. "What brings you to my humble home on such a fine morning?"

"My lady," he said, bowing. He could not quite bring himself to answer her question directly; the matter needed some preparation, and he had not yet thought about the ideal phrasing. "I trust you are well?"

"Quite well, my lord. As you know, I am not given to fevers or fatigues." The note of sarcasm was faint, but definitely there.

"Of course, but one can suffer discomforts of the mind, as well as the body . . ."

"Arlian," she interrupted, "get on with it. You do not request my earliest convenience for a mere social call. I did not want to be bothered with it last night, but curiosity has been eating at me all morning, and I am now thoroughly impatient. Why are you here?"

"My caravan has returned from Arithei," Arlian replied.

She shifted on the divan. "While this is doubtless very welcome news, I do not see how it involves *me*. Is there news of dragon attacks in the Borderlands, perhaps?"

Arlian shook his head. "No, nothing like that," he said. "Listen, Rime, you remember that Enziet held off his transformation for some time—months at the very least, perhaps years—with drugs and sorcery. It occurred to me that if sorcery, subtle but weak, could do that, then perhaps other magic could do even more."

She tilted her head and stared at him silently for a moment. "Go on," she said at last.

"My employees have brought back an Aritheian physician—a magician trained in healing. She has brought all the devices and spells she uses in treating taints and corruptions of the blood, of the sort caused by magical poisons and venoms."

"Taints and corruptions," Rime said slowly. "And why are you telling *me* this?"

"Months ago, you said that if I ever tried to kill you, you would try not to resist," Arlian said. "Suppose instead I try to *cure* you?"

"Have you tried it yourself?"

"No," Arlian admitted. "I admit it, I would prefer the first trial be made on someone else, so that I might observe the effects before undergoing them myself."

"And you chose me as your subject?"

"Well, I can scarcely expect Lady Pulzera to volunteer."

Rime smiled wryly.

"Will you do it?" Arlian asked.

"Have you any idea what the method is, or what the exact result will be?"

"To be honest, no," Arlian said. "Will you retain your extended lifespan? I doubt it. But you would presumably be restored to a full and normal humanity, and live out the remainder of your natural life."

"Or I might die horribly, if your Aritheian witch doctor has overestimated her skills."

"Yes," Arlian admitted, "you might."

"So you're asking me to give up perhaps five hundred years of life, and that supernatural charm that has allowed all of us who possess the heart of the dragon to become wealthy and powerful, in order to prevent the birth of a dragon centuries from now."

"Yes."

"Do you think I'm enough of a fool to do that?"

"I hope so," Arlian said. "I believe *I* am, once I know it works."

She smiled again, a crooked, uneven smile. "And do you know," she said, "it's possible your hope will be met. But not today, Ari. I need time to think about this. Surely, there's no need to rush into it—we have centuries, you and I."

"Indeed," Arlian agreed, "but our Aritheian physician does not. She is an old woman, and I cannot say whether there will be another, when she is gone, who can do as well."

Rime nodded. "Not centuries, then—but surely, you can give me hours."

"Of course."

"Despite the possible cost," Rime remarked, "it does sound preferable to someday having my throat cut, or allowing a monstrous worm to tear its way out of my bosom."

"I would think so," Arlian said, encouraged.

"Should I agree, I will want some time to put my affairs in order, in case this experiment of yours does prove fatal. When will your Aritheian magician be ready?"

"Whenever you please," Arlian said.

"Then let us speak of other matters for now, and you will have my decision when I have made it."

Arlian could scarcely object to that. The remainder of the visit was passed in idle discussion of gossip and trivia.

Three days later, Arlian received word that Rime would submit to the experiment.

And two days after that Rime arrived at the Old Palace, where Oeshir had prepared a bedchamber, fitting it with an assortment of talismans, enclosing the bed itself within a circle of iron and silver chains to shut out any hostile magic.

"Probably not needed here," Isein said apologetically as she moved the chains aside so that Rime could reach the bed without entangling her wooden leg, "but she needs these back home, and they make her feel safe."

"Hmph," Rime said, as she settled onto the bedding.

Oeshir herself was not there yet, but Arlian was—he and Isein were the only others in the room with Rime. Black was in an adjoining sitting room with Lily, Kitten, and Brook, who had volunteered to provide the clean blood the magic required.

Arlian, of course, could not donate, since his blood was tainted; Hasty had hesitantly suggested she might, but had been refused—as a nursing mother, she needed her strength. Cricket had shuddered at the idea and refused, while Musk had backed out at the sight of the crystal blade Oeshir intended to wield.

"You must remove your clothing, my lady," Isein said apologetically.

"I'll leave," Arlian said, as Rime glared at the Aritheian.

"You might have mentioned this sooner," Rime said, standing up again and reaching for the buttons of her gown. "Ari, I want you here to keep an eye on these two. I'll trust you to keep your eyes off me."

"As you please," Arlian said, stepping back from the door.

"Now, Isein," Rime said, as she undid the buttons, "*why* must I remove my clothing?"

"So that no blood will stain the garments, my lady," Isein said. "And so Oeshir can cut your flesh without harming them."

"Cut my flesh? Then this spell won't just involve an incantation or potion?"

Isein glanced uneasily at Arlian. "Perhaps we should have explained."

"I think you should explain *now*," Arlian said. "Before we go any farther. I knew that the spell required drawing clean blood and using it to replace the tainted blood, but is there more than that?"

"I am . . . that . . ." Isein struggled for a moment with the unfamiliar language, then said simply, "Yes."

"Please do explain, then," Rime said.

Isein looked at Arlian, then back at Rime.

"Long ago," she said, "there were many wizards who roamed the lands around Arithei."

"There are still many wizards around Arithei," Arlian pointed out.

"There were more once. Not so settled. They fought each other, and of course they fought the creatures in the Dreaming Mountains and elsewhere."

"Yes?"

"Yes. It was very dangerous. Many were killed, and some of them made a trick so they would not be so easy to kill. They took their hearts from their chests and stored them away safely at home when they traveled. It was very difficult to kill a wizard with no heart. You could still burn him, or cut off his head, but he could not die of bleeding, or of a stab in the chest, and poison could not reach his heart to stop it."

"Wait a minute . . ." Rime began.

"But the wizard could not live for long without his heart," Isein said quickly, before Rime could complete her sentence. "The heart would be restored to the chest in no more than three days, or the wizard would die. If a wizard was poisoned, then, he must remove the poison before he restored his heart. *That* was how this magic became known, and the magicians of Arithei stole the knowledge from the old wizards."

"You're going to *cut out my heart?*" Rime demanded.

"Oeshir is," Isein agreed.

Rime looked past her at Arlian. "I said you could cut my throat, but this is a little more than that . . ."

"You will live!" Isein insisted.

"Damn you, woman, stop interrupting me!" Rime snatched up her legbone and slapped at Isein's hand with it. "Let me think about this."

"She will take out your heart," Isein said, "and wash it in water and fill it with clean blood to purify it, and use a charm to draw all the poison into the hole in your chest, where it can be removed. Then she will put the heart back, and heal the wound."

"And I'll live through this."

"Yes!" She hesitated, then admitted, "In Arithei, the people live through it. Here, no one has ever tried."

"Oh, how *very* reassuring," Rime said. "And tell me, will it *hurt* to have my chest cut open?"

Isein looked unhappy.

"Yes," she said. "Very much."

"And do you have any magic that will help with that?"

"Herbs," Isein said, pointing at a collection of glassware on a bedside table. "They will make you unable to move, and deaden the pain."

"Deaden it."

"Some. It will hurt."

"Rime," Arlian said, "I didn't know all this. If you want to curse my name, dress yourself, and go home, I will not take it amiss."

"The old wizards cut out their *own* hearts," Isein said. "They could not use the herbs because they needed to stay alert, but they could still work the magic, despite the pain. It cannot be *that* bad."

"I'm not a wizard," Rime said.

"But you're a sorceress," Arlian pointed out.

"And a dragonheart," Rime said. "Damn you, Arlian. Very well." She reached for her buttons again, and Arlian looked away.

When she was naked, even her wooden leg removed, Isein handed her a cup of herbal brew; Rime drank it slowly, but without hesitation.

"What does it taste like?" Arlian asked.

"Pleasant, actually," Rime said. "Somewhat like . . ." She blinked, as if puzzled. "Like mint." Her voice was slightly slurred.

"Lie down," Isein told her.

Rime obeyed. Isein carefully took the ancient bone from her numbing fingers and laid it on a table, then looked up.

That was when Oeshir finally arrived.

She wore the strange, bright robes of an Aritheian, and bore a blue glass bowl, roughly the size of a man's head, held out before her as she marched ceremoniously into the room. She set the bowl on the foot of the bed, placing it beside Rime's remaining foot.

Rime lay unnaturally still; the herbs were clearly taking effect.

Arlian didn't see where Oeshir had carried the crystal knife, but suddenly it was in her hand. Arlian's hand slipped under his coat to the waistband of his breeches, where his own hidden knife waited—one with a blade of gleaming black stone, just in case something about this magic went wrong.

Oeshir had not spoken a word since entering the room; now she began a chant, gesturing with her crystal knife. The blade seemed to glow white, but Arlian was unsure whether that was his imagination, or the crystal catching the sunlight, or the magic at work.

She laid the knife on Rime's chest, and despite the paralytic herbs Rime twitched at its touch, her hands and foot jerking slightly. Then Oeshir brought forth two talismans—again, Arlian could not see whence she drew them; they seemed to simply appear in her hands. One was red and vaguely heart-shaped, while the other was a tiny white stone carving of a woman. Oeshir did something with her hands, and it appeared to Arlian that the heart talisman somehow passed *through* the white stone, emerging from the other side.

And now the red talisman was pulsing gently. Oeshir placed it on Rime's throat, then picked up the crystal knife again.

Then she plunged the gleaming blade into Rime's chest.

Rime convulsed, arms and legs flopping uncontrollably; her eyes and mouth flew wide with shock, but no sound emerged. Blood spurted, soaking the magician's knife and hands—but only once.

Arlian's vision blurred at the sight; he blinked and swallowed, feeling ill.

Oeshir paid no attention to the blood or Rime's movements, but continued to chant. With one hand she sawed the knife through Rime's body, through flesh and bone both; with the other she held the red talisman on Rime's throat, holding the thrashing woman in place.

Arlian swallowed again, struggling not to intervene.

Isein watched calmly from the side of the bed opposite Oeshir.

Then Oeshir pulled the blade out, and Rime's movements subsided. The magician laid the bloody knife on Rime's abdomen and reached one hand into the gaping chest wound, while the other picked up the red talisman.

Rime should be dead, Arlian knew—such a wound would have been almost instantly fatal. She was *not* dead, though—her eyes were wide and staring but alive, her fingers clenched and unclenched despite the herbs.

The air around the bed seemed to ripple, and the colors of the bedclothes shimmered unnaturally; Arlian remembered the waves of wild magic that he had seen flashing through the sky in the lands south of the Borderlands. He had never expected to see anything like that here, in his own home in Manfort. He thought he could see Rime's severed ribs flexing like snakes to make room for the magician's hand, but he was unsure whether that was illusion or reality.

Oeshir tensed, and pulled, and her hand emerged from Rime's chest clutching something red and bloody. Her other hand instantly dropped into the wound, inserting the red talisman in place of Rime's excised heart.

Then she took the bloody, still-beating heart in both hands, leaving the talisman in the wound, and placed it reverently in the waiting glass bowl.

The chant ended. "Water," Oeshir called.

Isein stepped forward, pitcher ready—Arlian had not seen her pick it up. She poured clean water into the bowl while Oeshir turned her attention back to Rime's chest. The white stone talisman was in her hand again; she held it to her lips and kissed it, then rested it across the gash in Rime's chest.

Rime's eyes were beginning to focus again, Arlian thought. Her fingers were still moving erratically, and her whole body had begun to tremble.

Oeshir said something in Aritheian. "The stone is drawing the poison," Isein translated.

"Will it take long?" Arlian asked.

"She doesn't know," Isein replied. "My lord, we will need blood soon, to keep the heart alive."

"Of course." Arlian hurried to the door and called, "Black!"

He was relieved, in truth, to have an excuse to look away. The knowledge that he had inflicted this horrible, unnatural, excruciating thing on his friend was churning his stomach, making him physically ill.

Black came to the door between rooms, and Arlian was suddenly appalled at the thought of letting his steward see Rime lying there, naked and mutilated.

"In here," Arlian said, pressing Black gently away from the bedchamber. "For modesty's sake."

Black nodded. "What do you need me to do?" he asked.

Arlian glanced back at the bed, where Isein had plunged her hands into the bowl, and was washing Rime's heart as if it were a cabbage. "We'll need blood soon," he said. "I don't know how much."

"Half the bowl," Isein called.

Arlian closed his eyes, sickened by the thought of drawing that much blood from his guests. Then he opened them again.

"I'm sorry," he said. "I should never have done this."

"Yes, you should," Brook said. "It won't kill us."

"I'll do it," Black said. "Isein gave us a bowl."

"My lord!" Isein called, her voice suddenly desperate. Arlian turned to find both the magicians staring in motionless horror at Rime's chest.

The white talisman had turned dark red. It had wrapped itself in a curtain of blood that now formed translucent wings and birdlike talons. Its shape had already changed, and it shifted further as Arlian watched—from the form of a woman to that of something else.

The new form was crooked and misshapen, its head too large for its body, its legs like twigs, but it was unmistakably a miniature red dragon. In that shape it was crawling across Rime's body, down across her shoulder onto the blood-soaked bedclothes.

Arlian snatched the obsidian dagger from his waistband and leapt to the bedside. There he hesitated, as the dragon-thing turned to face him.

"Will it hurt her if I kill it?" he asked.

Isein looked at him, then at Oeshir; she was clearly in no shape to translate that, and Arlian decided that it really didn't matter. If killing the thing killed Rime, at least it would end her pain.

He stabbed it, driving the knife down between the thing's shoulder blades, between its wings, pinning it to the bed. It squealed, a thin, high-pitched sound like the cry of a wounded rat, and the bloody shape dissolved, leaving the stone woman—or rather, the shattered fragments of the stone woman; the obsidian knife had broken the talisman into a dozen pieces.

The tip of the knife had broken, as well, and a triangular splinter of black glass stood in the tangled bedclothes.

And the white stone had turned black. The bedclothes beneath those fragments smoked, and Arlian smelled something he did not recognize immediately, but then placed.

Dragon venom.

Oeshir babbled wildly in Aritheian, but Arlian interrupted her, pointing his knife at the bowl. "Now what?" he asked.

Oeshir caught herself. She fell silent, took a long, deep breath, then let it out. She turned to the bowl and slid her thumbs under the rim.

Then, to Arlian's surprise, she lifted out a clear inner bowl; what he had taken for a single blue glass bowl was two bowls, one nested tightly inside the other. Now Oeshir had separated them. She placed the removed, water-filled inner bowl beside the empty outer one, then lifted Rime's heart from the murky, bloody water and placed it in the empty blue bowl.

It was still beating strongly. Arlian's breath came a little more easily when he saw that; Rime was not dead.

"Blood," Oeshir said.

Arlian nodded, and hurried back to the sitting room door.

"We need the blood now," he told Black.

Black was kneeling before Lily, holding her arm over a silver bowl; blood was running down her wrist into the bowl. Brook was sitting in a nearby chair, looking very pale and holding her own bandaged forearm. Kitten was sitting on the floor with her face to the wall, determinedly not watching any of the gory occurrences around her.

Arlian hurried over and looked at the silver bowl.

"That might be enough," he said.

Black nodded, and reached for a waiting bandage.

Arlian lifted the silver bowl carefully and hurried back to the bedside, where he proffered it to Oeshir.

She looked at the quantity critically, then nodded and accepted it. She poured it into the blue bowl and began chanting again as her hands massaged Rime's heart.

Arlian did not want to watch this, and his eyes roamed, searching the room for something else to look at. His gaze fell upon the clear bowl, now sitting on a bedside table, out of the way.

The blood was swirling in it, beneath a mirror-smooth surface.

Arlian blinked.

The motion was not natural—but he had seen it before. "By the dead gods," he said, as he stepped over to it.

The image took shape.

This was not a dragon he had ever seen before, but it was nonetheless a dragon, and Arlian could understand its thoughts as clearly as he had the others. He could feel its anger and hatred.

And then he heard its thoughts.

"You have killed my child!" it said.

45

The Dragon Enraged

Isein and Oeshir started; they had plainly heard the dragon's thoughts, as well. Oeshir's chanting wavered, but continued uninterrupted.

"You have killed my child!" the dragon repeated.

"As you killed Lady Rime's husband and children," Arlian replied, meeting the intense stare of the image in the bowl.

"As I will kill you. I was awakened by the pain of my child's death cry, and you shall pay for that agony. You cannot be permitted to teach others how to do this. To kill my child and let its host live is wrong." The amount of disgust and loathing it conveyed in the concept "wrong" was overpowering. *"It is obscene."*

Arlian marveled at how completely the dragon had forgotten its own presumed human ancestry, and how little it comprehended human values.

Or perhaps it understood human values, but rejected them.

"Dragons have threatened me before," Arlian said. "I still live."

"You have not faced me," the dragon replied. *"Now you will. You will die, your palace burning around you. That abomination that performed this obscenity will die with you, and all the outsiders who dare to intrude in the lands of dragons with their mockery of wizardry as well.*

The creature who permitted this to be done to her will die. Even now, I am on my way to destroy you."

Arlian opened his mouth to speak fresh defiance, but before the words came the image in the bowl shattered—and the bowl itself shattered an instant later, showering blood and water and venom across the table and the floor beneath.

He turned to see what was happening on the bed.

Oeshir had placed Rime's heart back in her chest and was frantically working to close and heal the wound; her hands and voice trembled, but she continued the gestures and incantation.

Isein was staring in horror at the broken bowl.

Rime's lips were drawn back from her teeth in a hideous grimace; her hands gripped the coverlet beneath her so tightly the knuckles were white. Her eyes were focused on the canopy over the bed.

Arlian turned again and saw Black in the sitting room door, a dagger in his hand.

"What was that?" Black demanded. "What spoke?"

"A dragon," Arlian said. "The one whose venom flowed in Lady Rime's veins. It would seem our little experiment succeeded."

"It's coming here?"

"So it says."

"I can have the coach ready in . . ."

"I'm not fleeing," Arlian interrupted. "I've been looking for a way to fight these monsters since I was a child; now that one is finally coming here to face me, I am not going to run away!"

Black nodded. He started to speak, but Arlian interrupted him again.

"You should get the women out of here, though—coach, wagon, whatever you can find. Alert the household, tell anyone who wants to flee to go *now*. Anyone who stays should be armed with obsidian." He smiled tensely. "And see that someone loads spears into that machine out front."

The chanting stopped. Arlian turned.

"It is done," Oeshir said, stepping away from the bed, the red talisman in her hand. Then she spoke to Isein in rapid Aritheian.

"She cannot be moved for a day and a night," Isein translated. She hesitated, then asked, "When will the dragon arrive?"

"I don't know," Arlian said. "I don't know where it lairs, or how fast a dragon can fly. It could be days, or it could be mere minutes."

Isein looked unhappily at Rime. "If it is less than a day and a night, our work was for nothing."

"I'll see to it that it wasn't," Arlian replied. He, too, looked at Rime.

Her naked body was drenched in sweat, and from throat to crotch she was smeared with blood; blood saturated the coverlet on which she lay. She was trembling uncontrollably, despite the herbs.

The wound in her chest was closed, though, and her eyes were alert.

"Do whatever you can for her," Arlian said. A thought struck him. "And can Oeshir heal those two women who provided the blood?"

Isein quickly translated the question into Aritheian; Oeshir did not bother to answer, but hurried to the sitting room. As she did Isein fetched a cloth and pitcher, and began to wash Rime.

Arlian wanted to stay, to see that Rime was cared for, to reassure her—but he had more urgent matters to attend to.

A dragon was coming to kill him.

"If I live, I'll be back for you," Arlian told Rime quickly; then he turned and ran for the door.

Two hours later the spear-throwing device was prepared, standing in the forecourt with six of Arlian's longest and best obsidian-tipped spears loaded, ready to be launched by tripping a single lever. Arlian stood beside it, scanning the sky, another spear in his hand and two obsidian daggers in his belt.

Kitten, Brook, Cricket, Hasty, Vanniari, Lily, Musk, and most of the servants had been hastily packed up and sent off to the Grey House—Black had seen to that, and had accompanied them to ensure their safe arrival. Messengers had been sent to the Citadel, and to Toribor, Spider, and Shard, warning them that a dragon was on its way. Everyone remaining in the Old Palace was armed with at least an obsidian dagger.

Everyone, that is, but Rime, who could not yet close her hand to hold a knife. Isein and Oeshir and Rime were all still in the upstairs rooms; Rime could not be moved, and the two magicians would not leave her, though they happily accepted the stone knives.

Arlian was unsure where Qulu, the third magician, was; he had not happened to cross his employer's path. Arlian hoped that the dragon had no special means for locating the Aritheians, and that Qulu was somewhere safe.

Arlian had considered sending a message to the remainder of the Dragon Society, but had dismissed the idea; after all, they might well decide to *help* the dragon.

Everything was as ready as Arlian knew to make it, and as yet there was no sign of the dragon.

That meant that Arlian had time to think, and to see just how feeble his preparations really were. Yes, he had his spear-thrower— but the thing was too big and heavy to be moved by a single man, and even a team of four could not turn it quickly enough to have any hope of hitting a moving target. The only way Arlian could hope to hit a dragon with it would be if the monster walked or flew directly into its path.

Of course, he might be lucky. The dragon might do exactly that. Arlian remembered that Rime had come from the northwest, and had guessed that the dragon's lair lay beneath the western mountains; he had therefore, before Venlin and the other footmen left, had the spear-thrower turned to point west, almost directly toward the front gate.

If the dragon came from the east or south or north, the spear-thrower would be useless—but Arlian could not see anything he could do to remedy that.

The general commotion in the Old Palace had not gone unnoticed by the rest of Manfort; curious crowds were beginning to gather at the fence, staring at the spear-thrower and at Arlian standing beside it with his strange stone-headed spear. People of all ranks, in homespun or velvet, wandered by and watched for a while, perhaps shouting an insult or two before growing bored and moving on.

Horn appeared, watched Arlian for a moment, then departed again.

Arlian ignored them all and watched the sky, which was growing dark. The sun was still high, but thick clouds were gathering, blocking the light. The day, warm to begin with, seemed to be growing unnaturally hot.

It was not true dragon weather yet, but that was clearly coming.

Arlian had thought since the previous summer that the dragons somehow *created* dragon weather, rather than waiting for it to occur naturally—that long period of time when they had roamed freely had been too convenient to be mere coincidence—but he had never imagined a single dragon could bring it about so swiftly.

The dragons were powerfully magic, no question about it—like the things beyond the border, the wizards and demons and monsters, they could manipulate their environment in unnatural ways.

But they did have limitations. Perhaps they did not merely prefer hot, dark weather, but *required* it. He scanned the sky, west to south to east to north.

Then his thoughts were interrupted as a voice called from the gate, "Obsidian! What is this all about?"

Arlian turned, dropping his gaze from the clouds, and recognized the bald, eyepatched figure standing just outside the fence. He smiled. "Belly!" he called. "Come in, come in, the gate's open."

It was odd, perhaps, that he should be so pleased to see a man he had once sworn to kill, a man he had twice dueled, but nonetheless he was very glad to see Toribor. This was at least one man who shared his hatred of dragons.

Toribor entered the forecourt, looking up at the spear-thrower in bemusement. "I knew you were working on machines, but I had not gotten a good look at one before. Is that thing supposed to kill a dragon?" he asked.

"I hope it will," Arlian said. "If I can get one in position."

"You can't aim it?"

"No."

"You could probably rig up something with ropes and pulleys that would let you aim it however you please."

"If I had more time, perhaps," Arlian said—though in fact, he had not thought in terms of turning it with ropes and pulleys, and he now realized he should have. "Alas, a dragon is on its way even as we speak."

"So your message said. You neglected to explain how you know this."

"The dragon told me," Arlian said. "In a bowl of bloody water."

Toribor turned his one good eye on Arlian. "I thought they no longer spoke to you."

"This one was provoked," Arlian said. "I believe we may have found a way to remove the heart of the dragon without killing a person." That description was uncomfortably literal, though Toribor would not yet know it.

"I take it you tested this method?"

Arlian nodded. "On Lady Rime. The dragon that spoke to us is the one that killed her family four or five centuries ago; it did not take the death of its unborn child well."

"Ah," Toribor said. "But you weren't deliberately luring it here?"

"No, of course not. If I were going to lure a dragon deliberately, I wouldn't do it in the middle of Manfort."

Toribor shrugged. "There are probably worse places." He looked up at the spear-thrower again. "So you don't have a way to guide the dragon into that thing's path?"

"Suggestions would be welcome."

"Is it coming specifically to kill *you*?"

"And Rime, and the Aritheian magicians, yes."

"You'll have to tell me about this method of yours sometime."

"Of course; I certainly wasn't planning to keep it secret. At the moment, though, I have other concerns."

"Do you know when the dragon will arrive?"

"No."

"If you stand right where you are, the most direct path to you takes it in front of this infernal device of yours."

"If it comes from the west, yes. If it comes from north or south, no. And I need to strike it in the heart, not the face, which complicates matters."

"Indeed." Toribor studied the situation thoughtfully. "Can those magicians of yours do anything? Steer the spears, perhaps? Use illusions to guide the dragon into range?"

"I don't know," Arlian admitted. "Two of them are upstairs with Rime; the third . . ." His voice trailed off. Qulu might be useful here after all; using illusions to lure the dragon to the right position might work.

Then he heard the first screams. Startled, he looked past Toribor at the little crowd in the street beyond the fence.

Several of them were staring at the sky, pointing upward—to the north. Arlian turned and stared.

A thin black shape was visible against the overhanging gray clouds, a shape like a winged serpent, long and narrow, tail waving, crossed by broad, flapping wings. It was growing larger at an alarming rate.

It was unquestionably a dragon.

"By my blood," Arlian said. "It's fast!"

"Give me a spear," Toribor said, turning to face the approaching beast.

"I don't . . ." Arlian hesitated, then handed his spear to Toribor. "Here."

Toribor accepted the weapon.

The crowd beyond the fence was screaming, milling about wildly; some of the people had fled in terror, but others seemed too fascinated to move, and yet others were actually running up to get a better view of the monster. Horn had reappeared, this time in company with Opal and Post; the three of them were standing on the far side of the street, staring at the northern sky.

"The Duke!" someone shouted, loudly enough to be heard above the hubbub. Several faces turned to the south, toward the Citadel.

If the Duke really was coming, Arlian did not see that it mattered. What could the Duke or his guards hope to do against the creature? They had only steel blades, no obsidian.

And, Arlian realized, all *he* had was his spear-thrower and a pair of knives—he had just given Toribor his spear.

Toribor apparently had every intention of using it; he had clambered up on the frame of the spear-thrower, to be closer to the dragon's own level, and was now standing on the loading platform, eight feet off the ground.

"Belly!" Arlian called. "It's not after *you*!"

Toribor glanced down at him. "It doesn't need to be," he replied. "A dragon took my eye, and it's past time I repaid that. I swore to fight the dragons, and by all the dead gods, I intend to!"

Arlian knew better than to argue. He wished Black were here to help, but his steward—his *friend*—had not yet returned from the Grey House.

And then, as suddenly as a summer cloudburst, the dragon was upon them.

46

The Dragon's Vengeance

As the great black shadow fell over him Arlian drew one of his daggers, but looking up at the dragon's belly he knew the gesture was absurd. The creature was immense; the dagger was no more use against such a thing than a pin would be.

The audacity of trying to kill such a creature at all suddenly overwhelmed him. Who was he, to attempt it? He was just twenty-two, while the beast had lived for millennia; he was but a single man, armed with a stone knife, against a creature as large as a wing of the palace, a beast that spat flaming venom, a beast whose every talon, even the tiniest dewclaw, was longer and sharper than the obsidian blade Arlian clutched.

He was about to die. He knew it. As soon as the creature noticed him he would perish in a burst of flaming venom, or perhaps be snatched up by those dreadful jaws and devoured.

But the dragon did not strike at him immediately; instead it dove at the roof of the Old Palace itself, talons outstretched. A cloud of venom sprayed from the dragon's jaws and burst into flame.

Fire washed over the roof of the Palace; even over the fading screams of the fleeing bystanders Arlian could hear tiles popping and shattering from the heat and pressure.

Then the dragon's forelimbs struck the roof with a tremendous rending crash. Arlian could not see what was happening, but he could hear heavy beams creaking and snapping, plaster falling, glass breaking. A cloud of dust and debris rose, mingling with the smoke of dragonfire, drifting over the eaves. He could catch an occasional glimpse of wing, but most of the creature was out of sight.

"What's it doing?" Toribor called.

"It must be after Lady Rime, and the Aritheians," Arlian called back—though in fact, the dragon had apparently struck at the center of the Palace, and the three women were in the south wing.

"Your machine is pointing the wrong way."

"I noticed that," Arlian agreed. The spear-thrower was pointed directly *away* from the palace, which had seemed reasonable at the time—it was intended to stop the thing before the dragon reached its target.

Except he had never had a chance to try it. The dragon had come from an unexpected direction, and faster than he had anticipated.

It was ascending again, and Arlian could hear the crackle of flames—the palace was ablaze, and the fire was spreading fast. The crackling quickly became a roar.

That made sense; why should the dragon hunt and dig out its prey, one by one, when it could simply burn them all to death? Arlian remembered the village of Obsidian, on the Smoking Mountain—every house had been burned, and the people who escaped the fires had been killed as they fled. The dragons had not bothered to dig anyone out.

Arlian remembered how a dragon had killed his grandfather. It had not used claws or teeth; when it noticed the old man standing in the burning house it had simply sprayed more burning venom in at him, then moved on.

This dragon would smash and burn the palace and kill anyone who fled from it. It might not take the trouble to dig anyone out.

If the Aritheians could get Rime or themselves to somewhere relatively safe—the wine cellar, perhaps—they might yet survive.

If the dragon could be lured away from the palace . . .

But the only thing that might lure it would be one of its

intended targets, and the only one available, the only one outside the palace, was Arlian himself.

Arlian hurried to the edge of the loading platform. "Belly," he called, shouting to be heard over the roaring fire and the screams from the street, "I'm going to try to lead it away from the palace, away from the women. If it follows me into position, you can shoot it . . ."

Toribor glanced down at him, then at the release mechanism.

"I've never seen this thing shoot," he said. "I don't know how it works, what its range is, any of that."

"But it's simple," Arlian shouted frantically. The dragon had circled once, high overhead, and was starting to slip sideways into a steep dive, back toward the Palace for another attack. "You just . . ."

"*I'll* lead it away," Toribor shouted, interrupting him. "*You* shoot it. You know how." He jumped down from the platform, spear in hand, landing beside Arlian.

"But it won't . . ." Arlian began.

This time Toribor did not interrupt him with words, but with a hard shove in the chest, pushing Arlian back beneath the loading platform.

"You get down there out of sight until it's chasing me," Toribor said. Then, before Arlian could regain his balance or begin to reply, he ran out in front of the spear-thrower, bellowing at the top of his lungs.

"Yah! Dragon! You stinking worm, you monster! Come and get me!"

The dragon was plummeting toward the palace, but it spotted the running figure and swerved toward him.

It was taking the bait. Arlian didn't understand why at first—Toribor was not on the list of enemies its image in the bowl had recited, and he was a dragonheart, carrying an unborn dragon in his own blood.

But then he realized, even as he lunged for the release lever, that the dragon was probably not thinking that clearly. It saw someone running, trying to escape, and it pursued without stopping to consider. It was not a human being; it was a predator, a destroyer, and its instincts told it to attack anything that fled.

The beast was dropping, wings spread; it flapped, and dust and smoke swirled around Arlian and the machine, half-blinding him. The wind from a second flap almost knocked Arlian off his feet.

Toribor had reached the gate, and had slowed; he threw a glance back at Arlian, and Arlian realized that he wanted to be sure he was still well within the machine's range.

The device could easily put a spear a hundred yards past where Toribor stood, and the dragon was dropping fast. Its shadow blotted out the sky, the wind from its wings staggered Arlian and tore his hat away.

"*Go!*" Arlian shrieked. "Run!"

Toribor ran—but not far enough, not fast enough. The dragon was suddenly there in the forecourt, its flank toward Arlian, its neck outstretched, its head reaching for Toribor. Its jaws opened.

It was perfectly positioned, its right flank fully exposed to the spear-thrower.

Arlian tripped the lever, but the cloud of flaming venom blossomed forth and washed over Toribor. Sparks spiraled up from the iron gates, dust and smoke rolled across the yard, and the glare of the yellow flame almost blinded Arlian. He flung one arm across his face as the weights dropped and the huge wooden arm swung upward, rapidly gaining speed.

Then it slammed against the framework with a single earth-shaking thump, and half a dozen obsidian-tipped spears flew toward the dragon as it rose again.

Four of them struck—at that range, it would have been difficult to miss entirely. A fifth skidded across the dragon's back and vanished spinning end-over-end into the roiling cloud of smoke and flame that had engulfed the gates; the sixth disappeared without touching the beast.

One of the four hits pierced the dragon's right wing; the spear passed almost completely through, then dangled there. Another lodged in its shoulder, just above the foreleg.

And two embedded themselves solidly in the creature's side—but apparently neither one reached the heart.

The dragon screamed, a sound like nothing Arlian had ever heard before—the cry of a full-grown dragon was infinitely deeper and louder than the shriek of a newborn. Windows shattered behind him at the sound, and he thought his ears might burst.

Clearly, he had hurt the monster—but he had not killed it, only angered it. As it whirled to face the source of this indignity it seemed fully as terrible and magnificent as ever.

The hideous stench of venom reached Arlian, mingled with the scents of dust and smoke and burned flesh.

You, it said—though it spoke without sound, as had its sorcerous image.

"Me," Arlian shouted back, drawing both his useless stone daggers. He was going to die, he knew that, and he intended to die defiantly.

The spears hadn't reached its heart. One of them had pierced the creature's scaled black hide behind its foreleg, and penetrated a foot or more into the flesh—that surely must have been *close*, Arlian thought.

But then, how big a heart could a dragon have, to be so cold and ruthless?

If that spear had gone deeper, perhaps it might have . . .

Arlian had no time to finish the thought; the dragon's head was swinging toward him. He ran—and partly because the spear-thrower blocked him, partly because the wall of the palace blocked him, and partly from mad inspiration, he ran *toward* the dragon, toward its spear-pierced flank.

The dragon wouldn't spit flaming venom on itself, he was sure—after all, dragon venom was the one thing that could scar a dragonheart, so might it not be able to burn a dragon, as well? And the venom was never ignited until after it had left the creature's jaws, so perhaps the flame could burn them even if the venom could not.

The neck curved around, the head followed him, and he ran as he had never run before, and then leapt, both arms outstretched, still holding his two obsidian daggers. He intended to cut the thing, hurt it more, before he died.

He slammed into the monster's side, between two of the protruding spears; his daggers bit into the scales and gave him purchase as the dragon thrashed, trying to reach him, trying to shake him off.

He hung there, feet dangling, belly pressed against the immense smooth scales, and plunged each dagger in turn as deeply into the beast as he could.

He clutched the hilts for dear life as the dragon screamed again and flapped its wings. The right wing smashed down over him, like a great black leather blanket pressing him against the creature's side, and he turned his head at the last instant, so that his nose was not broken against the scales.

The spear that had penetrated that wing twisted upon impact, tearing the leathery flesh of the creature's wing; thick dark blood sprayed across one side of Arlian's face. And Arlian saw that the blow of the wing drove the two spears in the dragon's side deeper into its flash, though it snapped off half the shaft of the farther one.

That must have hurt, because the dragon promptly lifted its wing as high as it could, screaming in pain and fury, and did not flap again.

That meant it couldn't fly, Arlian realized. He had done *that* much, at least. If others could find more of the obsidian weapons, perhaps they could wear it down, pick away at it . . .

If this dragon died here, then the Duke might be convinced. Humanity might fight.

That would be a legacy worth leaving, Arlian thought. He could cut no deeper with the daggers, both were embedded up to the hilt, but the spears in the dragon's flank and shoulder were within reach. He released his left-hand dagger and reached for the shaft of the nearest spear.

The dragon had finally brought its head around to peer at him.

You have courage, it said, *but you are a fool. Do you think you can hurt me?*

"I think I *have* hurt you," Arlian gasped, as he gripped the spear-shaft and pushed.

The shaft sank into the dragon's flesh, not as if piercing any natural flesh, but like a stick driven into earth, like a shovel thrust into the soil of a garden.

The dragon's mouth fell open, and its eyes widened in what was unquestionably a grimace of pain.

Yes, it hurts! the dragon said.

"Good," Arlian said, grinding the spear deeper.

Stop it!

"Don't be ridiculous."

If you kill me, the others will destroy you all.

"They may try," Arlian said grimly. The spear's head had disappeared and the shaft was now driven a good three feet or more into the creature's black flesh—almost half the shaft's length. He had no idea whether it would reach the thing's heart, but all he could do was keep on pushing.

And then, when he had pushed the spear a few inches further, he felt a deep, slow throbbing in the spear's shaft, like the beating of a monstrous heart. A great wave of gloating triumph surged up within him.

At last, after half a lifetime spent pursuing vengeance, he was finally going to kill a dragon—not a stumbling newborn, little more than an apparition of blood and magic, but a full-grown monster with the blood of hundreds of innocents on its claws.

It was not one of the three that destroyed Obsidian, but they would have their turn. Even if this one killed him with its death throes, he would have shown the world that dragons *could* be slain, and he had faith that his fellow men would someday use that knowledge and exterminate their ancient foes.

He shoved on the spear again, and a gout of dark blood erupted from the wound, spurting along the shaft, washing over his hand and drenching the black velvet and white lace of his sleeve.

And the dragon fell. Its legs folded under it, its upraised wing collapsed like a falling tent. A final gout of flaming venom and oily black smoke burst from its mouth as its head dropped to the ground; Arlian felt the heat, but the fireball did not reach him.

There were no sudden spasms, no desperate writhing, no last-minute slamming or clawing. The creature simply crumpled. The hard scales beneath him were suddenly soft and yielding; the dagger in his right hand ripped down through the dragon's flesh as if it were cutting through rotten cheese. Arlian slid down the monster's side beneath its wing until his feet reached the ground; he staggered, then stood upright, using the dagger to slice open the wing so that it parted and fell down around him.

The dragon had not exploded into blood and air, as the newborns had, but neither had it died after the fashion of a natural creature. Arlian remembered how rapidly Nail's body had decayed; the dragon seemed to be doing the same, but even faster. As he watched he could see its flesh shrinking, the bones already protruding.

And it stank of rot and death. He climbed and cut his way free and stepped out into cleaner air.

And then he heard the cheers.

47

Bones and Ash

Bones and ash were all that remained where Toribor had stood; a figure knelt over them, but wore a woman's skirt and was far too slender to be Lord Belly. Arlian was too stunned for a moment to recognize that person through the drifting smoke and ash, but then she looked up at him before rising and turning to flee.

Lady Opal.

Dazed as he was, Arlian still knew what she had been doing, bent over Toribor's remains—she had been after venom, and she might well have found it.

In the street beyond the gate, which had been deserted a moment before, it seemed as if a thousand people had appeared out of nowhere, cheering and applauding.

"Obsidian! Obsidian!" they called.

Arlian stared out through the fence at them, astonished. He was dazed, and it took him a moment to recognize Black, pushing his way through the throng.

And down the street men were shouting orders—guards clearing a path.

And he could hear roaring behind him, as well; he turned, and realized that the dragon's death had not meant the battle was over.

Flames and smoke were billowing up from the Old Palace; as he watched, a section of upstairs wall sagged and fell in with a crash.

"Rime," he said.

"Ari!" Black was bellowing at the top of his lungs to be heard over the cheers and the fire. "Ari!"

Arlian whirled. "Water!" he called. "Fetch water! There are still people in there, and one of them can't rise from her bed!"

Black had finally managed to push his way through the gate.

"Forget it, Ari!" he said. "You can't put that out—look at it!"

"I don't care about putting it out," Arlian said, "but we need to get Rime out!"

Black hesitated, then turned.

A line of guards in the Duke's livery were clearing a path and an area around the gate, and walking calmly along that path, a broad grin on his face, was the Duke of Manfort, in a powder-blue coat with silver and white trim.

"Obsidian!" he called. "Magnificent! Just magnificent."

"Your Grace," Black called, "we need men to fetch our comrades out of the house—could you spare us a few?"

"Of course, of course!" the Duke called. "And the rest will fetch buckets—I'm afraid the Old Palace is beyond hope, but we can keep the fire from spreading, eh?" His grin broadened even further. "Magnificent, Obsidian! Just splendid!"

"Thank you, Your Grace," Arlian said. "You men, follow me!"

Later he could never remember all the details, but he knew he must have led the guardsmen in through the kitchens, then up the servants' stair to the bedchamber in the south wing.

There Isein had insisted that Rime could *still* not be taken from the bed, under any circumstances—Arlian remembered *that*, and he remembered what he had said, though he did not recall any conscious thought before the words came from his lips.

"Then bring the bed," he said. "A man at each corner, another on each side, and cut through anything in the way."

By the time the bed reached the safety of the street the bedposts and canopy had been hacked away, but Rime and Isein and Oeshir were all safe, well clear of the flames.

The fire was still roaring, the walls crumbling, despite scores of people, guards and servants and simply people who had been nearby, flinging buckets of water at it. Black was directing them—he had clearly taken the matter in hand while Arlian had gone after Rime. That was when Arlian realized his memory was failing him; he could not say when he and Black had separated.

Rime was safely out, though, and it was time to get back to his friend's side. Arlian took a step, planning to join one of the bucket lines.

And then the Duke was clapping Arlian on the back, exclaiming that he was magnificent, wonderful, superb, and the street was once again crowded with people shouting, "Obsidian!"

"Your Grace," Arlian said. He looked around, and realized that although a few courtiers had accompanied the Duke, Lord Hardior was not among them—nor were any other dragonhearts. "Is Lord Hardior not with you?"

"That fool? *No*, he isn't here! He called you a madman, said you would bring disaster on us all, and here you've *killed a dragon*! By the dead gods, man, do you realize that? You've killed a dragon, the first man in all of history to do it! Hardior said it wasn't possible, but you've done it!"

"Yes," Arlian said, turning to look at the dead monster.

The black flesh was rotting away rapidly, melting from the bones—the ribs and the top of the skull and the long, thin bones of the wings were already exposed, gleaming white in the afternoon sun.

And the sun was out; the clouds had parted and were rapidly dispersing. The dragon weather was dissipating as the dragon's body did.

Toribor's bones lay by the gatepost, also exposed. Arlian swallowed. The last of the Six Lords was dead.

The spear-throwing device had been smashed by the dragon's death throes, and now stood broken, collapsed in upon itself and smoldering as sparks and burning debris drifted down onto it.

"I should help with the fire," Arlian said.

"Damn the fire, Obsidian—you've done enough! You look exhausted, man."

"I am," Arlian said.

And then he fainted, and the Duke himself caught the city's new hero in his own two arms as he fell.

48

Aftermath

It was just as well, Arlian thought as he lay newly awake in an unfamiliar bed, that he never had found a buyer for the Grey House. At least he would still have a home.

He looked around, trying to identify in which room of the Grey House he had been placed, but nothing gave him any clue.

In fact, he realized when he looked at the broad window, he was not in the Grey House at all.

He vaguely remembered being loaded into the Duke's carriage, and riding somewhere, and being half carried to a bed, and he had assumed it was in the Grey House—but this was *not* the Grey House, where none of the windows were anything like the one across the bedchamber from where he lay.

He sat up, puzzled, and realized that he was not alone in the room; two servants had stood by the door, one of whom was now turning on his heel and leaving—presumably to carry word that Lord Obsidian was awake.

Both of them wore the Duke's livery. Arlian turned and looked out that many-paned window, checking the view, and knew where he was.

He was in the Citadel.

"Is there anything you would like, my lord?" asked the servant who had remained.

"News," Arlian said. "Explanations. And food."

"I can have food brought," the servant replied. "What would please you?"

Moments later a tray of bread, meat, and wine arrived, accompanied by word that His Grace the Duke of Manfort would be honored if Lord Obsidian could grant him an audience.

Arlian marveled at that as he ate.

"I will speak with him shortly," he told the messenger between bites.

The interview that followed was odd, almost dreamlike—the Duke was so utterly cooperative, so eager to please, that any question Arlian asked was answered immediately and directly, any request granted. Their relative stations—the aging noble who was hereditary master of all the Lands of Man, and an escaped slave, little more than a youth, who had made a fortune by investing stolen gold in foreign illusions—seemed to have reversed themselves.

The fire was out, the Duke told him, but little of the Old Palace still stood—a few walls here and there, the ovens and hearth in the kitchens, a portion of the north wing.

The spear-thrower was destroyed, but several obsidian weapons had been recovered, and the Duke's men were combing through the ruins, collecting more, as well as salvaging whatever they could of Arlian's belongings. Flame, smoke, and water had destroyed much, but the contents of boxes, drawers, and trunks had often survived almost unscathed.

The dragon's bones still stood where the monster had died; most of Toribor's bones still lay against the gatepost, but someone had stolen his skull.

Arlian knew who had done that—not which individual, but what group. Toribor's skull would join the others on the shelf in the hall of the Dragon Society.

No more dragons had been seen; the weather remained clear and had turned slightly cool.

"Then we have time to prepare," Arlian said.

"And we *will* prepare," the Duke agreed. "We will build a hundred, a *thousand* of your machines! We will place them all around the city walls, and in every other major city in the Lands of Man. If any dragon approaches, it will be met with a *hail* of obsidian blades! At *last, we* will accomplish what none of my ancestors could! We will *kill dragons*! We will rid the world of their evil, once and for all!"

His enthusiasm was somewhat overwhelming, but Arlian smiled happily all the same. After a lifetime of being told he was mad, that his vengeance was impossible, Arlian had finally convinced someone that the dragons *could* be destroyed.

And it was someone who could *do* something about it.

"If we can find their caves," he said, "we might be able to get at them in the winter, and kill them while they're asleep."

"*Excellent* suggestion! Magnificent!"

Arlian looked around the audience chamber, and noticed that once again, he was the only dragonheart present. "Has Lord Hardior . . ." he began.

The Duke's smile vanished, and his expression turned harder than Arlian would have thought possible.

"Lord Hardior has been informed that his services will no longer be needed," the Duke said coldly. "Do you know, he and some of his friends were trying to *talk* to the dragons, by sorcery, to negotiate terms? They were ready to *surrender*. He told me about it when we first received word of the monster's approach—he was ready to give the beast whatever it wanted, if it would but spare the Citadel."

"Oh," Arlian said.

"But *you* were ready for it! A spear in the heart!" The grin was back.

"In the heart," Arlian agreed. That reminded him of another concern. "Might I ask, Your Grace, where Lady Rime was taken?"

"To her own home. It seemed best."

"And did she seem well?"

"I'm afraid I didn't see for myself, my lord—those two foreigners of yours kept everyone away."

"I'll want to visit her."

"I can have her brought here, if you like . . ."

"No." Arlian shook his head. "She needs to recover—she was the subject of strong magic. All I did was . . ." He blinked, as he realized what he was about to say; then he grimaced and completed his sentence with a wry smile.

"All I did was fight a dragon," he said.

Black and Brook and Hasty and Vanniari and Lily and Musk and Kitten and Cricket were all safe at the Grey House; Qulu and Stammer and Venlin and Ferrezin and Wolt and Chiril and the rest were there, as well. Miraculously, no one had died in the Old Palace, and only Toribor had died outside it.

Isein and Oeshir had gone with Rime, though, rather than joining the rest of Arlian's household.

It was upon his first return to the Grey House that Black took him aside.

"Ari," he said, "there are words that need to be said between us."

Arlian blinked at him. "Are there?" he asked mildly.

"I think so."

"Then say yours, dear Beron, and I will do my best to say mine."

Black hesitated at the sound of his true name, then said, "I may owe you an apology. You have relied on my loyalty, and counted me as your friend, and I do not feel as if I have been true to those expectations."

Arlian stared at him in astonishment, too startled to speak at first. Finally, he said, "In what way? You have done everything I asked of you, and more!"

"But my heart has not been in it. When first we met I aided you because you were young and charming and clearly needed a friend, because you had the heart of the dragon and an amazing determination, and because you paid me well. I thought you had the potential for great things, and your obsession with revenge fascinated me, so I guided you, taught you the sword, and accepted the job as your steward. I thought I might rise with you in the world."

"Indeed," Arlian said.

"That lasted until Enziet's death. On the journey home to Manfort I began to wonder whether I had made the right choice. You had satisfied as much of your need for vengeance as could reasonably be satisfied, and yet you wanted more. You wanted to slay dragons."

"As I always have."

"And I have always said you were mad. Well, I began to *believe* it."

"I probably *am* mad, Black."

"But the shape of your madness seemed more forbidding, more unhealthy, after Enziet's death. You spoke of your own damnation, and I realized that you meant it—but if you were damned, what was I? You had power and wealth and a lifespan of centuries stretching before you, all of which you seemed determined to throw away, and what did I have? The life of a servant."

"A steward," Arlian corrected. "And a lord yourself, if I died."

"Still, a life in your shadow, in the shadow of a madman."

Arlian spread his hands. "What could I say?"

"You could have said, when we spoke of your plans, that you had come to your senses. You could have said that defeating the dragons was too much to ask. You could have said to me that you wanted to keep my services for longer than a mortal lifetime, and would I mind drinking a mixture of blood and venom? You could have spoken of hope for the future, rather than a centuries-long campaign against the dragons, a campaign that must certainly last well past my own death. You could have considered the possibilities of *life*, rather than death."

For a moment Arlian gazed silently at his friend.

"Would you have accepted it if I had?" he asked at last. "Would you have drunk the elixir?"

"Yes," Black said miserably. "I would even now. *Especially* now, when you have found a way to reverse the transformation!"

"I think I would consider that a betrayal," Arlian said slowly.

"I know," Black said.

"Why did you stay with me?" Arlian asked. "If you did not believe in me, why did you stay?"

"I still *like* you, Ari. And you still pay well. And you mean well. And most of all, Brook lives in your house."

"Ah." A great deal became clear.

"We expect a child in a few months."

"She is as free to leave as you are," Arlian suggested tentatively.

"But her friends live with you, and the other reasons all apply. We could not live so well anywhere else."

"So you stayed."

"We'll leave if you wish it."

"No, I don't wish it!" Arlian frowned. "Why are you telling me this now?"

"Because now you have done the impossible. You have killed a black dragon. You have proven that I was wrong. You don't need me anymore—you have all the Duke's men at your bidding. And you have only this house now, instead of that vast rambling palace, so you might want to reduce the size of your household. The time has come to admit my error and clear the air, and for you to decide whether Brook and I should go or stay."

"It is not for me to decide," Arlian said. "It is your choice, Beron. I would be happy to have you stay on as my steward, and for you to remain my heir. I would be delighted to see Brook bear her child under my roof. But you do understand that my life is still dedicated to destroying the dragons."

"Of course," Black said. "And you do understand that I would still be tempted if offered the elixir, and might well accept it."

"I think men can have a few disagreements, yet remain friends," Arlian said. He clapped Black on the shoulder. "Come on, then, and let's be about the business of putting this place to rights."

It was three days after the dragon's death before Arlian was finally able to get free of the Duke and the demands of his own household and ride the Duke's carriage down the street to Rime's home.

He did not dare walk—any time he set foot out in public now he was mobbed by admirers. And although his own coach had not burned, it was covered in soot, the paint and gilding cracked from the heat.

The carriage was just pulling away from the gate when he heard a voice calling, "My lord! Lord Obsidian!"

Such cries were common now, but this voice was familiar, and Arlian leaned out the window to see who spoke. He saw that two of the Duke's guards, sent to accompany the carriage, were holding back a man who was waving a sheaf of papers over his head and calling for Arlian's attention.

Arlian recognized him—Shuffler, Lord Wither's clerk.

"Let him come," Arlian called.

The guards hesitated, but their captain repeated Arlian's command, and they stepped aside.

Shuffler ran up to the side of the carriage and reached the papers up to the window.

"My lord," he said, "these are your inheritance from Lord Wither. Lady Opal forbade me to deliver them, at least unless I let her read them, and Lord Wither had forbidden that, and I knew I should bring them to you all the same, but I . . . she said . . ."

"She said I was a traitor," Arlian said.

"Yes," Shuffler agreed. "She did. But when you killed the dragon, I . . . well, I stole these, to give to you. Wither meant you to have them."

"Thank you," Arlian said, taking the papers.

"Thank *you*, my lord—you killed the dragon!"

"My lord . . ." the captain said.

"Yes, Captain," Arlian said. "We should go; I mustn't tie up you and your men any longer than necessary. Thank you, Shuffler, and may the dead gods defend you." He pulled his head and arm, and the papers, back into the carriage.

As the horses started forward and the carriage began to roll, he glanced at the top page, where Wither had written clearly, "Enziet,

Rehirian, and I used this long ago. As Enziet's heir, I thought you should have it."

Below that, and on the three pages following, was an explanation in ancient, faded ink of a system for enciphering and deciphering messages. Arlian stared at it for a moment, then smiled.

Now he could begin decrypting those notebooks Enziet had left him—at least, those that had survived the fire.

There were more pages, though; he flipped through them quickly, then stopped and began reading more closely.

These were notes on exactly when and where dragons had been seen over the last few centuries. They did not give the exact location of any draconic lair, but they provided some information on where to begin looking.

Arlian folded the papers carefully and tucked them inside his coat, and sat staring at the empty seat opposite him.

He was the one being honored as a hero, and he would be the one to lead the war against the dragons, at least initially, but there were others who deserved honor, as well. Lord Enziet, heartless monster though he was, had provided the weapons; Lord Toribor had made the first great victory possible at the cost of his own life; and Lord Wither had left essential information. Arlian owed them all a debt he could never repay.

And Rime, of course—Rime had perhaps sacrificed hundreds of years of life and had put herself through intense torture to destroy the dragon she bore, and in so doing had lured the elder dragon to its death. She, at least, was still alive to receive his gratitude. He looked forward to seeing her, and telling her the news; he looked out the window just as the carriage pulled up to her gate.

Rime was still in bed when Arlian was admitted to her chamber, but awake, alert, and clad in a proper dressing gown. She sat up when he entered.

She was still Rime, her grey streaked hair pulled back in a tight ponytail, her eyes bright, but something seemed to have gone out of her. She seemed smaller and weaker than before.

But that was hardly surprising—her heart had been ripped from her chest. Recovering from that, even with magical assistance, would surely take more than three days.

"Enter the conquering hero," she said.

"It seems to me that *you're* the hero," Arlian said as he approached the bedside. "Words cannot express my gratitude. Believe me, my lady, I had no idea what the magic involved when I asked you to attempt it."

She smiled. "Arlian, do you *ever* know what you're getting involved in?"

Arlian smiled back. "Do any of us?" he asked.

"I suppose not, but you seem to be an extreme case. I understand you are now the Duke's chief adviser?"

Arlian shook his head. "No," he said. "*You* are—at my insistence. I don't know how to advise him on ruling the Lands of Man; I don't have the experience, the maturity, for that. *I* am merely his warlord."

"Warlord?"

Arlian nodded. "We are at war, my lady—the Duke has declared it so."

"With the dragons." Rime did not make it a question.

"Of course. In truth, we have always been at war with the dragons, though Lord Enziet forced a seven-hundred-year armistice upon us—and then gave us the knowledge we need to win someday."

"Then you think we *will* win?"

"Rime, there are millions of us, and perhaps a few hundred of them at most, and they need a millennium to gestate more. Now that we know obsidian in the heart will kill them, they have no real chance."

"They will probably kill thousands of innocents in the process, though."

"I know."

Rime saw the expression on Arlian's face and said no more on that.

"There will be a *few* more dragons, you know," she said. "Some three dozen dragonhearts still live."

"More than that, after last summer—but you, my lady, are no longer one of them, and the rest will be offered a choice, to undergo the same process you have or be killed. The Duke will insist. Over the past few days I have told him something of the nature of dragon-hearts—not everything, but much of it. He suspected some of it, and I filled in some gaps, and he has agreed that the dragonhearts must submit to the procedure—or die. We cannot have those among us whose loyalties are divided. We cannot allow our foes to breed."

Rime was silent for a moment, then said, "It's incredibly painful, you know. I thought I would go mad. Death would have been welcome."

"I know."

"And I believe I will now be as vulnerable to aging and disease as any ordinary woman."

"I assume so, yes."

"Do you really think the others will agree to it?"

"Probably not—and they'll be killed. The Duke has decreed it, and I will enforce it."

"So you'll destroy the Dragon Society completely."

"Yes."

"Enziet, Drisheen, Iron, Nail, Wither, Belly, Voriam, me—you've made a good start."

"Yes."

"And you—will you have your heart cut out, as I did?"

"Eventually. When the war is won. Until then, I cannot afford it."

She smiled wryly. "Then I foresee a long war," she said.

Arlian stared at her humorlessly, and her own smile wavered, then vanished.

Her little joke was not funny, she realized. Winning this war was Arlian's vengeance, the vengeance he had devoted himself to since he was a boy, and more important to him than his own life—*far* more important.

Further, the long life that most of the dragonhearts prized, that Lady Opal sought so avidly, Arlian saw as his corruption, his contamination with the dragons' taint.

And the longer the war lasted, the more innocents would die in dragonfire, as Arlian's family had—as her *own* family had. Arlian knew that. She had, for a moment, forgotten.

Her joke was not funny at all.

"I hope you're wrong," he said. "I really do."

"So do I," she said.